W9-AFX-038

The Golden Arrow Mysteries, Book 1

MEGHAN SCOTT MOLIN

47NORTH

This is a work of fiction. Names, characters, organizations, places, events, and incidents are either products of the author's imagination or are used fictitiously. Any resemblance to actual persons, living or dead, or actual events is purely coincidental.

Published by 47North, Seattle

www.apub.com

ISBN-13: 9781503904187 (hardcover)
ISBN-10: 1503904180 (hardcover)
ISBN-13: 9781503904194 (paperback)
ISBN-10: 1503904199 (paperback)

Cover design and illustration by Danny Schlitz

Printed in the United States of America

First edition

To the incredible Dr. Liechty, and to Noah Wayne . . . the two real *superheroes in my life.*

CHAPTER 1

Instead of finalizing his coffee order, the schmo ahead of me in line is reading on his iPad, the headline MYSTERY DRUG BUST AT DOCKS splashed across the screen. While I can't fault him for being sucked in, if we don't hurry, we'll all get stuck on the 110, having to contemplate peeing into our cups. As irked as I am, I can't help but look over his shoulder. I read about the drug bust this morning in my Twitter feed, but I didn't see a picture of the crime scene. It's a doozy. Who doesn't love when two street dealers are trussed together, back-to-back on the Long Beach docks, left with a note for the police? *Actually* trussed together. Like in a comic book. I squint my eyes, lurking over the guy's shoulder probably a little too long, but . . . Is that an outline around the criminals? It can't be. But . . . if I tilt my head just a little, it *does* look a little like a rabbit. And if so, this tableau bears a striking resemblance to something I've seen before. It is probably a glare in the shop or a trick of the light, but my poor little writer brain has no defense against this sort of nerdy imagining. All I can see is a panel from my favorite comic come to life.

"All that's missing is a golden arrow," I mutter, giving the picture one last look as the line shuffles forward. I dutifully shuffle . . . straight into iPad Guy's heels.

He snaps the iPad closed. "What did you say?"

Oh crap. iPad Guy looks straight at me with the typical "I disapprove of your purple hair" frown on his face and completely ignores the counter girl yelling, "Next!" There's a lull in the shush and hiss of the coffee-making orchestra that suggests they're ready to make the next order.

"Nothing. Just that news story reminds me of a graphic novel. Are you ready to order?" I paste a smile on my face. I know better than to upset the Muggles. Even when they are *seriously* inconveniencing the rest of us in line.

Tap, tap, tap—Order-Taking Girl isn't pleased. Someone's getting spit in their foam, and it's not going to be me.

"No . . . I'm still decid—"

I step around the man and belly right up to the bar. "Tall cinnamon dolce latte, coconut milk, dash of chocolate on top." I already have my card out before Order-Taking Girl asks, and she knows by now not to give me a receipt. I don't need more paper filling up my messenger bag. Thank God for online banking.

I'm startled when iPad Guy sidles up next to me while waiting for the barista to finish his drink. I look him up and down, taking in the slightly rumpled dark bedhead, five-o'clock shadow, jeans, and rolled-up sleeves of his nice-ish work shirt, and peg him as an Americano guy. Okay, so he didn't really *sidle*. He's more businesslike than that. But he's definitely not hanging back in the typical stranger zone. I use my Genius Comic messenger bag as a blocker, putting it firmly between us. At least make it hard for the creepers to cop a feel.

"Hey," he says, looking at me again. Only his gaze doesn't linger on my short purple hair. It takes in my whole self, moving from my Converse sneakers to my black skinny jeans, messenger bag, Wonder Woman tee, bright-red blazer, and actually ending at my eyes, in a "I did not just look at your boobs, and here I am looking at your eyes because I value women as people" look.

I narrow my gaze in return. So it's like *that*, is it? I detest false altruism. Just stare at my boobs and get it over with, like every guy at every convention I've ever attended. I can never just live my life; I have to be boobs first, comic book writer second—if a guy even gets that far. I get weary of being a novelty in my world.

"What were you saying before, about a book, Miss . . ."

I ignore the blatant fishing for my name and huff a breath, glancing at the time on my iPhone. I'm running late for the office, and I need time to let the coffee soak up some of my morning grump. "A *graphic* novel. A comic book. The scene reminded me of a panel from my favorite one." Cue the disbelieving stare when man realizes woman has read comic books . . . and there it is. Game, set, match. If he's surprised I read them, it'd turn his hair platinum to find out that I *write* them for a living.

"MG! Cinnamon dolce latte!" Saved by the barista. I reach out, snag the cup sans to-go collar—*ouch*—and keep right on motoring out of the coffee shop. I hear "Herbal tea" called out behind me, and I snort. Not an Americano guy after all. *Herbal tea?* Hipster much? Or maybe it's for his sick girlfriend. He seems the type.

Through the glass storefront, I hear a symphony of honking peppered with angry yelling. The traffic outside is already picking up for morning rush hour, and downtown LA is a bitch in May. It's why I ride my bike whenever possible.

Heading for the door, I weave my way through a dude pitching a screenplay and a stay-at-home mom bitching about no "me time," even though she's clearly here without her children. Or they're off terrorizing the other patrons—a distinct possibility, seeing as LA fuels itself on broken dreams and hypocrisy. The dirty glass door screeches, letting a blast of gritty, gasoline-scented wind in as I push it open with my hip. It never closes behind me. I'm surprised when an arm reaches out to hold it open. I don't even need to look to know that it's Herbal Tea Guy. Usually the Muggles aren't this tenacious. Time to level up my game.

"Hey, I know you seem busy, but—"

The guy doesn't take a hint.

I turn to face him, my sassiest hip thrown to the side. *Rip off the Band-Aid, MG. Sometimes there's no other way.* With one look, I can tell this guy's interest is severely misplaced. I usually date the type of guy who can dialogue about Batman's backstory, and I'm definitely not J.Crew enough for Herbal Tea. I have a meeting to get to, coffee to consume, and regret for breaking my usual silence in the waiting line.

"Look." I stop him in his tracks with a glacial glance, right over the top of my fire-engine-red wire-rimmed glasses, a look I've perfected at comic convention open-bar nights. "I'm sure you're a nice person, and you're cute and all"—*if you're into the rumpled, sensitive, tea-drinking type*—"and I am sure you have a lucrative hipster job that allows you to drink cof—er, *tea*, at all hours of the morning, but I'm not interested."

He steps back, shock and a lot of embarrassment registering in his eyes. He's not used to being brushed off. Score one for the home team. "Well, that's prickly," he says, going blotchy red at the collar of his shirt.

"It's not prickly. I just don't put up with bullshit. And there's a lot of bullshit in this world." I spin around to continue my trek and don't look back. I have bigger fish to fry this morning. "Winter is coming," in the words of Jon Snow.

Stuck, stuck, *stuck*. À la Gregory House, MD, I throw the ball even harder against the wall of my office. To be more specific, the half-height modular wall that separates my working pod from Simon's. It's supposed to foster creative collaboration, but it just allows us to annoy the living daylights out of each other. Kyle and Andy have been talking the story from this morning to *death*—the one with the tied-up drug dealers. Neither one of them has noticed the rabbit outline or overall resemblance to *The Hooded Falcon*, and instead of coming up with something brilliant for my project, I'm wondering if I should jump into the conversation with my tinfoil-hat theory. It surprises me that Simon is silent on the topic; usually if someone is wearing tinfoil alongside me, it's him. But my problem is solved momentarily when Andy gets a call and leaves the room. I sigh.

Thwack, thwack, thwack.

"I think if you throw it harder, you'll figure it out. Maybe you'll hit yourself." Simon doesn't even raise his head, and I'm surprised he can hear me over the music screaming through his headphones. I stick my tongue out at him. Of course, like a good kid, Simon polishes his pages while I am sitting here with *nothing*. Well, not nothing. I have my basic outlines, but I'm stuck on the last frame of the page. It refuses to fill itself in, no matter how hard I try to bleed something brilliant onto the page. There's an idea that's been cooking in the back of my brain since my run-in with Herbal Tea Guy yesterday, but for the life of me I can't pull it out. I can only hope it's genius when it emerges, because I'll be just under the wire for this week's green-light meeting. And unlike the last three times, I have *got* to nail this presentation. My brilliance seems to go unappreciated in meetings. Just last month, my boss, Edward Casey Junior, was unable to overlook the *tiny* fact that I'd insulted the current story line—a beast of Kyle's making, not mine—before offering my own ideas. So I *may have* called the villain—my boss's favorite to date apparently—a direct copy of our competition's and *may have* used the words "trite" and "tired." What I saw as honest feedback he took personally. Fine. I need to work on my delivery, that's all. I'll keep working on my presentation for this month's green-light meeting, wow them with graphics, and prove I have the best ideas. Because I do . . . when I can figure them out.

I resume my throwing, and even Kyle shoots me the stink eye from across the room. He's just in a bad mood because he got all banged up playing *Pokémon GO* on Sunday night. He insists he was trying out parkour—from the new "nerd fitness group" he and Simon had joined—to nab a Jigglypuff, but my guess is he was staring at his phone and walked into a tree.

"Are you finished annoying the rest of us? You're not the only one with a deadline this week, you know." He's absentmindedly rubbing what looks like rope burn on his arm. I narrow my eyes. Kyle is about the nerdiest, most nonathletic guy I know, next to Simon. Papercuts would constitute an emergency in his book. *Rope burn? Has he taken up slacklining too?* That doesn't seem likely. Maybe he was injured in some *bedroom* parkour instead of at the park. Certainly something I'd lie about to coworkers too. I raise my eyebrows at him and throw the ball against the wall, maintaining eye contact. I can't say I'm always proud of my antics, but being the only woman in this office, I sometimes stoop to their level of boyish tactics.

Thwack, thwack, th—

The ball bounces off the wall funny and flies over my shoulder into the aisle near the printer. I'm halfway under the printer when I hear my name called. Busted for workplace "distraction" again, I bet.

"Oh, eff off, Andy. My draft idea for the green-light agenda isn't due until three p.m., and I have at least—" I pause mid-kneel, holding my red ball, and stare up at Herbal Tea Guy. What. The. Hell. I climb to my feet awkwardly, complete with hitting my hip on the table holding the printer.

"You have a visitor," Andy says. He's trying to smooth his flyaway curly blond hair. It would be surfer hair on a cooler person. "I had to go get him from reception."

"I can see that," I shoot back. Simon surfaces from his ad markers, staring at me. I don't think he's ever seen me with a guest in the office, *ever*. That's because I don't bring them. On purpose.

Herbal Tea Guy looks different than he did yesterday. He's wearing slacks and a neat work shirt, though I note that it's still rolled up at the sleeves. Even his skinny tie is fashionable. His five-o'clock shadow is gone, and I catch myself pondering whether I liked him better with scruff before I yank my mind back to the important question at hand: *Why is he here at all?*

"I brought you a coffee. Cinnamon dolce latte." He offers it to me like an olive branch.

My eyebrows shoot up, and my traitorous hand sneaks out to take the cup. Caffeine is my body's drug of choice, and it seems he's found my weakness. *And* remembered my order.

Andy is still staring at us, and I don't blame him. I still haven't said anything. He shifts from foot to foot and straightens his woefully rumpled button-down in a self-conscious way. "I, uh . . . I'll be over there if you need me." He motions to his desk, the central one in the pod as befits his team art director status. Andy's never been big on dialogue. That's my specialty. Usually. Except right now, when I'm gaping like a fish out of water. We watch him go in a growingly awkward silence.

"Must be nice to have a hipster job where you can drink coffee at any hour," the man says with a wink, looking pointedly at Kyle—watching us shamelessly in return, feet propped on his desk, large travel coffee mug in hand. Touché, Herbal Tea Guy.

And just like that I'm back, shields powering up. "Takes one to know one, I guess." *Or* go with childish insults. Whichever.

He smiles, and damn it if I'm not back to thinking about whether the scruff made him more attractive. Smiling definitely does. You know, if you're into hipster stalkers, *which I'm not.* The last part is a dictate to my subconscious to quit being ridiculous.

I'm finally about to boot this bozo out when he ups his ante again. "Is there a conference room or something that we can go talk in?" The question is quiet instead of suggestive, and his face is serious. Intriguing, and not at all how I picture hipster seduction taking place. He holds out a business card. This one seems to be a . . . gentleman stalker? I take it automatically and glance down. *LAPD. Detective Matteo Kildaire.*

Oh *crap*.

CHAPTER 2

"So, uh, how did you find me?" I sip my latte and try to suppress my moan of satisfaction. It's the perfect temperature and exactly what I want right now, stressed as I am about my deadline.

"It wasn't hard." He sets his coffee cup across from mine, spins one of the chairs, and sits down opposite me. We're jammed in the small conference room dedicated to our team just off the main workspace. The bad news is that everyone in my office seems to be taking every opportunity to walk past the glass door and glance in. The good news is that I love this room for the view. LA stretches out in front of the large window that makes up the back wall—the textile and fabric shops off Wall Street, my favorite part of the city.

"I thought you were an *herbal tea* guy." "Americano" is scrawled across his white cup, along with something that looks suspiciously like a scrawled phone number. Order-Taking Girl, you go-getter, you.

"I've been trying to quit drinking coffee, but work has . . . amped up since yesterday, and I'm off the wagon," he admits, taking a sip and meeting my curious stare. Studying me. I'm a little undone by his intense hazel gaze and long lashes. "It was easy to find you. Detective, remember? I noticed the Genius Comics name on your bag, called to see if anyone with purple hair worked here . . ."

"Et voilà," I finish for him. Seeing as I'm the only woman in the office most days, and well . . . the purple hair. Not exactly rocket science. Something tells me that despite the pretty gorgeous set of peepers this Muggle has, he's here on business. "All right, Sherlock, let's cut onions. What can I do for you?"

"I need to talk to you about what you said in the shop."

"You mean my completely ridiculous remark about the crime scene missing a golden arrow?"

"Yes. That."

Our silence spans two sips. *There's no way.* "You *found* a golden arrow?"

"Yes."

Internally, I'm scrambling. They *found a golden arrow.* And my tinfoil suspicion suddenly doesn't seem so coated in, well, tinfoil. But, then, why would the *police* be at my work? "So I'm, what, under arrest for guessing?"

An annoyingly infectious smile toys about his lips. *It's a legitimate question, Officer Herbal Tea, thankyouverymuch.*

"No, if you were under arrest, I'd need to have just cause, proof, and read you your rights. I'm here purely on personal interest. I want to know how you knew that there would be an arrow at the scene. The LAPD hasn't released that evidence to the media. No one knows but the crime scene investigators. Tell me how you knew."

Well, that's another thing I didn't see coming. I bite back an acerbic response. *Just answer the question, and he can leave and I can get back to my* real *work.* I delve deep to distill all I know and love about my favorite comic. "I mean, it's kind of a leap of imagination, but the picture I saw in the news looked so much like a panel out of a comic. *The Hooded Falcon.* Two goons trussed up on docks back-to-back. Classic superhero move. And there's this . . . I don't know . . . outline around the thieves that looks like a rabbit, which in the comic sometimes happened so the reader knew the goons belonged to Falcon's nemesis. So you can see how an imagination in my employ would jump to a fantasy of comic book come to life. In the comic, the scenes are always marked with a literal golden arrow sign, Falcon's signature."

Officer Herbal Tea looks up from his notes. "And this is a new comic? One your company is working on?"

I sigh. There's no way to package this conversation for a comic newb. Reboots are often beyond the comprehension of non-geek folk. "It's tricky. The original Falcon—based on Robin of Loxley—was written in the eighties and was less popular than his better-known *Justice League*–era compatriots: Batman, Wonder Woman, the like. Brilliantly illustrated—well, the originals anyway. They've been rebooted by a new artist since then. The new ones suck. I work on those," I add.

He's scribbling, and I note his furrowed brow, maybe at my candor about the current issues. Maybe I should learn to sugarcoat my words. But I'm just being honest.

"So, in the comics, the golden arrow is a what? A drawing? A pin? Only on bad guys? Does this Falcon character ever attack police, or is he simply out for crime fighting?"

Another tricky question, but I'm impressed by the level of his inquiry. If I were a Muggle policeman, I'd have listened to about three seconds of this before tuning me out. "Falcon and his sidekick, Swoosh, are vigilante heroes, fighting on the side of social justice. They often use the symbol of a golden arrow to mark their busts. Usually in the form of a golden arrow anchor running through the ropes holding the criminals, or the arrow—shot from his trusty bow—pinning the criminal to a wall. Was it *on* the criminals?"

"No." He glances up at me, then presses his lips together.

"It's a two-way street, this information thing. You're the one here asking for help."

"Drawn on the pier. Gold sharpie, maybe. And it wasn't even finished. My guess is they ran out of ink, or the wood chewed up the pen."

"And the outline thing, was that just in the picture? Like a flash or a glare or something from the camera? Did it look like a rabbit?"

The officer's lips narrow into a line, and I can't tell if it is amusement at my knowledge (or lack of) of photography or annoyance with being the questionee. "We noted a chalk outline, but I don't think anyone saw it as the *shape* of anything. Just a chalk outline. People just do morbid stuff sometimes." He sounds dismissive, but a thoughtful look flashes over his features, and he scribbles something in his notebook. I bet he is planning to reexamine the outline, which will probably be completely pointless.

Though there were similarities in the panel, to be sure, I figure that without the rabbit outline, I am back in tinfoil-hatsville. I'd been hoping for something more concrete when we started this conversation—a harpoon in the shape of an arrow tying the goons together or something. Not a measly scribble that could have been there for years before someone got the gumption to tie up a couple of passed out drug dealers or whatever. I'm not the only one with an active imagination, it seems, and as much as I love sharing my theories, it is time to come back down to earth. "So you think because someone drew *part* of an arrow on the pier in *sharpie*—"

"*Gold* sharpie." His full lips are now toying with a frown.

I ignore him and continue, "—that this *really* has to do with *The Hooded Falcon*? It's a stretch." And that's putting it mildly.

"I'm just following a lead and trying to weigh everything equally. You were the one who said the scene reminded you of this comic, and you knew the arrow was there," he responds, his lips pressed into a line again. I stare at them just a moment too long.

As much as my little heart desperately loves *The Hooded Falcon*, this line of thinking is useless. Real criminals don't mimic comics. This scenario is something that happens only *in* comic books, not everyday life. It's a good story, though. My brain is off and racing away with the new possibility. Brilliance strikes, and it punches straight through my writer's block. *It* could *happen in the project I'm working on. A copycat comic book crime scene. It's perfect.* And just like that, I'm feeling rather kindly toward this interruption. I could kiss Officer Herbal Tea.

I need to get back to my desk, stat. "LA is full of street artists. I suggest you go ask them who drew it. Now, I have a deadline and need to go. Is this all you wanted?" I don't realize I'm standing until I'm halfway to the door and catch the look of annoyance on his face. He's probably not used to other people calling the shots or walking out on him.

"Not really." He looks down at his notes then back at me with earnest eyes. "Rival drug dealers were cuffed with zip ties and then tied back-to-back with some packing materials from one of the crates on the dock. Our guys undercover say that there's a possible drug war brewing. Each side suspects the other and has threatened to kill the person who turned them in. Things could get ugly in a hurry, and it's my job to follow every lead—no matter how far-fetched—to keep that from happening."

I kick my hip against the door to the conference room. "I get that this is important to you, but to me it just looks like someone saw the criminals tied up and reads too many comic books. Thought they were being funny. Or it was already drawn there and it's a coincidence. There's no way that this is related to a thirty-year-old comic book."

"You said it was a current comic."

"Our latest issue had space aliens in it. The panel we're talking about is from the originals."

The last remark hits home, and he nods slowly, wheels turning the logic of it over in his mind.

I hold the door to the conference room open. With one more look at me, he tucks his notebook in his pocket, grabs his cup, and exits the room.

"Can I call you with any additional—"

"Email only. I don't do phone calls," I cut him off, holding up the business card I snagged off the conference room counter.

His eyebrows raise.

"Interrupts my creative flow," I state cryptically, ushering him out the door to reception.

Like a pack of hyenas, the guys in the office watch him leave. One makes a wolf whistle. I can't see who, or I'd already be using the rubber-band gun at my desk. "Shut up," I say to the room at large. "I left something at the coffee shop yesterday. He was returning it." I don't address the fact that I'm not holding anything except my coffee and slink to my seat.

But then I smile. Officer Herbal Tea didn't just bring me coffee; he brought me something even better. An *idea.*

CHAPTER 3

The smell of chemicals stings my nose as the chair swivels to face the mirror, and Lawrence's gorgeous dark face comes into view. I take a deep breath and let it back out, willing all the tension, all the stress and *baggage* I tend to carry around, out of my body. I have T minus three days to the green-light meeting that will make or break my promotion. I can't seem to stop seeing superheroes in every shadow. I'm obsessed with the news, hoping to catch a glimpse of a certain cop in the follow-up drug-bust stories.

"If loving the smell of hair dye in the morning is wrong, I don't want to be right," I say.

Lawrence makes a cluck of approval and runs his fingers through my short locks, finger-combing a part for the foils. "Don't I know it, *girl*." He stretches the word out extra long in a way that's habit, even when he's not in costume. "How's work?"

I open one eye against the scalp massage. "Pass. Next topic, please."

"That good?"

"It's not bad. I at least made my deadline for sketches for our internal review. But work just gets me all . . ." I wiggle my head back and forth, unable to articulate how extra draining my job has been lately. "I'm hoping to get that promotion, and I think Casey Junior is going to announce it next week . . . but I've really got to nail my presentation at the exec meeting so the whole board can see that I'm the better choice. And, of course, Andy gets to approve my ideas for the executive green light—that historical reboot thing I told you about last week—and he doesn't like it. He said I could present it as is if I wanted but that he'd offer suggestions to change it if I was interested." I throw my hands up. "He doesn't even *get* what I'm saying half the time. I hate that he's my team leader and that we're both up for the same job." Lawrence was the first to get an earful when I found out months ago that both Andy and I had applied for the newly created art director position within Genius. I'd been giddy at the prospect of finally getting to be Andy's boss—the team directors would periodically have to answer to the art director. I'd be an executive at Genius, and finally people would have to take me seriously. I'd thought it was *perfect* . . . until I found out that Andy's seemingly lost sense of ambition had reared its ugly head and that he'd applied for the position too. Since then I've been paranoid that Andy is out to sabotage my ideas, just so he can appear the better candidate.

"Being fierce all the time takes its toll on you, honey."

"Preach, sister."

Lawrence steps away to mix the dye at the mirrored station in front of the chair.

I sigh, already missing his hands. "Seriously, L, you need to teach Trog how to give me scalp massages, and I'll never need another date as long as he lives."

Lawrence raises a penciled eyebrow. They're not as dramatic as when he is in full drag, but they're more than you'd expect a six-foot guy with a boxer's build to have. "Should the next topic be dating?"

My mind goes directly to Detective Kildaire's hazel eyes. "Hard pass."

A rumble of thunder outside shakes the windows to the tiny shop. I'm glad I called Ryan to see if he could pick me and the bike up in my car. Nothing's worse than getting your hair done and instantly having it ruined by acid rain. I'd been trying to get in to see L for a few weeks, but L's business has been going through the roof in the year since he was on *Drag Race*. RuPaul herself offered to help Lawrence franchise, but he still likes his quiet, slightly run-down shop, taking one customer at a time. He says it's *him* and that sometimes queens like to feel at home instead of like they're performing.

"How about religion?" Lawrence asks.

I raise my eyebrow right back at him.

He slathers the gel in my hair, wraps it with foil, and chuckles. "Politics? Or if you prefer the arts, I can practice my opening number on you." He bounces from foot to foot, aggressively humming something that reeks of Broadway. "You need to start making my new costume, you know. I'm thinking gold lamé *anything*. I don't care if those other bitches think it's outdated."

I laugh. I can never stay grumpy around Lawrence. He may be my singular most favorite human being on this planet. "I have some ideas I'm working on. Are you sure you're okay bartering colors for costumes? I feel like I'm getting the better end of this deal."

"Girl, my tips went up fifty percent wearing your stuff. Plus, when you're a world-famous designer, I'll sell mine for millions."

I nod and close my eyes, thinking about this possible promotion and how it smooths the way for me to do more costume creation for both movies and video games. For years I've been doodling my own takes on all the Genius characters. Flashy new revamps of their costumes. Sketches for cosplay adaptions. At first I thought it was my way of fleshing out my writing. But lately . . . well, I've been dreaming of doing it for work too, *without* the writing. Despite my distaste for following "traditional" stereotypes, I can't help loving costuming. The colors, the fabrics, even the sewing itself. It slowly turned from an augmentation of my "real career" to something I privately think of as my true calling. It's why I secretly applied to a fashion design competition specifically targeted at nerds, part of San Diego Comic-Con. I'm curious if I'm any good measured against "real" costume designers. But if I get this promotion, I'll get to have my cake and eat it too . . . I won't have to prove anyone right by quitting my job as the only female comic book writer at Genius to go design clothes. I'll be able to mold and shape my job into something I want. Plus, I'd be Andy's boss, and I'd finally win the long-standing stalemate of the difference of our ideas.

My eyes pop back open a minute later. "Actually! Speaking of politics, did you see that Edward Casey is planning a huge charity auction for the thirtieth anniversary of *The Hooded Falcon*? It's all over the Twittersphere today. It's going to take place at San Diego Comic-Con!" As much as I dislike the man, he does a lot for the fans of Genius, and this charity auction promises to hold some of the most monumental *THF* memorabilia that exists. I nearly rub my hands together in greed and issue maniacal villain laughter. At least *one* item will be mine.

"Mmmm." Lawrence makes a noncommittal noise and spins my chair to the side. It's not like Lawrence to clam up, and I turn my head, trying to see his face. I get one huge hand over each ear to hold me still for my trouble.

"*You* brought up politics," I grumble.

"I didn't know about the anniversary."

"Um, hello, I've been talking about it for months. In fact, I've told you three times about the gala you're attending with me. My boss says dates are *required*. I RSVP'd. I need you. Come on, come be my date, celebrate a comic that used to be awesome, and make my boss happy."

Lawrence pulls a face.

The only work events I can ever drag Lawrence to are ones involving *The Hooded Falcon* or ones with copious amounts of free food. This one would have both; it should be a slam dunk.

"So you don't want to be my date, or you don't want to make my boss happy?"

Complete silence from Lawrence.

"Come on, L. I know I make him sound awful, but he's not *that* bad. I know; I'll introduce you. Maybe he'll give us some insider knowledge about what's being auctioned."

The sour look on his face when I suggest introducing him goes beyond the typical bored-sympathetic look he wears when I rant about the patriarchy at work. I've told Lawrence stories about how I've been asked at every meeting for a year to take notes like a secretary or get coffee for the team. I know he doesn't love that Casey Junior can't seem to remember I like to be called MG and insists on calling me Michael. And he's always clammed up, but for years now I've just assumed he doesn't want to interrupt. That he is being a BFF by listening to me vent without judgment. This is the first time I've had the idea that maybe he's been clamming up about *something* and not just being supportive. But Lawrence is largely an "accept everyone as they are" kind of guy. He was once sabotaged onstage by another queen and proceeded to not only finish his act but use the ruined costume to his advantage—sincerely thanking the other queen afterward for helping raise his game. There's not a hateful bone in his body, so the slightly bitter look on his face takes me by surprise.

Lawrence is still silent, so I reach out and spin myself around. "I've already assumed you'd be my date. You or Ryan *always* come with me to stuff; it's too late to back out now." I study his face, which hasn't lost its look of pure distaste. "So it's my boss? You *actively* dislike my boss? I always thought you were just being supportively antisocial so I didn't feel awkward. L, you don't dislike *anyone*. Well, except that no-good Cleopatra Foxy."

"There's only room for one Queen of Egypt, and that's Latifah Nile," he says, followed by a characteristic hair flick, sans wig. "Now. If you'll face front so I don't wreck this mess." He turns me forward and pulls another foil. He's silent a long moment, like he's chewing on his words, then hesitantly offers an explanation. It's like a dam is breaking and these words have been stored up, waiting to come out. "I'll come, but don't introduce us. We've already met. He's always been a bit of an ass, so no, I don't like him. And he's not wild about me." L's mouth snaps shut, and he's got an "Oh shit, the cat is out of the bag" expression that makes me widen my eyes.

It takes a moment for Lawrence's words to register in my brain. Everything in my heart screeches to a halt. The way he said "we've already met" went beyond "we ran into each other at the artichoke dip at the Christmas party." There was a depth and a complexity there that spoke of true knowing. Which is beyond my comprehension since I've known L for *years* without him divulging that he knew my boss outside of my work.

"You know my boss? Like for how long?" I attempt a look over my shoulder.

"It's nothing." L forces my head forward and attacks my hair with a comb like the Hulk at an all-you-can-smash buffet. "I don't like or dislike him. I'm just saying I preferred his daddy. Now leave it and let me do my work."

I reach back over my own shoulders and grip Lawrence's broad arms, stopping them from their movement at the nape of my neck. I am most *certainly* not letting this go. "Whoa, whoa, whoa, you know this how? Like *preferred* preferred his daddy?" I spin back around, ignoring the yank on my hair, and quirk my eyebrows up suggestively. My mind is reeling. Do Lawrence and Casey have a lovers' past? Is that why he couldn't care less about other comic books? It would certainly explain him clamming up about my work woes.

"You are going to look the wrong kind of fierce if I don't get these foils in. You're a damn Tasmanian devil today." He finishes the processing in silence, then goes to the sink to rinse his brushes, letting me stew in my thoughts and chemicals. It is an unspoken pact between us that I don't pry into Lawrence's past. L accepts people as they are and expects the same from his friends. Some queens fiercely guard their real-world identities—understandable when some are high-powered lawyers or doctors afraid of losing credibility or business just because they enjoy performing drag. Lawrence isn't quite that tight-lipped, but he has always been cagey about his past. Of course, I've fished a few times. I asked him about where he grew up, went to school, all the normal small-talk questions at the gamer convention where I met Ryan—dragging Lawrence along against his will—at the Genius table and Lawrence was performing at an after-party. And a few times after our *Game of Thrones* drinking games (one drink for death, two drinks for boobies). But he always passed it off with good humor, saying he'd been "born with sequins and a tiara." It got to the point where I didn't even ask; I just accepted Lawrence as is . . . except this isn't something I can just set aside. This is *my* comic, *my* personal hero, and apparently one of *my* best friends is involved. Rule or no rule, I have to push.

"I'm waiting."

Lawrence gives me a look that says he regrets having said anything.

"*You* were the one that brought it up, L."

"Which I am regretting. It wasn't like *that*, though Senior was eccentric. He'd been known to wear women's underwear long before it was cool." A small smile flits across his lips before he meets my eyes in the mirror and his face closes off again. "I worked for Senior, case closed."

"You—what? You *worked* for Edward Casey Senior? The man who wrote *The Hooded Falcon*? The man who basically saved my life as a teenager? And you never thought to mention this in the *years* that you've known me?" I could understand maybe not telling me right away, but my feelings sting under the weight of how many opportunities L has had to divulge this information. I sure expounded on several occasions what the comic had meant to me as a teen.

The comic book store I worked in when I turned sixteen was the first place that had ever felt like home. Even though I wasn't allowed to run the register because I was a girl—*how 1950s can you get?*—I put up with it because I loved the stacks of adventures waiting to be read and the conversations about Falcon and Swoosh I had with customers while stocking shelves. It was where I dreamed about living the life I wanted instead of the life my parents dictated, the place where I made my first comic friends, both on the page and in real life. That was until my mother discovered my "retail" job had to do with the comic books she was trying to divest from my life and forced me to quit.

Without Edward Casey's comic, I never could have applied to work at that store. I'd never have dreamed of living my own life or had hope that my awkward teenage years could turn into something else.

Lawrence's eyes are focused on some point in the distance, and he seems lost in thought for a moment too. "Mr. Casey Senior was a good man."

The bell tinkles above the door as it opens. We both turn to see Ryan step in, his jacket held above his head against the rain spattering the sidewalk outside. I know by Lawrence's suddenly straight posture that we have to hold our conversation—for whatever reason, L is loath to let anyone else know that he worked for the Caseys. Something I'll respect, at least until I understand *why* it is some big personal secret.

Ryan is oblivious. "Hey, L." He waves, then takes in my foils. "It's a good look for you, MG." His own dirty-blond hair is tousled from the jacket over his head, but I'm the bigger person and fail to point it out.

I stick my tongue out at him but smile. "Shut up. And thanks for coming to pick me up. It's going to be a few minutes. I forgot to text you and let you know we are running late." L throws me a glance that says it's *my* fault for the monkey business.

Ryan looks outside at the driving rain. When it rains here, it means business. "I was going to go to a spin class for cardio day, but . . . I'll just stay and answer emails on my phone instead." He settles down on the uneven red pleather sofa in the corner near the ancient register and pulls out headphones. "L, I wanted to check if you still wanted to play in that *Assassin's Creed* tournament this weekend."

And there's why I love Ryan. He doesn't pigeonhole Lawrence or me into any box—comic book girl, drag queen, or otherwise. I'm finally free to be myself and am accepted in my own home. My cup runneth over; I really love my strange little family.

"I'm all in, and those bitches are going down. Could use the cash. I have an eye on a new microphone setup—those things are expensive." L wiggles his fingers like a pianist about to play. And he's serious too.

"You could start work for me next week, you know. I'd kick Dave right off the team." But he's smiling when he says it. Ryan keeps trying to get Lawrence to play video games for him as a professional. They rarely lose a tournament, which means good cash prizes, and now that Ryan is helping Genius Comics develop the newest Hooded Falcon video game—thanks to *moi*—he really could get Lawrence a job with his development company. Which L keeps refusing. Not all of Ryan's gaming friends are as cool with queendom as Ryan, and L loves being the reigning queen of wild color dye jobs in East LA. My friends have found their niches and success in their careers. I haven't. Not really, not until I get to wear that executive badge.

"I'm good," Lawrence responds, as always.

"What are you two girls talking about?" Ryan asks, picking up his headphones again. "Looked serious."

"We're talking about Edward Casey Junior," I say before Ryan can put on his headphones. Maybe L will tell him about knowing Casey Senior too, if given the open door. Seeing as Ryan recently started as a contractor for Genius Comics, I thought the conversational opening particularly suited for everyone involved and high-fived my dialogue-writing genius.

Ryan glances between us, then grunts, a sour look on his face too.

"What the hell. You two are being *so* weird today. It's like I don't know you." I throw my hands up as I watch Ryan clamp the bulky Dr. Dre phones over one of his ears.

"Men," I mutter.

"So have you done anything about that yet?" Lawrence addresses me, raises an eyebrow, and looks pointedly at Ryan. And by "done anything," he clearly means "hit that." I can tell he's trying to change the subject, which I don't want to do, but he's hit an Achilles' heel.

Lawrence has been hoping for a Ryan-MG ship for a long time. Which I get. On paper, Ryan would be perfect for me. He runs his own business, he nerds out with the best of them, he's not bad looking, he's not horrible to live with, and he's open-minded about his friends and clients. But. My feelings of my roommate-found-at-a-gaming-con situation possibly turning into something *more* led to a best friend. Not a romantic love. Lawrence just always holds out hope since Ryan and I are still single.

We've had this mini conversation a million times. "No. There's nothing that needs to be addressed. Look, I know we live together amicably and shared one *teensy* kiss, but I think that boat has sailed romantically. I love Ryan, just not in that way. In fact, last night he went out with a girl from his gaming group. I'm happy for him." I shrug, thankful that Ryan isn't listening, and try to shove the thoughts of Matteo out of my head. We need to get back to the matter at hand. Maybe a little humor will grease L's tongue. Sass *is* his first language.

"So. Casey Senior. Were you his colorist?" I'm teasing, but I'm surprised to see a flash of something haunted in L's gaze. It's an expression I haven't seen cross his usually jovial features.

His eyes flick to mine, and his shoulders sag an inch. I get the feeling that he *knows* I'm not letting this go. "Not his colorist. I was his security guard. You say he saved your life when you were a teenager? Well, he saved mine too, and he was a damn fine man for it. He got me out of a bad situation when he didn't have to, took me in, gave me a job, accepted me as a person." Lawrence's voice is quiet, and he avoids eye contact.

I sit back, letting that wash over me. I never knew. The million or so times I spouted off about *The Hooded Falcon* and he never said anything. For all the angst I have when people try to label me, I never considered Lawrence as anything but a lipstick-loving queen. *Security guard.* He certainly looks the part. I'd never mess with Lawrence in a million years, unless I wanted to get scraped off the street. The guy still worked out twice a day—he and Ryan went to the same CrossFit gym. His arms literally bulge out of the black tank top he's wearing today, and I saw him win a bet that someone could bounce a basketball off his abs.

There's so much story here, I don't know what to ask first. "Let me get this straight. You *worked* for Casey Senior? As a security guard? Why did you quit? . . . Oh." Edward Casey Senior died of a heart attack, amid rumors of a huge change in the plans for his comic book. Of course his job would have ended. "Lawrence, we have to talk about this. You have to tell me *everything*. How could you keep this from me?"

Again, a flash of something I don't understand crosses L's face. "Girl, sometimes the past doesn't need to be examined. Mr. Casey was a good and kind man, but he died on my watch, and I don't want to talk about it."

"But he died of a heart attack. No one can help that." I just reread the big *LA Times* article yesterday when doing research for my write-up on the thirtieth anniversary. Stress-induced heart attack.

Lawrence doesn't say anything for a moment. "Maybe." There's a shadow behind his word, but he moves on with a shrug. "Junior blamed me for it. For bringing trouble into their house, for adding to his father's stress. And Junior sure didn't appreciate my . . . extracurricular activities and dismissed me. I don't love that my life led me back to dealing with him, but I make it work. LA is a small town. End of story. Now, let's get you to the wash sink before your hair ends up like a trashed purple weave."

By the set of his shoulders, I can tell Lawrence is finished talking about his past, and this time I have enough to ponder that I let it drop. I wonder what else he's kept from me. It's nuts how complicated my life has become since Matteo appeared with his questions. I lean back over the sink and let the hot water and L's humming momentarily wash away my worries.

I snort at one of my own wayward thoughts. "Now at least I understand your willingness to go to Hooded Falcon stuff. I always assumed you just liked the spandex."

"I may not love comics, but I can appreciate the art. I loved the drawings that Casey Senior did in his journals. The messy ideas, the scribbles, the colors, the costumes." Lawrence shrugs, then meets my gaze in the mirror and gives me a small secret smile. "*And* the spandex. In fact, Senior gave me one of his journals right before he died. He knew I loved watching him work, drawing the characters. He'd said he wanted me to have it."

"Wait—like you have original memorabilia? And I don't know this." I'm a little jubilant, mostly deeply offended.

"I told you we were done talking." The blow-dryer clicks on, and we're forced into silence.

"Can I see it?" I ask the moment my hair is dry. Lawrence tries his best to hurry me out of the chair, but I'm not finished.

"It's just a journal. An *old* journal. Aren't we done talking about this?"

"If you show it to me, we can be."

"You're so stubborn."

"Back at ya."

Lawrence throws down the brush with a scowl, leaves me sitting in the salon chair, and trudges off to the back hallway without another word. I can hear him clomping upstairs to his apartment and . . . silence.

Ryan eyes me over his phone in puzzlement. He removes his headphones and motions to the back of the shop. "Are you done now?"

"Almost. Lawrence has an *original* journal from Casey Senior he's going to show me!"

Something sparks in Ryan's gaze, but his words are blasé. "And you care because . . ."

"*Ryan.* Seriously. Because I love *The Hooded Falcon*? Do you know me at all? You're working on the video game! Aren't *you* interested?" It takes all my willpower not to divulge the entirety of L's secret.

Ryan's lips press into a thin line, and something odd passes over his face. My friends are acting so *weird* today. He clamps the headphones back on his ears just as the creak of stairs announces Lawrence's descent. Lawrence reappears moments later and shoves a worn black moleskin notebook in my face.

I can't help myself. I squeal like a Whovian at the start of a new regeneration. "Lawrence, it's *real*!" I flip the pages, taking in the pen and ink sketches, the messy notes, the odd torn-out page. I have notebook upon notebook exactly like this of my own work. I recognize the thought process of a fellow comic book writer; familiar sketches call to me at the beginning of the journal—sketches from the last issue ever published. This is a *gold mine*. It's likely one of the last journals Senior ever drew in. I flip faster, wanting to see everything this treasure holds.

A scene near the back, fully and artfully wrought, especially for a sketchbook version, catches my eye. It's an all-black panel that spans two pages, the pen lines of a hatch fill in all the white, leaving just two lone figures in the center. It's the Hooded Falcon, kneeling before Swoosh and handing him his bow.

I do a double take and look again. I flip to the back, then forward again to the sketch. "When was this written?" I've never seen this sketch before, but its significance is undeniable, and it's *definitely* not in the canonical issues.

"Girl, don't you mess up my keepsake." Lawrence taps his foot. He reaches for the notebook, but I parry and spin the chair around, using his shins as a push-off point.

"I need a date; I need a date—ah-ha!" I find a little sketch that Casey Senior dated a few pages back, do a little quick mental math that only someone truly obsessed with the comics would know, and shake my head. "This isn't possible."

"It's real, if that's what you mean. He gave it to me himself, right after a meeting with his son." L sounds offended now.

I spin the chair back around and meet his eyes with my own wide gaze. "I believe you. But according to this, Casey Senior was retiring the Hooded Falcon. He was going to stop the Falcon series." I look around. "Can you copy these two pages for me? I promise I won't show *anyone*. I want to do some research if I can. This is the biggest news in the comic industry in *years*."

"But . . . the comic is still going, isn't it?" Lawrence looks confused and extremely hesitant to share his journal.

I catch my breath. "You said that Casey Senior argued with his son the night he died. What if it was about his plans to stop the comic? What if my boss knew his dad wanted to stop the comic and has been covering up and hiding the original creator's wishes? It'd be a *huge* deal if Casey Senior finished the series and his son hid the issues in order to capitalize on the franchise. I need to find out if anyone else knew about this."

There's a moment of coiled violence where I think Lawrence is going to rip the journal out of my hands. Instead, he takes a deep breath, and his shoulders relax a fraction of an inch.

"No one else sees this unless I say so." Lawrence takes the journal to the copier at the register and runs off two sheets for me. He's muttering about how I should just leave the past alone again, but I can tell he's a *little* glad we talked today. It takes a really good friend to dredge up your former life drama and maybe relieve a bit of misplaced decades-old guilt. Or maybe it's the thought of Casey Junior getting caught doing something wrong. Either way, I'll take it.

"I promise."

Without permission, my mind wanders to Officer Herbal Tea and his crazy theory centered around the same comic book. By some weird twist of fate, the original Hooded Falcon is in my life yet again. I can only wonder at what change he'll bring this time.

CHAPTER 4

"You have *got* to be kidding me."

My front door stands open the next morning, and there, like my own *Groundhog Day*, is Officer Herbal Tea. Trogdor yaps like mad, and I have half a mind to move the leg I'm using to block the door and let this guy's shins get nipped by my dog. I can't even hear OHT's response over the barking.

"Trog! Inside! Now!" I point and watch with satisfaction as his Wonder Bread corgi butt trots into the living room. Even after five years together, it still makes me laugh to watch his little purposeful stride.

My gaze runs over OHT.

"It's not the pizza! Or Lawrence!" I shout to Ryan in the living room before stepping outside and closing the door behind me. I would much rather have Lawrence at the door, but his afternoon appointments are running late, something about acrylic gel that sounded painful. Instead, OHT and I are nestled on my snug front porch, a little too cozy for my comfort, but what are you going to do in four feet of space?

"Am I interrupting?" he asks, trying to allow me room on the porch and failing miserably. His shoulders look the "lean and fit" type, but right now they *feel* like the "huge and hulking" variety.

"No, I often greet guests on my spacious veranda. I'm sorry the iced tea is still brewing," I say before I can catch the snark from coming out. "What? Now I'm under arrest?"

"No, of course not." He looks uncomfortable and plays with the cuff on his shirt. It's *not* cute, I decide. Not even a little bit. "I tried emailing you."

"It's a work email. I only check it on workdays."

"I have additional questions to follow up on. This case is extremely time sensitive."

"So you came to my house." I cross my arms over my ample chest. "You have thirty seconds to prove you aren't a stalker before I call the police. The *other* police, I mean."

"I needed to ask a favor. It shouldn't take much of your time."

I arch my eyebrow in clear indication of my dubiousness.

"There's been a development in the case I told you about. I looked up that stuff you talked about. *The Hooded Falcon* and the Justice Liaison."

"League."

"Yeah, League. I'm trying to find some of them to read—"

"Any newsstand will probably have the latest copy. Or Meltdown on Sunset."

"No, the ones you talked about. The older ones."

I laugh, my hands dropping to my sides. "Good luck with that. They're Bronze Age collectibles." At his look I add, "They've been out of print for years and years. Sometimes I have to sit on eBay for *months* to find one." I don't want to be accused of obstructing justice, even if "justice" is taking up an annoyingly large part of my tiny porch.

"So I discovered. Hence the favor." Sarcasm fairly drips from the comment.

In the interest of divesting my porch of said officer, I decide to play nice. "Okay, don't get snarky, Herbal T—er, Detective. How can I help you?"

"I've looked online, at the library, everywhere. I want to read the one with the scene you recognized, and Google says the only place I'm going to find one is in a private collection. I just happen to know this person who collects comic books *and* works at a comic book company . . ."

"A stunningly lovely purple-haired person that must be plied with copious amounts of free coffee in order to help you?"

A smirk starts at the corner of his lips and spreads into a quick smile. "So you know her too?"

I pretend to study my aquamarine manicure. Despite a small quickening of my pulse, smugness is most definitely *not* cute on his tan skin. Definitely not. Even when he's just agreed that I am stunningly lovely by omission.

"So can you help me?" His hazel eyes are wide and boyish. I find myself swayed by his gaze. Plus, free coffee.

I reach backward for the door handle. "Fine. I happen to know that Genius Comics has some of them in their library. I'll give you thirty minutes. Why you want to look through them is beyond me. I mean, it's not like there's someone out there in a cape and tights trying to be the Hooded Falcon."

When he doesn't join my laughter, I roll my eyes. "Oh Jesus, you think there's a man in tights and a cape." I lean inside the door, snag my keys off the hook, and yell to Ryan that I'll be right back.

The muffled noise from inside and the clank of sword fighting tell me he's forgotten about the pizza and has returned to playing video games. "In the zone," as I call it. Singular focus. He won't even notice I'm gone.

"All right, Detective, your vehicle or mine?" I motion to the old-school Schwinn bicycle locked to the outside of the porch, complete with bell and tassels.

He laughs, a good deep laugh with a wide smile that his face wears well. "You are quite the force to be reckoned with, aren't you? Are you sure *you* aren't donning a cape at night?"

"Let's not talk about my nighttime habits during official police business," I tease, shoving the keys into the pocket of my red skinny jeans. I'm amused to see a blush creep up his neck. Interesting again, OHT. Maybe there's some red-blooded man behind that altruism after all.

"To the police car," I say, giddy despite my dedication to remaining aloof. And I wiggle my hips just a little extra as I jog down the stairs, just because I can. I smile a self-satisfied smile when he joins me and I see the neck blush still in evidence. That joy falters as I see what vehicle we're walking toward.

"I thought you said this was police business?"

"I only drive a marked car for patrol. My car *is* a police car." There's a silent *thankyouverymuch*.

He opens the passenger door of a white Toyota Prius and helps me inside. First herbal tea, now this. If it were possible for this guy to be getting less and less my type, he's doing it in a hurry. Worse than a Muggle, he's a *vanilla* Muggle. An herbal-tea-drinking, Prius-driving, vanilla Muggle policeman with gorgeous eyes. I guess we all have our redeeming qualities.

"So what prompted the need for the comics?" I ask mostly to avoid sitting in silence. This car is *really* quiet.

"I got a piece of evidence back from forensics today, and something tells me that it's more than coincidence. Trust me."

"Cop's intuition?"

"Something like that."

I'd argue with him, but something inside me is enjoying this adventure, and I'm loath to cut it short, even if he's dead wrong. Soon enough we're hurtling with the speed of a turtle down the 110 toward downtown LA and Genius Comics.

We're back to silence. "A Prius, huh?" I look around the neat interior. Like brand-new off-the-lot clean.

"I don't actually think someone is running around in a cape," he says, his eyes still on the road. "And yes. A Prius. It gets good gas mileage."

"So does my bike," I say, looking out the window. Palm trees whisk by, hazy in the strong summer sun.

"I'd love to bike to work, but I live too far out of the city. It's not the distance but the traffic."

"Oh, I drive when I need to. And yeah, that's smart—I've seen a lot of wrecks where the bicyclist didn't end up on the upside."

"I thought you only had a bike?"

I shrug. "I wanted to see the inside of a cop car. I didn't *say* I didn't have a car. You drew your own conclusions."

Rather than get angry, he laughs again. It's infectious, and I find myself smiling back at him.

"So your boyfriend doesn't mind you leaving with a strange person?"

"Ryan's my roommate." I glance at him to gauge his intention. "My corgi, Trogdor, is the love of my life."

"You're really something," he says.

It doesn't sound like an insult, so I accept it as a compliment.

Usually people say that to mean that I'm *too much*—too colorful, too passionate, too smart, too dramatic, too sarcastic. It's what people say when they don't know how to categorize me, as if I should just fit into the social box of a woman who wants a picket fence and two kids, just like my mom.

I know from my failed attempts at dating that even when people *say* they are okay with my dyed hair and career choice, they usually aren't. After my last disastrous breakup, I decided I was going to stop letting other people's expectations bring me down. I was going to be full-tilt *me*, come hell or high water. I'd colored my hair a bright pink, the most shocking color I could imagine for my mother, to signify my dedication to being nontraditional and never looked back. Instead of being intimidated, Matteo seems genuinely . . . charmed by my quirks. It's been years since I've felt charming instead of like a spectacle. Charming is a nice change. Another two points for the detective.

I pause for a moment, surprised by my own next question. Officer Herbal Tea has intrigued me, which catches me off guard. I'm so used to fending off the overzealous comic-book-nerd attendees at con parties or actively avoiding the stuffy guys my mother tries to shove on me, it's been years since I've even wanted to fish about a guy's dating life. "How about you? Does your girlfriend know that you pick up strange women and drive them around in your car?"

His face remains passive. "I don't usually follow up leads in this way, and"—he shoots a quick glance at me—"I don't have a girlfriend to care that this one is a little . . . different. The case, that is. I live alone, I mean. I like the quiet." Again the red blotches appear under his collar, giving away that maybe this line of questioning isn't strictly business. I'm not willing to admit I enjoy getting a rise out of poor Officer Herbal Tea. And even if I do admit it, he's going to look at these comics, decide he's completely in left field, and go back to normal vanilla life. And I'll go back to focusing on the green-light meeting that could mean my promotion instead of cute neck blushes. The trade-off doesn't sound as good as it should.

I motion that he should take the next exit, even though he's clearly been to my office before. I'm a terrible side-seat driver. "Living alone for the peace and quiet. Sounds charming. I bet you have stellar houseplants."

"I do. And I bet my plants have better breath than your dog."

I pause. "Was that an actual *joke*?" I'm smiling again. I can't help it. Witty banter is my Kryptonite.

CHAPTER 5

I point to a lot on the far side of the building. "Park over there. It's near the off-hour entrance."

"Quite a few cars here for a Saturday," he says, turning off the car and unbuckling his seat belt.

"Creative work waits for no woman," I answer, slipping out of the car, then walk up to the side door. A quick flick of my ID badge and we're in like Flynn.

"Let's avoid mentioning the case, if that's okay?"

"Secrecy works for me," I agree.

The Genius building rises above us in the glass-and-steel style of every headquarters building in comics. Nondescript but impressive. Not quite Stark Tower, but we use seven floors of the total eleven, and that's saying something in a town where rent for a closet can be as much as a bedroom in other parts of the country. I know that fact personally. After quitting my first "real" job out of college—in a law office, just like my dad had wanted—to work at Genius and being cut off by my parents, I lived *in* a friend's closet for three months. If only my time in a cupboard had made me a wizard. I'm still bitter about that. I want a magic wand.

I hold the door to the back office open for him. I'm also an equal opportunity door holder, and I'm pleased to see that he lets me hold it for him without comment. "So anything in particular we're looking for? You never did elucidate."

Matteo's eyes dart around as he steps through the door. A few people walk through the almost-empty break area, probably working on last-minute deadlines. Something I'm familiar with. "Let's wait until I'm sure we're alone."

It's a cagey answer, but I understand why minutes later when I follow him off the elevator. I've been praying for zero peanut gallery, but no dice. I can see Kyle's feet propped on his desk as soon as we arrive on the fifth floor. During business hours we have our own floor receptionist to make it look fancy, though I like to think of our cubicles with the small bank of windows in the work area as the low-rent district. Smoke and mirrors up front, Walmart in the back. It's hard to believe that as *Office Space* as our corner of the universe looks, we produce some of the most colorful and dynamic media in the world.

"Shouldn't you be playing on your phone at home?" I glance pointedly to the phone in his hand where the *Sim City* app blinks—the guy is addicted. Kyle is wearing the male version of the office uniform: graphic tee, jeans that don't fit quite right, and some sort of grungy tennis shoes. I like to hold myself to a higher standard and at least always cover my tees with colorful blazers. Andy and Kyle perpetually look rumpled. Despite Kyle being my coworker and Andy being my supervisor for five years, it's like they roll out of bed surprised *daily* that they have to get to work—the fact that he looks the same on a Saturday proves my point. Kyle is the ultimate Peter Parker sans Spidey.

"Yo, MG. And . . ." Kyle swings his feet to the ground, his chronically broken chair tilting with a crunch of cracked plastic, then glances behind me. His eyes widen. Seeing the same guest twice is unprecedented in the years we've worked together. And I know exactly where Kyle's brain has gone when his gaze darts between us and a slow smile spreads across his face. Time to nip this in the bud. I don't have time to play the star-crossed lover or the lovely maiden or look like anything less than one of the guys in this office when I am up for a promotion. I work too damn hard to have it undermined by a man who drives a Prius. At least until after the "important announcement" scheduled for next week's executive green-light meeting, which I suspect is when my boss will tell us whom he's chosen for the newly created art director position.

"This is just—" But to my horror, Officer Herbal Tea crosses the room and holds out a hand to Kyle, leaving me standing like a sidekick with my mouth open.

"Matteo," he says, shaking Kyle's hand.

"Here, let me introduce you," I grit through my teeth. I can't believe this guy is running right over me. Doesn't he trust me not to blow his cover, as agreed? "This is Kyle, my coworker."

"Hey, man," Kyle says, doing the stupid guy thing where he puffs up his chest to act more manly around another dude. I hate when guys do that, especially since I know for a fact Kyle's favorite movie is *The Princess Bride*. And sometimes while he's working, he watches it on repeat on his iPhone for background noise.

"What did you do to your arm?" Matteo asks in a way that reduces them to thirteen-year-olds comparing fight scars in my eyes.

"Oh, um. An old lady. Hit me." Kyle forces a laugh.

I snort. "An old lady *hit* you? I thought you said you'd been doing parkour."

Kyle's face flushes briefly. "Oh yeah. I mean, I was. There's this old lady who does parkour with us."

"Whatever," I mutter. I don't have time for Kyle's weird stories. For a guy who writes and draws for a living, he certainly is a dollar short in the imagination department today. Time to cut bait and run while the going is good.

I struggle not to say "Officer Herbal Tea" out loud. Matteo's real name feels odd on my lips, like saying it makes him an actual person where he wasn't before. "Matteo is just—"

But *Matteo* has other plans and interrupts me again. "Hey, looks like the hydraulic lift on your chair is broken. Be careful. I'm guessing a free fall wouldn't be a good thing in your profession." He motions to the pens and paper scattered on the desk. Kyle is doing some final inking on a panel; I bet he's all prepared for our smaller team meeting this week *and* our bigger presentation next week, rumpled Goody Two-shoes. He's probably got three options, all fully fleshed and ready to go to the execs if Andy gives the go-ahead in our internal green light. It's the reminder that I need to get this little visit over with and go back home to work on my own stuff.

"Yeah, I've already done that once this week! It was *epic*." Kyle laughs and proudly points to an almost-finished panel ruined by a stray marker stroke across the entire page. Boys. Thankfully they stop short of chest-bumping.

I sigh, throwing my keys onto my desk to break up the man party and return the focus to why we're here. My bad luck holds out, and they slide between Simon's wall and mine. Just great. I bend to retrieve them, knocking the stack of papers on my desk onto the floor in the process. My research for the article on the thirtieth anniversary of *The Hooded Falcon* scatters like a game of 52-card pickup, further complicated by the pile of *crap* Simon has under his desk. I must have left the pages for the article on the edge of my desk without remembering, unless Simon has been snooping. He doesn't seem the type, but I *had* let it slip that I had a major idea. Maybe he got curious.

I frown at the rope, black hoodies, and clutter piled on the floor. Simon and Kyle must have been up to some sort of nerd mountain climbing for *Pokémon GO*, because who keeps this stuff under their desk? I sort through a small stack of dented cardboard, several wrapping-paper tubes, and duct tape. *Murderers. That's who keeps duct tape and hoodies under their desk.* Or nerdy ninjas who say they're learning parkour but are into team Pokémon bondage. My discovery of a pack of *Magic* cards, along with a pattern for homemade chain mail underneath the sweatshirts, seals the deal for me. Ninja Nerd City. I emerge from under my desk with a further understanding of just how far down the nerdom path my coworkers are. I remind myself to tease them mercilessly on Monday.

"I could look at it for you, maybe fix it." Matteo squats, peering at Kyle's chair with what I assume is a fake aura of professional capability.

"Cool." Kyle jumps off the chair, and they start all sorts of pointing and prodding. I do *not* have time for some pissing contest where they pretend to understand how a hydraulic whatever-it-is works. I am about to inform them of this when Kyle crows with satisfaction. There is *no way* Matteo actually fixed something that fast. Kyle's been fiddling with that chair for the better part of two months.

"Right on! I didn't think of rotating the supports that way! Thanks, man." This time when Kyle is back on his feet and shakes Matteo's hand, he's euphoric.

"No problem," Matteo says, pulling out an honest-to-God *handkerchief* from his pocket to wipe his fingers.

Kyle turns and gives me a grin and double thumbs-up. "Seems like a keeper, MG."

Everything's so effed up that I sputter something incomprehensible while Mr. Herbal Tea, Fix-It Man himself, walks back to my side and peers down at me with the most infuriatingly benign look on his face.

"Sorry about the delay. Didn't you want to look at something in the library?" Matteo asks. And dammit if there isn't a smile lurking in his eyes. This man is thoroughly *enjoying* watching me sputter. This man has my head spinning so fast, I'm losing track of what I'm reacting to. In fact, he's steering me toward the back of the office before I even realize that Kyle thinks OHT is my *special someone*.

I turn to defend my reputation, but OHT slides his arm around my shoulder and leans his lips near my ear. This maneuver is far more effective in stilling my protest than I'd like. My mind drops Kyle like a hot potato, and OHT's proximity takes precedence. I'm trying to remember just *when* it was someone had last caused goose bumps to rise on my neck in such speedy fashion.

"I don't want your coworkers to know I'm a cop, remember?" Matteo says in my ear. From Kyle's perspective, I'm sure it looks like sweet nothings.

I give him a look that clearly says, "No duh, I'm not a dunce."

With an adoring smile, he opens the door to the back hallway, ushers me through, and drops his arm from around my shoulder. The charade is up, and he steps a normal distance away from me, though I'm still calculating how long it's been since someone has whispered in my ear. Six months? A year? Probably since I dated Ryan's gaming pal for three months, before realizing he'd been vlogging all his dates with a "real hot comic chick" and uploading them on YouTube to gain followers. Complete with analysis of my physique, which superheroine had a rack like mine, and comparison pictures. Needless to say, it didn't work out.

I catch a glimpse of Kyle. He's grinning at me through the window in the door. It's going to take months of normalcy to regain my carefully cultivated resident-badass, no-personal-details-in-the-office, no-bullshit persona. I want to prove I'm ready for the promotion to art director. No one respects a boss who has office dalliances on a Saturday.

I welcome the space between Matteo and me. It allows me to regain my wits. "Let's go, *Detective*. The library is right through here."

CHAPTER 6

"So are you British?"

"What? No. Why would you even ask that?" I'm digging through the filing cabinet in the airless room that serves as our library of past work.

"You have one of those short dogs, and you have a picture of a telephone booth on your desk."

"First off, it's a TARDIS. Second off, Trogdor isn't short. Well, he is, but it's on purpose."

"A . . . TARDIS?"

I ignore him.

"Your desk and your card say 'MG.' You don't like your first name?"

"Is this twenty questions? How would you like it if you had a girl's name as a first name? I got called a boy all the way through elementary school. My first name *is* Michael-Grace. I don't have a middle name. Doomed to a life of stumping fill-in forms." I take a breath, realizing I'm dumping stuff on him that I usually keep to myself.

"No, I don't like my name," I say. "But it got me this job, anyway, because my boss thought I was a guy in the résumé portion. I guess all's well that ends well." I stop short of telling him that in my final interview with Edward Casey Junior, president of Genius Comics, he assumed I was a secretary. He actually asked me to get a pitcher of water and glasses for his meeting with Michael Martin, having missed the "Grace" portion of my name on my résumé. I've always wondered if the debacle contributed to my landing the job, and I spend every chance I can proving to him that despite my gender, I'm the best writer he has on staff.

"We're supposed to be researching your theory, remember?" *Not talking about my personal life.* I pull out the plastic-covered book and set it on the table. I slap his hands away from touching it, shove a pair of disposable gloves from a box on the table into his hands, and slide a pair on my own before carefully slipping the comic out of the protective wrapping. This is why I don't date non-nerds. I shudder to think of the skin oils that would find their way onto these beloved possessions—outsiders just don't *get* the magic of a pristine issue.

With a scent of the ink and paper, I'm swept back to the first time I held *The Hooded Falcon*. Some girls get moony-eyed about first boyfriends. First kisses. Me? The boys *called* me a boy but wouldn't hang out with me either. Well, at least until I was fifteen and the "girls" popped out. Then boys just wanted to hang out with my chest. No, for me it is comic books that make me weak in the knees.

I catch Matteo watching me. "Didn't you say there's a new development in the case that made you think of the comic book? Care to share it with the class so I know what I'm looking for?"

Matteo laces his fingers and leans his elbows on the table, bringing us closer together. "I need your help because I think someone here is in danger."

I'm not sure if the tingle running down my spine is because of his words or his intense gaze locked on to my own.

"Danger?" I try to play it off and force a laugh. "Thanks, Professor Trelawney, for your prediction. Now *you* sound like the one in the comic book."

"I mean it." His gaze doesn't change intensity, and another chill spills down my back. "I got the case file back from forensics today, and the note left at the scene? It references Genius Comics."

"That's crazy."

"Is it?" Matteo's eyes have a light of certainty in them, and it dawns on me how intimidating it would be to be interrogated by him. He comes off as this L.L.Bean catalog cover model, but there's this depth of conviction in him that is gripping at moments. Muggle waters run deep apparently. I squint at him. Maybe I'll upgrade him to Squib.

"You don't have to be a Genius to chase the White Rabbit," Matteo says.

I blink. "What?"

"That's what it said. The note left at the crime scene. The 'G' in 'Genius' is capitalized."

I see the Genius connection, sure, but my mind instantly jumps to the White Rabbit bit. The White Rabbit, a.k.a. the Hooded Falcon's nemesis. Surely this note couldn't be tying together drug dealers, my favorite comic book, and a White Rabbit–esque villain? *Not possible.* Okay, it's *possible*. But highly improbable. Comic books don't come to life. I know. I spent half my teenage years hoping for that very thing.

Detective Kildaire takes my silence as doubt. "See where I'm going? Genius Comics? You already confirmed for me that Genius Comics is the current producer of Hooded Falcon comics. And didn't you say you thought the chalk outline looked like a rabbit? I looked at it, and I'm not as convinced it's a rabbit, but maybe our vigilante is a lousy artist. Or White Rabbit could reference the street name for the specific brand of heroin these dealers are selling. Still waiting on lab results on whether or not it's the same designer drug formula. We've had a rise in its popularity recently."

My shoulders give an inch. *Okay, relax, MG. No need to see boogeymen around every corner. This theory makes a lot more sense than the White Rabbit outline indicating the* actual *White Rabbit, THF's nemesis.*

"Unless . . . you have other theories tied to the comic?" His gaze is shrewd. He leans farther forward, bringing his face close to mine across the table. Can he read my thoughts that easily? "These criminals are bad guys. I know you understand that concept. I don't want some overweight guy in spandex with a hero complex to get killed because he thinks it'd be fun to play superhero. Right now the drug rings are just pointing fingers at each other. And it could be that's it and that I'm chasing phantoms. But. If this is a real person trying to live out some superhero fantasy connected to this comic, I'm not sure how long that will hold if this masked avenger continues his antics. I'm trying to take the shortcut if this is a real person trying to tell us something using this comic."

I'm silent, a war raging inside me. It could be complete coincidence that the note mentions both the words "Genius" and "White Rabbit." More than likely it's what Matteo said: it's the coincidental street name of a drug. My brain can't even comprehend what would make someone play superhero with real villains. It has to be a coincidence, and the more time Matteo—*Detective Kildaire*—wastes on this crazy theory, the longer the bad guys are out there. Real people don't wear spandex and tie up drug dealers, do they? My mind flashes to Kyle and Simon and their injuries. Surely not. I can't picture either of them deciding to take down a drug ring instead of Jigglypuffs. This has to be coincidence or a joke.

"I still think it's a long shot," I say in all honesty. He's been quiet, letting me sort through his words while we lean over the comic spread on the table.

Eventually, Matteo sits back, breaking the connection of our gazes, and I feel the gulf between us. Like I've let him down. "Can you at least show me the episode that you recognized?"

His blunder brings a smirk to my face and a lightness back into the room. "It's an *issue*, not an episode, and yes. I think it's about midway through this one—one of my personal favorites, actually. THF was the first socially conscious hero that Genius published. Rather than fictional villains, he focused on *real* social crimes. Rape, drug production, addiction, corrupt politicians and cops, stuff like that."

I look at Matteo to make sure he's following me. He's nodding, so I continue, "This comic has two story lines coming together. It's a bit about THF running for mayor in his 'real' life, but it's also about his brush with a supervillain. This issue in particular is a real turning point in the Hooded Falcon's career. It's where he decides he'd have more power working *with* the law instead of outside it. You see, he'd caught these guys last issue laundering money and drugs already. They got off on a technicality, so he had to *re*capture them. He'd done his job, but the cops hadn't done theirs—what?"

OHT is staring at me with something like amusement on his face.

"Aren't you even paying attention?"

"You're so different when you talk about this. Like *The Hooded Falcon* is real to you."

That irks me more than anything else he could have said. I'm so *sick* of ComicsGate and everything this industry throws in my face about being a girl who loves comics. My mother said the very same thing to me at seventeen, two years into my *Hooded Falcon* obsession: "These aren't your real friends, Michael-Grace, and comic books won't earn you a living or bring you a husband. Go to school, make real friends, and meet real boys." Why does everyone assume I can't tell reality from fiction when it's my job to write? And isn't this *his* lunatic theory in the first place? Even though my geek heart would love a real-world vigilante superhero, I'm the one arguing on the side of logic.

I snap the comic closed, forgetting to be gentle with the copy.

He backpedals, sensing blood in the water. God help him if he tries to salvage this with a patronizing statement. "I know you know it's not real. I just meant it's nice to see you passionate about your work."

"Because I'm a freak show? A woman who loves comics, so I automatically can't tell reality from fiction? You're the one who asked me for help, and you're sitting here making fun of me. I think we're done here. You can just leave." I stand to excuse him from the room and am shocked at his audacity when he reaches across the table and grabs my arm with his gloved hand.

"I'm sorry, MG. Really. All I'd meant to say is it was really neat to see how passionate you are. Not because I'm surprised to see a girl reading comics. It's neat to see *anyone* passionate about this beautiful work. It's magical to you. I can see that. I don't get to deal with beautiful art or passionate writers in my job. That's it. I promise."

"Oh." A hot flash of shame fills my face with what I assume is bright red to match my glasses. After a minute, I clear my throat. I definitely gave him a dressing down he didn't deserve. It wasn't his fault that he chose the exact words that had galvanized my desire to prove I *could* make comics my life.

With a squeeze on my arm, he turns back to the copy on the table. "Can you show me the panel you thought you recognized?" Business it is. And I appreciate it.

"Um, sure." I sit back down and focus again on the copy. It takes me a few moments to find the page because my brain is buzzing from the fervor of my reaction. "Here it is."

I slide it across the table to him. He looks dutifully down at the page, a frown creasing his brow. "What am I looking at?"

"Okay, well, here is the panel I thought I recognized." I point to the lower left where a long panel shows a group of men tied at the pier. "In the comic, the guys are tied together with jesses—those are the leather thongs used to secure a falcon—and the golden arrow is the stake in the middle they're tied to." Not painted on the street. "The aura around them isn't actually there. It's something the author used to help the reader identify who the criminals worked for." I point to the white shining rabbit around the panel.

We both study the drawing. "I see the similarities, but it's not enough to convince me that ours was an intentional copycat." He rumples his hair with his hand.

I nod. "I can see it just being a drug deal that went bad, and one side tied up the other for the police, no crazy wannabe superhero needed." Or several vigilantes. My mind slips back to Kyle's wrist and the rope under Simon's desk, but I force it out of my mind. My writer's brain is taking this way too far.

The corners of Matteo's mouth are firmly turned down. "Out of curiosity, what happens in the rest of the comic?"

I thumb through the copy, letting the story come to me in snips and glimpses. "Well, these particular guys are laundering money. That panel shows him catching the thugs with the drugs, and then Falcon and Swoosh follow the ringleaders into a warehouse. This issue also deals with how the Hooded Falcon uncovers evidence that one of the other superheroes may be behind the drug operation and *may* be his nemesis."

"Kind of a Scooby-Doo ending?" Matteo is scribbling in his notebook, and I give a short laugh.

"Yeah. It's old Mr. Jenkins with a ghost mask. He's so helpful the whole episode, you should have seen it coming."

He snorts. Another two points: laughing at my jokes.

"Actually . . ." I flip forward in the comic and show him a panel where the Hooded Falcon and his sidekick are in full fight mode, complete with a dozen "KAPOWs." "There's this big battle scene. It turns out the rival drug lord knew all about the Hooded Falcon's plans to set him up. Since the Falcon's superhero partner was the only one who knew his plans, he figures out his own partner is leaking information to the gangs, like a double agent. Not only that, but the corrupt superhero plans to arrest both gangs and take over as the resident drug lord. He winds up looking like a hero for putting that many people in jail, and he gets to control a very lucrative, very illegal business. Falcon suspects his partner is not only a double agent but his nemesis, the White Rabbit."

"The White Rabbit."

I bite my lip. "It's the name of his nemesis in the comic book."

Matteo makes a note. "Coincidental?"

I shrug. "Or the chemist is a fan of comic books?"

"Maybe." Matteo doesn't seem convinced. He's still wearing a "thinking" frown. "Is that the end?"

I flip a few more pages. "Well, Falcon breaks into the double agent's lair and finds drugs hidden in his safe. Falcon tries to unmask the double agent and threatens to expose his real identity to the police, and they fight. Typical unbelievable crime-fighting stuff."

"Yeah, that doesn't seem plausible, does it? Though the tie-in with the street name of the drug and the dueling gangs fit. Maybe that's what the vigilante wanted us to find with the comics. That it's not just one ring; it's two."

"But you already knew that?"

He shrugs. "Yeah, but maybe our vigilante didn't know that. The rest of it with the superhero stuff is pretty out there." He sits back in the chair, and I replace the comic in the plastic cover and file it into the cabinet.

I agree. "Pretty far-fetched for reality, and nowhere to go with the story line, really. In fact, this is the next-to-last issue for the original line—Casey Senior died without completing the story arc."

It was a dark day in my young life when I found out I'd never get to see the Hooded Falcon beat the White Rabbit or win mayor of Space City. The new issues published after Casey Senior's death were wildly different and barely acknowledged the old series.

Yet White Rabbit is now a street drug, and someone's tying up competing drug dealers. Something wiggles in the pit of my stomach, dangerously close to belief.

We slip back through the now dark office. Kyle is gone, and I can't help glancing at Simon's desk and the pile of stuff beneath it. Perhaps a tiny bit of my own sleuthing is required to make sure Kyle and Simon aren't being vigilante idiots in spandex. Just on the off chance that Matteo is correct. Which he isn't.

"I'm sorry I wasted your time, but thanks for being willing to help," Matteo says as I climb out at the curb at my condo. I can hear Trogdor yapping from inside. I hope Ryan left me some pizza—it's our weekly nonhealthy food splurge, and I look forward to it.

I was anything *but* willing to help, but he put up with it admirably. "It was kind of fun to see the old Falcon again. I mostly read the new ones for work, and they're awful. I can't believe they're selling so well. Kids these days just don't appreciate good comics anymore." I'm rambling, and I sound crotchety. Am I nervous? My stomach *does* feel a little fluttery.

"See ya around, Detective Kildaire." He hasn't said I can call him Matteo, so I don't. He's watching me, and I swallow. "I had fun, actually. Sorry I couldn't help you more with your case." I have the ridiculous urge to ask if he wants to meet up for coffee sometime, but I stall so long, the moment passes. Some kind of brave new age woman I am.

He waves as he drives off in his ridiculous tiny car, and I turn to greet my ridiculous small dog. I'm maybe just a *teensy bit* sad that I won't see Matteo again. Or maybe, just maybe, fate has some fat man running around in tights and a tunic who will throw us back together again.

CHAPTER 7

I'm hopping on one foot, trying to jam my ballet flat on, when my phone rings. I hate Monday mornings. "No, no, *no*," I mutter, almost falling over. "I do *not* answer calls." I glance at the number. It's one that I don't recognize, so I push the silence button. Maybe my mother has signed me up for online dating again; that had been behind last year's rash of unrecognized callers.

"Bye! Have a good day at work!" I yell to the living room. Trogdor is already up on the couch, snuggled next to Ryan in his typical 8:00 a.m.–2:00 p.m. spot. The little traitor doesn't even look up. Ryan barely acknowledges me either, but I'm used to it.

Ryan briefly raises a hand, then shouts, "No, Dave, dammit, we can't have a hole here. It's the first thing someone will check! Add that to the list of bugs to fix this week."

I slept terribly last night, my mind working overtime on this *Hooded Falcon* thing that I keep trying to convince myself isn't a thing, and I slept through my alarm. I should have set two. I should have set *three*. I haven't slept through an alarm since college. Not only did I lie awake pondering the case, but Ryan and Lawrence had been out late all weekend with their tournament. I never sleep well with Ryan gone, and I'd basically been a zombie for two days. I hate an empty house—it's one of the reasons I got a roommate. Trogdor would basically show anyone who broke in where the electronics were kept, as long as they had food. Traitorous fluff-butt. So last night, with Ryan finally home, I guess my body went into hibernation mode. Not helpful.

I don't have time for breakfast, and I'm balancing my cup of crap Keurig coffee with my messenger bag as I dash for the door. Thank God I'd obsessed about this meeting enough to plan—a mustard-colored pleated skirt, black and white–striped shirt, and plaid scarf—days before and that pomade and short hair made my personal toilet less than a minute. I've spent *so* many hours in the last week perfecting my drawings, running over my less aggressive approach in my head, and imagining getting the promotion, I can't believe that something as mundane as sleeping through an alarm could put that all in jeopardy. I'm not just cutting it close; I might not even be there when the meeting starts. Most days it doesn't matter when I arrive. Today? Today matters, and of freaking course, my plan has been derailed.

I whip open the door and am immediately met with a wave of humidity. The sun breaks through a heavy mist, and it feels and smells like an urban jungle. I can hear a soft drizzle falling on the large broad leaves of the plants near the curb. I swear and swiftly turn around. I can't risk my pages, carefully placed in my bag the night before, getting wet. The messenger bag is waterproof, supposedly, but I'm not keen to put it to the test for an entire bike ride this morning. Not only that, but my hair would never survive. Bedhead can be masked. Drenched hair, not so much.

I reach inside the door, snag my keys, and hurry to my brown 1990-something Ford Aspire. "Come on, baby. Come on, baby."

I crank the key twice and am rewarded with the rich perfume of a flooded line but also the sputtering of the engine coming to life.

"One of these days I'm going to have to replace you." I pet the wheel as I pull out onto Santa Bonita Avenue and speed toward the freeway. That purchase has to wait until I pay off my college loans. Until then, it's the Hurtling Turd, as I affectionately call the Ford. I just can't warrant spending money on a car when I use my bike 90 percent of the year.

I'm lucky in avoiding too much gridlock, probably because everyone else is *already at work*. The car screeches into a parking spot outside my building—literally. I have to push the accelerator while I'm braking, or the engine dies. And that's when it starts raining.

I'm trying to gather up all my meeting prep and dash into the building, while pulling out my ID under the tiny canopy, when my phone vibrates and my cup of coffee topples off the top of the stack. I look down and see the splatter of my breakfast like a body laid out on the concrete.

"Dammit!" I yell, but there's nothing to do but heft open the door and get my bag and self in out of the downpour. I all but fall into the front entrance, where I find the group of executives I'm supposed to be meeting. They look polished. I look like Tinkerbell went through a car wash. Fan-frickin-tastic.

"There you are, MG! This meeting was supposed to start seven minutes ago." It's Andy, and he looks alarmed at my late arrival. Or maybe alarmed at my arrival in general, given my soaked and coffee-splattered appearance.

He's managed to tame his flyaway long curls and wears a suit jacket. He looks like a polished supervisor should, ready to present our team's work. I'm *never* late. I'm *never* anything but polished and together. Especially for a meeting with the main executives of Genius. It's what I *do*. It's who I am at work. Show no weakness, give no quarter, prove women are up to all tasks, not just getting coffee.

Except this morning.

I'm at a loss to explain myself with the truth, not without going into the lunatic theory of a real-life vigilante superhero or a thirty-year-old journal keeping me awake at night. I start to mutter something pithy about the rain and my prints and make my way through the open conference room door.

"Honey, you left your coffee in the car," a voice cuts me off mid-explanation. Already the executives are looking over my shoulder at the door behind me.

Andy's face registers shock, then something like . . . glee? "Oh. *Oh.* Hello again."

I whirl around because I have the sneaking suspicion that I'm going to find a tall, dark, and handsome tea drinker behind me.

"You—" I sputter, unable to form words. I'm infuriated he's witnessing my bedraggled situation and at the same time mortified to find I'm almost *glad* to see him. My gladness slips into nerves, eyes darting to where Simon and Kyle stand. Has Matteo somehow figured out that I've kept my suspicions about them a secret? Has he found out that I'm in possession of copies from a secret notebook? Maybe I'm under arrest. I do *not* love the slightly sexy daydream that plays out in my head entertaining that thought. I'm obviously delusional, paranoid, and desperately in need of my morning coffee. I try again to speak. "You—"

"Are too sweet. Yes, I know. Have a good day at work, pumpkin." He throws me a look that says he's apologetic about cutting me off, but then, to add insult to injury, he gives Andy a conspirator's smile. "I'm sorry she's late. Completely my fault."

The peanut gallery . . . no, my *bosses* titter.

Andy seems at a loss for words. "Um, yes, well, collect your things for the meeting, MG, and we'll see you inside." He hesitates, then *winks* at me. The group of executives, led by Casey Junior, heads toward the boardroom amid laughing and storytelling at my expense. My reputation is burning up and crashing to the surface like the USS *Enterprise* on Veridian III.

My fury from my morning implodes—detonation starting in T minus two seconds. OHT called me honey. In front of my boss. And pumpkin. And what the *hell*, also insinuated again that he and I are dating. No. More than dating. My mouth flaps open and shut. There are literally *so* many words I want to spew, they're stuck in the back of my throat. This man has cut me off for the last time. "The *hell* are you doing coming into my work?"

Matteo leans in while I wind up for the pitch and gives me a hug. His lips graze the sensitive spot just under my earlobe as he mutters, "You and I need to talk. It's important. I *did* try to call you."

I shove him backward. "I *don't* answer my phone, and you *didn't* need to make my bosses think I was late because we were . . . *you know*," I hiss back.

Matteo thinks a moment, and I can tell he's replaying the conversation in his head. The skin around his collar grows blotchy. "Okay. Maybe I could have chosen better words—*much* better words. I didn't mean to undermine you. I'm sorry. I don't usually have to contact our consultants like this, but it's time sensitive. I brought a peace offering?" He hands me a steaming-hot paper cup. I smell cinnamon. Damn this man and his knowledge of my weakness. My hand reaches out and takes the cup automatically. "If it's okay, I'll pick you up for lunch? We can talk then."

"No."

"I really think you'll be interested in what I have to say."

I hesitate. And finally nod my head. Then *he* gives me a wink and squeezes my elbow before amping up his voice. The man could be a damn actor. "Go get 'em, tiger." He gives Simon and Kyle a mock salute and walks back out the door.

Kyle and Simon have matching grins spreading across their faces. I am now the butt of every joke I never wanted to be a part of.

"I'll be ready in five minutes," I snap. And damn if I don't hear one of them laugh as I bolt down the hallway to the elevator.

Once the jokes die down, the meeting starts out well enough. Kyle, Simon, Andy, and I present green-light ideas for the smaller comic series we write individually. My pet project, *Hero Girls*, is the bestselling girls' comic book on the market. Unfortunately for me, comics aimed directly at tween girls make up the lower portion of the sales chart, a fact Edward Casey Junior brings up twice during my eloquent, insult-free speech. I've practiced my approach tirelessly. I'm not going to screw up this time; I'm as complimentary and politically correct as I can manage—the very epitome of what an art director at a major company should be. My presentation turns into a conversation about reducing my time on *Hero Girls* in favor of Kyle's more lucrative project while I lobby that the only way girls' comics will *gain* market share is to present more of them with relevant social topics. In the end, my brilliant idea for an offshoot limited-run graphic novel about origin stories is completely shot down. I avoided using the word "douchenozzle," which was on the tip of my tongue, and I deserve a damn Tony for that performance. But this is what being a leader is, right? Sure, sometimes I get a tad combative about my ideas because I'm passionate, but this morning it can hardly be considered my fault. Yet I refrained. I won this round . . . well, not really *won* but avoided catastrophe. And the next part of the meeting is what will make it or break it for me. I've groomed the *Hooded Falcon* idea *just* for Casey, and I am sure he is going to love my historic reboot.

I tuck the *Hero Girls* pages back into my folder, deflated but not surprised. Casey Junior has hated *Hero Girls* since the beginning. The only reason he lets me keep working on it is the interest Netflix has in a possible TV spin-off. I leaf through the pages and catch sight of the *Hooded Falcon* sketch. It's gritty, loose in all the right ways. It shows action, and it uses many of the vintage stylings for text and action tags. It's the perfect cross of the modern hero and all that makes vintage comics popular. My heart lifts again. *This* is the idea I had while talking to Matteo, and my gut says that it's going to put me on the board.

It's still drizzling outside, and I fight to keep my mind on the meeting. It's the kind of day when I like to curl up and daydream plot ideas or sketch costumes, but this morning's encounter with Matteo has me rattled. I keep thinking about his voice in my ear instead of focusing on the single most important meeting I've had in a long time. It's unlike me. Instead, I fill my head with possible story lines for my historic reboot. Maybe I'll pitch a few to show Casey Junior just *how* prepared I am. To show him *how* dedicated I am. My mind runs down a rabbit trail of stories, and I scribble madly on the side of my notes, nearly cackling with personal pleasure at the sheer genius I'm channeling at the moment.

It takes a moment of silence around the table to draw my attention back to Andy. He's stopped talking, and everyone is staring expectantly at me. My brain flies into overdrive, and I try to piece together the last words I heard.

"I agree," I say as firmly as I can. Authority is good in an art director, right?

Edward Casey Junior sits forward and steeples his fingers on the table. "I'm glad you agree with Andy's proposition that you go first. So would you like to present your ideas for *The Hooded Falcon*, or would you like us to come back to you?"

Thor's hammer. I mentally shake myself and gather my professionalism around me like a cape. I can do this. Small bobble. Back on the horse, or the speeder bike, or whatever. "Yes, of course." There. Perfect delivery. Professional. Not at all apologetic like I've been daydreaming.

I flick copies of the panel I drew last night across the table. Andy catches sight of the panel and shoots me a look. This is the idea he didn't like. I do, though, and if I'm going to be art director, I have to learn to take risks. Champion my own cause. March to my own drummer.

"The current direction of *The Hooded Falcon* differs from where the comic started, what originally made it popular. I'm proposing a historic reboot. A story line that would take us back to the roots of *The Hooded Falcon*, away from the c—" I stop myself short of calling what we've been currently writing crap. "—current story line with the alien overlord and back to social justice. We can reawaken the love people had for the first series, especially those that have stopped reading the comic because it's so different. I want to bring back an old story line but in a unique way, using current crimes to copycat the Falcon's iconic battles."

Edward Casey Junior frowns, shifts in his seat, then tucks the panel into his notes. It's a death knell. "I don't see how that would tie in with the current story line."

Ah. I prepared for this. "It wouldn't have to be in canon. It could be a time to use a special issue—"

Casey Junior waves his hand, not even hearing me out. "I want to keep continuity, especially with the video game coming out." He looks at me, his gaze inscrutable. "Someone up for an art director position would need to think globally about marketing, product branding, and momentum."

Was that a dig at my proposal or my application for promotion? Or both? Dammit, I was prepared for this, and he didn't even *listen* to me. Everything I rehearsed, the story lines I brainstormed. All wasted.

There's a rustling of paper as the other executives follow suit and tuck my beautiful rendering of a modern *Hooded Falcon* into the notes from the meeting. I've been dismissed. Color me Batman in *Knightfall.* I'm fighting the good fight but getting my rear end handed to me. How does this keep *happening*? My ideas are *good*, dammit.

"But—"

Casey Junior has already moved on and looks at Andy expectantly. Instead of moving ahead and presenting his own green-light proposal, though, Andy glances down at my drawing.

"Retro is in these days," Andy starts, as if he knows *anything* about what is "in these days." The guy thinks Hawaiian shirts are the height of fashion. "Everyone is into reboots. *Star Trek*, *Sherlock*, *Batman*. We'd be missing out if we didn't capitalize on what's popular."

I snort. Hadn't I just said that? Sure, I said we needed to move away from the current story line, but what I meant was adding a retro flair.

That was obvious when I said historic reboot. Historic equals retro. Retro is popular.

I expect the same rebuff, but Casey Junior nods thoughtfully at Andy.

Andy sees the nod and continues, patently avoiding eye contact with me. "Jumping off MG's idea, what if we did a reboot celebrating the thirtieth anniversary of *The Hooded Falcon*? A limited-run graphic novel. It wouldn't have to be in the main story line. Something fun like the Falcon solving the same kind of crimes from the original series. Get people thinking about the good old days of comics—nostalgia? It would tie in perfectly with the anniversary, and we could keep continuity in the canon for the video game."

What. The. *Hell?* That's *my* idea. No, my *ideas.* The limited-run graphic novel from *Hero Girls*, mashed with *my* idea for the classic reboot and the copycat crimes. Mine, mine, *mine.* Sure, Andy somehow managed to make it sound flashier than I had in my presentation, but surely everyone at the table realizes that Andy just presented my idea *again.* The idea they'd just shot down. The idea he shot down last Friday. My mouth flaps open then closed. "Jump off MG's idea" my ass. "Switched a few words and served it up" was more like it.

Casey doesn't bat an eye. "I like that. We could market it as limited edition, crank up the price. It will appeal to our major market." Casey Junior drums his fingers on the glass-topped table once, then bangs his hand down, making the glasses of water and coffee jump. "Done. Have your team move forward on it. Good thinking, Andrew."

I can't just let this pass. "Sir. I—" Half the heads swivel in my direction. I don't even know what I'm going to say. Accuse Andy of stealing my idea? Rail against them for giving Andy the time to respond to his criticism and not me?

Andy sees the look on my face and knows I'm about to out him. He also can probably read in my face that I'm gearing up to make a scene worthy of a comic book panel: *KAPOW—MG slugs her newly minted nemesis across the table*. I push myself out of my chair so fast, I startle the man next to me.

Andy's Adam's apple bobs frantically, panic etched on his face. "Thank you, sir," he says, whipping his attention back to Casey Junior. "But it wasn't just me. I mean, MG had the idea for the limited edition."

He might have just saved his own sorry butt. I relax backward, just an inch, as he prepares to continue his confessional. Maybe Andy had just been trying to help me defend my project?

Casey Junior doesn't let him finish, though. He waves his hand. "Spoken like a true director. Of course it's a team effort, but it takes a special someone to take the individual strengths and ideas and put them into one cohesive plan for the product. It's something an art director would do. Now, I hope one of your remaining team members has a good suggestion for the next arc for the current Falcon story line?"

"Team effort, yes. Exactly that," Andy parrots back and gives me a small smile like that's going to soothe my soul. The soul that at this very second is burning with such ferocity, the Human Torch would be jealous.

Not only has he *stolen* my ideas; he's getting praised for stealing them. It also sounds suspiciously like he's getting *my* promotion because of *my ideas*. It's unacceptable. I won't stand for it. I'll stay after the meeting and talk to Casey Junior privately.

Kyle and Simon are sinking in their seats; they know I'm about to explode. They were privy to the conversation in our team meeting when Andy told me my idea was boring. Andy suggested we bring in one of the other superheroes for a team storytelling arc, like Superman versus Batman. Which would be great if that hadn't been done by our competition three times last year.

In fact, that's the very idea that Simon presents—which, of course, Casey eats up. Andy must be feeling *pretty* good about himself. Jerk. It fuels my fire just thinking about him getting promoted, and I don't even listen to Kyle's presentation. I'm too busy stocking up my defense arsenal in my head.

Casey Junior says he has an announcement, but when it's not about the art director job, I quit listening again. Something about a new vice president of marketing. I look around as everyone else in the room rises with Casey. They're all gathering into some sort of receiving line. We've never done this for a new VP before, but I'm okay with it. It means I can get to Casey Junior without seeming pushy or overbearing.

"I'd like you to meet Lelani Kalapuani, our new vice president of marketing. She'll be attending the team meetings from now on and will be helping us select the art director." Casey claps Andy on the shoulder in unofficial congratulations as he says this.

Fury nearly blinds me. I'm near him now, at the back of the group of executives gathered around the main door to the conference room. "Sir—"

Casey glances at his Apple watch, then up at me. "I have another meeting in here in five, Michael."

I grit my teeth and push onward. Do or do not; there is no try. "Sir, I need to talk to you about the ideas I presented. It's important."

Casey sighs, and his gaze meets mine for the briefest of moments. "Yes, yes. I realize that I may have been a bit unfair in the meeting today."

That shuts me up. *Really? It was that easy?*

Casey pushes through the crowd to the door, and I elbow through behind him. He turns over his shoulder to speak to me. "I know how much you girls like having your own comic books. So go ahead with the limited-run graphic novel spin-off. If sales are good enough, we'll consider more projects like it in the future. I wouldn't want to be accused of being sexist. Girl power, right? That's what Lelani's here for."

It's gone so wrong so fast that I don't even respond to his patronizing smile but instead follow his gaze and catch sight of our new VP through the dwindling crowd. Casey's words sink in. *She'll* be at team meetings. Andy fawns over a slim woman, expertly dressed in a tailored white suit that somehow doesn't look out of place against her flawless mocha skin, dark almond eyes, and cascade of black hair. *A woman.* Casey has hired a woman executive, finally. Maybe, just maybe—if one disregards his girl power comment—things are changing around here. I hope this is more than a show to placate the affirmative action people, though I wouldn't put it past my boss. Maybe my influence has finally been felt. *Michael-Grace Martin, gender equality superhero!*

Casey is almost out the door, pushing past the remaining pack of executives. "Oh, and Michael? My next meeting is with an investor. Can you please take these water glasses with you to the kitchen when you go back upstairs? And have the secretary bring new ones in. Thanks."

Or not.

CHAPTER 8

"Did you have a good meeting?" Matteo asks when I walk into main reception. I'm expecting a smug smile, but instead he looks anxious.

"No, I didn't." *And it still stings.* I cross my arms, and the receptionist looks up to glance between OHT and me. More fodder for the peanut gallery.

"Let's go outside." I don't look to see if he follows me but stalk through the door and into the humid afternoon. It's not raining anymore, but it feels like it could start again at any moment. Just like my mood.

I whirl to confront him. "Do you want to explain yourself?" We're standing between his Prius and my brown Aspire. From the building, it could look like we're trying to decide where to go to lunch. *I'm* trying to decide where to punch him first. It could be that I'm keyed up from my horrible morning stuck in an office with three people who refused to make eye contact with me. Or it *could* be that *someone* embarrassed me right in front of my bosses and threw off my mojo.

"I realize that this morning was awkward."

"Awkward? Do you have any idea what you've done?"

"Other than my job, you mean?" He's confused now, a furrow between his dark eyebrows.

Everything is jammed inside of me, rattling around like Pac-Man in a block jail: the continual internal abrasion of Casey's dismissal and how I have to try twice as hard as Andy to be taken seriously. Andy's ability to sell *my* ideas better than I did. And while he *is* a douchenozzle for stealing my ideas, I'm just a teensy bit afraid that he's getting the promotion because he's better at being director than I am. That Andy *actually* presented my ideas better, and I hate it. Also rattling around is the fact that Matteo let them think I was late because I'd lost track of time with my boyfriend, insinuating I'm not serious about my job or at the very least that I'd throw over a meeting for a man. I've become the butt of the office jokes. Add in Matteo's breath on my neck and how it makes me secretly *want* that reality to be true, and the little block jail can't hold all my thoughts and grievances anymore. There's no room for Matteo if I want to keep everything contained. I don't have time for dalliances. I need to focus on my job.

Matteo patiently watches me chew through all of this, his eyes infuriatingly concerned.

"You just don't get it, and you never will."

"Condemned without trial, it seems." Delivered offhand, with a ring of simple truth . . . and somehow that statement seems *sexy* instead of patronizing. I'm getting internal whiplash from how fast I seem to swing from wanting to punch OHT to wanting to kiss him. I blame the "hot cop" trope that is shoved at us from every crime show ever. I shouldn't be fantasizing about kissing the cop that could arrest me for what I'm keeping from him: Kyle's and Simon's injuries, Lawrence's background with Casey Senior, the journal pages.

Matteo's hand sneaks up and rubs the back of his neck. I've made him a little nervous, even though his gaze is unwavering. "I'd like to explain myself?"

I raise an eyebrow. This is new territory: I'm not used to levelheaded discourse when I yell.

"I brought you a drink, hoping to catch you before work. Then I saw you drop your coffee. When I went to see if you needed help, it was obvious that your boss was mad you were late. It's the first thing I thought of. I did all of that because I tried to call you and you didn't answer."

"I *don't* answer calls." But I realize that *perhaps* I'm using him as a scapegoat. He threw me off, sure . . . but the rest of the meeting was a creature of my own making.

"I needed to actually *talk* to you about the case. I can't write down what I need to show you in a text. *Or* an email." He's caught my caveat before I can even say the words.

That stills the string of retorts that I have. "Did something else happen?"

He glances toward the building, then back at me. "Yes. If you're okay coming to the station, I'll bring you back after lunch hour?"

My stomach plummets. He found out about Kyle and Simon. Or the journal. "Am I under arrest for real this time?"

He laughs, and I'm glad for it. "No, MG. Although I kind of feel like *I* should be read my rights for upsetting you so much. This is just to ask you some more questions about a new development."

"Oh." His half apology smooths some of my ruffled feathers, and I make a concerted effort to lower my hackles. Recovering a little of my normal spunk, I blow out a breath, ruffling my purple bangs. "You may proceed. To the station, Alfred."

"How was your meeting, really?" We pull onto palm-lined First Street. White arched windows, red roof, and gorgeous front lawn mark the historic downtown headquarters of the LAPD. Behind it, glinting in the sun, sits the glass cube and impressive gray metal building that houses the new station. Horrendous traffic for years while they completed it, but now it's a building any comic hero would be proud to defend.

I shoot Matteo a glance. He's got an adorable worried crinkle between his eyebrows. I shrug, not up for explaining Andy's deceit. "It wasn't your fault my meeting went badly. It's mine. *They* thought your little stunt was funny."

Matteo's gaze is serious, though I tried to be lighthearted with my delivery. "Either way, I'm sorry. I kind of lost my head when I saw you. Struggling with the door, I mean. I apologize if I came off as unprofessional and for making you look unprofessional too."

My heartbeat picks up, and I want to roll my eyes at myself. No matter which gorgeous lips, with beard-scruffed cheeks, are doing the apologizing, "no apologies" is my number-one rule, so I'm baffled as to why I find this apology sexy. Matteo waves his badge at the guard as we pull into a parking lot full of police cars and park along the side of the building. The tallest part stretches up into the sunshine, past the tops of the swaying palm trees.

I stare up through the windshield, first at the building, then covertly at *Detective* Kildaire. The full weight of his job and why we're here hits me like a punch from *The Thing*. I've now yelled at, thought about kissing, and threatened the physical well-being of an officer of the law. Without the station and the car, he's just a cute, slightly annoying guy. Now, watching him climb out of the car, throw his suit jacket on, and check to make sure his badge is in his pocket . . . it's *real*. I fight back a groan. I've made a pretty awesome idiot out of myself. My palms are sweating, and my nerves resurface. Keeping things from Matteo seems logical. I'm protecting my friends. Keeping things from *Detective Kildaire* at the *police station* seems like less of a good idea. Maybe it's time to come clean.

"MG?" He's peering into the car again, concern wrinkling his forehead. "Are you getting out?" I love and hate how familiar my name sounds on his lips, as if we've known each other for years and it's normal for me to be interrogated on my lunch hour for funsies.

He ushers me from the car and through a set of glass double doors bearing the insignia of the LAPD. I'm so busy gawking at the people surrounding me in the lobby, I barely register when I'm handed a guest badge at the front desk. Clerks are carrying stacks of papers, officers typing reports into computers. And a few . . . saltier people are sitting in chairs lining the wall near the front desk—a homeless man with two suitcases and three coats, a teenage girl passed out with her hat over her face.

"We'll go back past intake, and it'll be quieter." He leans close for me to hear over the din. "We have more than three thousand officers on the force. It can get pretty noisy in here."

We weave through a labyrinth of short halls and open work spaces until we reach a bank of rooms with glass doors. They're comfortably furnished with tables, chairs, and sofas. Not exactly the dingy single-pendulum-light-fixture rooms from TV, but my palms still start to sweat.

"Right in here. You can put your coat on these hooks if you'd like. The air-conditioning is out today. The last brown-out fried something. Gotta love this city." But I can tell he does.

After he closes the door, it's deafeningly quiet in the room. And warm. I shrug out of my black blazer and hang it on the hook next to his suit coat. It looks cozy—too "his and hers" for my taste, like I'm admitting that we fit together, so I take it down and toss it across the back of the sofa. No need to remind me of my parents' house where everything is monogrammed, matchy-matchy, gender specific, and *just so*.

It's the embodiment of my parents' stuffy-if-comfortable marriage. My mother gave up her true passion as a nurse to be a "lady of the house" and raise privileged, polished, perfect children. Think Emily Gilmore without the quaint East Coast charm. It's everything I don't want in a relationship. I want depth, breadth. I want messy and colorful. I want sitting on a couch and watching *Star Wars*, not sitting at a fancy dinner with sixteen forks. Matteo gives me a weird look when I move my coat, but I ignore it.

He sits in a chair across from the sofa and slides a glass of water across the oversize coffee table toward me. "I ordered you lunch. Is a veggie pita okay?"

"Yeah, sure." Rabbit food. Probably without dressing.

He notes my displeasure, though I try to hide it. Is he this observant with every person of interest or just me? My blood sings a little, contemplating the possibility. Maybe he feels the same fascination that I feel when I'm with him.

"I just assumed you were vegetarian. You know, being fit and riding your bike to work . . ."

I laugh. "No, I only ride my bike to work because I'm allergic to other forms of exercise. I hate the gym. I hate treadmills. I hate yoga. I love biking, so I can eat whatever I want." I eye him a little askance. It's rare that my slightly curvy form is considered the epitome of "fit." In fact, I don't even own a scale. My personal philosophy is eating in moderation; feeling good over numbers; and if I don't enjoy an exercise activity, I'll never repeat it. Not exactly a poster child for workoutaholics. I'm afraid he's up to that false altruism again, but the gaze he sweeps over my figure is appreciative, and it buoys my pride enough to allow the rabbit food to slide.

"I'll split my BLT with you, then."

I smile. "Deal."

He fiddles with something that looks like a voice recorder. "So what do you want to believe?"

The question takes me completely off guard. Had I spoken when I hadn't meant to? About my pondering an attraction to him? About the information I know? My heart races under my breastbone, and I feel my own neck grow hot. "W-what?"

He's still studying the recorder. "Your shirt. It says 'I Want to Believe.'"

First a surge of relief, then a tingle. He's referring to the "I Want to Believe" T-shirt I changed into after the meeting. The shirt with the words across my bust, which I now realize he had to be staring at to ask the question. I can feel my ears growing hot, a telltale sign that I'm blushing. "My eyes are up here," I joke. "It's from *The X-Files*."

He shuffles a few papers in a businesslike manner. "Why else do you put words on a shirt if you don't want people to read them?"

True. It's a legit question, but there's that telltale blotch at his shirt collar, so I have to wonder if I wasn't *a little* right about it too. Look at us. Matching his-and-hers blushes.

Matteo clears his throat. "Are you okay if I record this? There's a video recording for the room, but I wanted a copy for my use as well. This comic stuff can get complicated." Now he's all business, and it's a little disconcerting. *Detective Kildaire* is back.

"That's fine." I swallow twice and perch on the couch facing him.

He goes through a list of statements: today's date, my full name, his name, a case number that sounds like gibberish, and the time of our interview. Then he reaches across and pats my arm. "It's okay. You don't need to be nervous. It's just you and me talking. You look like you're going to throw up."

Yeah, that's what they tell all the prime suspects on TV right before they catch them in the lie that seals the case.

"Oh good. Glad that's on tape." It's my best attempt at levity.

His lips quirk up, and it does funny things to my stomach. I nearly toss my cookies with the added jolt. I have *got* to get a handle on myself.

"All right. Michael-Grace Martin, can you confirm for the record that you have not told anyone of our previous conversation?"

It's weird to hear my whole name come out of his mouth. It's even *weirder* that it doesn't sound weird. I hate my name; from him it sounds normal, like he says it every day. The familiarity eases my tension, and I resign myself to being interrogated—even if kindly. He is *good* at his job.

I lean toward the recorder and say, "No," in a clear voice.

"The recorder can hear you fine from the couch."

"Oh. Okay. Then, no. I didn't have a chance to tell anyone I met you. I mean, not that I had a reason to . . ." I'm flustered, so I scrunch up my face. "No." There. Pretend like it is an office meeting. Clear, concise answers. It's good practice for me.

"Can you tell me where you were Saturday night?"

I think. *Not good.* I'm *that* person on the TV show—a lame alibi that can't be proven. "At home, in bed."

"And can anyone verify that?" Cue color blooming under his collar, but he remains the passive professional.

"I was sleeping alone." *Thankyouverymuch.* "So unless you can interview my *dog*, you're out of luck—oh!" I snap my fingers. "Wait! Trog! He went out around eleven, and my neighbor yelled at me to get him a bark collar. So, yes! My neighbor can confirm that I was home." Victory.

He takes down her name and address. "And your roommate?" I may be imagining it, but Detective Kildaire's voice becomes steelier when he mentions Ryan.

"He and my friend Lawrence were at a video-gaming tournament. They played all night."

He nods, makes a note, and sits forward. "Have you noticed anything unusual around your office? People doing something they shouldn't?"

My mind goes directly to Kyle and Simon. I swallow hard. "I—uh—" I stall for time, trying to figure out a way to tell Matteo without telling him what I suspect. Is it cool to make your coworkers major suspects in a vigilante drug-busting case before you know for sure they're behind it? "Unusual like what?" *Rope, duct tape, black hoodies, and bruises?* I'm so wound up; my head is about to start spinning around like R2-D2.

Matteo runs his hands through his hair. "I'm not sure what we're looking for exactly. I brought you in because we're worried about your office. That note that I told you about at the first crime scene? Someone leaked its contents to the drug ring."

"You can't be serious. So the drug rings are stupid enough to think that someone from Genius is running around and tying them up? They're smarter than that, surely?" I bite my lip, mind churning through what he said. One word stands out to me. "Did you say this was *leaked*?"

"Yes, we're still trying to figure out what happened."

What he's not saying is that a *leak* means a cop told the drug dealers what is on that note, whether intentionally or by accident. One of Matteo's own is possibly a double agent, and I watched enough *Castle* to know that rarely works out well.

"And now you think they're going to come after Genius Comics? Just because of some note?"

Matteo doesn't answer. Instead, he reaches for a tablet on his side table and opens it while I watch with eyebrows raised. He flicks through video files, then sets it on the table in front of me.

"We've been following a few different leads. Someone stopped a purse-snatcher Friday night, though we can't confirm it was the same person. Only interesting because it fits your theory of a social-justice vigilante. However, Saturday night there was another bust. This time it was some middle-ups. Our superhero tracked them to the warehouse district, and a security camera caught some footage."

A grainy black-and-white video plays on the tablet, and I squint. "What am I looking for?"

"Just watch."

A few figures come into frame, and I scan the screen intently. It's too far away to make out any identifying features. I'd be hard-pressed to even determine gender and height, much less identify someone in a lineup. Is someone from Genius recognizable in this video?

"I still don't see—" My breath catches in my throat. Something flashes across the camera. Something that looks suspiciously close to a figure *flying* through the air.

Matteo's mouth presses into a line when I glance up. The rest of the video is useless. The figures on the street move out of frame, and the flash doesn't reappear. I reach forward, swipe my fingers left to run the video back to the flash of dark movement I saw. I stare at the screen in shock, and the last vestiges of my resistance crumble like the shield around the USS *Enterprise* in every mid-episode fight sequence. "That looks like a person *wearing a cape*, flying through the air."

Matteo skips the "*I told you so.*" "The problem is, now both drug rings are looking for this person, and they think they're connected to Genius Comics. We haven't seen a feud like this brewing since the massive drug busts in the eighties. It isn't a good thing for an untrained civilian to be involved in."

This guy doesn't look untrained to my eye. He looks like he's *flying*, and he captured the bad guys. My brain stutters. There's actually someone out there in a *cape.* Someone I might know fighting crime.

Matteo's words strike me too. *Drug feuds. Possible double agents.* The past and the present rattle around together in my head. It seems like this comic book is everywhere I look: drug wars, just like in the original *Hooded Falcon.* The discovery that Casey Senior had planned on ending the comic but his son kept it going. Then there are my coworkers. Kyle or Simon is potentially in bodily danger for some ill-placed role-playing, if that's what they've been doing. And to top it all off, there's the possibility of a dirty cop—a story line straight out of the vintage *THF.*

"We need to talk," I say to Matteo. He's been silent, letting me stare at the tablet, where I've frozen the blur into a smudge of black suspended on the screen. First the bust on the docks. Now a bust in the warehouse district. The cape. The similarities between the comic book and reality are too much for me to deny any longer. Someone is out there masquerading as the Hooded Falcon, following a drug ring that seems to mimic the original books. But can I trust Matteo? Would he tell me there is a dirty cop if he *is* the dirty cop? Doubtful. I refuse to admit that I make snap judgments about people, despite what Lawrence says, but I will admit to having fantastic instincts about people. And all my instincts about Matteo say he's as true-blue as Captain America.

I blow out a breath. He's not going to be happy when I tell him I've been keeping stuff from him. No way out but through. I open my mouth to spill my inner demons when we're interrupted by a knock at the door, and Matteo motions in a younger officer carrying a white paper bag.

"Ah, here's our lunch. Ms. Martin, I'd like you to meet our youngest narcotics officer. Officer James, our comic book consultant for the case, Michael-Grace Martin."

I smile at the sandy-haired officer, but he doesn't return the gesture. He simply shoves the food at Matteo and mutters something about not being a delivery driver. Oh, how I can identify with that. I *am* Officer James at my office. The fetch-and-carry kid.

"He seems nice."

Matteo rolls his eyes. "He's in a hurry to make detective and doesn't take kindly to things he sees as beneath him, but he's good at his job. Uncanny instincts when it comes to drug dealers. Now, what were you saying before?"

I tell him about everything—from Kyle's and Simon's sudden interest in a nerd fitness group to Lawrence's journal—as quickly as I can. I feel a pang of remorse about betraying L's confidence, but I stop short of mentioning that I have copies of the journal in my possession. I told L I wouldn't *show* anyone else; I'm simply letting Matteo know it exists. Technically I'm keeping my promise.

To Matteo's credit, he doesn't break his calm and professional demeanor while listening to my list of confessions but runs his hands through his hair and over his stubbled chin. When I finish, he closes his notebook and sits back. "This is likely someone you work with—maybe Kyle or Simon. Someone who knows the comics as well as you do. Someone with either something to prove or a misplaced Robin Hood complex. We've got to stop whoever this is before they get themselves killed."

"But why can't you just be glad someone handed you some bad guys, throw them in jail, and go your merry way?"

"Because this person is ahead of us. And while it works in comic books, it doesn't work in the real world when citizens take the law into their own hands. Truly, I'd like to figure out who this masked avenger is, find out what they know, and either work with them or take over. I get the feeling there's a reason they're tipping off the police instead of making a report. It doesn't seem to me like this is your average backyard role-player."

I raise my eyebrow, impressed that he even knows those words.

He ignores my incredulity. "It's close enough to what you're telling me about the comic to drive me mad—we're looking at a road map but don't know how to read it. These criminals are not nice people. I want to keep our vigilante from getting hurt, so we need to find him."

His serious face is doing serious things to my insides when I should be more concerned that *I'm* the one they hope knows how to read the road map.

Matteo continues to study me. "Are you still willing to consult on this case for us, assuming, of course, that your alibi checks out? I'm sort of breaking procedure by bringing you in so early, but time is of the essence with this case."

The chance to watch a real-life comic book plot unfold and help save my idiot coworkers from repeating history and stirring up a drug feud that could land LA on its backside? Not to mention the apparent capes and costumes in play? A *real-world* superhero. It's like my entire life has led to this. My name is Inigo Montoya, and I've just found the six-fingered man.

"I wouldn't miss this for the world."

He freezes me with his gaze, and a zing of electricity shoots down to my toes. It isn't a quick once-over or the analytical scan of a cop looking at a suspect. This is deeper. Matteo takes stock of my *person*—everything from my ballet flats to my sarcastic quips, sizing me up as a partner. The way he inclines his head in an indistinct nod gives me the impression that I haven't come up wanting in his appraisal. "I have some paperwork for you to fill out while you eat your sandwich."

His next words have a ring of finality to them. They sound suspiciously like the opening lines of a comic book introducing a new hero: "Welcome to the LAPD, Michael-Grace."

CHAPTER 9

Matteo pulls up to Genius Comics, and I'm surprised when he parks in a visitor's spot and turns off the engine instead of just dropping me off. "I know this is awkward to ask."

My heartbeat zings in my chest. Is he going to actually ask me out? I'm shocked to find that I'd readily accept. I'm slightly desperate to put my finger on just what intrigues me about this man. And bonus points that he doesn't seem the type to secretly tape, analyze, and try to market dating a geek chick like some of my more recent relationships.

He keeps looking ahead, fingers fidgeting on the steering wheel. He's *nervous*. My body responds in kind, releasing a horde of dragons into my stomach.

"I need you to keep the fact that you're helping us a secret." He leans forward.

I'm waiting for the other shoe to drop. "Okay, but what do I tell everyone?"

And now he looks *really* uncomfortable. "You said your coworkers already think we're seeing each other. We could let them draw their own conclusions and just not correct them? That way we don't have to out and out lie. You can help with the investigation if need be, and I can just drop in if I need to?"

So he *is* asking me out, but only as a cover. My little stomach dragons blink out of existence. It makes sense—he'd gain access to my coworkers, be able to come by the office without alerting anyone to the fact that the police are watching Genius. But it doesn't mean I'm happy about it. "You will *not* distract me at work. You will text any and *every* time you are coming, whether or not I agree to your scheme."

He slides out, opens my door, and insists on walking me to the lobby.

I try to tell him every which way to Sunday with my eyes that it's *not* necessary. That it's chauvinistic. That I won't be attacked in the one hundred feet to the main door, but he insists by ignoring me pointedly.

"So is that a yes?"

I eyeball him, trying not to note how good he looks with his work shirt rolled up at the elbows and his noon-o'clock shadow. I've got a lot going on right now, and I hate to admit that maybe, just *maybe*, my feelings are hurt about being only a pawn. A work tool. Not to mention the fact that there may be a double agent out there. Though it's unlikely, it *could* be Matteo. My instincts don't seem to be firing right around him, muddied by the electricity I feel. If I play along without doing my own bit of sleuthing, I could be leading the bad guy right to my friends and coworkers.

"It's a 'we'll see.' I don't have time for a boyfriend, fake or otherwise. Especially not one who drives a Prius. My friends would *never* buy it."

He ignores the Prius dig. "Can I stop by the office and look at the new comics? We need to get a feel for where we think this is headed, now that we know more about what we're dealing with."

"You *could* buy them yourself. I have a lot of work I need to do this week. Not only am I writing a new issue; I have to try and figure out how to get this promotion. I thought my boss was announcing it today, but he didn't, so there's still a chance. And there's this huge gala thing we're hosting for the thirtieth anniversary in a few weeks." A ball of stress forms in my stomach. As much as I said the words to make an excuse, I really *don't* have time for a boyfriend right now. Or a pretend boyfriend.

"But I need you to look at them and tell me what you're seeing. You're the expert." He's wearing that damn look on his face that makes me think of puppies.

"Fine." I hold up my finger before he can crow with victory. "But not at work. You've already shot my week to hell. You can come over to my house later this week and look at mine. I work from home Thursdays." This way I can keep him away from my coworkers and boss . . . but then he'll be in my house. I'm not sure which is worse.

"Deal."

I pull open the large glass doors, and of course, my full team—Kyle, Simon, and Tejshwara—are gathered in the front lobby, so they see us walk in.

"I'll see you later," Matteo says.

"Yeah, okay." I give a half wave and turn to flee to the safety of the elevator, but not before my coworkers muck up the situation even further.

"Hey, Matteo!" It's Kyle, and he's crossing the room to the main door before it can close. I note a fresh bandage on his wrist. From his newest escapade swinging in over a warehouse in his Spider-Man pajamas, perhaps? "We were thinking about having a movie marathon this weekend, and we wanted to invite you and MG. Saturday, at my house. From eleven to eleven."

My mouth actually falls open. This is unprecedented territory. I don't get invited to work parties. Other than Christmas, but then I just bring Lawrence or Ryan with me and hang out by the artichoke dip for four hours.

Matteo doesn't look surprised. He looks infuriatingly calm and *normal* about this. He says, "Oh, that's so nice of you. I think we could make—"

At the same time, I say, "No."

The peanut gallery looks between us.

"I thought you had that *thing* on Saturday?" I say through gritted teeth. This is getting out of hand. I didn't realize we'd face the pretend dating thing directly after our conversation.

"I think I can move it around, that is, if *you* want to go? Doesn't it sound fun? Movies with friends?" Innocence. Pure innocence.

And now I'm the bad guy if I say no. Frickin' brilliant. "Can I see you over here for a moment?" I grab Matteo's solid arm and pull him closer to the door. It's the first time I've grabbed him instead of the other way around, and I don't like contemplating asking him how often he has to work out to be a detective. It must be often from the feel of his muscled arm beneath my hand. My palms are sweating again. *Fake* relationship, MG. *Fake relationship.* I can no longer deny my attraction to Matteo. But now he's my partner? Boss? There are rules against these things. "Are you *trying* to undermine me at every turn, or is it just a particular talent you have?"

Color appears at his collar, either from my accusation or the fact that I'm still touching him. I release him like I'm holding molten steel, accidentally brushing his hand with mine as I retract my arm. I pull my hands into my chest, likely resembling an off-balance *Tyrannosaurus rex.*

"It might be the perfect opportunity to look into your coworkers. Get to know them." I know he's thinking about the bandage on Kyle's wrist, and I have to admit, I'm curious too.

I've stayed silent while Matteo has interrupted me too many times, and the gloves are coming off. "Then maybe do you want to *ask* me instead of barging right through and trying to control my life?"

He looks suitably ashamed but meets my eye. "Can we go to your work party?"

It's at this point that I realize we're being watched by all of my team. They might as well have popcorn, they look so entertained. Here I am, a novelty again. This one of my own making, though. Surely it won't be that bad to go hang out for a few hours in the name of helping solve this case. I'm hoping the "greater good" works out better for me than for Dumbledore.

I address the peanut gallery first, "Thanks for the invite. I think we'll be able to make it." I lower my voice and address Matteo, "As long as *someone* behaves themselves, capisce?" My world. My rules.

Matteo nods once in agreement to me, then waves to Tej, Kyle, and Simon before heading out the door. Why, when this comic has helped my life for so many years, is *The Hooded Falcon* wreaking such havoc this time?

CHAPTER 10

No matter how hard I try, I can't get Ryan or Lawrence to vacate the house on Thursday. Ryan's office day moved to Friday, so it's to a full audience that I open the door before Matteo can knock.

I need to keep this meeting brief, especially since we're going to be relegated to my bedroom instead of the living room. "I'm giving you thirty minutes."

He takes in my bright-blue cheetah yoga pants and black T-shirt. "Looks like a real ballbuster day at the office."

I will *not* laugh. We're serious work partners now. This is a business meeting. But I smirk, and he sees it and looks satisfied. Every time I try to put him into a box, he goes and gets all witty and charming again.

And dammit, he smells good. Who wears . . . I sniff . . . awesome-smelling laundry detergent to a work meeting? Look at me, weak-kneed from laundry detergent fumes. I definitely have been dating the wrong people if clean clothes are a turn-on.

"I *am* working," I say, closing the door behind him.

"I don't doubt it. You are a woman of your word." He reaches down to take off his shoes, and it's oddly intimate to see him in stocking feet in my entryway.

"Thirty minutes," I say again, and I turn to lead him into my room when I come nose-to-chest with Lawrence. And Ryan. Holding Trogdor.

"This is your big work meeting, huh?" Ryan looks at Matteo like he just stepped out of a spacecraft from Jakku. There is no skirting this introduction.

"Matteo." Matteo leans across me, easy as can be, and holds out his hand to Ryan and Lawrence. He doesn't even wince when Lawrence gives him the squeeze of a lifetime, his signature "don't mess with my girl" move. He also doesn't bat an eyelash at the bedazzled paisley headscarf Lawrence has wrapped around his head today or the bright-silver polish on his nails. Two more points for him.

"Ryan," my roommate offers in return, then continues to stand there.

The intro doesn't budge Ryan or L, so I let out a blustery sigh. "What's with the third degree?"

Ryan feigns innocence. "No interrogation here. We're just being friendly, MG. Where are your manners?" says the guy who grunts instead of forming words while he's gaming. Unless, of course, they're curse words. Those emerge perfectly and often.

I want to keep *everyone* away from Matteo, especially Lawrence. What if Matteo mentions that I've told him about Casey Senior's journal? "You've met Ryan. This is Trogdor and Lawrence." I motion to each of them in turn, then look at Ryan. "Satisfied?"

Now Ryan's got some sort of smirk on his face. Great. "Supremely."

"So glad I could entertain you," I say dryly.

"Trogdor. Like *Homestar Runner*?" Matteo asks. I whip my head around and eye him. I know he has no idea who Trogdor is. He must have googled it after he met Trog last time.

"Yeah." Ryan turns the dog over, little stub legs in the air. Like a man possessed, he starts doing our personalized imitation of the Trogdor dragon video, altered for the dog. "First you draw a loaf of bread, then you draw anodder loaf of bread, and then you draw two pizza slices on the head for ears . . ." Trog licks Ryan's face.

"Not to break up the comedy act, but we have things to do in my bedroom."

I close my eyes as both my friends chortle and Ryan says, "*Things*, huh?"

"Move it or lose it, Ryan." I shove past him. "That's not what I meant."

He closes rank behind me and blocks Matteo in the entryway. He's still smirking, but now he and Lawrence remind me strongly of two big brothers; I'm more than mortified.

"So what do you do, Matteo? Are you with Genius too?" Ryan sizes up Matteo's button-down shirt. It's not normal Genius fare, and I want to smack my own head. *Work meeting.* Right. Matteo would have to work with me for it to be a work meeting.

Matteo clearly picks up the same vibe I do but handles it like a pro. Completely casual. "I went to school for architecture." He hangs his head sheepishly and looks at Ryan and Lawrence. "Actually, this isn't for work. I met MG in a coffee shop. She and I got to talking, and I told her I wanted to read some comic books, so she invited me over to give me a few suggestions."

Lawrence's and Ryan's heads swivel to me in tandem. It's *creepy*. I know how implausible this seems. I *never* invite guys from the coffee shop to my house to show them comics. My home is my sanctuary, and Ryan and I have a strict no-hookup policy in the house. My mind spins, trying to figure out how to tell them about our work without spilling the beans. Maybe Matteo won't mind if my roommate knows about the ruse.

Lawrence busts up laughing instead of questioning Matteo further. "I bet she did."

Somehow they are buying it. After giving me a good once-over, Lawrence opens his arm to let Matteo past. "Best not keep a woman waiting, son." He goes so far as to clap him soundly on the shoulder.

"It's nothing. Seriously, guys. Just go do whatever you were doing." I comport myself with every ounce of dignity I can muster until Matteo and I are safely in my room. I leave the door wide open.

"*That* went well," I mutter, glancing around my room. In my head I'm cursing myself for not cleaning up. I didn't really plan on bringing him in here. I see the rubble of my room with fresh eyes. Not too much laundry. The bed is half-made. Some papers and drawings on the floor and on my nightstand. I walk over to the dresser, stuff a pair of undies back in, and shut all the drawers.

Trog trots in and hops on my bed with a jingle. The white duvet is peppered with the copper-and-white hairs that incessantly fall from my dog, and when he lies down, a cloud of them fly into the air.

Matteo must decide that looks like a good idea because he walks over to my bed and sits next to the dog. I'm left to fend for myself and end up sitting awkwardly facing them in the wooden chair that holds a plant near the window.

"Now what?" I ask, looking at the man and dog on my bed. Matteo looks far too at home with my dog. On. My. Bed. Can I even count the months—nay, years—it's been since I've had a guy in my room other than Ryan or Lawrence? Voldemort—the guy who filmed our dates for profit—was the last one, so two years? Quite the dry spell. I have the insane urge to push him back onto my bed and sink my hands into those artfully disheveled locks of his, fake relationship or no.

"I guess we could always do what your roommates are expecting and . . ." Matteo purrs as if reading my mind. For the briefest of seconds, something sparks in his gaze that looks suspiciously like desire, but it's gone in a blink. "Look at comic books?" he finishes.

I let out a small chuckle, and it breaks the tension, though my stomach has yet to unclench from my vision of us rolling around on my duvet.

"Fair point. Work. The case." My closet is a disaster area, and I want to shield him from too much of the mess, so I open the sliding door farthest from him and reach in to look for my stack of comics. "They're here. I just have to find—whoops." I knock over a stack of watercolor sketches. I'm not the most neat and tidy of women. I cultivate the "creative chaos" style of housekeeping.

I dig for a few more minutes. "That's weird. I swear I thought I'd put them in here." I look around my room in hopes of inspiration and spy the comics on the top of my bookshelf. I guess I moved them at some point. Yet I could have sworn I put them in my closet. Maybe Ryan wanted to look at them as reference material for the video game? He's the only one who ever comes in here. I shrug my unease off, anxious to get to the business of looking through comics so I can stop sneaking glances at Matteo petting my dog on my bed.

Nabbing the comics off the shelf, I sit in front of Matteo. Trog is now on his back, laying it *all* out for the world to see. He has zero modesty.

"So this is the first of the new ones, and I thought we could look at where Casey Junior picked up and Senior left off. Show you the difference between the two comics just so you have an operating knowledge of the series as a whole."

It's incredibly awkward for me to turn the comic book halfway between us. We're both craning our necks at angles that aren't comfortable, and I let out a huff of frustration before picking up the stack of comics and plopping myself between Trog and Matteo. My hip presses into Matteo's, but I imagine a stone wall there. Partners don't focus on how aware they are of other partners' legs, right?

I look up and our eyes meet. I should say something about the comic book. I reach for another, and instead, I end up sliding back a fraction of an inch when my weight lands on the issue instead of grabbing it. Something flicks in his eyes, a switch going from cool to hot. He helps me to sit up again, heat searing through my shirt sleeve where his hand rests like a lightsaber. He's close. He's *too* close. Matteo leans forward, his eyes on my lips. It feels like I'm standing on the edge of a cliff, like this is something *big*, exciting, and suddenly scary. My heart stutters to an absolute halt in my chest. Frozen. It's Castle Black in there. Something thaws, a trickle at first but picking up speed until it's a torrent. My body automatically returns his lean. Matteo is so close, his face is blurry. Then his breath is on my cheek, and . . . he reaches right across me and grabs the framed picture off the bedside table.

I'm getting whiplash. First I think he's going to ask me out; then he asks me to pretend to date him. Then an almost-kiss, but now he's studying this picture frame like it's a clue to the damn mystery. It's a picture of Ryan, Trog, and me at Halloween. Looking at it through his eyes, I realize how cozy we look. Like I fancy my roommate, even though to me he's family. Aren't you allowed to have pictures of your family next to your bed?

I swear the muscle in his jaw tightens ever so slightly.

"It's my favorite picture of Trog," I say by way of explanation. It's probably best to get back to business. "Anyway, this first issue of the new reboot is the only issue that addresses the old story line with the smugglers and the double agent—"

"Is Trogdor in a box?"

I blink. "Yes."

"Is that another one of the jokes I don't get? Like a Japanese cartoon thing? Or an online meme?" He says "meh-muh," and I stifle a laugh.

"It's anime, and a meme," I say, correcting his pronunciation. "And no. That was his costume. He was a box."

"A box of . . ."

I shrug. "Just a box. This year he's going to be the demo-corgan from *Stranger Things* . . ."

Matteo throws his head back and laughs, interrupting me. Trog gives an indignant snort and sneeze, wiggles on his back, then slides off the bed and trots out the door. Fuzz-butt traitor. "So you're saying that you're a comic book writer, have purple hair and a million inside jokes from movies and books I've never seen or read, and that your dog was a plain ol' box for Halloween?"

"I thought it was funny." I'm defensive now, and not a little put out.

"It *is* funny. You just keep surprising me is all." His face is warm, open, and inarguably magnetic right now.

"Oh." I refuse to return his grin. We're dangerously off the rails here.

I open the comic and scan the pages. Instead of the beautiful yellows and greens the originals were drawn with, these are an in-your-face, gratuitous riot. I love me some colors—just look at my hair—but after years of having rainbow-hued locks, I've learned an important lesson: *judicious* use of color is key. "Here," I say, pointing at a page. "This is where they return to the warehouse and fight with his partner. And here"—I open the first of the new issues—"here's where it moves away from the old story line. It's also where they find the secret portal to the alien planet, and . . . Are you listening to me?"

Matteo replaces the picture on the table and leafs through the stack of drawings. "Did you draw these? And yes, of course I'm listening. They find the lair, tie up the double agent. And I have a question about that. But I also want to know if you drew these."

I reach out, snag them, and stuff the drawings for L's new costume into my desk drawer. I'd rather have him rifling through my underwear. My drawings are *private*. "Yes, I drew them. And why don't you go ahead and ask your question about the comic book and leave off snooping."

He wears an innocent look that I'm not buying. "Fine. Touchy. I thought you said the other day that we didn't know what happened to the double agent." The words "double agent" send a tingle up my spine. A dirty cop. Brewing drug wars. White Rabbit. There are too many odd coincidences these days between *The Hooded Falcon* and real life.

I wiggle forward so my feet dangle off the edge of my bed, trying to extricate myself from the force of gravity that Matteo's larger person exerts on my smaller frame. I fail miserably and seem to only draw attention to the fact that we're pressed together in the middle of the bed for no reason now that Trogdor is gone.

"That's what I'm getting at. The story line was basically dropped in the new series. In the old ones, it's set up as a big reveal. They find the drugs. Falcon is going to unmask him. They're going to expose him to the public. Then the new ones"—I flop my hand around, searching for a word—"tie it up in a matter of pages. They simply go to a warehouse owned by the double agent, find the stash of drugs, and capture him for the police. They never reveal in the comic who the superhero was to Space City, even though we're told he was a double agent. We know he was *someone* important to the book. This cliffhanger has always bothered true followers of the Falcon. And now we know why. Casey Senior died before his final comics could be run." I pause, still feeling guilty about revealing L's secret to Matteo. "Lawrence's journal proves that Casey Senior planned to unmask the double agent, end the comic, and retire the Falcon."

"But the new one didn't."

"No."

I'm starting to recognize the super intense gaze as Matteo's thinking face. "Why change the new one so drastically?"

"I suspect because either Edward Casey Junior didn't *know* what his father had planned or more than likely didn't care. I told you that it was in this episode that they launched the new cycle. New villains, new weapons. Even the costumes changed drastically. Being a Robin Hood character isn't cool anymore; kids aren't interested in social justice. If you don't have aliens and stun guns, you aren't selling, I guess. Really the only thing he kept was Swoosh, the sidekick, and the fact that the Hooded Falcon uses a bow and arrow."

I bite my lip, a thought occurring to me. "You don't think that Casey Junior . . ." I can't even finish my sentence. Son killing father certainly isn't an unheard-of story line in comics.

Matteo frowns, picking up my thought anyhow. "Hurt his father to keep the comic running? Possibly. Your friend Lawrence said that Casey Junior was pretty bent out of shape about his father's death, right? I don't really see him murdering his father in cold blood, but we'll have to add it to our list of possibilities. I'm not sure that we have enough to question him yet, though, anything to tie him to the *real* reason we're investigating these comics." He rubs his hand over his stubbled chin, making a rasping noise.

"I guess," I say, not convinced. Casey Junior is my number-one suspect, internally. Kill your father in cold blood to keep him from ruining the empire he's built and take it over to reap fame and fortune? Add a few capes and some spandex, and it seems like a Hollywood blockbuster plot to me.

"It doesn't help my theory if the story line never really got finished for our masked avenger to replicate or follow." Matteo glances over the comics, then up at me. "Can we go over the order of events in the issue that we're loosely following? Let's try to get ahead of our misguided superhero before he gets killed in the crossfire."

"Yeah, sure. I think I have that one, actually. Well, half of it. It's old. It fell apart years ago." I dig around in the pile I brought over and hand some papers to Matteo to hold while I sort through issues. My copy is battered compared to the pristine one in the work library, but I love it just the same.

I flip to the page. "Okay, so if I were to guess about what were to happen next? It would be something in a warehouse. Or on a boat. We already know that our suspect was in the warehouse district. We could guess he tracked these guys to where they stash their drugs, either when they get them in or when they're being sent out."

Matteo nods, flicking through the papers I handed him. He's not paying attention *again*. "Warehouse or boat. I'll look into those. Can I borrow that issue from you?" He's still focused on the pile of papers, frowning like he's looking for something right in front of his face.

I'm kind of offended that he's brushing off my predictions. That's the whole reason he's here, right? I'm starting to think that maybe he has superhuman powers to focus on two things at one time, and he's *very* interested in my papers for some reason. I hesitate. He's not asking for the original series, but it's still against my rules. "Yeah, no problem. Just get them back to me."

"What is this?"

I eyeball the pile of papers. "My research for my article on the thirtieth anniversary of *THF*." It's about the LA heroin war that framed the backdrop for the rise of *The Hooded Falcon*'s popularity, and I can tell the eerie similarity to the comic isn't lost on Matteo. He flips to the next papers in the bunch. "And these?"

My heart flip-flops, recognizing the acceptance letter I received in the mail. I still can't believe it is true. "Information on San Diego Comic-Con. I entered a costuming contest held there." I stop short of telling him all about *the* biggest geek-girl fashion design competition in the country and how excited I am. Matteo seems to inspire conversational tangents, making me want to prattle on like a schoolgirl. I have to keep course correcting my brain if this is a business meeting. I am an LAPD consultant now, after all.

"This." He sits up straighter and nearly throws the paper at me. "This we can go in with."

"What on earth are you talking about?" I pick up the folded printout of the list of memorabilia for the charity auction. Casey Junior's face smiles from the too-polished-to-be-candid picture of him sitting at his father's desk in their LA mansion. "The charity auction?"

"No, the picture."

I study it, then glance up at him, still baffled.

"Beside the desk," Matteo nearly crows.

I look back and do a double take. It's a glass cabinet tucked into the corner of the room housing a perfect replica of the Hooded Falcon's costume—cape and all.

"You think . . . my boss?" I can't imagine Casey Junior running through the streets in a cape.

Matteo shrugs, but his eyes sparkle. I'm pretty sure it's the same look I get when a great idea strikes me at work. "It's enough to question him. Let's see if your friend's information holds water. Thank you for your help, Michael-Grace. I'll be in touch about the interview with Casey and let you know if I find anything on the warehouse front."

I pad to the door behind him. He slips on his shoes and heads outside with a wave. A second later he sticks his head back in. I'm still standing there, fighting the insane urge I have to run after him like I don't want him to leave.

"Oh, but I guess I'll see you this weekend. I'll call—er, *text* you about it. I'm looking forward to meeting your coworkers." He winks.

I smile, relieved that this isn't fully goodbye.

CHAPTER 11

I shut the door behind him and turn to find Ryan and Lawrence standing in the entry again. These guys are *sneaky* for large men.

Lawrence's mouth hangs ajar. "He's meeting your *coworkers*?"

"It's not like that." Then I realize that it *is* like that and that I sound stupid. "Well, I mean, he's already met them."

I might as well have announced I'm selling all my electronics and living an unplugged life—Ryan looks *that* weirded out.

"He already met them because I left my wallet at the coffee shop, and he returned it to me at my office. Then he fixed this chair, so Kyle has a man-crush on him now and invited him to a movie thing. It's not a big deal." I'm being disingenuous about more than just the wallet. I *like* Matteo. He's funny and smart and makes me laugh, and even though he's not my type, he just . . . sneaks up on you. I remember the flash of heat in Matteo's eyes and wonder if after all this hoopla dies down, maybe I *should* invite him out for a drink. Sure, he wouldn't know Trogdor from Smaug if they bit him in the butt, but he sure *is* cute. And now I'm thinking about his butt. *Stop it. Stop it. Stop it.*

Maybe it's time to change the type of guys I date. I haven't had such great luck with the geek crowd. The last con party I attended, a guy walked up to me five or six times before finally telling me my Codex outfit was "neat," then followed me into the bathroom, resulting in me threatening to beat him with my papier-mâché staff.

Ryan stares at me as I mull through my thoughts, then calls me on my bluff. "Right. No big deal. Because you always invite people over to read comics in your bedroom when they return your wallet at your office."

Lawrence doesn't look put out like Ryan does. He looks *gleeful.* "Girl, that man is Atlanta, Georgia, in Ju-ly, and he can come and build me a tower anytime."

"Oh come on, give me a break. We'll probably never see him again." *Lie.* I seem to be lying to everyone these days.

"You didn't see how he looked at you." Ryan crosses his arms.

My pulse quickens in my veins, but a familiar anxiety washes over me, breaking down the hope spawning in my stomach. Dating a non-geek means they might want to normal-fy me. I am terrified of someone constantly telling me my shows or comics are dumb, wishing I'd "tone down my hair a bit," or asking me to give up my job like my mom. I did the normal-guy thing once. It took a botched engagement to wake me up. No, it is better to continue flying solo, and far fewer entanglements for the police case this way.

I shove my reaction back into the padlocked box it belongs in. "Let's all go back in the living room. I have something I want to show both of you."

I reemerge from my room several minutes later with a stack of papers, which I present like a trophy on the coffee table while standing in front of the TV.

"You make a pretty crappy window—aw, sonofa, L! You're supposed to kill the aliens, not our team members!" Ryan leans around me, and I hear the sound of video game gunfire at my back. More specifically crossbow fire.

"Well, I *wouldn't* if somebody wasn't standing in front of the television."

They both throw their controllers down and grumble.

"You guys can go back to killing imaginary—"

"We're working on a real project. This is my *job*, MG." Ryan still sounds like a petulant four-year-old.

"I know. I'll keep this brief. But I want to show you what I just finished filling out." I hold out a paper to Ryan.

"Congratulations, you learned to fill out a form." Ryan barely glances at the paper as he takes it. This drives me crazy about Ryan and is why I can't date a gamer. His job is all-consuming at times. It's like pulling teeth to get *anything* out of him when he's focused. And how much he identifies with his gaming heroes verges on unhealthy. Like a lot of guys who game, I feel like he wants to be heroic in real life but decides it's safer to be a hero in a fake world rather than face judgment. Plus, the regulations for crossbows are murder, I hear.

Lawrence, thankfully, isn't acting like a toddler and takes the sheet of paper. "Girl, is this what I think it is?"

"Yes! I got in!" I can't contain myself any further. "And, L, I would so be honored if you would be my model. I only have two months to come up with *the* best costume design of my life."

Ryan finally glances up and grabs the brochure off the top of the stack of papers on the coffee table. "San Diego Comic-Con, Miss Her Galaxy," he reads out loud. Realization dawns on his face as he flips through the pages. "Oh, this is that fashion show you were talking about entering."

"Yes. And thanks to L's encouragement and my drawings for his costumes, they've accepted me! More than fifteen hundred applicants, and they only select twenty!" This couldn't have come at a better time. I entered on a whim, but now I need to see if I'm *really* any good at fashion and costume design. If I win, I'll get a deal designing for Hot Topic stores . . . I wouldn't have to get the promotion. I could give a one-fingered salute to Genius . . . but that is a big if and something I don't want to bank on quite yet.

As good as my ideas are, my presentations at work *haven't* been going so well. The more worked up I get about them, the worse they get. I am the better writer—of this I am certain—but *maybe*, just maybe, Casey's favor of Andy doesn't have everything to do with the ideas themselves. I'm concerned that even if I *try harder*, nothing will change. That this is how Genius is, take it or leave it. And I'm contemplating leaving it, which is something I never thought I'd do.

This contest would be something just for *me*. If I win, I'll become a household name for geek girls everywhere. I'll support my fellow femmes and rub elbows with the best. It's time to take a risk on myself and possibly on my future.

"MG, that's really impressive." Ryan looks up, all trace of toddler gone. "Seriously. I thought you weren't even going to apply." He stands up and scoops me into a hug. It's so warm and comfortable, I forget any weirdness between us.

Lawrence is next and swoops me up. MG sandwich. My absolute favorite spot in the universe.

"So you'll do it, L? I'll make you look fierce."

"Will I be the only queen?"

I shrug. "I think so. Cleo definitely won't be there; that's for sure."

"I'm in."

Excellent. L is the Fezzik to my Inigo, and I need him there with me. "And we'll need our cheering section. How about it, Ryan? I brought you all sorts of info." I cut off Ryan's response before he can roll his eyes. "I *know* you hate cons. I get it. But this one isn't a gamer convention. It's just general geek merriment. I think Jean-Luc Picard is going to be there."

Ryan's eyes gain a hint of interest. "I'm not promising anything." But he takes the brochure from me.

"I have a color at eleven," Lawrence announces, stretching up and touching the ceiling. "I need to go open the shop. Ry, I'll see you at the gym later."

Ryan grunts in agreement. It's their guy-love language, though I don't understand how one grunt can say so many different things. It's one of the things that makes Ryan and Lawrence closer to an old married couple than friends.

Ryan was originally L's roommate but ended up moving out because a spiteful lover had dumped a bottle of wine on their PlayStation when L beat him at *Call of Duty*.

Ryan didn't mind L's eccentricities—L was the first person who befriended Ryan at the gym after he'd moved to LA, and Ryan seems to have something dark in his past that makes him shy about meeting people. We don't talk about it much; he clams up big time whenever I ask. Maybe it's why he and L get along so well: they have that in common. He always says that he has a fresh lease on life here and that he's making amends for his past any way he can.

Lawrence slips his shoes on, and I note the letter "L" written in sparkles on the black leather. That bitch has been bedazzling without me.

I blow him a kiss as he leaves, lock the door behind him, and walk back into the living room to sink onto the cracked pleather couch. I prop my feet over the end, grab one of the woefully mismatched couch pillows, and settle into Ryan's side.

Ryan's answering grunt means I'm clearly inhibiting his ability to make a living today. "Hang on, everybody. I'm going to mute. MG is back." He pulls the headset off and looks down. All sorts of horrible commentary starts pouring from the TV as the other gamers in his group start catcalling and suggesting video game–based sexual positions. I catch the term "paladin missionary style" before Ryan manages to silence the channel.

"How's work?" I ask.

He raises his eyebrow, and his eyes say that it would be going better if I stopped interrupting, but he decides to be diplomatic. "The job is more challenging than I could ever have imagined. How about *you*?" He draws out the syllables, obviously fishing for the reason I'm back on the couch instead of working like a good girl.

Two of the characters on screen pretend to do a striptease, and Ryan runs his avatar forward to knock them over.

"My big presentation didn't go as well as I wanted." I tell him about Andy basically stealing my idea.

"You have so many talents. So many skills. You can smell a story a mile away. Fastest brain this side of the galaxy. But maybe this isn't your superpower. Maybe you're not General Leia. Do you even really want to be a team leader? Less time on your own work? More time with the executives? Maybe this isn't the only solution."

My glance must give away my skepticism because Ryan rolls his eyes to the ceiling. "For instance, if Andy gets the promotion, wouldn't there be an opening for team captain or whatever? You'd still be Kyle and Simon's boss."

I contemplate that. "True." Before he can crow with satisfaction, I hold up my hand. "*But* Andy would still get to be executive, *and* I want the promotion so that I can do costume design."

"I get that, but . . . surely if Andy gets the promotion, you use that genius brain of yours to figure out another way to do what you want to do? And maybe it will be better than your plan A?"

I press my lips together and meet Ryan's brown eyes. His hat is on backward over his blondish hair, so he looks like a teenager, but the words coming out of his mouth are surprisingly grown-up—and almost exactly verbatim what I've just been telling myself. When did Ryan turn in to the adult of this relationship?

The players in the game are now testing what look like vials of potions on one another, and Ryan leans forward to yell into the mic. "Quit that, you guys. We need to test those against the alien horde . . . Aw, dammit, Lee, now you've attracted the band of rogue archers, and you know they're still glitchy."

"I'll leave you to it." I hop back off the couch and smirk. Ryan is already completely immersed again, his fingers flying over the controller. Something has shifted, though. Ryan seems older, wiser. Have I missed something in his life while I've been sidetracked with the case? Must be that girl he's been seeing. "Love you, Ryan."

He smiles, still staring at the screen. "I know."

CHAPTER 12

It's Friday morning just after breakfast. I've already walked Trog and have the television on, hoping to hear something related to my case.

"The Golden Arrow strikes again. This seems to be the latest in a recent string of vigilante justice . . ."

I turn from the sink, glass of water halfway to my mouth. It can't be. The Golden Arrow? Is that what the media has decided to call our masked civilian? I roll my eyes at the general public's lack of creativity with naming superheroes, seeing as our competitor already has an "arrow" superhero with a different-colored moniker.

"Moments ago we got word that this warehouse had been chained shut by persons unknown, and an anonymous call was placed to the police claiming that they would find more than just criminals inside. We suspect a drug bust of large proportions. Police have surrounded the area with crime scene tape, so we can't get any closer, but it looks like teams are arriving to transfer dangerous individuals to the police station." The reporter is gleeful, her red suit standing out against the grays, blues, and rust hues that make up the warehouse district alleyway. I recognize the building they're standing in front of. It's the same one I saw in the video at Matteo's office.

My phone buzzes. I can't tear my eyes away from the screen where the news feed cuts to a chopper view of the warehouse near the docks. A brilliant gold arrow painted across the front of the building and doors, at least twelve feet long, gleams in the morning sun. The bold gold glitter paint makes me think of Lawrence. This is a hero right up his alley.

My phone buzzes again, and I glance at it. It's a text from a number I don't recognize, but I'm not surprised by what it says.

I'm going to call. Answer your phone, we need to talk.

A smile tugs at my lips. Matteo's learning.

As I read the lines, the screen transitions to the active call icon, and I thumb "Answer."

"I see it. On the news," I say without preamble.

Matteo doesn't waste time on formalities either. Chopper noise beats in the background of his call, indicating he's already at the scene. "I'd like you to come look. When can you get out of work?"

My heart starts to thud a staccato rhythm in my chest. "I guess around three?" This is *real.* It's insane, but *real.* My very own comic book come to life.

"That's late, but it'll have to do." He hisses out a breath. "I'll let you get ready for work. Call me when you're out. You're going to want to see this." Then he's gone, leaving dead air between us.

"I'm glad you made it. Traffic is horrible today. Everyone is a lookie-loo." Matteo holds my car door open for me as I climb out into the smoggy, nasty air that is LA's inversion layer. I sputter on the smell of too many cars, too many fast-food hamburgers, and the lurking scent of wood decaying in the water. It's why I avoid the Santa Monica piers like the plague. Everyone always lauds the "fresh sea air." For me, I'd rather be at home with my air filter.

It's three o'clock on the dot, and I did everything short of faking sickness to get out of the office today. Everyone wanted to talk about the upcoming gala and the Golden Arrow on the news.

"What do I need to bring with me?" I shove sketches into my Genius messenger bag, then reach in the back seat to grab the original *THF* issues I smuggled out of Genius. They would *kill* me if they ever find out. I have to hope I keep them pristine and use them only if truly needed. The new ones can be replaced. The originals can't.

Matteo leans in and pins a media pass to the lapel of my jacket, and I go still. I am inordinately fascinated with his fingers fastening the pin, though it takes no more than fifteen seconds. My heart careens in my chest like a Mario-kart around a curve.

Matteo, on the other hand, looks cool as a cucumber. All business. This is a crime scene, after all. "There, you're all set. Come on, let's get you across the line. We've been trying to keep the media out all day. I think reporters are about to start rappelling in from the next building to get a look."

I raise my eyebrow at him.

"I like *Mission Impossible*. I'm a gadget guy."

I can see that about him.

He flashes his badge to the patrol officer standing near the street. "Kildaire, narcotics," he says by way of greeting.

What am I? *Martin, superhero consultant? Comic specialist?* At the patrol officer's nod, Matteo holds the yellow tape up, and I duck under, resisting the urge to snap a picture of myself and post it to Instagram. I'm *inside a crime scene*. Just call me Temperance Brennan. And Matteo is *so* Seeley Booth. He's wearing a brown felt fedora today over his dark locks and sun-kissed brown skin. It looks very twenties throwback. Very noir detective. Very, *very* sexy. I mean, I'd find Worf drinking prune juice attractive if he put a fedora on. Be still, my twenties era–loving heart.

Thinking about *Bones* brings me to my only worry about the crime scene.

"The people inside aren't dead, are they? I do *not* do dead bodies."

"No. They're all alive and in custody. I'm not sure they'll be appreciative, given the jail time they're facing."

The afternoon sun shines directly in my eyes, and I squint. Perpetually wearing glasses means no sunglasses. I'm also afraid I've overdressed for the weather. I wish I'd worn a hat, and I'm regretting the navy-blue coat over my "Don't Let the Muggles Get You Down" graphic tee. It's my silent homage to the person who's quickly becoming my favorite Muggle. I couldn't help myself today when I saw the shirt in my closet. I thought of Matteo and had to wear it. Would it be inappropriate for a crime scene investigator expert to wear just a tee, though? I decide to swelter it out in my jacket for a bit, even though I already feel a drop of sweat sliding between my shoulder blades. Ah, Los Angeles. I hate being hot, but I hate being cold more. And as hypocritical as it is for me to hate this city and love it too, there it is. I'd never live anywhere else.

Matteo leads me over cracked and rutted asphalt, around the corner of a metal building, and to the front door of the building I recognize from the news. The golden arrow looks spray-painted, and a few other police in uniform still work to photograph and document it.

"Ah, Detective Rideout, Agent Sosa, this is Michael-Grace Martin, the comic book expert I was telling you about." Matteo ushers me forward, his arm behind my back, toward two people in suits standing by the far end of the building.

"Hi," I say. I reach forward for a quick handshake from both, used to leading out. God help the man if he does that limp-finger "lady handshake" thing.

"Detective Rideout assists me with the LAPD narcotics portion of this investigation."

By the look of him, this Rideout guy's not thrilled I'm here, but at least it's a firm shake.

Matteo then gestures to a dark-haired agent wearing a bright-blue coat. Her hair is cut short into a stylish but severe page cut that would feel like shackles to me. All that maintenance, no movement, no creativity, just morning after morning of the same smoothing and straightening. "Agent Sosa is from the DEA and is evaluating whether or not the FBI needs to share jurisdiction. Copycat crimes aren't common, so Detective Rideout and I are leaning toward asking for a federal profiler to help out as well."

I snort. "Well, it's not like it's often that someone pretends to be a superhero."

"Actually"—Detective Rideout levels a gaze at me—"it's not unheard of. What's uncommon about *this* case is that they're good at it. I saw it before on patrol. Isolated incidents, and because bad guys don't have moral compasses, the would-be hero is beat to a pulp in four seconds flat and ends up at the hospital in an embarrassingly tight spandex suit."

Matteo shades his eyes and glances toward the building. I follow his gaze. My eyes wander over the golden arrow, lingering on the lower part of the door where more graffiti is partially obscured by a crate and a pile of crime scene tape.

"Should we show the lady comic book expert the stuff we found inside the Lair of Justice?" Detective Rideout gives me a once-over that clearly shows he's interested in two assets of my person in particular, and not the smarts. He leans over, under the guise of opening the front door, and says in a low voice, "That's a reference to *The Hooded Falcon.*"

My brain flashes back to my conversation with Ryan. I need to be a professional here. A team player. I don't want to default to insults. But years of this treatment while working in the comic book store and at Genius cause an automatic stiffening of my spine. Mansplaining comics is literally *the* most annoying thing in the world to me.

I halt at the door to the warehouse, and the group turns to look, a smug smirk on Detective Rideout's face. He thinks he's made his point. I'm about to make mine.

"No, you shouldn't show me inside. First off, I currently write for Genius Comics and have worked in the industry for ten years—I think that far outweighs your weekend trips to the comic book store." Matteo looks horrified, though a little fascinated at my outburst.

I can't help myself. The words just tumble out of me, just like they do in my meetings when I get defensive. "Secondly, the *Hall* of Justice refers to the *Justice League*, which is a competitor's property. Falcon's personal hideout was called the Glen, until the new series when they changed it to the Falcon's Nest, which personally I think is a dumb name, but whatever. I wasn't there for that vote." I take a deep breath, fully aware of the uncomfortable set of Detective Rideout's shoulders.

"And thirdly, no, you shouldn't take me inside because you are about to walk straight past something important. Do you see that graffiti there? To a *true* comic book expert"—I can't help but add the dig—"that mark tells us who these criminals were selling to, or who the Golden Arrow *thinks* they're working for."

They turn in unison to look at the graffitied white rabbit, and I bite my cheek to keep from smiling.

"And *that's* why she's here," Matteo confirms.

I walk over to the heavy metal door, kneel low where kids have been tagging the building with several colors of spray paint, and point to the outline of a white rabbit.

"The Easter Bunny?" I don't even have to look to know it's Rideout's dulcet tones.

"You see how this looks as fresh as the golden arrow? I don't think it's a mistake. This is the White Rabbit."

The DEA agent frowns and looks at Matteo.

"You mean the Hooded Falcon's nemesis? As in a real person?" Matteo asks. "Are we chasing *two* vigilantes now?"

I chew on my lip, unsure. I decide to go with my gut because that's what I'm here for. "I don't think so. I think it's a reference *to* the White Rabbit, but it's hidden. It's like our suspect—the Golden Arrow, I think they're calling him—didn't want just anyone to find it." A prickle rises along my neck. Is this meant for *me?* Is it a warning? Matteo said that these drug cartels wouldn't think twice about killing someone to keep their silence. And here I am, willing mouse chasing a cat in a game with ever-heightening stakes.

I continue with my explanation, though Detective Rideout looks like he's about to glaze over. You can always tell a true comic book fan by their knowledge and love of a good origin story. Falcon's is the best in my opinion, and Rideout has sunk lower in my estimation for his failure to latch on to the tie-in.

"In the origin story of the Hooded Falcon, he's an average Joe who stumbles upon a drug deal at a dock. Instead of walking past, he calls the police to stop it. The drug dealers see him, abduct him, stow him in the ship, then ultimately leave him on a deserted island where he has to fend for himself for months before a ship comes back. It's where he hones his hunting skills to survive. The same smugglers come back to the island to pick up the stash. He sneaks aboard and ends up commandeering the ship, steering it into the port of Space City, and turning over the entire ship, crew, and drugs to the authorities." I point to the rabbit. "The rabbit is the sign of his archnemesis—the White Rabbit, a Chinese drug lord. It's accepted as a reference to China white, or a slang term for heroin."

I look around, and all three of them are blinking at me. Suddenly I'm not so sure. "Didn't you say that White Rabbit is what the street drug is called?"

"Yes." It's Agent Sosa who answers. Her mouth has puckered like she's sucking on a Sour Patch Kid. "We did the field tests, and it's positive for heroin. Possibly other elements, though more than likely that's contamination from the scene. We have yet to do a full scan at the lab. It's more likely that this drawing is in reference to the street drug."

I bite my lip. Other contaminates like a designer drug? But . . . Occam's razor. I suppose it's possible I'm stretching this too far. I look at Matteo, who shrugs. We're all in the dark here. Until I am sure that the Golden Arrow is trying to identify a specific nemesis, I should keep to the simpler explanations. "Probably."

We tour the rest of the crime scene, but I don't see any further indication of hidden messages or Hooded Falcon trivia. Towering stacks of boxes and crates, most of which are being sorted through, cataloged, and photographed by officers, fill the warehouse. The warehouse stock sheet says there are twenty bays of other goods to inspect, everything from books, magazines, and comic books to KitchenAid mixers, machine parts, and—I laugh—cereal. Crates and crates of cereal.

"Maybe they're putting heroin in Cap'n Crunch. I've suspected it for years." My joke earns a smirk from Matteo but not even an eye roll from Rideout. Great. He's grumpy *and* he has no sense of humor. *Detective Dursley* it is.

Matteo points to the largest group of people in the warehouse, gathered around a small stack of crates on the floor. "We discovered the uncut heroin. Agent Sosa here has explained that more than likely it's from Mexico, since we're so close to the border and it's not unheard of for illegal shipments of drugs to come on small boats from Tijuana."

I frown. That doesn't line up with the White Rabbit from the comics, but I'm still not sure how literal to take the story line. "Could it be from another country, say China?" Just the other week, Ryan pointed out an article online about the rise of the designer drug culture in LA. It said that countries like China, Laos, and Vietnam were hotbeds for synthetic drug production and that US port cities were starting to see more of them. Now *that* could be a nod to the White Rabbit in the comics. Something moves deep in my subconscious, and the image of the boat from the panel with the people tied to the dock surfaces.

"Could these drugs possibly be readying for *export* instead of going to other states?"

Agent Sosa squints at me.

"Well, it's just that the initial drug bust was down by the docks, and in the scene it reminded me of from the comic, the drugs were being loaded onto a boat, not off."

Agent Sosa flicks a glance at Matteo, then sweeps her dark page cut behind one ear and gives me a small smile that looks a *teensy* condescending, like she's humoring a kindergartner. Which I practically am, since the most I know about drugs is that Tylenol Cold & Sinus wipes me out for three days. "We're going to proceed as if it's a standard drug trafficking case until proven otherwise. In my professional opinion, that's what we're dealing with."

"It's just . . . it's a lot like the plotline with the White Rabbit in the series. Enough that I think you should look into it?"

Agent Sosa narrows her eyes at me, and I feel like I'm overstepping my bounds on my first day at work. "This is cut-and-dried. We'll test it and send a report to the narcotics team, but it's your basic pure heroin. Next it would have been cut, packaged, and trucked out to the surrounding area. I don't even think it's what the street teams are labeling White Rabbit. The lab will have to tell us. We're wasting our time in this warehouse looking for clues, past testing the product."

"One of the dealers from the first bust is with a notorious Mexican cartel," Detective Rideout adds. "And I agree that the connection to the comic book is weak. We should move forward with the cartel theory."

I'm *not* convinced. Or my gut isn't. I shoot a look at Matteo. "The Golden Arrow is obviously a fan of the comic book. What if he's trying to tell us something? In the comic, it has to do with China, and it has to do with shipping."

Matteo nods slowly. "I agree that it's too soon to dismiss the idea. That's why we have MG here. She's the expert. If she says there may be a connection, let's follow up—no matter *how* out-there it sounds, Detective." Rideout was muttering under his breath but stops short when Matteo calls him out.

"As I was saying, there's no harm in checking which ships were in port the night of all the busts. See if there's a connection. Agent Sosa, just test the sample, and let us know if there are any anomalies that would point to this *not* being Mexican cartel for whatever reason."

Rideout could double for Cyclops, his laser gaze nearly slicing Matteo in half.

Agent Sosa looks likewise displeased to have her *authority* questioned in such a manner. "Fine. Whatever. I'm telling you to leave it alone. You're wasting your time."

Leave it alone? Her acidic tone gives the distinct impression that I've made an enemy, or *two* if I count how Rideout's lip curls up right now. Yet something pools in the depths of my stomach, buoying my spirits. Matteo heeded my thoughts. He stood up for me to his partner. *He* thought what I'd said was worth following up on.

Something in me says I'm on the right track here, even if in their professional *opinion* I'm off my rocker. If this lines up and we are literally chasing rabbits, then we are also looking for the crooked cop. My head moves as if on a swivel to take in first Rideout, then the group of police working over the crate of drugs. How easy would it be to fiddle with the crime scene? There are so many cops, it would be hard to pin it down . . . but the note from the Golden Arrow was leaked by a member of Matteo's team. So Rideout; that younger officer I met, Officer James; or Matteo. Or any one of the other fifty cops here involved in the case. I'm not even sure how widely known the note's contents are.

My eyes narrow as I recognize Officer James among those bagging evidence. He slips one of the baggies into his coat pocket, and my hackles rise. It could be coincidence, or it could be tampering. I open my mouth, about to ask Matteo to watch James, when I see Agent Sosa approach James. They exchange words, his hand fishes back into his pocket and produces the tagged evidence, and they both bend their heads over it. Sosa nods and puts the bag into her own pocket. No drama. No other cops shouting or pointing. No sirens, and *no* Golden Arrow swooping down to say, "Aha! I've got you now!"

I thank my lucky stars I haven't blabbed to Matteo yet. *Apparently* I'm seeing the comic book everywhere. Poor Officer James. How would he like to know that I suspected him as a dirty cop just because he is the low man on the totem pole?

Agent Sosa moves off to meet with the other teams inspecting crates while Matteo takes me to the area where the men were locked up. It's a large utility closet housing mechanical equipment—nothing tying that to the books.

"Do you have pictures of how you found the men? Were they tied with rope again?" My brain jumps to the pile of rope under Kyle and Simon's desk. I'm looking for anything that will point me in a direction. Any direction. Why draw a rabbit? Is it really *the* White Rabbit, or is it in reference to the drugs? It may just be more lunacy, but I feel like I know the Golden Arrow. Like he or she leaves these clues for *me*, and I'm not smart enough to decipher them.

"They were handcuffed with zip ties and chained to a large welded pipe," Matteo answers, pressing his phone's camera on and showing me pictures of the scene this morning. I flip through, looking for anything that catches my eye. I feel useless here; I add questions instead of giving the cops any direction at all. In fair imitation of my work presentations, my one thought about the source of the drugs has been shot down, and it seemed simple: our vigilante wanted to alert us to drugs in this warehouse. Maybe end of story. No need to look further.

"Wait. Wait. Scroll back. This one here. Do you have any other pictures of him?" My stomach lurches as I catch sight of something on one of the guys' hoodies. It's slightly obscured by another person chained to the pipe, but I see enough of the white to think it may be a rabbit.

Matteo frowns and flicks through the pictures on his phone. "This is a little better, but not great."

It's enough. My eye for lines helps where Matteo's eyes fail. It is the exact same rabbit we saw outside. "This guy has the same rabbit on his hoodie."

Matteo shoves his face closer to the screen to verify my claims. "So what would this mean?"

"I don't know yet." I bite my lip, thinking.

"Well, we took everyone in for questioning. I'll find out who he is. Maybe he's the leader and our suspect marked him. Or maybe he's a graffiti artist who spray-painted the same image from his hoodie onto the building."

Again my gut tells me it's more than coincidence, though I don't know what it means . . . yet. I'll get there. I feel like I'm *this close* to getting it. Getting what the Golden Arrow is playing at. And my writer's sixth sense says the story isn't done; there's another act coming. We just have to figure it out before someone gets killed.

Daylight mingles with twilight by the time Matteo walks me back to my car.

"No matter what my partner says, we have lots to check in to. You saw stuff that we would have missed. This is getting serious. If the cartels suspect that this dude landed their whole stash of pure heroin at the PD, it won't go without retaliation. We need to do some digging to see if your coworkers have costumes. Anything that would suggest research on drugs in LA. Rope, gold paint, stuff like that, and the party is the perfect opportunity. Do you want me to pick you up? That way we can discuss the case on our way there. Make it look more like we're seeing each other if we arrive together." He shoves his hands in his pockets and scuffs his shoes. Honest to God shuffles his feet. I feel an answering blush stain my own cheeks.

Then I think about Lawrence, and Ryan, and how I don't want any more questions because I don't want to lie to them any more than I have to. "How about I meet you at your house?"

A look of surprise crosses his face, then curiosity, then acceptance and something that looks like amusement. Like he's figured me out. "I'm all for equal opportunity driving, so sure."

"Just text me your address, and I'll be at your house around nine?"

"Sounds good." He pauses and looks at the sky, then back to me. "That was pretty impressive back there, Michael-Grace. I think you definitely proved your worth as a teammate today."

My heartbeat zings a little in my ears, and I smile back, opening the door to the car. "I did kick a little ass, didn't I?"

I start my engine, and the headlights cut a swath through the gathering night like Captain America's shield deflecting enemy fire. I watch Matteo walk back toward the crime scene, a feeling of isolation washing over me. The media frenzy has died down, the reporters have gone home, and a blanket of eerie silence covers the street. Not a car in sight. It rained while we were in the warehouse, a late-afternoon squall that has heightened the smell of gasoline and rotting fish. I roll down my window, trying to ventilate my car, and glance out at my now clearer view of the alleyway.

Is that the flapping of a cape up there on top of a warehouse? My heart stops in my chest.

I squint, sure I am seeing things in the dying light of the evening. But no, my eye catches it again. The flap of fabric on the rooftop. The Golden Arrow? Come to watch us piece together the puzzle?

Immediately I throw my car into reverse, hardly looking behind me as my tires squeal on the pavement in my zeal to back up. I *have* to get my headlights to illuminate more of the alley. When I think I'm far enough back, I throw caution to the wind and get out of my car, cell phone clutched in my hand. If I can get a picture of him, we'll have something to go on. I race forward, eyes on where I last saw the fabric. I can now make out the form of a person, but it looks . . . wrong as I approach. The Golden Arrow isn't moving. He isn't *on* the roof; he's dangling from it.

I gasp and run forward, hand at my throat, disregarding the drizzle of rain pattering on my head. The figure doesn't move at the sound of my approach, but I finally see why. The dim light of my headlights reveals a stuffed dummy, hung by its feet off a fire escape. A cape dangles down toward the street below, a huge golden arrow stuck straight through the chest. The words "You're next, Batman" are written in black paint on the cape. Or at least I hope it's paint. A shiver runs down my spine. The warning is clear—the drug dealers know that there is a civilian defender involved, and they're threatening the well-being of whoever is interfering with their business. Too bad the Golden Arrow could be someone I know, and *I'm* stuck in the middle of this mess, and Matteo too. It's the first moment I realize that I could seriously get hurt helping with this case—what if the drug dealers are hanging around waiting for someone to leave the crime scene who would be easy to kidnap? I punch Matteo's number before sprinting back to my car. I don't want to be caught anywhere near this ominous sign. I tell Matteo what I've seen and hang up the phone.

This is no cat-and-mouse game; this is life or death comic-book style, and since the rest of the team seems to be refusing my advice, it's up to *me* to figure it out before someone I know ends up like that dummy.

CHAPTER 13

A peppering of sand hits my car as I cruise down the lonely desert road. The address that Matteo texts me is outside the city. *Way* outside the city. I'm feeling like I could take one wrong turn at a cactus and end up on the planet from *Dune*. In fact, when I pull up to the modest walled house that Siri insists is the right one, there's not another building in sight. In any direction.

I would have pictured Matteo in a trendy downtown loft drinking sangria on his rooftop garden patio with his neighbors. It's so quiet out here, my steps on the gravel sound like something out of a badly produced horror movie.

"Glad you made it!" Matteo stands at the front door across a courtyard landscaped with a plethora of rocks, colorful blooming cacti, succulents, and tall spiny grass—a little capsule of the best of the desert. An oasis. "Come on in. The gate is unlocked."

"Paranoid much?" The gate swings open on silent hinges, even though it weighs at least twenty pounds, and I close it behind me with a clang. Although if it were just a tiny gate between me and endless desert, maybe I'd be paranoid too.

He shrugs. "I bought it this way, and it keeps out the coyotes."

"Coyotes?" I shoot a trepidatious look over my shoulder. I'm all for small, fluffy, lovable dogs, but I'm not a wildlife lover. It's why you don't *ever* catch me at the beach. Or in the pool. In addition to my translucent pale skin that burns in the merest suggestion of sunlight, I may or may not also be convinced that sharks can and will live anywhere. For instance, in swimming pools.

Matteo laughs. "They're not out right now. They're mostly nocturnal." He turns to go inside. "I mean, unless they have rabies."

I skitter up the path to the porch. "Yeah, that makes me feel better."

"Hence the gate," he says with a wink, sweeping the front door wide.

The house is simple and contemporary on the outside and wide open, daylit, and clean on the inside. We stand in a living room filled with square gray furniture, a glass fireplace flanked by huge windows with views to the desert, and an art deco lamp. To the right sits an open kitchen—simple, modern—and to our left is a short hallway to what I assume is the bedroom and the bathroom. It's so neat, clean, and contemporary, it looks like I walked straight into a design magazine. The magazines I like to glance through, not the ones dripping tassels and jacquard. Sleek and professional. Grown-up. I slip off my bright-yellow flats and set them next to his leather shoes.

"Come on in. I'm about to make some coffee. Not the fancy coffee shop stuff, but it's not too bad."

"It's okay. I'll take a cup. I can't believe you live all the way out here, on purpose."

He busies himself in the kitchen, putting an actual kettle on the stove. I haven't seen a real kettle since I left my mother's house.

"For five years," he confirms.

Five years driving this far out of the city to go home? No way. I'm too instant-satisfaction. If there were a transporter available, even if it were only questionably safe, I'd be the first to use it.

He catches me looking at him and frowns. "I know it's not glamorous, and most people live in LA for the city and the nightlife, but I like how quiet it is out here. I like to think."

"Think about . . . coyotes?"

Humor sparks in his eyes again. "Mostly my job. I take work home, review cases. I find answers and make connections I can't make while I'm in the office where it's busy. Sometimes I think about the universe. You are reminded how small you are out here in the desert. I like that. Puts everything in perspective after a tough day."

Spines ebb and flow beneath my fingers as I run my hand down his bookcase. Even the books are neat, orderly, and I think even organized alphabetically and by category. The architecture section is particularly prodigious, and I read the titles *The Small House*, *The Sustainable House*, and *Desert House*. "So you really did go to architecture school?"

"Mm-hmm." He's pouring the water into a French press, so I keep looking at the books.

"Did you design this house?"

He laughs. "No. It's midcentury modern by a local architect really into passive solar design. Not too many people want to live this far out, so I got a deal on the place. Really, no one recognizes what a work of art and science a house like this is. Or not many people. But someday I'd like to design my own house out in the desert."

"It's like camping every night."

"You say that like it's a bad thing."

"I've been camping exactly once. Let's just say we refer to it as the Great Misadventure of 2012. It involved carrying a thirty-pound cooler with no handles more than two miles, a pillowcase with my clothes in it, a lopsided tent that trapped every mosquito inside, and Lawrence being mistaken as the suspect in a carjacking and arrested in the parking lot on our way home. We didn't repeat it."

Matteo snorts. His hair is a little more tousled than I've seen before. He's relaxed in jeans and a new button-down shirt, his cheeks clean-shaven, his dark eyebrows furrowed over the task of placing the mugs and saucers on the counter in a neat line. It's . . . *adorable*. And that odd sense of intimacy hits me again before I'm ready for it. Like I'm peering into his soul without his permission. I turn back to the books, afraid of what he might see on my face if he catches me looking this time.

The rest of the bookshelf is filled with psychology books, crime scene investigation books, and a big fat tome of federal codes, which holds zero interest for me, so I wander into the kitchen.

"How did you end up being a detective if you went to architecture school?"

He pauses, and I can see the internal debate about how to answer. "That's a long story. I didn't know it until I was grown-up, but my mom had been a drug user. She missed her family in Mexico, felt alone and bored. It's not that uncommon for housewives, actually. It made me want to help prevent others from making the same mistakes she did. So I joined patrol, and then when I discovered I was really good at narcotics, I put in for the promotion to detective."

From the shadow behind his eyes, I'm guessing there's more to this story, but I don't pry because we haven't exactly crossed the gulf between pretend significant others into the realm of "Tell me your deep dark childhood secrets." Even superheroes guard their origin stories in comic books.

"We have to wait until the timer goes off," Matteo says as I slide onto a barstool. The concrete counter is smooth and cool under my elbows as I prop my chin in my hands awaiting liquid sustenance.

A chiming sound emanates from my pocket, and I pull my phone out. It informs me that it's searching for a signal and that I'm currently roaming. No joke; it's a regular safari out here. It's apparently been searching for a while because I can practically see my battery charge draining.

"Do you need to make a call?" He's eyeing my phone as he pours the coffee into cups. The rich aroma fills my nose, and my mouth actually waters. *Coffee, coffee, coffee.* The song of my people.

"No, my phone is just searching for a signal. It's draining the battery."

"Service here can be tricky. I have a landline if you need." He motions with a spoon to the corded blue telephone attached to one of the stained wood columns that separate the kitchen island from the living room.

"You have a *land*line?"

The spoon clinks as he swirls something into each cup then places mine in front of me. He doesn't answer because, well, duh, he just told me he did. After a quick scan, I don't see a television either. Definitely no towering stack of video games like *my* living room—thank you, Ryan—or any of the memorabilia junk that fills my friends' houses. Or any of the typical accoutrements of router, modem, and cables.

"You don't have Wi-Fi." Beyond judgment, I'm in the horror zone.

"Nope." And he seems entirely unperturbed about his caveman status. He licks the spoon and tosses it in the sink. "Now, I made you a breakfast blend with coconut oil and a sprinkle of cinnamon. Don't knock it until you try it."

He laughs at the face I make. Hipster status fully reinstated. "Coconut oil?" Though the scent of cinnamon tantalizes my nose.

"It makes the coffee taste even better. Would you like a biscotti?"

I nod my head. What man even has *biscotti* in his house? Double hipster points awarded, even if they are *awesome* hipster points. I can't think of any other way to phrase it, but Matteo is the *adultiest* adult I've met in a long time. He's a real grown-up. Fully in the man category, unlike some of the borderline perpetual teenagers I seem to meet.

If my life is *Firefly*, my crew consists of these forever-young people—they're playful, they're geeky, they're always up for a marathon of *Arrow*. But in a way, it's refreshing to meet someone who made the leap—Matteo's the novelty in my world. Usually I am repelled by the thought of dating an adult. I picture being a grown-up as stuffy, no room for play, fun, or *color* in life. It's "go to the office, kiss wife on cheek, read the news, go to bed, repeat until you die," as modeled by my parents. But Matteo . . . His version of adult is different. It's polished, sophisticated, and sure, he owns more than one pair of shoes and a couch made from something other than plastic, but he seems *alive* still. Maybe it's his job, that he brushes shoulders with danger. Maybe it's that he seems to not only accept my quirks and my hair and my comics but is charmed by them. Or maybe it's just him.

My eyes stray to my yellow flats sitting next to Matteo's shoes on the step. Out of place, but a welcome relief against the gray background. Like his house needs my splash of color. The thought takes my brain all sorts of places and gives me a pang of wanting I shouldn't feel with my *work* partner. I mentally pull myself back from the edge.

"But what do you *do* out here?" No online gaming. No Reddit. No Instagram. No Netflix.

"I read. I sit out on my patio and listen to the desert. Work on my cases. Think."

"So you work, and then you come out here and you work. But don't you get—" I snap my mouth shut, realizing how personal and inappropriate my question is going to be.

"Lonely?" He thinks for a moment, then sips his coffee. "Yeah. Sometimes. And I know everyone else loves the city, but it fills up my head. I get this wired energy, and I can't relax. I *can* relax out here, and I need it. I'm not a great person otherwise. I've met that Matteo. I don't like him." He looks . . . wistful? Bitter? Resentful? His eyes find mine, and we sit in silence as the steam from our cups rises between us. "But yeah. Lonely sometimes."

It sounds like an admission. A *personal* admission, like maybe he feels less lonely with me here. My stomach does a flip-flop. He hit the nail on the head with how I've been feeling lately. Wired up and pulled in a lot of different directions. Maybe I need some time in the desert too. Complete with a bodyguard to protect me from coyotes and all the bad guys who suddenly sprang to life in my world.

But no Netflix. That seems extreme.

I take a hesitant sip of my coffee to fill the thoughtful silence that's fallen. It's . . . good. Better than good. This is the best damn cup of black coffee I've had in ages—no milk, sugar, or caramel needed. Just like Matteo, it's simple, straightforward, and unique. I moan in delight.

Humor is back in his eyes now, the flash of vulnerability and heat gone. "I *told* you it's good." He takes another sip to make his point. "So if we're supposed to be dating, I should probably know more about you. What exactly is it that you do for work?"

I shrug. "Perhaps I'm a woman of mystery."

He looks out the window, so I can't tell if he's teasing. "You most certainly win that title. I know you know a lot about comics. But what do you *do*?"

"I write," I say simply. "In big comics it's often split up into two pieces. The art and the writing. Some people get to do both. Quite a lot of the commercial stuff is published so fast that it's easier for one person to do one, and one to do the other. I lay out a general story line and break it into pages and panels. Then the artist draws what they think matches with the story. Sometimes it's a two-way street and they feel really strongly about a panel they want to draw, and I adjust the story or the structure of the page for it."

We lapse into silence. I can't quit contemplating my damn shoes at his house. Like a splatter of yellow paint from a dropped brush on an otherwise pristine page of line drawings. A puzzle to figure out, like there's something to put together. The feeling his house has been *missing* my shoes.

"Were you ever married?" My words fall out before I check them.

"Going right for the big guns, huh?" But he doesn't look upset.

"It seems like if we're supposed to be dating that I would know."

"I was engaged for a few years."

"Oh. What happened?" I want to smack myself. "Wait, you don't have to answer that. That's really nosy."

I catch a flash of white teeth as he laughs again, and my spirits buoy. "It's okay. And you don't need to be sorry. I'm glad I figured out it wouldn't work before we got married and had kids. She was an actress—"

"Ah. No need to explain further. They are a breed apart." LA is swimming with wannabes, almost-wases, and has-beens. Neck-deep. Can't throw a rock without hitting one.

He smirks. "She wanted to live in the city and constantly be out for exposure. When I sold my place in LA and moved out here, she didn't like having to drive in for auditions or shopping. She was wonderful and vibrant and fun. Cliché as it sounds, she was like an exotic flower. She didn't fit in the desert, which is where *I* fit."

My mind goes directly to his lush courtyard full of exotic-looking vegetation. Did he plant them just for her? An oasis for his love? I'm admittedly a *little* jealous of said exotic flower, but I push it down. I get what he's saying. It resonates deeply, like a chord struck in me. "Dreams have to match up. Or at least be compatible side by side." I'm not sure what else to say, but it seems to be enough.

He nods. "How about you? Ever married?"

"God no." I snort. Then I feel bad. He's told me about his; I can at least return the favor. "I was almost engaged once when I was too young—my first year of law school. He didn't 'get' me, and I had the good sense to end it before we made each other miserable. There hasn't been time after that. Or anyone who seems pleasant enough to deal with for a lifetime."

There haven't been a pair of shoes that could sit next to mine in a doorway for more than a few months. Tom worked for my dad while I was in law school. My first *real* love, forever trying to change me. The night he asked me to marry him—two kids in love who had no idea what they wanted in the world—he told me that if I said yes, I "wouldn't have to write those comics anymore—not work at all when we had kids." It was my moment of reckoning, looking at a future just like my parents'. No fun, no color, no passion, no room to be crazy into geek fandoms. Tied down. Boring. Typical. I didn't *want* to be typical. I wanted to be a superhero. I told him *no thank you*, dropped out of school, colored my hair the next day, and never looked back, even after my parents told me they wouldn't give me another dime if I didn't finish law school.

Enter the Hurtling Turd, my new crew, and the job at Genius I landed after three years of freelance writing that had finally made my dream come true. But here I am thinking that just *maybe* something has been missing. Maybe I like how my shoes look next to Matteo's. He intrigues me, makes me feel a way I haven't before in my life. Longing for stability. For permanence. For partnership, where before I was a content party of one. Pretty heavy stuff.

"I've been thinking about the case," I say, not taking my eyes from his face. "And I read some of my old comics last night looking for the White Rabbit." I want to see how crazy he thinks I am away from the crime scene and away from his partner.

No sign of a smirk. "And?"

"I can't help but feel like this bust is more than what it seems on the surface. Everything has lined up with the comic books, maybe too well. This person, the Golden Arrow. Why not just call the police, report drug activity, and call it a night? It's like they're trying to indicate that they're following a certain person or story line. It's like trying to read tarot from a normal deck of playing cards—like I'm looking for something that isn't there. But. My gut says it's worth following the *story*, not just the crimes. The connection. The presence of a drug war, then and now. The heroin in a warehouse. It's going to sound crazy, but I'm a writer, and I draw off of real life all the time. What if Casey Senior wrote about a real drug ring? And somehow the Golden Arrow figured it out?"

Silence.

"But why would the crimes repeat themselves if they already happened thirty years ago?" Matteo takes another sip of coffee and mulls over his next words before speaking. "Right before Casey Senior died, there was a huge bust of the biggest heroin rings in the city. The streets were cleaned up. I'm not saying you're wrong. It's just how would we ever go about proving it's all related?"

I let out a breath. His willingness to listen frees up my mind to start piecing story threads together. That bust he's talking about—the city was rid of its most notorious criminals. But maybe *someone* has survived and had their pickings of a marketplace conveniently cleared of competitors. "In the comic, the next steps are catching smugglers on the boat and chasing the White Rabbit. I think we'd be smart to look at the shipping logs. Stake out the warehouse. Search to see if there are connections to China."

Matteo nods slowly. "As it stands, I'm set to interrogate the man from the warehouse who had the rabbit on his hoodie. It *was* painted on. We just need to figure out why, or if he saw the person responsible. If all this is more than coincidence, we're also possibly looking for a double agent. Maybe *that's* why our Golden Arrow can't come to the police," Matteo adds.

I give one nod, unwilling to comment. It's true. If we are following this story to its extent, we are also looking for a dirty cop. I keep thinking this seems designed for . . . well, *me*. Like the Golden Arrow expects *me* to put together these clues, and it's unsettling.

Matteo shrugs. "I'm just glad you stumbled upon me in the coffee shop to help us out. We'd have no clue without you. We'll call it divine providence until we see a reason to think otherwise. Ready to go?" He drains the rest of his cup, and I follow suit.

"We'll review what you know about your coworkers in the car. Yours or mine?" He pats his pants pockets, looking for the little notebook he carries everywhere.

"Let's take mine," I reply. But as we walk briskly to the door, I can't help but feel oddly sad about leaving. Though this whole case is complicated, my thoughts feel more in order here, in this quiet place with this quiet man. There's something serene that would possibly become addictive. I can picture sitting with Matteo, each of us with a book in front of the fireplace . . . and I slam the door shut on that vision. Again I am reminded that Matteo isn't just some guy I keep hanging out with. We have a crime to solve, and we are both in uncharted territory.

CHAPTER 14

"So we're looking for a costume, a cape, anything that would suggest knowledge about drugs and crime, and Hooded Falcon *anything*," Matteo reminds me on the doorstep of Kyle's house.

"Roger that. I hope you're ready for geek immersion."

As the door opens, I school my features, trying to look like I'm not snooping in my coworkers' lives in order to solve a drug-related crime spree. We make it perhaps two feet inside before we're attacked by geekery. A small herd of people descends on us wielding wands and a large floppy brown hat—bringing forcefully to mind the time I was attacked by geese at MacArthur Park. I hate nature.

Before I can defend myself, the large floppy hat lands on my head, covering my eyes, and the darn thing starts to *sing*. When the hat ceases its wagging, it crows, "*Better be . . . Hufflepuff!*" much to the delight of those standing by. I recognize Kyle's sarcastic snort.

"I would have bet Slytherin." Most definitely Kyle. I lift the brim.

"You'd better be glad I don't have my rubber-band gun, Kyle. Plus, what a lame welcome. I'm *obviously* a Gryffindor. I demand a retrial."

A titter of laughter ripples around the group, and the hat is replaced on my head. It does its jiggly dance, and I stand patiently until it crows, "*Better be . . . Gryffindor!*" More laughter as it's pulled back off and transferred to Matteo's head.

He ducks so that a tiny elf of a girl can put it on him, ever gracious even while wearing a clear WTF expression.

The sight of the large pointed sorting hat on Matteo's head causes dragons and glee to bang around my ribcage in a death match. "I don't know about this one . . . I think he might be a Squib."

Matteo knows he's been insulted and throws me a playful dirty look.

"Better be . . . *Ravenclaw*!"

I'm already clapping. "Yes! That's perfect! You are *so* a book nerd!"

He still looks baffled. "What is a Ravenclaw?"

The same woman who put the hat on his head holds out her hand. "It's your Hogwarts house! You may now enter the party! I'm Nina, Kyle's fiancée, and a Hufflepuff. We've heard so much about you, Matteo. And you too, of course, MG. I'm so glad you could make it!"

Her perkiness goes beyond normal irritation and into the realm of . . . infectious. I find myself smiling back. "Thanks for inviting us." I lean over as if I'm telling her a secret in a stage whisper. "Matteo is new to a lot of this."

She squeals and claps. Kyle wanders up behind her and throws his arm around her shoulders. "MG. Matteo. Welcome!" He points to the kitchen. "The house-elves are in there." He points over to a large living room where five or six people are sitting, already engrossed in conversation. "*Star Wars* marathon starts in about ten minutes in there." He opens a door directly to the right of the entry, which reveals stairs. "Downstairs will be a mix of *Settlers of Catan* tournament and random episodes of *TNG*. There's a Charmander nest down the street for those in the office *Pokémon GO* competition, and"—he glances at his Apple watch and finishes off with an announcement at large—"pizza will arrive at four p.m.!"

I give a mock salute, and Matteo follows me like a puppy into the kitchen, where the masses have descended.

"What do you do, Matteo?" Nina munches on a baby carrot.

"I went to architecture school," Matteo responds with his pat answer, and I pray for a diversion away from his job description because while *he* can hold it together, I can't lie to my coworkers that well. Any diversion. Some kung fu vampires to pop up from a grave who need slaying. Anything.

"He's an *architect* and he fixed my chair in two seconds flat," Kyle responds. Total bromance.

I clear my throat. "How about you, Nina? What do you do?"

"I'm an actress—theatre, not movie. *Hamlet.* Neil Simon. Stuff like that. And then I help do some production management stuff to actually pay the bills." She laughs.

"That's really neat. Actually, I've always wanted to do costumes for theater but have never pursued it."

"You do costume design?" She looks impressed.

"I take a few commissions. Mostly drag shows right now, but I want to get into art direction so that I can help design superhero costume adaptations. Maybe do costume work on the side." I bite my lip and cut a look at Kyle, hoping I haven't said too much. This is why I don't attend work parties. I suck at playing politics.

Kyle doesn't even bat an eyelash at my work comment but dives right in about the costumes. "That's really cool. I didn't know you did that. You'd be great at costume design. Your costume sketches are the best on our team." His straightforward vote of confidence nearly bowls me over, especially given my role within the team is usually the dialogue, and his is usually the panel art. He shoves chips into his mouth and turns toward the Crock-Pot.

"Stock up. This looks like serious business," I say to Matteo, eyeing the spread of a humongous Subway sandwich bar and several homemade-looking sides. My stomach literally growls as I spot a huge bowl of my favorite artichoke dip from the Christmas parties.

"So, MG, if you do costumes . . . can I talk to you about something?" Nina moves closer to me and drops her voice. Her eyes dart to the Crock-Pot as if attempting to gauge whether Kyle can hear her.

"Sure, what's up?"

"Well, Kyle will kill me for asking, but I know he and Simon have been doing this extracurricular stuff, and they need to make it official. With costumes. I was going to try to hack something together myself, but . . . Well, if you're a professional, we could just hire you to do it."

My heart races, and I channel my mental energy into *not* gaping at her like a fish. I didn't even have to snoop! Proof that Simon and Kyle are two superheroes in want of costuming! On one hand, I'm shocked they've managed to elude police thus far, but on the other hand, I'm glad that this mystery can finally get solved. They can just *tell* us what they know about the White Rabbit. I school my features. "Oh, yeah, um, of course. I'd love to. What kind of costumes are we talking?"

Nina eyes the floor. "Well, you're a fellow geek. I'm sure you'd understand, but I need chain mail."

I blink. "Chain mail?" Wouldn't that be a little heavy when scaling the side of a warehouse?

"Well, a whole knight costume really. I know it sounds silly, but they are having so much *fun* learning to sword fight."

"Sword fight."

"It's this whole LARPing group they joined to keep fit. Sword fighting, metal working, rope making, stuff like that."

Live-action role-playing. I've heard of it. Never done it myself, but I don't hold it against anyone if they want to nerd out in costume. But this negates what I thought would be a big break in the case and possibly means Kyle and Simon are up to nothing more than hitting each other with wooden swords. Or cardboard tubes, like the ones under their desk. I inwardly groan. I need to tell Matteo.

The man in question now leans so close to me, I can smell his aftershave. It's a heady scent, and my brain swims with his closeness. Is he playing up the dating thing? Is he possibly going to kiss my shoulder? Or give me a hug from behind? I am so lost in *that* role-playing fantasy that when he speaks he takes me by surprise.

"*What* is a pufflehuff?"

I snort. "*Hufflepuff.* It's another Hogwarts house, from Harry Potter," I whisper back, reveling in his aftershave awhile longer.

"Is that the wizard thing?"

"It's a person. And yes, he's a wizard. Why do you ask?"

Matteo nods toward Andy. "That guy over there said that he'd thought for sure I'd be in that Hufflepuff house. I told him it sounded girly." He lowers his voice until just I can hear him. "Plus, I need to be making notes about your coworkers, so maybe you can introduce me?" I bite my lip but nod, and we shuffle around the kitchen until we're in a corner between the sandwiches and the artichoke dip.

I keep my voice low, anxiety pooling in my belly. It's normal that I introduce everyone to my guest, right? *Act natural.* I point in turn at the people in the room with us. "That's Andy. He's essentially my boss. He presents our team's work to the executive art directors at Genius. He really doesn't seem the type to chase anyone, much less bad guys, but that's your area of expertise." And the guy who steals my ideas to get *my* promotion. Even if he did do a *teensy* bit better job packaging my ideas. I'm not quite ready to forgive him, though, so I'm going to just continue to studiously avoid him today.

"Next is Kyle, who you met. He's an illustrator, and he works on the new *Hooded Falcon* and whatever other current Genius comics are tying in. There's Tej over there; he's the most charming guy you'll ever meet. He works on adaptations for films, coordinating with developers, marketing, press releases, that sort of thing. He's not always a part of our work team, but he's awesome." He's also gorgeous, geek or not. Mocha skin, dark hair always updated with the trends, immaculate clothes, and black plastic-frame Clark Kent glasses. He's laughing in the living room with a woman I assume is his girlfriend or wife. I'm newly ashamed that I don't even know if my coworkers are married.

Simon steps into the kitchen, so I introduce him, hoping it comes off as natural. "And this is Simon. He's the illustrator I work with the most. His desk is right next to mine, and he's helping me with *Hooded*

Falcon and *Hero Girls* right now, although I hear tell that he's going to be pulled onto a revival of *The Green Monster*. Version six hundred million."

"Version six hundred million and *one*," Simon corrects, reaching out to shake Matteo's hand before pointing to the girl deep in conversation with Nina. "And that's my wife, Isabella—no relation."

Matteo looks thrown. "No relation to . . ."

"*Twilight*?" Simon smirks. "Sparklepires?"

"Let's not destroy Matteo's perfect and pristine mental canvas with that," I say, looping an arm around Matteo. His middle is solid, and I can't keep myself from wondering if he has a six-pack like the cops on TV have. A moment later I let it drop, unsure if the contact is appropriate.

"You've never heard of *Twilight*?" Simon asks.

Matteo gives an affable grin. "Unless you mean the Zone, no."

Simon studies Matteo the way a scientist studies a curious specimen. "So what fandoms *are* you into?"

"Fandoms?" The word is obviously foreign in Matteo's mouth.

"It means, What are you a fan of? What do you watch? Who do you ship?" I pop a baby carrot in my mouth, devilishly relishing his squirming under the question.

"Ship?" he asks finally, rubbing the back of his neck. He shoots me a look that plainly says, "Help!"

"Ships are couples. Shorthand for 'relationship' originally, but now just means two people you want to see get together." I really should help him. Really, I should. Simon watches us with naked glee on his face.

Matteo frowns. "I liked that Arwen lady and Strider? Is that a ship?"

I struggle not to correct him that Arwen was an elf and not a lady. Though kudos to Matteo for being able to even name Arwen from *LOTR*. I try to hide my distaste. Those books are long and boring, with a few exciting dragon chapters followed by long and boring.

Simon nods. "Ah, so you're a fantasy geek. I can dig that. Sorry it's not *D&D* downstairs."

"Don't you like *The Lord of the Rings*?" Matteo asks me, puzzled.

"Not my favorite. I'm more of a space geek. *Trek*, *Wars*, *Battlestar*, *Firefly*, *Doctor Who*—science fiction, space opera. That sort of stuff." I turn to Simon. "He's new to all this."

"So there are *types* of . . ." He probably wants to say "geeks," but I can see he's afraid of offending Simon.

Tej leans in around Simon and dips a chip into the French onion dip. "Geekdom? You betcha. I am a fellow fantasy geek." He executes a mini bow. "People come at geekdom from different directions. There's the Japanese anime lovers, like my wife. Then there's the band and music geeks—"

"Guilty as charged." Andy waves a hand. We've attracted everyone's attention apparently. "I played oboe." *He would.*

"Music geeks like to dabble. A little of this, a little of that," Simon finishes.

"And then there are the space geeks," Tej adds.

I raise my hand. "Although every once in a while, if I've had some wine, I do like *Game of Thrones*. Or should I call it 'Death and Boobies'? Brienne of Tarth is my Patronus."

Tej cracks up. "Yeah, you need to drink for that show."

At this point, Matteo has his arms crossed over his chest and is staring between us like we're speaking a different language. "What on *earth* is a Patronus?"

"Well, technically our animal counterpart when you use the *Expecto Patronum* spell. But it can also mean a character you love. Or admire. It's pretty standard in the geek world. For example, if you ever need to *find your people*, it's totally legit to yell out, 'Who's your Patronus?'" Simon makes it a point by yelling the last words. It's a game we play in the office from time to time.

"No one could possibly be prepared for—" Matteo is cut off by a chorus of answers from various rooms in the house.

"Giles from *Buffy*!"

"Katniss Everdeen!" This from Nina, who looks pretty fierce for a wee one.

"Neil deGrasse Tyson!" Simon answers his own question with a smile.

Kyle steps into the kitchen and taps Matteo on the shoulder. "Hey, do you want to play *Settlers* or just hang with the lady friend and watch the movies? I can sign you up if you want." He holds up a clipboard.

"Absolutely Ron Swanson from *Parks and Rec*," Tej answers.

"Dana Scully," Tej's wife calls.

I offer her a fist bump. "Word. Dana Scully is amazing."

Matteo turns to me, wide-eyed. "How do I know who *my* Patronus is? Can you look it up somewhere?"

This brings a wave of laughter from everyone gathered.

"Okay, okay. Nothing to see here. Move along." I try to fight my own laughter. "Babe, we'll visit Pottermore sometime. For now I think"—I tap my chin—"Wash from *Firefly*."

Kyle arrives back in the kitchen carrying the *Settlers of Catan* box. "Okay, I'm headed downstairs after I start the movies."

After the spirit animals conversation, Matteo sticks to me like glue. I'm his life raft in this sea of awesome. "Oh good, I'm curious about these *Star Wars* movies. I've heard about them a lot since meeting MG."

You could have heard a pin drop.

Kyle sucks in a breath. "You've never *seen Star Wars*? Like, *ever*?"

"Never seen them, no. Is that bad?" Matteo has failed his entrance exam to my world. *Never seen Star Wars.*

"We've got ourselves a *virgin*!" Kyle grasps Matteo's shoulders in his hands and shakes him back and forth with enthusiasm. "Don't worry. We'll be gentle. Well, at least I'll be gentle. The jury is still out on MG."

I cough to cover the rush of heat spreading on my face, and beside me, Matteo's hands spasm.

"Where on *earth* did you find him?" This question is to me, and I can tell that Kyle is baffled I'm dating someone so far outside our world.

"You'd never believe it," I say with a smile. I turn to Matteo, having a bit of a hard time meeting his eyes after the virginity comment. "Shall we?"

I escort him into the living room. This should be more than interesting. I've never seen *Star Wars* for anyone's first time.

Matteo pops the bottle cap on a beer and takes a swig. "Let the beatings begin."

"We will watch these movies in the only order that should ever be presented," Kyle announces while slipping the first Blu-ray disc into the player. "Today will be episodes IV, V, VI. Next weekend I, II, III, and *Rogue One*." There is some mild booing from the crowd at this, and Kyle waves his hand. "I know. We all have to deal with Jar Jar together, but I'm a purist, and we can't skip them. And *then* we'll watch the new ones, starting with *The Force Awakens*."

Matteo leans over. "Why would we watch episode IV before episode I?"

"So much to learn have you, young Padawan. It's the historical release order."

Matteo's eyes dart to the side, then back to mine. His tone is confessional, his eyes furtive. "I wasn't expecting this to be so much . . . fun. It makes it hard to do my job. Your coworkers are a blast."

I'm having fun too, and Matteo makes it hard for *me* to focus on the case. He's *too* good at playing boyfriend. I smile and bump his shoulder with mine. The fun is just starting. "Just wait until you see the movies."

I've seen these movies at least twenty times, and I'm used to making snarky comments and pointing out filming errors. I haven't watched *Star Wars* without a liberal dose of cynicism since I was ten years old.

But something funny begins to happen when we start *A New Hope.* The words scrawl across the screen, and Matteo reads them out loud, and a shiver runs down my spine. This whole universe is about to be opened up to him, and I'm the one who gets to introduce him to the marvels of the *Millennium Falcon*. And R2-D2. And I'm seriously hoping this is the old cut with the non-remastered Jabba. I realize I'm giddy. It feels magical. Like the first time I saw them myself and got caught up in the wonder of it all, instead of wondering where the stormtroopers got so much PVC to make their armor in space.

And it's not just me. The enjoyment level amps up across the room. No one goes downstairs to play *Settlers*. Everyone is up here because it feels new and exciting. Instead of being on the outside, I can feel Matteo being encircled by my coworkers, and it fills my insides with warm fuzzies. I snuggle onto the couch, trying to walk the line of looking like a couple without crossing professional boundaries. I settle for legs touching, but no cuddling.

"These aren't the droids you're looking for" launches a whole conversation—which requires pausing the movie—between Matteo and Tej about the Force. Kyle jumps in, explaining the finer points of robotics in the Empire. I sit back and watch all of this unfold, feeling like a spectator on several levels. I'm grateful that my coworkers invited us and teased Matteo a little but then welcomed him into the fold. They didn't *have* to do that. Heck, I don't think *I* would have done it if the tables were turned. How many guys have I dumped after the first date because they just "didn't get" my life or my geek culture references? I didn't have time to educate people. Matteo kind of forced my hand, but he's *into* it. My own universe expands a smidge.

Matteo laughs at the right times, sits forward at the right times. He's not just pretending. I catch myself watching him more than the movie, my heart beating in my throat, pulse pounding in my body. This is *sexy*. Instead of being repulsed by his non-geekdom, I'm inarguably attracted by it. A wave of heat suffuses my face, and I sit against the back of the couch, needing a breath of air, a small moment to gain my composure. My heart is pounding like I've just run a mile.

"You okay?" Matteo leans his head into mine as the movie hits a quiet spell. He pats my knee in a way that is meant to appear classically affectionate but ends up shooting spirals of energy right through my middle. I'm having an internal meltdown because he *touched my leg*. How *thirty going on thirteen* can I get?

"Yeah. Of course. You?" *If by "okay" you mean "melting inside."*

"I'm having a great time." The words sound affable and normal. But our eyes meet, and there's *something* that catches there. Something that sparks in his gaze to mirror my own unguarded reaction. His hand stops patting and holds my knee, his long fingers nearly encircling my leg. The gesture is no longer a play at affection. It's a searing brand on my leg. The heat between us isn't make-believe. In this moment it's real and palpable. Our gazes lock in the slowly waning afternoon light. It's the first moment that I know for certain he feels this crazy pull too. The crazy pull that we can't do anything about because we're solving a crime together.

The sounds of scuffle—Obi Wan disarming the ruffian threatening Luke—return us to reality, and we turn to regard the screen. Matteo's hand falls off my knee, and he sits back, intentionally putting distance between our bodies. I don't blame him. My own chest is rising and falling faster than sitting on a couch warrants. That was some sort of intense moment, and I know we need to focus on why we're here, not give in to my urges to make out on the couch.

"So do you guys do this every weekend?" It's a casual question for Matteo to ask, but I sense he's going somewhere with this, like he just read my thoughts. Are we that in tune?

Kyle grabs a pillow off the couch, presses pause on the remote, and leans against the coffee table, Nina snuggling under one arm. "Nah. Once or twice a year."

"It seems like there's so much I need to learn," Matteo says, eyes still glued to the TV. "What did you watch last weekend? I need to start keeping a list." Matteo not only has an ulterior motive, but he's a skilled professional when it comes to gaining information and feeling out alibis.

Kyle laughs. "We'll get you squared away. We actually didn't watch anything last weekend. Nina had her fifteen-year high school reunion, and I took work along for the hotel."

"It was so romantic," Nina intoned, not batting an eye.

Matteo muffles a laugh with a cough. "I bet. Was the hotel nice, at least?"

"Holiday Inns aren't too bad. Good Wi-Fi."

Nina ignores him. "We were in San Diego. The weather was awful, though. Kyle actually left the party really early and drove back up here because he worried about moving his artwork around in the rain."

Only I see Matteo's attention snap to Kyle. Because I can read *him* now too, I know he's wondering if Kyle was up in LA in enough time to get to the warehouse district. But has he *seen* Kyle? The guy couldn't wrestle a squirrel. He's shorter than me, wiry, and about as nonthreatening as Trogdor. Not to mention that I found out about the sword fighting, which shoots my theory to hell.

"It's my *job* to care about my art," Kyle says, rolling his eyes. "Now quiet. This part is *so* great."

"Maybe you were late for a sword fighting lesson?" I ask sweetly, batting my eyes at Kyle.

"No—wait. How did you? Nina, did you *tell her*?" Kyle eyes Nina with mock horror.

"I asked her to make you and Simon costumes, so relax." Nina rolls her eyes, shoves a chip in her mouth, and turns back to the TV.

"It's no big deal," I say, "but it sure puts my mind at ease about why I found cardboard tubes under my desk the other day. But what do you need duct tape for? I assumed it was something kinky. Now I'm assuming it's something dorky." I hope Matteo's picking up my intentional mention of the clues.

Simon's face has turned red now too. "The duct tape holds our cardboard armor on. I didn't realize you saw that stuff."

"Cardboard . . . armor?" Matteo looks between Simon and me, completely baffled.

I make a show of turning to Matteo. "You see, it turns out that Kyle and Simon are learning to sword fight and make ropes and draw pictures like medieval times. It's called role-playing."

Matteo turns to Kyle, comprehension dawning on his face. "You said an old lady hit you. Is this actually what happened to your arm?"

Kyle chugs the rest of his beer in what I take as a ploy to look more manly. "Sword fighting. Yeah."

Simon cackles with glee. "It really *was* an old lady. Kyle got his ass handed to him."

"Hey, man, you have to partner with her next week, so shut up." Kyle tosses the empty can onto the coffee table.

"So you guys have been fake sword fighting with old ladies." Matteo looks part gleeful and part disappointed. Exactly my feeling. No lead on the Golden Arrow, but a damn fine story.

Simon scoffs, acting offended. "Sword fighting is *hard*. And we do other stuff too. We're learning to write with quill and ink, illuminations, stuff like that. There are guilds and crafts, and it's all very historically accurate. Scientific, even."

This doesn't mean that Kyle or Simon *can't* be the Golden Arrow; it just makes it less likely. I'm relieved but bummed. I never wanted Kyle or Simon to be the vigilante, but here we are back at square one. At a dead end with no promising leads.

"Can we go back to watching the movies, please?" Kyle shoots Nina another dirty look and presses play just in time for my favorite scene: Han in the cantina.

I usually roll my eyes about the alien-Muppet costumes, but this time is better because I get to watch Matteo recognize young Harrison Ford. And again, I get the distinct impression that he's truly *enjoying* this, even if he's also finding a way to question each of the couples about their past few weekends. When he gets up to use the restroom after the first movie, I wonder if it's to make notes.

"You guys are cute together." By the accent, I assume it's Tej's wife behind me. She went to the door to grab pizza between films.

I smile. "Thanks."

"I've seen you before at work functions and at the office Christmas party, and you always seemed so reserved. Focused on work. I don't know you well, but I can tell you're different around him."

She may not know me well, but she's hit the nail on the head, and that freaks me out. I *am* different around Matteo. Where I'm usually too busy to take time away from furthering my career, Matteo is a breath of fresh air in my life I didn't even know I needed. Something to turn me on my head and give me a fresh perspective. I always tell myself how happy I am with my party of one, but tonight I've glimpsed a version of me that would hang out for movie marathons with coworkers. He's opened my eyes to some of what I've been missing to uphold my persona at work. I'd never have come except for Matteo, and I realize just how lonely a party of one can be sometimes. How can one person affect me so much in a matter of a week?

My phone buzzes in my pocket, and I seize the opportunity to escape. "I'm sorry. I have to go grab this." I hold the phone to my ear even though I received a text message, say "Hello?" loudly enough to be heard, and step out the front door.

The text from Matteo is short:

Come upstairs.

I wait a few moments for effect, then head back inside, shooting a quick glance to the kitchen, where the pizza is quickly disappearing. No one will miss me.

I find Matteo in a bedroom upstairs standing at a closet. He's not just taking notes; he's *snooping*.

"Isn't this illegal?" I hiss, poking my head back out the door to make sure no one followed me upstairs.

"I got lost on my way to the bathroom. Come look at this."

I stand beside him and peer into the closet. Costumes of all types line the wall. Including a Hooded Falcon, complete with hooded cape. I chew my lip. "We go to a lot of conventions. It's a part of the job."

"There you guys are. The second movie is starting," Nina's voice comes from the doorway, and I jump about a mile high.

"Oh, um, we were just . . ."

Nina gives me a bawdy wink. "It's fine. I see you've discovered our costume closet. We just got that Hooded Falcon one last week off eBay. I thought it would be fun for Kyle to go as the Falcon for the anniversary gala, although I'm going to have to do some sizing work. Maybe you could help with that, MG. Right now Kyle would trip and fall on his face, the cape is so long. Are we going to get to see you in costume, Matteo?"

I shoot Matteo a look. "Oh, I, um, I've already invited my friend Lawrence." I haven't even thought about inviting Matteo to my work party. Silly me, as I didn't *have* a fake boyfriend two weeks ago when I invited Lawrence.

"Maybe I'll just have to change her mind about that. I look dashing in a cape, or so I imagine." Matteo plays the ever-doting boyfriend and pulls me against his chest. My heart does somersaults. I bet he *does* look dashing in a cape.

"Second movie is starting!" Kyle yells from the living room.

"Come on, let's go. I don't want to miss anything." Matteo grabs my arm, and we follow Nina downstairs where we settle back onto the couch. I end up leaning against the armrest, my feet across Matteo's lap. It's cozy, and some of my ruffled feathers settle. I'm fairly certain Kyle isn't the Golden Arrow. He and Simon never seem particularly *up* for fighting crime in the real world. They're more fit for the Dork Squad than the Justice League. The case remains a mystery. My gaze returns to Matteo.

Watching the second movie is just as endearing as the first, even as I mull over the case in my head. And my fake boyfriend. I'm a little afraid he's taken my heart by surprise and not just my mind.

CHAPTER 15

I bang my head slowly on the desk in hopes of reawakening all my carefully cultivated brain cells. Ever since the work party this weekend, my mind has been a gooey mess of crime stories gone wrong, developing L's costume for Comic-Con, and hot cop fantasies instead of focusing on the circus of deadlines parading through my week. I still haven't started my *Hero Girls* pages, and the rough outlines are due to Andy by Wednesday. I'm still fiddling with the ending for my *Hooded Falcon* pages—those are headed to the printer for a test run on Friday, come hell or high water. And speaking of, I still haven't said a word to Andy, even though it's 2:00 p.m. on Monday and we've been in the office all day together. My mind feels stuck, swirling, and I blame it all on Matteo. So what if I like him? More than like him. No biggie, just solve something the DEA and LAPD can't crack; then I can ask him out. There's no reason for this creative stagnation and romantic angsting. Especially since I've heard *zero* from Matteo since I dropped him off at his house after the party. He's obviously not pining personally or professionally. No updates on the clues. No updates on the warehouse. Nada.

I've been drowning my woes in sewing sequins . . . something that normally drives me batty but has been like a life raft for my fingers, which have been itching to pick up the phone.

"Yo, MG. You all right?" This from Simon, who has removed his headphones and can hear me banging my head.

Show no weakness. Give no quarter. "Yep." I continue to bang my forehead.

He pauses. "You don't look okay."

"You've obviously never seen creative genius at work." I sit up and slap my palm to the desk, sick of my own mental waffling. Would Buffy just sit home and wait for a vampire to show up? No, ma'am. She'd strap on her favorite halter and go patrolling. It's time for stomping boots. I'm going to get my work done. Then I'm calling Matteo to ask for an update. Yes, *calling*.

As if summoned by my thought, my phone buzzes, and Lawrence's face pops up on my screen. One of the only people I ever answer for; God help me if I ever take a call from my mother again. I forgo formalities because he's my bestie and I know why he's calling. "Sorry I didn't deliver those costumes last night. I ended up restitching that cummerbund. Twice. I'll get everything to you Friday before the show, I promise."

Silence greets my words.

"L? Did you pocket dial me?"

"Did you come to my house last night?"

"I—what? No. I didn't get a chance to drop off the costumes. Why?" A chill of foreboding makes its way down my spine.

"I don't know. I think someone was in the shop. It's very strange. A few things are moved, but all the money is here."

My mind goes back to my room, where I felt the exact same sensation. My stuff had been moved, but nothing taken. Surely this couldn't have anything to do with the case? That would be ridiculous. Yet . . .

I probably should come clean to Lawrence. Tell him about the case, about Matteo. About how I told the police about Lawrence's journal. Could Matteo be the one who broke into Lawrence's? Can cops even do that? Or maybe the dirty cop is responsible. Or . . . the Golden Arrow. My paranoia's amping up because it seems like I am at the center of this somehow. That the Golden Arrow is watching me and those I love. Watching the case. Watching but waiting for . . . what? Better to ask Matteo first then talk to Lawrence.

Time to throw some shade, even though it kills me to do it. Stall tactic. "Do you think you're being paranoid?" I don't; Lawrence is probably spot-on. But what if Lawrence ends up like that hanging dummy? I need to talk to Matteo, stat.

"Maybe." Lawrence doesn't sound convinced.

"I'll see you tonight, right? We can talk more about it then. Just . . . make sure to double-lock your door. Maybe it was some homeless person who got in and took a nap on your couch again." I force my voice to be bright and cheery.

I hang up just as a text message comes through. As if called by my bat signal, Matteo's name appears.

> Scheduled interview with your boss at the station. Can you be here around 3 to watch on closed circuit? You might have to prompt comic book questions if it's needed.

I punch my affirmative reply and straighten my shoulders. I'm Janeway. Captain of my own destiny. I have things to do, friends to save, and gold lamé hot pants to finish before the show tonight. That thought lifts my doom and gloom a smidgen. Sometimes glitter and men in drag are exactly what a girl needs to be set right again.

And sometimes all it takes to make your day is seeing your jerk of a boss in an interrogation room at the police department. The satisfaction I feel watching him nervously sip the water on the table makes up for a lot of the grief he's given me over the years. I'm heady with power as I realize I can have Matteo ask him *anything* I want. I fight the urge to do a villain laugh. I will use my powers for good, but I'm going to watch him sweat first.

Literally. Casey Junior is a big-boned man, and I can see beads of sweat forming at his receding hairline. He keeps his head buzzed to hide his balding, but the dark stubble forms a wicked widow's peak. Otherwise he looks comfortable in his navy suit and brown shoes. Always together. Always the boss. Even when he's nervous.

"Thanks for agreeing to speak with us," I hear Matteo's voice before I see him on the compact TV screen. He tucks his tie as he slides into the chair across from Edward Casey Junior.

I'm in the next room but could be watching this anywhere. Rideout is supposed to be watching with me to pass along any questions I have, but so far I haven't seen him. Not that I'm too bothered by it. We already had a small powwow and decided Matteo would question Casey alone, unless he thought he needed a "bad cop" to play against.

Casey gives Matteo a winning smile despite his moisture. "Anything for the LAPD. Though I can't think why you would need to interview me, I'm happy to give my time." Add "always the politician" to his list of attributes.

"Well, we have a fascinating case on our hands that seems to be something in the way of your expertise. We could think of no one better to ask advice from."

"Oh. Ask away." Casey Junior's shoulders relax instantaneously. His face gains color. Matteo's methods are spot-on; even I know that a relaxed suspect shares more information. Let him think we're on his side then *wham-o*. Got your nose.

"I'm sure you've seen the news about this Golden Arrow?" I can see only part of Matteo's face—the camera is aimed mostly at Casey—but by the set of Matteo's shoulders, he's watching Casey as closely as I am for any hint that he knows more than he should.

Casey barely covers up a snort of derision. "That lunatic probably makes your job hard to do these days. Damn shame, but it's driving up Genius business, so I can't complain. How can I help?"

"Well, we think the Golden Arrow may be taking on the persona of one of *your* superheroes. We're hoping you can shed light on why they may have picked this particular comic book."

"I'll do what I can, of course, but there's no point in trying to figure out why someone who is mentally unbalanced does whatever they do. They could have picked any superhero."

"We think there's more to it than that. That's where you come in. The vigilante has been busting drug dealers and re-creating panels from one of the last *Hooded Falcon* issues your father published before he died. Do you know if your father wrote about any real crimes at all? We're looking for a connection between this drug ring and the comics your father wrote."

This question stops Casey dead in his tracks. He swallows noisily and sits back, jovial manner gone. "I, uh, that's an interesting question to ask. Certainly he was inspired by real events. Constantly poring over the newspaper for inspiration. But what does that have to do with what you're investigating?"

The warning light in my head flashes. There's something *more* here.

"Here's the thing: the media isn't reporting this because we haven't released the information, but there was a note at the first scene that indicated a connection to Genius Comics. At the most recent warehouse bust, there was a white rabbit spray-painted both at the scene of the crime and on a suspect. We're trying to determine if there's a *real* White Rabbit out there, and you are one of the only people who would be able to help us with that, Mr. Casey."

Dead silence. I didn't expect Matteo to take this tack at all. It raises the hairs on the back of my neck. He hasn't asked about a costume or an alibi. He's gone in with my suspicions and gone in swinging, presenting them like fact and not wild speculation. Calculated, professional, to the point. This is Detective Kildaire in all his glory, traces of "my" Matteo gone.

"I . . . You're sure?" He doesn't seem surprised. His ashen face looks closer to *terrified.*

Matteo leans forward, and I can just see the compelling and serious expression on his handsome face. "Deadly sure. It's why we need to get to the bottom of this. The drug lords are after this wannabe superhero, and they've picked up on the comic book connection too. They could target your staff and your building if we don't shut this down. If you think you know something, I suggest you share it."

"I-I was younger when my father wrote it. Dad didn't discuss everything with me, but yes. Honestly, I think he wrote about something real."

"What makes you think that?"

Casey takes a deep breath, holds it in for a long count, then lets it back out slowly. He raises his eyes to Matteo's face. I know that look. I see it in the boardroom monthly. He's taking Matteo's measure. His fingers cease fidgeting on the table, and Casey seems to take hold of himself. From my vantage point, it looks like he's about to be truly honest with Matteo.

"My father *did* always use the newspaper for inspiration; that's true. And the drug culture in LA in the eighties was insane. The comic book was his way of trying to change the ills of the world. I mean, he was constantly trying to help out kids from bad situations. He'd hire them or mentor them when he could, but it was more than that. My father saw *himself* as some sort of superhero." The last came out with a note of bitterness.

Matteo doesn't respond, allowing Casey room to continue. I shift on my feet, heart pounding. It's a good thing I'm not in there. I'd be halfway across the table to get answers.

Casey continues after a sip of water. "Something about that last story line was different, though. My father was *different.* Gone a lot. Lots of . . . questionable personal decisions. At the time, I thought he was going senile, that he finally thought he *was* the Hooded Falcon . . . We were fighting more. But I think he'd based his last comics on something real that he was investigating. He didn't tell me about it, and if he told anyone about it, it would have been the equally crazy kid who lived with us—he was trouble. There were other kids he'd hire for odd jobs—helping with his typewriter or gadgets or whatever. But this one . . . got to my father the way no one else had, and he used him until the day he died. I told my father that every chance I got, even though my father wouldn't listen to me."

My stomach turns over. The kid who lived with them. He has to mean Lawrence. There's true bitterness in Casey's voice. If he's involved in this case somehow, could *he* be the one to have broken into Lawrence's place? *My* place? Could my boss *be* the Golden Arrow?

Rideout picks this moment to burst into the room where I'm standing, sloshing a cup of coffee all over the floor. He mutters an expletive as he jams a headset on and tries repeatedly to get the earbuds inserted properly. He shoots me a look like it's *my* fault he's been getting coffee and missing the interview. "Kildaire, ask him about the arguments. Possible motive."

Before Rideout even finishes speaking, Matteo's voice—quiet, calm, and without a hint of being prompted—comes out from the TV screen, "You were fighting. Fighting about what?"

Casey Junior shrugs, and for a moment I glimpse the younger man he must have been when his father was alive. Not the big bullish businessman but the awkward teen. "I was fifteen. We fought about everything. His comics. His eccentricities. How embarrassing it was to have me invite friends over and have him show up in a cape and tights. About this kid he had live with us for a little bit. He just brought people in off the street and fed them and stuff. It was stupid and dangerous. Though he'd never invited any to live with us before. I had to nip it in the bud."

Rideout watches the TV screen like a hawk now. "Use the journal," he growls. We talked about Casey Junior possibly being the culprit, but my stomach clenches at the fervor in Rideout's voice. He's like a hound on a scent. If this is how Rideout questions people, no wonder Matteo does the interview first.

Matteo gives an almost imperceptible nod. "And did you fight about how he was ending the comic?" Matteo's words slide home, and Casey Junior's jaw tightens.

"What do you mean, 'ending the comic'?" Casey Junior's face has shuttered, his features completely controlled.

"We found evidence that your father planned to end the comic after the current story line. Did that make you angry?"

"You found—how could you know that?"

"We found a journal for an issue of *THF* that shows the Falcon retiring."

Casey Junior's face floods with color, and his hands move to grip the table. "You found a journal? Show it to me." It was an order. A demand.

"We can't share evidence—"

"If you want me to say another word, you show it to me." Casey's face is a dusky red, his voice shaking. I've never seen him unhinged like this. He is . . . furious? Scared? I can't tell which.

Matteo doesn't say a word but rises from his chair and exits the room.

My heart races a mile a minute, and I know Matteo is coming in here even before the door opens.

"We need that journal. There's something here. Something he knows. Something he's not willing to share for some reason."

"It's at my friend's house," I stammer. I hate using L's name right after he was mentioned in the questioning.

"I'll send an officer to go get it."

Oh crap, oh crap. Not only have I *not* told Lawrence about the case or about telling Matteo I've seen the journal; now Matteo wants to go get it by *force.* My best friend won't be my best friend anymore if that happens. I need to fix this. Lawrence would end up a suspect, and it would all be my fault. My mind flies to my messenger bag where I tucked the copies.

"How about the copies I have?"

Matteo's eyebrows draw together over my withheld information, so I plunge ahead with my explanation. "We can just tell Casey that we can't show him the whole journal, but this will prove we have it. I'll ask to borrow the journal tonight and bring it to you tomorrow."

Matteo thinks for a moment, then nods and accepts the copies before walking out the door, saying, "This will work in a pinch. Thanks."

I wait with anxious breath for him to reappear on the TV screen.

"Interesting how much inside information you keep coming up with," Rideout comments, not removing his eyes from the screen.

My stomach plummets. "Happy coincidence," I manage to respond, following his lead and keeping my eyes on the screen.

"There are a lot of happy coincidences where you're concerned—" Rideout continues but is interrupted by Matteo's arrival back on the screen.

I didn't miss the veiled accusation from Rideout and just pray he is the only one who thinks I am involved further. Matteo *must* know there's no way I could actually *be* the Golden Arrow.

"Here are a few pages from the journal." Matteo hands the photocopies over to Casey Junior, who studies them.

"Where did you find this? I've been looking for *years* for my father's journals. Where are the rest of them? I need to see them. All of them."

"We only have one. Are you telling me there are more?"

"Yes." Casey Junior rubs his hand over his head so hard, he'd yank out hair if he had any. "Yes, and I need them. Where did you find this? It's important."

"Why have you been looking for the journals? To hide the fact that your father planned to stop a comic that put millions in your pocket?" Matteo drops the bomb like it's no big deal, but Casey Junior explodes.

He stands up, knocking over his chair, and I think for a moment he's going to rush Matteo. "I loved my father, and I didn't know he was serious about ending the comics. I could never find his notes after he died to wrap up the story line. But this!" Casey Junior returns to the table and grabs the photocopies. "This proves that he *had* notes. Detective, you have to find them. The other journals. I don't know how this ties in to your current case. Really and truly, I don't. But these journals contain the identity of the person I think killed my father."

Goose bumps race down my arm, and I gape at the TV screen. *Killed his father?*

Rideout, on the other hand, is in his element. Calm. Steely. "Chase it, Kildaire."

"Murder? Mr. Casey, your father died of a heart attack."

"That's just what the police report says." Casey Junior has regained some composure and sits back in his chair. "I'm sorry I didn't tell you this at the beginning. It just sounds so ludicrous. I don't expect anyone to ever believe it, but it's my firm belief that my father was killed by the man he was following. The man he intended to write into his comic book as a villain. I've been searching his belongings for *thirty years* to find clues."

Rideout grimaces. "Kildaire, this is starting to sound implausible. I suggest . . ." Then he throws the headset at the TV because Matteo has taken out his earpiece and leaned toward Casey.

"You believe your father was murdered? For writing a comic book?"

"Yes."

"And that the police covered it up?"

"Yes."

"And you think these journals hold the notes including the identity of the person who killed your father?"

"Yes."

"Mr. Casey, I have to ask . . . If you suspected murder, why didn't you file a report?"

"I-I think it was a double agent. A cop he saw dealing drugs." Casey runs his hands over his head, then places them back on the table. His eyes harden. "He was going to publish the cop's real name when he unmasked the other superhero in the comic, but I could never prove it. I heard my dad and the kid arguing about it once, and I was afraid of coming forward without an identity or proof. In case . . . you know."

"In case the cop who took over was the double agent and killed you too?"

"Yes." I think I hear a note of relief in Casey's voice. Like he's just removed a splinter that has been a pain in his ass for thirty years.

"Okay. If we can find this kid, we'll bring him in for questioning. We'll do what we can, even though the time to search for him would have been right after your dad's death. Can you give me a name?"

"I've tried to find this guy for years. Never knew his last name. I only know his first name is Lawrence."

Fear curdles my stomach, forming a pit of doom. Lawrence not only worked for Casey Senior; he was a part of the shenanigans that got Casey Senior killed. At least that's what my boss believes. I guess I'm not the only one keeping secrets, but this could get Lawrence sent to jail. Or killed by the drug lords if they figure out he is involved. I frown. Unless Lawrence *is* the Golden Arrow and is avenging Casey Senior's death, but wouldn't he have told me that?

Matteo clears his throat. "Lawrence. Okay. Description?"

"We were both pretty young, but he would probably be a big black guy these days. Over six feet probably. That's all I know. I don't know why someone has been following drug dealers or making reference to the White Rabbit. Maybe the White Rabbit was a real person too. We won't know until we find those journals. I've looked everywhere in my father's belongings for them. Will you please let me know if you find more?"

Matteo's face doesn't give anything away, but I'm already dying inside. He jots in his notebook, then tucks it into his shirt pocket.

"Thank you, Mr. Casey. I appreciate you weighing in on this. We'll take your counsel seriously in this matter. Would you mind giving a written statement?"

Casey Junior hesitates. "Is it necessary?"

Matteo sits forward in the chair, bringing him within inches of Casey Junior's face. "Mr. Casey, I assure you this case is my number-one priority. The safety of citizens is at stake, the safety of *your* employees, and now possibly the solution to your father's death. I need a written statement."

Casey blows out a breath. "Okay."

"Excellent. In light of your new information, may I also have permission to look at your father's office?"

"Sure. I've looked through there a million times, but be my guest. I hope you find something I've missed."

Matteo shakes Casey Junior's hand and stands up to leave. He tosses a look at the camera that is clearly meant for me. "Stay where you are; we need to talk" is written *all* over his face.

He arrives shortly and shuts the door with a click behind him. Rideout starts yelling about how Matteo removed the earpiece, but Matteo has eyes only for me. "MG, did you know about this?"

"Of course not. I had no idea he thought his father was murdered."

"That wasn't what I was talking about. I'm talking about your *best friend* being a person of interest in this case."

I chew my lip. "Not really. Lawrence did say he'd worked for Senior. It's why he had the journal, but that's it. I didn't know the rest. I promise."

"We're going to have to bring him in for questioning."

"Can't we just—"

"MG, he's a *suspect*. You should be thankful I'm not saying we need to arrest him." He pauses to study my face. "Do you think he knows more than what he told you?"

I shrug. "Maybe. I didn't even know to ask. Matteo—he's not the Golden Arrow. I *know* him." I'm outwardly vehement, but . . . do I really know Lawrence? Look at all I've learned in a week about my so-called best friend. Talk about secrets and lies on all sides these days. I bite my lip. "But . . ."

"But." Matteo looks less than thrilled.

"Well, it's just that Lawrence called me earlier and thought maybe someone had been in his shop. And, well, the day you came over to my house? I thought maybe someone had been in my room."

Matteo's mouth presses into a line, a clue to his suppressed fury. "And you're just mentioning this?"

"I-I didn't think about it before." Which is stupid since Matteo increased patrols at my house and I've been feeling for a week now like the Golden Arrow is taking my involvement personally.

"Was anything taken from your room?"

"No, maybe just some comic books moved around. And really, I'm not even sure about that. Lawrence said the same thing. If nothing was taken, it's not a big deal, right?"

"What if someone is trying to find out what you know about the case? Or found out about your friend's journal and suspects that he has something to do with the case too? Did you think about that?"

I frown. "Well, *now* I'm thinking about it."

"That's why you're not a cop," Rideout says with a pointed look at Matteo.

Matteo runs his hands through his hair. "And keep me in the loop next time, will you? We need that journal. We need to question Lawrence. And now that I know that someone could be watching him, it may be safer to take him into custody."

My hands make fists of their own volition. This has gone sideways so fast. "Don't do that. Don't put him in custody, Matteo. He hasn't done anything wrong." I hope.

Matteo looks unconvinced. He glances at Rideout, who gives him a shrug that I read as "It's your own funeral." "Fine, we won't put him in custody unless something comes out of the questioning. But we *are* going to bring him in to the station. He's a bigger player in this than we thought."

I nod, but inwardly I'm dying. If the police show up at Lawrence's door before I can tell him what's been going on, I'll never forgive myself. Also, I want to see the entire journal before the police have it. What if the crooked cop loses it on purpose? A plan hatches in my head. I need to get to Lawrence before the police.

Rideout seems oblivious to my plight. He's staring at the TV screen with a scowl that would make any comic book villain jealous. "This just keeps getting more complicated. Now we're trying to solve a thirty-year-old possible murder as well?"

I chance a look at Rideout, then address Matteo, "I think it's all related. The last issues, including the journals. The drug dealers. The White Rabbit. We just have to put it all together. We're getting close. I can feel it." Even if it looks like my friends—no, my *family*—are involved and their lives are at risk.

Rideout makes a sound of derision in the back of his throat and pushes the TV screen and cart into the corner of the room before stalking out into the hallway. He grabs the arm of the younger officer, Officer James, the one I saw pocket evidence at the crime scene. I recognize the thinning sandy hair. He and Rideout have an intense discussion, and my interest piques. The younger officer looks angry about something, and I can't help my brain from going back to the warehouse. Two more officers walk by in the hall. One looks vaguely familiar too. This is the problem with my paranoia. Until we have a way to pinpoint the double agent, it could be literally *anyone* at this police station with knowledge of the case.

Matteo's fingers snap in front of my eyes, and I'm brought out of my thoughts and back to the interrogation room. "Hello? Get your coat. You and I are going to go look at Casey Senior's office while your boss is making his statement. I've told Officer James to take a *very* long time to complete this task so that your boss won't know you're our informant. Casey mentioned he's shipping many of the items in the study for a charity auction tomorrow, including the costume. It's likely our only chance." He motions to Officer James, who still looks cranky, but now I understand the heated exchange with Rideout. I would be upset too if I had to stay at the precinct and do paperwork while my partners went to search a suspect's office.

Rideout sticks his head back in. He barely gives me a glance and addresses Matteo, "Let's get this show on the road. We only have an hour tops before this guy heads home."

"Oh goody," I mutter under my breath. Instead of a cozy conversation in the car, I get to enjoy the dulcet tones of Detective Rideout singing all the verses of *subtle jabs about why MG shouldn't be here.* All the better for me to stew about Lawrence on my own.

Lawrence didn't just work for Casey Senior. He was a confidant. He *lived* with the man. If Casey Junior is right and his father was murdered, odds are Lawrence has seen his killer. Not only that; if there *is* a leak in the LAPD, it's only a matter of time before Lawrence becomes the number-one target. We need to wrap this up yesterday.

CHAPTER 16

The manor sits like a refined older gentleman—elegant, slightly sprawling, with the air of being worn in and relaxed—atop a hill overlooking a private greenbelt outside of LA. On one side, Griffith Observatory looms atop the same scrubby hill looking down on us, and on the other three sides, there isn't a house to be seen. Deep woods obscure the view of the nearest neighbor, and I contemplate the possibility of them being my favorite movie star.

"Rough place to grow up," I mutter, climbing out of the sleek dark sedan, a real undercover car this time. No Prius in sight. This is a serious investigation at this point. All it took was a flash of Matteo's badge in front of the camera on the front gate, and it opened straightaway. Now, a figure in a conservative black suit comes down the stone steps toward us. My parents may be rich, but they aren't "front gate with a camera, butler at the front door" rich.

In short order, we are escorted inside the spacious foyer, classic and distinguished with checkered black-and-white floors and a large arrangement of flowers. At first glance, it's the opposite of who I am. I expect to hate this house, to feel the overpolished, stuffy, overpowering feeling of Casey Junior in every room. Instead, it feels oddly like . . . coming home.

There's an aura. I *feel* the presence of a man I've never met, in this the birthplace of my favorite stories. He's everywhere. The old-fashioned brass light fixtures that come off as charmingly retro instead of tacky and outdated. A huge bust of a superhero cast in bronze and attached over a doorway like he's flying through the wall. The row of paintings between that door and the stairs that have the eyes cut out. I assume it's so someone in the room can look through them—it's classic comic fodder, kooky as all get out, and I love it. I not only feel Casey Senior's presence; it's like the house welcomes me. Sighs with relief that I've come. I shove away the thought that Casey Senior's spirit *wants* me to solve this case. That's crazy, right?

It also shows that Casey Junior has *not* redecorated in the thirty years since his father's death. I frown, thinking through his impassioned interview. Perhaps this house is the very proof I need to show that Casey Junior *really* loved his father. Wants his presence to linger.

"Are you coming?" Matteo's voice comes from the staircase in the foyer.

I realize I've been staring around the room and have completely missed all of Matteo's conversation with the butler.

"Oh, um, yes, of course."

Matteo turns to follow the butler up a curving staircase—quiet, with a worn and soft red velvety carpet runner. I make my way up the stairs behind him, taking in the house. *This* is the perfect superhero lair. Comfortable. Impressive. Homey. Huge enough to hide a batcave in the second living room. Heck, Casey Junior even has an Alfred.

"I know what you're doing," a voice comes from behind me, and I jump about a mile in the air, my mind going directly to ghosts, goblins, and the specter of Casey Senior's murdered corpse. Instead, it's the all-too-real, unpleasantly corporeal Detective Rideout.

"Climbing the stairs? You must have graduated top of your class."

"No, I *know*." His hand grabs mine on the railing, and the touch sends creepy crawlies straight to my soul. I yank my hand away and turn to face Rideout, careful to stay a full step above him and his impishly smirking face.

"Know *what*?"

"I'm not stupid. First you happen to meet Kildaire in the coffee shop. Then you *happen* to see those white rabbits that no one else saw. Then you *happen* to just have these journal pages on you, and your best friend is the key to finding the murderer. Kildaire may be blinded by your"—his eyes wander down to my chest, then back to my face—"finer assets, but I'm not fooled."

This man must have come from Mordor, and I wish he'd just go back to Mount Doom and the fires that birthed him. I turn my back to him and start up the stairs again. "I don't know what you're talking about."

"You're the Golden Arrow, and I will prove it. I don't know what you're doing messing with the case, but I'm going to figure it out."

I whip around so fast, I almost lose my balance. "What? Are you *insane*? I'm helping with this investigation. I'm the only reason you've figured anything out. Without me, you guys would have no idea."

Rideout shrugs and mounts the stairs with a relaxed manner that just sets all my creep monitors off. "Our profiler gave me the report today. He thinks it could be a woman we're chasing, not a man; the original thugs were drugged, not beaten . . . a woman's tactic. Intelligent, educated, well steeped in geek culture, and with a way to keep tabs on the police investigation to avoid being caught. Sound like anyone you know?"

I decide on bluffing outwardly. "You're barking up the wrong tree, Watson." But, inwardly, I'm panicking a little. It *does* sound like me. Could the Golden Arrow be trying to frame me for all of this?

Rideout's mouth presses into a line. "I'm watching you."

I let him get far enough ahead of me that I have the landing all to myself. It's back to quiet and comfortable, though I'm still shaken. If Rideout isn't just being an ass, if he *really* thinks I am the Golden Arrow . . . well, I could be in *real* trouble.

At the head of the stairs, I pause. I could have sworn Matteo and Rideout went to the right, but I hear a noise to my left. The house seems to pull at me, so I wander down the worn path in the deeply padded wine-colored carpet to the set of large double wood doors that takes up the entire left end of the hall. Casey Senior's study entrance is no less impressive than the house itself.

Matteo and Rideout are on their mission; I can already hear them knocking around in the study. I didn't think I'd gotten that far behind them, but then again . . . this house kind of sucks me in with its quiet and creative energy. I can feel the stories here, picture Casey Senior plotting and sketching, drawing on the ethereal ideas floating in the air. Something about the atmosphere in this house speaks to my writer's soul. I feel a bit like I've crossed into a fairy ring—one hundred years could have passed in a day, for all I know.

I pad up to the door and push down the brass lever. It's hard to open against the thick carpet, and I push my body weight against it. The hinges squeak slightly, and I pause, realizing I didn't hear that squeak when Detective Rideout and Matteo went in. Maybe the second door is more oiled or something. From inside the room, the noises stop.

I press again, and the door moves forward under my weight, swinging into the room . . . where I come face-to-cape with a figure who is *not* Detective Rideout or Matteo.

The yell that erupts from me is half scream, half war cry. For a brief instant, I think maybe I've interrupted a servant dressed in an odd uniform. But this figure is dressed all in black, wearing a *mask*, and a large golden arrow shines across the chest of the person's spandex suit.

I stumble backward at the same time the figure whirls around. I fall back, hitting my head on the wooden door, and land in the hallway. I scramble to my feet, but by the time I make it back into the study, Matteo hot on my heels, I glimpse only the edge of a cape as the person *jumps straight out a second-story window*. No hesitation.

"Matteo, it's *him*!"

"What? MG, are you okay?" Matteo's hands are on my shoulders, probably trying to see if I'm hurt.

There's no time to examine the splitting headache already developing from my fall. "Matteo, he's here!"

"He who?"

I'm frantic at this point, pushing Matteo's hand from my neck so I can get to the window. "The Golden Arrow. The Golden Arrow was right here in this room when I came in. And he just jumped through the window. He's *out there*, Matteo!"

Matteo gives me one quick searching glance and rushes to the window. Rideout puffs into the room seconds later, his eyes darting between Matteo and me.

"Jesus, what happened in here?" Rideout asks. "You yelled loud enough to alert the entire county to the fact we're here, and what the *hell* did you do to this office?"

I cut a look around the room, noting for the first time that it's been carefully ransacked. There's no other way to describe it. Everything has been pulled off the walls and arranged in orderly piles against the baseboards. The desk drawers are sitting out.

I blink up at Rideout, then look at Matteo. "I—he—Matteo, tell me you saw that. Saw him jump out that window."

Matteo returns from the window and crouches in front of me. "There's no one out there, MG."

"Interesting." Rideout regards me as if I'm Poison Ivy herself. His words echo in my head. *I'm watching you.*

In response to his silent accusation, I spit out a retort: "This room didn't do this to *itself.* And definitely not in thirty seconds." I want to yank out my hair. How did Matteo not see the Golden Arrow?

"No. Probably not." Matteo and Detective Rideout share a loaded glance, and my blood pressure increases. It's obvious they're having a conversation without talking.

"Well, aren't you going to go *look* for who jumped out that window?" I'm practically yelling again, and I don't care. Rideout has obviously gotten to Matteo with his stupid theory. Only it doesn't hold water because I just *saw* the Golden Arrow, and it wasn't in a mirror.

Matteo considers me for a moment. "I'll go look around outside, okay?" He shoots a look at Rideout. "We could be dealing with a possible B and E." Matteo makes a move to leave but pauses just short of the door, turning back to look at me. "Are you all right?"

"I'm *fine*, just startled having come face-to-face with the person we've been chasing."

After a brief pause, he nods before disappearing down the hall.

I stand in silence.

Rideout leans his shoulder against the wall and crosses his arms, watching me. "I have to hand it to you: this was complicated to organize. You had no way of knowing you'd have time alone in the study. What were you looking for?"

"What on earth are you talking about?"

"Getting us to bring you here but sneaking in to search by yourself first. Or give your accomplice time to get away. Pretty brilliant. What were you looking for? Evidence that would name you as the Golden Arrow? And then pretend like you saw someone? Bravo." He mocks me with a slow clap.

What. A. Dick. I throw my hands in the air. "I didn't do this. Do you really think I could have taken everything off the walls in thirty seconds? That's crazy, and you know it."

We wait in silence for Matteo to reappear, though I have a sneaking suspicion I know what he's going to say.

Matteo's face says it all before he opens his mouth. "Nothing. No cars left the gated driveway." He pauses, then continues, "The security cameras were experiencing some technical *difficulties*, and nothing from the last twenty minutes recorded."

Rideout grunts. "Heck of a coincidence."

"Yeah."

We're all silent for a moment. At least Rideout can't think I still did this, right? I bite my lip. I've had time to glance around the room while Matteo's been gone. There's order to the chaos; the room isn't just torn apart. The knickknacks that sit in neat lines are intact, no books pulled off the shelves. Mostly it's just the paintings yanked off the hooks, exposing the walls. The Golden Arrow was systematic.

"I think I know what he was looking for," I say to the room.

Matteo pulls on a pair of latex gloves and sets about taking pictures with his phone.

"Interesting that you *know*. But fine, elucidate," Rideout answers, raising my ire. Even Matteo makes an annoyed grunt.

I decide to just ignore him. "You know the issue we looked at? How they discovered clues to the identity of the double agent in the wall safe? I think the Golden Arrow is looking for the journals. Or something else that Casey Senior would have kept to identify the double agent or the White Rabbit. I think he was looking for a wall safe."

A chill chases down my spine, and I feel the house whisper an assurance to me. It's a *great* story line. One any comic book would be proud to own. One I'd be proud to write, and if there's anything I think I understand about Casey Senior at this point, it's that he loved a good story. Even if it's his own story. "What if this is what it's all about? Identifying the double agent? Or the White Rabbit? What if the Golden Arrow has figured out Casey Senior was murdered and that his killer is still at large?"

Rideout gives a full belly laugh. "This is ludicrous. Kildaire, you can't possibly buy it. This guy died of a *heart attack* thirty years ago. Old news. We work narcotics. You and I know that big eighties bust put all the big dealers in jail. White Rabbit guy included, if he ever existed. These rings are all brand-new, and no drug dealer runs a ring for thirty years unless you live in Argentina or Mexico. We are chasing a thirty-year-old wild goose, and we're losing the trail of the real drug guys by following this *girl's* false trail."

"What if we find a wall safe?" I ask. "What if the journals are in there?"

Rideout sneers. This guy is *not* the good-cop half of their team. "Okay, then, show us. Show us the proof."

I press my lips together, willing Matteo to feel what I feel in this room. Something in my head clicks into place. Call it intuition. Call it Casey Senior's spirit from the past. Whatever it is, I feel surer about this than I have anything about this case so far. I'm letting the story lead me, not the facts. Exactly how I write my comics. I get a nugget, a vision, then chase that story down its own path. I don't try to box it in. I'm open to wherever it wants to lead. Facts are Matteo's part of the investigation. Comic stories are mine.

I look around the room, my attention lingering on the painting behind the desk. "I interrupted the Golden Arrow before he could take all the art down. We need to look behind it."

Rideout snorts. "If this was an attempted burglary, this room is evidence. We can't move anything."

That figures. He asks for proof, then tells me I can't look.

Matteo turns to Rideout. "We'll wear gloves. We're here to look at the office and look for the journals."

Rideout mutters a string of words I can't hear before finishing with "It's your funeral."

Yahtzee. I accept the pair of latex gloves from Matteo before crossing to the desk and grasping the side of the ornate frame. It's almost as tall as I am. I recognize the panel drawn in the frame as the one I saw Casey Junior lounging in front of for the charity promotion article Matteo and I saw when we were looking through the comics in my room.

Matteo lines up on the other side of the frame. "All right. We'll lift it enough for you to look through the crack in the side. On three: one, two, three . . ."

Something inside the frame shifts as Matteo and I awkwardly lift the painting up and slightly away from the wall. My heart races. I'm convinced we've broken the antique frame, but it holds together enough for me to lay my head against the wall. It's an awkward angle. Even with my nose literally touching the frame, I can't see the wall clearly.

"I need a flashlight," I say.

"Rideout, if you wouldn't mind."

"Of course I *mind.* I'm a narcotics detective, Kildaire." But I hear rustling, and a cell phone with a flashlight appears near my head.

"A little farther down, more toward the wall—yeah . . . right . . . right *there.* Matt—*Detective Kildaire,* there's something on the wall behind the painting." My head pops up, nearly sending Rideout's phone flying.

Matteo studies me like I'm a puzzle, but after a moment he nods. "Okay, let's take down the frame. Let's look at what's behind there." We lift, but the five-foot frame is awkward and hard to manage. I don't think the Golden Arrow could have removed this one by himself, at least not in one piece. It explains why it's the only one remaining on the wall. Something clunks inside the frame again as we shift it wildly, trying to unhook the wire from the mounting device.

"A little help here, Rideout," Matteo calls. Rideout mutters about how this is "all a part of my plan" just quietly enough that I don't think Matteo hears. I'm so excited to be right at the prospect of finding the journals, at being one step ahead of the Golden Arrow, that I ignore Rideout's ridiculous allegations.

Finally the frame leans against the wood-paneled wall, and I behold in triumph a small safe in the wall behind the desk.

"Just like in the comic books." Call me Professor X. I'm a brain-*ninja* to find this.

"It could be coincidence," Matteo says, taking a picture of the safe with his phone.

"Or the perfect place to keep journals that contain the name of a drug lord and a dirty cop in league together." I study Rideout from the corner of my eye. Maybe *that's* why he's so unsettled. Prickles dance on my skin as I consider the very real possibility that Detective *Dursley* could be the dirty cop. And that he's annoyed with my clue-finding abilities, looking for a way to pin this all on me.

Rideout doesn't seem to notice me staring. He's talking over my head to Matteo. "You do realize that the journals can't be in there. Casey Junior said he's been looking for *thirty* years."

I cross my arms. "Maybe he didn't know the safe was here."

Rideout rolls his eyes at me like the teenage boy he is. "After thirty years? You don't think he knew his dad had a safe in here?"

Matteo watches us like a tennis match. "Chances are he knew it was here, *and* there's no way for us to unlock it without a warrant and a special team . . . Oh."

"Oh what?" I hold my breath. I know this is the answer. *This* is what the Golden Arrow wants. This is the key to the story.

"It's open." Matteo studies the wall safe, then extracts his pen from his pocket. He slides it up the side of the door, and sure enough, it swings forward. "It's been disarmed."

We all crowd around to be the first to glimpse whatever is inside the safe. Except it's empty. Completely. Well, that just takes the freaking cake.

"What now, Dexter?" Rideout's dry drawl comes from over my left shoulder. I hate that he's using nicknames like I do. Just because I use my knowledge of comics to catch a comic book criminal doesn't make me Dexter.

I ignore him and turn my face to Matteo's. "We need to find those journals." I beg him with my eyes to believe me. To believe *in* me. These journals are the key.

Rideout crosses his arms again. "If our vigilante is after the journals, we need to figure out how the Golden Arrow even knows about them.

I suspect help from the inside." He looks pointedly at me, and Matteo grunts.

"Funny, I think the same thing," I shoot back, not bothering to hide my glare from Matteo. Rideout is the one breaking the rules of professionalism here.

"Rideout, drop it. MG, he has a point. Who knows about these journals?"

"Lawrence showed one to me. I showed it to you and Detective Rideout, and you showed it to Casey Junior." A very short list. My stomach turns over again. All jokes aside, Rideout is a jerk, but possibly right too. How would the Golden Arrow have known to even look in this office if he didn't know the journal existed? Was he just going off the comic books? I press my lips together. It seems unlikely. It's like the Golden Arrow sees everything I do, and *that* idea gives me the willies. Am I under surveillance? Does the dirty cop on Matteo's team also feed information to the Golden Arrow? That idea seems more unlikely than the last. The Golden Arrow knows the case, that the journals exist, and has reason to want to find them. If it isn't Casey Junior, there's only one other common denominator.

Matteo nods slowly, his mind obviously chasing the same path as mine. "We'll need to inform Edward Casey Junior about what allegedly happened here today and see if he wants to make a report. It's possible that he left the room like this going through his father's office for the auction. But maybe not. And we need to talk to the only other person who seems mixed up in this."

I swallow hard. Lawrence.

CHAPTER 17

Cars clog the Hamburger Mary's parking lot by the time I pull the Hurtling Turd into a spot. A good sign. Everyone loves a full crowd, and an early-summer Friday night is prime drag show time for the locals. I reach in my back seat, gather the pile of fabric into my arms, and hurry across the lot. Usually I'm giddy about coming to a drag show, but tonight my stomach is a ball of nerves. I'll let L perform; then I'll have to spill the beans. So many beans. And hope he has beans to spill right back that will solve my case. And keep L out of jail.

I wind my way through the crowd as quickly as possible. I hope I can get back in enough time to snag a great table. I'm almost to the back of the house when I see a familiar face. Kyle's fiancée, Nina.

"MG!" She yells my name like we're old friends, and my heart instantly warms a little, easing my anxiety. Her enthusiasm is literally contagious. She waves me over.

"Hey, Nina. What brings you guys here?"

She takes a sip of the large drink in front of her. "Bachelorette party!" The girls all whoop. It wouldn't have been hard to guess, given the large tiara on Nina's head and the sash that says "BRIDE" slung across her middle. I'm a terrible human, I'd already forgotten that she and Kyle were getting married soon.

"Congratulations," I say, smiling. The group is already tipsy. They're in for a good time once the queens start performing.

"Kyle said no strippers. He didn't say anything about drag queens."

A girl after my own heart.

"What are *you* doing here?" Nina eyes the pile of gold lamé.

"I'm dropping off a costume I made for my friend. In fact, I'd probably better get back there so I can still get a table after."

"Nonsense, you'll come sit with us."

"Really?"

Nina grins. "I insist! We nerd girls need to stick together!" She leans over to me and whispers dramatically, "These are theater friends. They get it. They'll be happy to have you too!"

My heart warms just a bit more. Nina does seem cool, and Kyle never outright backstabbed me the way Andy did. Maybe a friend of the female variety would do me good. Again this case has pointed out to me that I've been alone on my own isolated island. I can't even remember the last time I reached out to my friends from college or my cosplay group. I suddenly miss them. "Okay. I'll be back."

Backstage *sounds* glamorous, but at a drag show, it's pretty much one tiny room stuffed full of panty hose, cosmetics, and men in wig caps. I stand at the door and try to locate Lawrence among the group of men. Someone is yelling about lipstick on the mirror, and someone else snips back, "At least it's not on your teeth like last time," but I don't hear or see Latifah Nile anywhere.

"L!" I wait, no answer. I snag one of the queens right by the door, a plump Filipino who I've seen several times do a great postwar-era pinup routine.

"Can you find Latifah Nile for me?" I hold up the pile of costumes.

He turns and shouts into the room, "Hey, queens! Has anyone seen La-tee-tee? You bitches just need to shut it for one second so that—"

Lawrence emerges from behind a dressing rack in the back corner of the room, one eye already done up in gold glitter, Cleopatra cat-eye style.

"Girl, you look *fine* tonight," he says, taking in my own penciled purple eyebrows, glittery purple lipstick, and chunky skull-and-crossbones necklace. "You're going to make these queens jealous. Is

Atlanta here with you?" The mention of Matteo both gives me butterflies and kills them with a ball of anxiety. L is a suspect, and it's all due to my meddling.

I flush. "No, just me. And a friend here for a bachelorette party. I needed to refabulous myself. I wilted a little this week." I lean in like I'm telling him a secret. "I learned from the best."

And it's true. I learned the art of super-dramatic makeup from Lawrence. Shockingly, there aren't many places I get compliments on my Violet Femme purple lipstick. Yet another reason I love drag shows. No one appreciates drama or makeup quite like queens.

"Well, my drag mama would be proud. And, girl, you're never anything less than fabulous. You just wear it different sometimes." Lawrence gives me a squeeze, then pounces on the fabric I have in my hands. He's already wearing the foam padding around his rear, reined in by layers of panty hose to make the look complete.

Outwardly Lawrence is completely normal, seemingly unfazed by his recent apartment scare. I'm trying to follow his lead, but inwardly I'm at war with myself. I want to talk to Lawrence, but there are so many queens around, I don't dare do it here. "Do you want to try it on in case I need to adjust it? Maybe the bathroom could give us enough room if we need to pin it." At the very least sans eight queens.

Lawrence beams at me, then makes a shooing gesture. "Nonsense. You just go get yourself a table before one of these queens steals you from me. One of these bitches can help me if I need to pin something."

I nod, swallowing my panic in an awkward gulp.

"Girl, what's wrong? You feeling okay?"

I open and close my mouth, unsure of how to approach this. *No big deal. The police are going to show up and question you, and I'm worried you might be playing superhero.* "Just something I wanted to talk with you about. It's nothing . . ." I turn to leave but think better of it. I need to know. Rip off the Band-Aid. "Actually, where were you today? Around five o'clock?"

Please have an alibi. Please have an alibi.

Lawrence pulls back, looking surprised. "Did something happen?" He taps his chin. "I think around three I was out getting lashes for tonight, but I'd have to check."

So . . . nothing solid, but my shoulders relax. There's nothing in Lawrence's face that suggests he's lying. Maybe I'm all bent out of shape with my suspicions for nothing. Yet there's still the police stuff to tell Lawrence.

L reaches out and rubs my shoulder. "Seriously, girl, are you okay?"

I almost divulge the whole story right there in the backstage area. I want so badly to come clean to L, but the plump Filipino queen sidles up to us and leans over the gold lamé.

"So *this* is your secret weapon, La-tee-tee!" The queen flicks a non-existent wig and gives me the once-over. "Girl, your costumes are on fleek. I need a new one next show. Any chance you take food stamps?"

The nearby queens laugh at the joke, and I crack a smile.

"Sorry, I only deal in lifelong indebtedness and firstborns, but I'll let you know when I start accepting Visa."

"You will *not*," L says firmly.

This isn't the time or place to discuss matters with the show about to start. I highly doubt Matteo is going to show up and pull L offstage mid-act, so I decide to let L perform without worrying. I pat Latifah on the padded rear before I leave. "Maybe we can chat after you're finished. We'll go to IHOP and have pancakes. Right now, you go show them how it's done."

I make my way back out to the table, where the girls are already enjoying another round of drinks. I slide in next to Nina and sigh, leaning my head against the booth back. The end of the night looms over me, and I hope I'll be able to enjoy the show. But I keep reliving opening that study door, catching a glimpse of the person in black. Ruminating about what the Golden Arrow knows and what he or she is looking for, trying to figure out just how I can help solve this case, especially now that Rideout seems to be gunning for me as a suspect. I need to start at the beginning. If this is all about Casey Senior, I need to start there.

Which is where Lawrence comes in.

Just as I finish this thought, my phone buzzes. It's a text from Matteo. We need to talk about the case. New development.

With an apologetic look at Nina, I type back, Not a good time. With some friends at Hamburger Mary's. Can I call you later? I have *got* to explain to my best friend why the police are after him first.

We're plunged into darkness as a voice booms over the loudspeaker, "Ladies and gentlemen, welcome to Hamburger Mary's famous Drag Review."

A spotlight pops on, and there's Latifah Nile standing center stage, hip thrown back, gold sparkly heels perfectly apart in a dramatic stance, and one ridiculously fantastic sequined top hat pulled down over her eyes. The sequined tailcoat I designed fits L perfectly.

"I am your host for the evening, Latifah Nile." L repositions the hat dramatically atop the afro wig, and the crowd cheers and catcalls like crazy. "And we have quite the show for you tonight. You can see we're doing some updating." L sweeps a hand in suggestive curves over her gold lamé and sequined bodysuit down to the gold sequined skirt and panty hose–clad legs. She looks like a mix of vintage twenties, sexy temptress, and a nod to Egyptian style with her signature eyes. "And tonight I'll be"—L produces an old-fashioned cane from somewhere behind her, cracks it on the floor, leans over it to better show her taped cleavage over the top of the bustier, and pouts—"putting on the Ritz."

The girls at my table yell and wave money in the air even as the music comes out over the loudspeaker for L's number. She's slow stepping, sashaying, and generally shaking what God—and foam padding—gave her to a cabaret-paced "Puttin' on the Ritz."

The crowd cheers as she makes her way slowly down the stage, mimicking bawdy versions of most of the lyrics. She pantomimes money, bends over a little, and snaps up like someone spanked her, much to the delight of the front row. L actually *sings*, which is unusual at a drag show, her voice smoky and seductive.

I holler with the rest of the girls as L stops with a drumbeat, waggles her hips, and pouts. It's a genius routine. At one point Latifah wanders over to us and puts her sequined top hat on my head while she leans on the cane and addresses Nina.

"Are you sure you want to get married, honey? There are so many men and so little time!" Shimmying her shoulders to the heavy drumbeat, she does a Ginger Rogers slide and makes her way back up to the stage.

"We have so many good acts tonight, and I can tell you are the *perfect* audience." She winks, and someone calls something from the audience. "You all behave now." She waves her hands and does a grapevine with the cane out in front to exit the stage.

I'm beaming, and I can't wait to give L a huge hug and a high five. No matter the case and all the shade going down, Latifah is *damn* good at her job. I turn to Nina, unable to contain myself. "What do you think?"

"The glitz, the glam, the costumes, the *eyelashes*. This is so much fun!" Nina laughs and fans her face. "This is the best bachelorette party *ever*!"

I laugh. "Yeah, not too many straight men come to these events, but when they do, it can get really hilarious."

Nina cracks up like she's about to fall off her seat. Boy, she must be really in her cups; she can barely catch her breath. "MG, isn't that your boyfriend over there? He might need saving. It looks like there are four or five gay men fighting over him."

"What?" I whip around, and like my eyes are powered by magnets, my gaze meets Matteo's. I feel it like a physical jolt all the way down to my feet. Then waves of nerves come crashing down on me. Is he here for L? Maybe he's come to pull L offstage midperformance and drag her down to the station. My heart hammers in my chest.

"Um, I'll be right back. I thought he was . . . working."

I make my way across the room to where Matteo is politely telling a tall gentleman in a crop top and a pink wig that he doesn't drink. I offer the tall man a smile, then turn narrowed eyes on Matteo. "What are you doing here?"

"You told me where you were, so I thought I'd just come . . ." He looks around, bewildered. "Where *are* we?"

"Hamburger Mary's."

The next act starts, and I pull Matteo back toward the table with me. "I can see why you're good at your job."

"I need to ask you about a suspect. The guy in the hoodie."

"So ask."

"Can we sit? It won't take very long, and then I'll be going back to the office tonight to follow up."

My shoulders relax. So this *isn't* about Lawrence. I sigh. "All right, come on." I drag him the rest of the way to Nina's table. If the show follows its usual pattern, we won't see L for at least three or four numbers.

The girls at the booth go gaga over Matteo and giggle to themselves while making room for him. Nina won't even let me apologize for crashing her bachelorette party and goes back to attacking her hamburger with glee.

Once Matteo and I are as alone as we can get, I turn to him. The faster we get this over with, the faster Matteo can leave. "Okay, Scotty, give her all she's got. Let's hear it."

I try desperately not to think about how I'm squished up against him, the thigh of my tight black pants against his slacks. *Bigger fish to fry, MG.*

"Scotty?"

"Never mind."

The next performer's music starts, and Matteo tries not to seem like he's staring, but who *wouldn't* stare at a five-foot-five Filipino hottie who literally just burst out of a clamshell? A campy mash-up of *The Little Mermaid*'s "Kiss the Girl" with Katy Perry's "I Kissed a Girl" booms over the speakers. The performer's forties, victory-rolled hair and sexy pink kimono-style maxi dress are perfection.

Matteo blinks. "I just expected hamburgers." His genuine confusion undoes some of the tension I've been feeling. Matteo is just here to talk. No ulterior motive. He didn't know this was going to be a drag show. Or that L is a performer.

"You do seem to have a habit of arriving at interesting moments. Is it something you come by naturally, or do you have to practice?" I take a sip of my beer.

He rubs the back of his neck. "Honestly, it just seems to happen around you. I can't find my feet sometimes."

He gives me a look far more searching than could be labeled "professional interest." My heart stutters in my chest. His gaze drops to my lips, and mine to his. It amazes me how fast we can go from my paranoia to banter to crazy sexual tension. His admission that he can't find his feet around me does impressive things to the dragons in my stomach.

The urge to kiss him overwhelms me. *We can't, we can't,* my brain chants. *Do it, do it,* my hormones insist. He's fighting the same battle. I see it in his face. *It's a bad idea. We work together.* Another part of my brain points out that it's dark, and no one would see one *tiny* little kiss . . .

Then Nina *screeches* inches from my ears. The finale of the song washes back into my reality, and Matteo and I lean apart. I study Matteo, not for the first time feeling like I'm on a roller coaster where he's concerned. Striking a balance between the case and my personal feelings gets harder and harder to manage. If he were a normal guy, I'd definitely invite him as my date to the work thing later this month. Matteo in a cape? Oooh, yes, please.

"You're a million miles away. What are you thinking about?" Matteo's face is still far too close for professional conversation.

"The gala at my job." I take myself by surprise by admitting this. I need to get him out the door, not talk about this right now. It's as if Matteo's presence continually inspires my candor, whether I want it to or not. I am far more truthful with him than practically anyone else in my life, save Lawrence and Ryan, at least until this case fell in my lap.

"Okay . . ." He frowns, not following.

"I think it would make more sense if you came to my work party."

Matteo's eyebrows rise—I've taken him by surprise with the change in direction too.

The can of worms is open, so I decide to roll with it. "It will be fun, I promise." Okay, maybe I'm trying to convince myself as well as him. "Costumes, capes, contests, all the free booze you can imagine. I mean, of course it's so you can check out more Genius folks, now that we don't think it's Kyle or Simon."

Matteo taps the table with his fingers before replying, his face looking strangely torn. "Are you asking me to come with you to your work party?"

"Yes, Captain Obvious. I just said that."

Matteo searches my eyes in that "more than professional" manner again that makes my heart turn to electric goo. "No, I mean, are you asking me to the work party for *you* or for the case?"

Applause fills the air around us as yet another act finishes up. I haven't even heard the song or seen the performer—the world always falls away when I'm with Matteo. I'm also not sure how to respond to his question. I'm not going to lie to myself; I want Matteo to come with me. I want to see him in a hot comic-inspired costume. I want to dance with him, laugh with him, do a normal couples-type thing with him . . . Only we aren't a normal couple.

We're a pretend couple, and we're trying to solve a thirty-year-old mystery. Unless I make a move. My thoughts distill. This may be my opportunity to change the pretend part, even if we have to wait until after the case is over to follow through. That's assuming we all live through this and no one gets arrested. I am *not* wearing a jumpsuit; orange clashes terribly with my hair.

I put on my big-girl panties and answer him honestly. There's that candor thing again. "Both."

He lets out a breath, and I see relief mixed with another emotion on his face. Anxiety? He reaches over and puts his hand on my knee like he did while watching *Star Wars*, and he gives it a small squeeze before returning it to the table. "Deal."

My heart stutters in my chest again. He's glad I asked him for me and not just for work.

"Wasn't that wonderful, ladies and gents? Another round of applause. You're really going to love this next one too, but first, I wanted to say a special hello to my dearest friend . . ." Gold sequins glint in the spotlight, and my attention is drawn to Latifah as she struts back onto the stage . . . and the double take she does when she lays eyes on Matteo. *Uh-oh. This is definitely not when L usually reappears. Not the night to go off script. This could be bad. So, so bad.* Here I am trying to keep these two apart, and Latifah is literally going to land in our laps. I can only pray that Matteo doesn't recognize Lawrence in drag.

I smile grimly as a vision in gold sequins sashays across the crowded floor in our direction. "I guess you're about to meet my friend, Latifah."

I see understanding dawn on his face the moment before he turns in the booth and comes face-to-bustier with Latifah. I say my prayers.

"Hello, sugar," she purrs into the microphone. "It seems my sweet girl here has brought Atlanta brisket for dinner instead of a hamburger." The crowd roars with good-natured laughter as Latifah makes a big show of sizing up Matteo's shoulders.

She holds up one hand, showing off her long golden nails. "Don't you know this is a bachelorette party? You are being very naughty by crashing it. Should I send you to my room?"

She winks at me, then squeezes Matteo's shoulders one more time before doing a dramatic shiver and wandering back to the stage. "Whew, I am burning *up* in here. This man sandwich is *hot*!" She throws another wink back at me. "You just let me know if you need help with it, sugar." She sashays back up to the stage.

Matteo is beet red now; I can even tell in the dark. Even as much as I'm freaking out, this is *hilarious*. I try not to laugh, but it's difficult when the table literally *shakes* with the mirth of the other girls.

"You should see your face," Nina says in gasps. Then she reaches around me and grabs Matteo's hand. "But you are such a good sport about it."

He really is. I offer him a small smile. "Okay, now we might be even for you crashing my evening." I relax just a *little*, realizing that Matteo doesn't recognize Lawrence as Latifah.

He rubs a hand over his hair and over the scruff on his cheeks. "You drive a hard bargain."

I shrug and sip my beer. "If you don't pay no tolls, you don't get no rolls." And at his baffled look I set down my beer. It's time to get Matteo out of here before Latifah comes back. "Sorry. *Men in Tights* reference. And didn't you have case developments to discuss?"

He shoots a look over my shoulder to Nina, who is clearly involved in counting her money with the rest of the table to figure out how much they have to tip the performers. He scoots in closer to me and bows his head so he's closer. To anyone else, it would look like a lovers' tête-à-tête. I shake off another ridiculous pang of longing over our *pretend* status.

Matteo doesn't seem likewise conflicted right now. He's back to business. "It's about the suspect with the painted rabbit on his hoodie. He didn't see the person who did it—dressed all in black except for some sort of cape. We ID'd the suspect, but it took a long time to find any reason the Golden Arrow would have marked him as different. We were looking, but nothing stood out. No priors, clean record, not even a parking ticket."

"That's it! He must have help on the inside. No one has a clean parking record in LA."

Matteo rolls his eyes. "Anyhow, I just finished looking through his family's records, and I came across something interesting. Do you recognize this name? It's his father."

I lean over and glance at the phone screen Matteo has pointed in my direction. "Song Yee?" I ponder this. "No, never heard of him. Yee, is that Korean?"

"His family is from China, all legally immigrated in 2012. Midfifties, married, teenage son named Huong."

The White Rabbit. I *told* Detective Rideout and Agent Sosa I thought there was a connection to China. My Spidey sense tingles. It's more than just a coincidence. I don't understand the drug part; that's Matteo's wheelhouse. Maybe this kid isn't just a drug dealer. Maybe his family *produces* the drugs. Ships them in to the dad or the son, who deals it. This would certainly fit the White Rabbit's story line. Maybe the Golden Arrow has tagged *the* White Rabbit; maybe it's that cut-and-dried. Over and done.

"Should I have heard of Song Yee?" I ask. There must be a reason Matteo is asking. Some connection to our case other than China.

"Not necessarily . . . except Song just bought into a printing company. He only owns a small portion, all on the up-and-up. Nothing shady about buying in, but I happened to look into the company's clients, and—"

"A printing company?" I'm confused.

"Marvelous Printing."

I sit back and think. My gaze meets Matteo's as it finally dawns on me. "They print some of our comics. They print *The Hooded Falcon*."

A beat filled with hooting, hollering, and "Uptown Funk" stretches between us as I absorb the information. I sit back and take a sip of my now warm beer. I bought it only to nurse something while I watched L, but I really wish it was something stiffer at this point.

"Could this be how the Golden Arrow discovered Yee, or as I'd bet, the White Rabbit?" I ask.

"I hoped your creative genius could figure that out."

"Flattery will get you everywhere." I pull off my glasses and tap them on the table while I think. "This has to be what the Golden Arrow knew about Yee's son. Too coincidental. But I'm still puzzled how this ties in to any of the other stuff. Maybe Huong or his father could simply be *the* White Rabbit we're looking for. It's not exactly like the comics, but they could be importing drugs from their family in China and dealing them out of the warehouse. But . . . how could this kid being a drug dealer relate to the printing of *The Hooded Falcon*?"

"We questioned him this afternoon—Huong Yee, the son. He's still in custody and had some interesting information to share in exchange for a plea deal. He told us that there *was* a cop working with his ring. And he'd give the identity in exchange for us dropping his charges. Not only that, he didn't think the drugs came from Mexico like Sosa's theory. We've arranged to speak with a judge on his behalf. I'd like you present when we question him again, for the plea deal. We've asked Agent Sosa to review the tape of the interview and be present for the next one too. She knows these bigger rings better than I do."

"The dirty-cop thing plays right into the comic book story line, but how could the Golden Arrow have known that?"

Matteo shrugs. "Maybe he didn't. Maybe you're right and the Yees are the White Rabbit, and that's all he meant to show us. But it sure seems more than a coincidence. *The Hooded Falcon* crops up yet again."

I tip the half-empty beer to the side, then let it fall back to the table. What I wouldn't give for my red ball and a desk wall to think right now. "But that doesn't make any sense. What does a printing press have to do with the drugs?" My mind works a mile a minute, looking for the thread of the story. Even if one of the Yees is the White Rabbit, neither of them seems old enough to be the same White Rabbit Casey Senior was chasing.

"I don't know, but we're going to add surveillance to the printing press until we figure it out."

Matteo jumps slightly as his phone buzzes in his hand. Frown lines crease his brow as he flips through a message. He shoots me a look, then glances back at his phone.

Nina leans over my arm and sloshes a drink toward Matteo. "You guys look *waaaay* too serious. This is a party." She executes a cute little wiggle in the seat next to me. "And, MG, your friend Lawrence was *so* good tonight. Your costume was divine!"

Matteo's eyebrows draw together, and I realize he's put two and two together. "Your friend . . . Lawrence." I can literally see comprehension dawning.

I sip my beer and try to look innocent.

Matteo sighs. "Well, I don't have time to talk to him, er, her, right now. Probably tomorrow by the time this all gets wrapped up, but I'll tell Rideout I located him. Her. Lawrence." He motions to his phone, picks up his water, and salutes the table. "My apologies, ladies. I didn't want to crash the party, just stopped by to say hello. MG, I'll catch you later?"

I spin to face him, relief and curiosity warring for dominance in my heart. "You're leaving?"

"Yeah, that was work." He stands, straightening his tie. His eyes slide past me, and I can tell he doesn't want to say anything in front of our audience. So I follow him out the door and to the parking lot.

It smells like a summer night just before a storm; a wet heaviness hangs in the air, and the clouds seem charged.

Matteo vibrates with an anxious energy. "There's a ship off schedule that just pulled into the dock outside the warehouse. It could be nothing, but patrol has been watching specifically for something like this."

"But you think it's something?"

He shrugs. "I'm not sure. Detective Rideout and Agent Sosa think we're chasing our own tail and wasting resources monitoring this warehouse. The drug operations know it's under surveillance, so Sosa thinks they'd never continue to use it." Matteo runs a hand down his face.

I chew my lip. "I can see her point." I hesitate. "But . . . the dock. The warehouse. The rabbit, then the boat. It's all the progression in the book. I think the ship thing is our best bet at following the Hooded Falcon. At least until we figure out the printing press angle. If you stop watching the warehouse, what happens if we miss the next clue? What happens if we miss the White Rabbit himself?"

"That's what I'm thinking too." He tucks the phone back in his pocket. "I'll call you if I find anything."

I cross my arms. "What if you miss it? The clue, I mean. You would have missed the white rabbit without my help."

He shoots me a look. "You're not coming."

Oh yes. I am.

"I didn't say I'm coming with you. I just asked what if you miss a clue." I watch enough true crime TV to know that he can't take a civilian along, but if I just happen to feel like strolling in the warehouse district of LA at night, well, then he couldn't stop me from exercising my basic rights.

He studies me, sensing a trap. His phone buzzes again, and he starts walking to his car, pushing the unlock button on his fob. The lights flash on a dark sedan that I gather is his undercover car. "I'll call you once I'm there and see what's going on."

"You should probably get going. Toodles." I wave at him and turn, making a show of walking back toward Hamburger Mary's.

"Michael-Grace . . ." Matteo can tell something's up.

"What? I already said I know I'm not going with you."

Of course I'm going. Just not *with* him. I'm the Captain freaking Janeway of my own destiny, and if he thinks I'm going to let him or that jerk Detective Rideout screw with *my* crime scene, with the masked avenger masquerading as *my* favorite hero, when it's *me* who tipped them off in the first place? Not to even mention the fact that Rideout thinks it's *me* working with the Golden Arrow? Forget Captain Janeway. Trekkies unite and all due respect, but she has to play by Starfleet's rules. I shove aside the niggling thought that I should play by the rules. I need to be a rule*breaker*. A vigilante hero of my very own. I am the Han frickin' Solo of my destiny now.

CHAPTER 18

It takes me a moment to debate. If I stay, I could catch L before the police talk to him. If I leave, I won't get a chance to talk to Lawrence until *after* my midnight stroll in East LA. I don't have time to dither, and Matteo is already at his car. My come-to-Jesus meeting with L is going to have to wait.

I yank my phone out of my purse as I run, ricocheting off any number of men, women, queens, and the rainbow in between as I go. Normally I'd apologize. Right now I have to get to my *Millennium Falcon* and get to a nunnery—er, warehouse.

I'm texting and running, a huge no-no, but manage to get one sent off to Lawrence.

> Something big came up, had to go. You were wonderful. Need to talk after your show, will text you later.

I'm startled when the phone buzzes not a few moments later. Usually L is MIA during a show. L's message makes me laugh out loud. Well you wouldn't want it to be small, would you? Have fun, I know I would.

Oh, L. Only he could make me truly belly laugh in the middle of chasing a police detective chasing a masked avenger chasing criminals unknown. L better still love me after I explain the mess I've gotten him into.

I skid in my heels on the pavement as I run down the poorly lit aisle toward the Hurtling Turd, now thusly dubbed the Millennium Turd. I am, after all, Han Solo. I catch sight of a set of taillights pulling out of the parking lot and breathe a huge sigh of relief. The lights belong to a dark new-model sedan, and I'd bet dollars to doughnuts that Matteo is behind the wheel.

I slide into my car and pray over the steering wheel, *Please, oh please, oh please, start.* The engine cranks on the first try, and I crow in triumph. Oh, how I'd give my left arm for light speed at this moment.

It's only several moments more before I too am out on the main street on my way to the warehouse. In fact, it's not too long at all before I can see the dark sedan ahead of me in traffic. Okay. I can do this. This is about stealth. I need to stay far enough back in traffic so he can't see—

My phone rings.

I don't need to look to know it's Matteo, but I look just so I can see his name on my phone. "I don't answer phone calls," I announce to my passenger seat, where the phone flashes. I reach over and send it to voice mail.

Surely he can't see me. There's no *way* he can see me. I intentionally let a huge pickup truck cut me off.

My phone rings again, and again I send it to voice mail. *"I don't answer calls."*

Matteo didn't say the words "You cannot show up at the crime scene" to me. He just said I wasn't going *with him*. Big difference. He must have figured out my loophole.

My phone dings my text message tone. Smart man. But I'm smarter. I glance at the phone, where Matteo's name is lit up on my display. There's a one-word text underneath: No.

"Oh, I'm sorry, Matteo," I say in my best stewardess voice, picking up the phone. "I don't text and drive either."

I click off the phone, toss it back on the passenger seat, and proceed in a blessedly quiet car toward the coast.

I decide I can't quite shadow Matteo directly to the warehouse district. Traffic thins. I get off an exit early and weave my way through dark streets, picking up my phone again and using my GPS to guide me.

"Okay, no big deal. Remember? I'm Han Solo." I throw the Millennium Turd into park and switch off my lights. Except now I remember that Han was supposedly frozen in carbonite for a *year* before his rescue, so maybe not the best battle cry.

I'm about a block east and a block north of the warehouse, and it's dark. Like the inside of Dexter's mind dark. Patches of low clouds block any moonlight, and surprise, surprise, the streetlights in this part of the city work only every so often. I reach over and grab my phone, wondering if I should predial 911. I mean, it's not like there are just people lurking on every corner looking to grab the next person that walks by. I don't want to be paranoid. But I also don't want to be stupid. I already know there might be some legitimately *bad* people in this area getting ready to move hundreds of thousands of dollars' worth of illicit substances.

I debate only a moment longer. Somewhere out here is a masked avenger. I'd bet my near-mint copy of *The Black Canary* number 1 on it. The heels of my shoes crunch as I step gingerly onto the gritty, cracked pavement, and I close my door as quietly as I can . . . which feels like the decibel level of approximately 6.7 air horns. I need desperately to get a new car. The Millennium Turd is just not a stealth vehicle. Speaking of, I'm not really dressed for stealth myself. The dark colors that happen to make up my outfit are sparkly as well. I'm about as well hidden as a disco ball at a flashlight festival.

I scoot across the street and into the deeper shadows afforded by the taller warehouse. Then I creep up the block. I jump out of my skin only once when something skitters away from me into a broken window, and once when a car door slams farther down the street. I see one other person hurrying in the opposite direction. I stay where I am, stock-still, until he passes. Not a few seconds later, a car engine roars to life, and headlights spill against the metal buildings.

After what seems like an eternity, I ease around the corner of the warehouse I'm looking for. A large semi idles in front of the huge bay doors, a shipping container strapped to the flatbed trailer. A crew of maybe eight men pack the container in an efficient manner, though I can't identify the crates from this distance. I wish I owned binoculars. I'm hoping against hope that this is the White Rabbit's crew. All of this will be over, and I can move on with my life, and my best friend and I won't have to be the number-one suspects in a crime Lawrence knows nothing about.

I peek around the corner again. This time I catch sight of a group of men moving toward the end of the building where I'm halfway hidden. One tall and slender, the other two built like refrigerator boxes with legs. Comic book criminals if I've ever seen any. I chance one more glance to confirm. They are most definitely headed in my direction. *Well, bantha fodder.* What am I going to do now?

Scanning the wall isn't much help. It's a metal building with windows higher up. But it's dark. Maybe I can just suck in my tummy and stand in the shadows and hope they don't turn the corner? I channel "Grecian Urn" with all my might, as if every warehouse has a sparkle-clad statuary that I'm blending into. My heartbeat accelerates to a slow gallop. *This* is probably why it's a bad idea for me to be here.

And then I see it. The little cove of a door along the wall, shrouded in inky darkness. It's a perfect hiding spot, thank the stars above.

Not one second too soon, I skitter on tiptoes to the doorway, and just as I catch the barest glimpse of the men round the corner, I step back into the alcove and let the shadows swallow me.

I land against something softer than a building, something that gives an audible grunt when I step on its foot. That something slips a hand around my face, covering my mouth, muffling my scream.

"You are in *big* trouble," a voice growls in my ear. My pulse beats so wildly, my head swims. I scrabble at the hand trapping my mouth and attempt to bite it at the same time. I am rewarded with another grunt and a slight lessening of the pressure. I squirm and wiggle, trying to get even a fraction of an inch of space to maneuver.

I was at a wedding once where a drunk bridesmaid accidentally drove her stiletto heel clear through another girl's foot on the dance floor. I might not make it all the way through the arch of the foot beneath mine, but I'm hoping if I replicate the move, I'll cause him enough pain that he lets me go.

I gather my strength, lift my foot, approximate the location of my captor's limb, and do a quick countdown in my head. Three, two . . .

I catch the slightest scent of cinnamon.

"Matteo?" Only there's a hand over my mouth, so it comes out "Mmm-mmm-ohmmmm?"

"Shhhh." I recognize the voice this time. "I'm going to let go. Don't scream, okay?"

I nod against his hand, and it drops from my mouth. He shifts me slightly to the side like we're hugging, and we melt into the alcove together, my heart hammering for several reasons. Most pressing is definitely the footfalls I hear on the pavement maybe twenty feet to our left. What if they are looking specifically for *this* door? The other reason is definitely Matteo's proximity. We're pressed together from thigh to shoulder. It's better than I imagined.

Matteo seems to have the same thought and shifts his body against me. My cheek presses against a hard material under his jacket. It's Kevlar, unless I miss my mark. I love a man in uniform—well, costume. I'm thinking now of expanding that admiration into hot space-cop tropes. The point still stands that Matteo is in Kevlar, and here I am parading around in pleather. I've *really* misread the situation's danger level.

Footfalls approach, and Matteo lifts his hand to his side. It's hovering just above where I assume his holstered firearm is. I hold my breath as we watch the group of three men walk past the alcove without even a glance. They're talking about their next delivery and joking quietly about mundane things. Drug smugglers wouldn't be telling dirty jokes, would they? They'd be searching every nook and cranny for cops. I almost give a mirthless laugh; right now they'd definitely find one.

They continue along the street, and I can feel Matteo relax a little bit. He takes a half step back, allowing me to right myself from the uncomfortable angle I've been standing in pressed into the corner.

"What are you doing here?" I ask, keeping my voice low.

"I'm out here looking for you since I knew that you'd be here." He doesn't bat an eye. A foregone conclusion that I'd risk my own neck. "I should ask you the same question. Why are *you* here?" He sounds mad. I glance up at him, and his face is carefully blank. Professional Detective Kildaire at my service.

"I went for a pleasure stroll? At night? In a crime-infested neighborhood?"

"And what was your plan if you happened upon an unsavory character?"

"Who says I *haven't* come across one? I had a plan." He's still basically blocking my body in the alcove, though I can't hear anyone else. His nearness intoxicates me. I can't control my breathing. I feel half-panicky, half-giddy, like I'm on the best and fastest ride at the carnival.

"You did bite me," he says, his voice close to my ear. Less mad this time. I hear a faint tone of amusement.

"That was part one. *This* was part two." I place the heel of my stiletto where I assume the arch of his foot is and jump half my weight onto it. "Only harder than that. I don't want to hurt you. I've seen a stiletto go straight through a foot."

A strangled noise escapes his lips, half pain, half laugh. Matteo scoots back in surprise, eyes wide as he looks down at me. "Only you would use fashion as a weapon, Michael-Grace Martin. You are singularly the most infuriatingly fascinating person I've ever met."

I chance a look up at his face because I can't tell if he's angry or amused. What I find there takes my breath away. He's looking at me . . . *really* looking at me. I'm hyperaware of our close proximity, the darkness of the alcove, the racing of my heart, and the mere inches that separate our lips.

"You are compromising my case." His voice is husky. I hardly hear his words because I'm too entranced by his five-o'clock shadow and the movement of his full bottom lip. Once the words do register, I'm not sure if he means I'm compromising *him* by our close proximity or the case by the fact that I'm chasing down criminals on my own when I should have been letting the police handle it.

He leans an inch closer, and I can sense the war within him. The inevitable gravitational pull our lips have against the sense that this is a very, *very* bad idea.

WWJD—What Would Janeway Do? She'd probably have a diplomatic answer. Screw her. Diplomacy is overrated. What would Han do? He'd kiss the girl. So that's exactly what I do. I reach out, slide my hands up his jacket, twine them around his neck, run my fingers through the slight curls at his nape, and pull his lips to mine.

The world bursts into color as my lips meet his. He's not hesitant to follow my lead. It goes beyond chaste first kiss. Instantaneously searing, the product of two people who have been dancing around this contact for weeks. I've never had one simple kiss undo me in milliseconds. His hand wraps around my waist and pulls me to him, firmly, possessively, the buckles on the Kevlar digging into my own chest. I want the vest off. I wish I felt his heart pounding against mine. I want more.

The sky behind my eyelids bursts a brilliant and ferocious orange and magenta. Thunder rolls across the sky. I'm breathless and flying through the stars, my body alight with a fire that stems from the point where my body meets Matteo's.

That is, until I realize that the fireworks and thunder aren't just in my head. They've actually happened.

Matteo and I jump apart, realization dawning at the same moment.

"W-what was *that*?" My voice shakes as I draw a deep gasping breath. Maybe because I'd just had the most intense first kiss of my entire life in the alcove of a warehouse? Or because things are exploding and the man I was just kissing is already holding a gun?

Matteo grazes my cheek with one hand. "You stay here, okay?" His gaze lingers on my lips for just a moment. He leans in, brushes my lips ever so briefly with his, then dashes out of the alcove, while I'm a little slower on the uptake. My brain still fights with the intense wave of lust that crashed through me, my head still spinning from the kiss, but my eyes are searching the street outside, looking for danger. And my ears are straining to put a label on the rolling, thundering noise I heard.

With one good mental slap, I'm back on my feet, all senses firing together. I don't want to stay *here* all by myself while someone's bombing the neighborhood. I feel vulnerable and alone without Matteo's solid mass beside me. He's already sprinting up the street, and I follow at a safe distance, constantly glancing behind me to make sure I'm not being followed. A plume of smoke and fire rises above the warehouse district. What looks like an explosion only a few blocks away.

Other people are running up the street now, but they don't seem to be chasing either one of us. The fireball in the sky even draws the crew loading the crates. I don't have much time to scan the faces because I'm already sprinting up the street after Matteo. *Don't trip, don't trip, don't trip* beats a staccato in my head as I run. One errant rock and I'd have road rash.

"What's going on?" I wheeze as I flop to a stop next to Matteo's dark sedan. He's already halfway inside, the key in the ignition, the radio in his hand.

"Jesus, MG. Do you ever listen to me?" He runs his hands through his hair in frustration, then seems to shrug it off. Bigger fish and all that. "I don't know what's going on. I'm listening to the scanner."

I fall quiet. Well, as quiet as an out-of-shape girl who hates running—much less in stilettos—can be. Which isn't very.

The fire's intensity already diminishes, though enough of it still burns for me to see clouds of smoke filling the sky. Even here I can smell the faint hints of burning wood and an acrid smell that reminds me of fireworks.

Matteo says a string of gibberish into the radio, letters and numbers that mean nothing to me. Matteo looks concerned. No, he looks pissed. A garbled response immediately, and somewhere in the distance a chorus of sirens lifts into the cloudy night.

"Get in." Matteo reaches over and pushes the passenger door open.

"I—what?"

"Get in the car, MG. Please." All business. "I need to respond to this. I don't know what's going on, and I'm not leaving an unarmed civilian here alone."

So now I'm not Michael-Grace. I'm hardly even MG. I'm an "unarmed civilian" he needs to protect.

His face softens. "I'm not leaving *you* alone. Not here. I need to know you're safe. Get in, please."

I cross quickly in front of the car, slide in the passenger side, and the car lurches forward before I even have the door shut. I glance over. Matteo clicks his seat belt, and I do the same. There is zero conversation as we speed along the street. At each stop he flips a switch for his lights and we fly through the intersection. A mess of static and different voices fills the radio. Some must be dispatch, and some are officers responding to the scene we are headed toward.

I catch a word I recognize among the gibberish. "Did they just say Marvelous?"

Matteo's face is grim, focused on the road as he drives. "Yes. There's been an explosion and a fire. While I was requesting backup at the warehouse and talking with the Coast Guard and . . ." He trails off, and I *know* he's reliving our kiss. My stomach drops through the floor of the car. "While I did all of that," he continues, "we guessed wrong. Not only were those guys loading crates *into* the warehouse; we missed the Golden Arrow. We chose the wrong lead, and it literally blew up in our faces."

We. At least we are still a team in his mind.

"What do you mean?" I rock violently from side to side as we fishtail into a parking lot filled with police cruisers and a firetruck. The sign that just flashed by my window confirms my suspicion.

"I mean"—Matteo throws the car into park and is halfway out the door before he turns to me—"the Golden Arrow just blew up Marvelous Printing."

He shuts his door with a slam, and my mouth falls open. How could he possibly know that? I start to open my door when I see it.

I know how he knows.

The fire inside the building has all but burned out, but on the lawn, just off the quiet commercial street where Marvelous Printing resides, there's a fire still burning. Artfully drawn with some sort of long-lasting fuel and set aflame, an arrow burns bright in the darkness.

CHAPTER 19

The smell of acrid smoke stings my nose and eyes the moment I'm out of the car. "Oh my *God*, it's a golden arrow."

"No. Absolutely not. MG, you get back in that car right now, and that's an order." He returns to where I stand outside the car, reaches behind me, and reopens the door to the sedan.

I cross my arms. I want to see this building. I want to know what's going on. This is my case too, dammit. And *my* friends are suspects, and Rideout thinks it's me, and someone killed my boss's father over it.

I swear a vein is about to explode in Matteo's head. He grits his teeth, looks swiftly around, then reaches for me. He drags me forward two steps until we're so close, I can smell his soap again, even over the scent of fireworks in the air. My heartbeat races wildly, thinking he's going to kiss me, right here, in front of everyone. Instead, he leans his forehead against mine, takes a deep breath, and speaks very quietly. "Michael-Grace, for the love of all that is good, will you *please* get in the car? I need all of my attention focused on figuring out what's going on, and I can't *do* that if I'm worried about you." He cuts off my argument before I can even make it. "I'm not saying you're not capable. I'm saying this is *my job*. You are not trained for a crime scene, and there may be other explosions. This case is important to you. I get that. But right now I need to make sure you're not complicating things further and that you're safe, okay?"

I snap my mouth shut. His sweetness sops up my usual vinegar, and my hackles lower. Fire crews make their way across the parking lot and cautiously into the building. It wouldn't be just my neck I'd be risking. If someone had to come looking for me, it'd be their neck too. It would be Matteo's neck I'd be risking. Without another word, I slide into the car and let Matteo close the door behind me.

He jogs off into the smoke, and I feel a twinge deep down in my stomach. Guilt? Over kissing him? Anxiety for his safety? Worry that our feelings are a complication to this case? Fear that I won't get a repeat of the singular most amazing kiss I've had in all my years on this planet?

I sit and listen to the radio, which chatters incessantly. There are so many buttons, I wouldn't even know how to turn it down. A few minutes later, Agent Sosa and Detective Rideout arrive.

My phone buzzes, and I jump. I guess I'm a little on edge watching all these police milling around. It's Lawrence. I look at the time and groan. It's already well past midnight. And rather than sitting at IHOP with Ryan and Lawrence, I'm sitting in the passenger seat of an undercover cop car listening to static about 10-30s and Code 10s.

Just checking on you. I hope your hot date is going well! Don't do anything I wouldn't do. Xoxo.

I chuckle. That wouldn't leave much off the table. I bite my thumbnail, then reply, You have no idea. I'm safe and sound, call you tomorrow. We need to talk first thing. My anxiety reappears full force. I got lucky diverting Matteo tonight.

Almost immediately the dots appear that show me L is typing back. It can't be going that well if you replied to my text. Get back to that hunk of man, and I'll talk to you tomorrow.

If only it were that easy. I tuck the phone away, lean my head back against the seat, and close my eyes. Guilt over sharing Lawrence's journal with the police and Casey Junior has me sinking in my seat. I broke my promise; now L is a suspect. If there's a dirty cop involved, Lawrence going in for questioning could be trouble. There's a murderer on the loose who could kill him for his journals. Or for that matter, kill me for putting it all together. Solving this case could very well mean saving my friend's life. Or my own.

An idea starts to form, a way to protect Lawrence. I sigh and stare at the ceiling of the car. If I execute the plan, it will mean lying *yet again* to Matteo and the police. I'm caught in the perfect storm of lies, truth, and thirty-year-old ghosts.

After what seems an eternity, Matteo climbs back into the car. I stifle a yawn, rub my eyes, and sit up from my seat a bit. He appraises me for a full beat in the relative dark of the car, but even so, I can tell his eyes are bloodshot from the smoke. He's brought the smell of burning campfire into the car with him. "Were you asleep?" he asks.

Despite being bloodshot, his eyes soften as they take in my appearance. That odd sense of familiarity passes over me—the feeling I've known this man for much longer than I have. Like he's seen me half-asleep in my Wonder Woman pajamas for a lifetime and still thinks I'm adorable. It's the first time I've given credence to past lives; maybe Matteo was more to me in another universe too.

"Mmmm, maybe dozed off a little." I sit up straight, wiggling my toes. I'd taken off my shoes in an effort to sit more comfortably, and now I regret it. "What's the word?"

He shimmies out of his jacket, then awkwardly out of the Kevlar vest. The shirt beneath is filthy, pressed to his chest with sweat and soot. One yank has the button-down shirt pulled over his head, leaving him in nothing but his slacks and a white T-shirt that clings to his shoulders. I'm suddenly *very* awake. Yum.

He tosses those in the back seat, then reaches forward, cranks the engine, and begins driving.

"The explosion was well contained in the front lobby. A lot of flash but not much structural damage. It looks like it was meant to attract attention rather than destroy the building."

"Like fireworks." I remember the acrid smell that wafted our direction.

The look he gives me is odd. "Yes . . . *exactly* like fireworks. How did you know that?"

"I didn't *know* it. I guessed. But it's good that the building is intact, right?"

"There's a fair amount of smoke damage, but yes. Largely, it could have been worse."

I sit back against my seat and stare out at the dark streets streaking past my window. "So . . . why would someone do that?"

Matteo looks tired. He draws a hand over his face. It's a thinking face, but more than that, it's a frustrated thinking face. "I don't know. I have theories, but each seems as unlikely as the next."

We're almost back to the warehouse. I vaguely recognize the street we shot down on our way to the fire.

"Do you think this is the Yee connection? That somehow someone found out?" I ask.

Matteo is silent.

"But why would he burn Marvelous Printing?"

Matteo eases up behind my car and puts the sedan in park. "Again, I don't know. It seems like it was for attention. Either way, I missed my mark tonight. And Detective Rideout isn't happy with me. He can tell I'm . . . distracted right now."

I've mucked things up more than that. No matter that it was two sets of lips doing the kissing, it was most definitely my idea to close the gap.

Matteo watches my face. Reading my mind. "Michael-Grace, I wouldn't have traded that kiss for anything. It's just . . . you could have gotten hurt. I let my feelings take precedence over my job, and my job, this case, is the most important thing right now, you know? Detective Rideout was right to call me on it. He also thinks that you somehow convinced me to be at the warehouse on purpose tonight. I don't know why he's so convinced that your motives aren't pure, but tonight didn't help disprove his theory. I told him he was crazy, but he's threatened to bring our . . . involvement up to the captain."

My face falls.

"MG, this case won't always be between us. But we need to figure out what's going on, and right now that's more important than how I feel about a kick-ass girl I met in a coffee shop, okay?"

All of a sudden it feels like the end of a date. And not the good kind. Matteo is quiet. He looks spent, and I don't doubt it's been a long day for him. I fight the impulse to reach across the car. To reestablish the connection I felt earlier.

"Okay," I say, making a production of putting my shoes back on my feet and jingling my keys.

Matteo takes a breath in, holds it for a few counts, and lets it back out. "MG?"

I turn to face him, keys in hand.

"You *didn't* have anything to do with tonight, did you?"

I hate that he has to ask, and my heart falls further. "No."

"And you don't know who set the fire?"

"No. I would have told you."

He nods slowly. At least I feel like he believes me, but he looks back up, and I can still see the smallest shred of doubt in those dark eyes. "Okay. It's just that this is serious business. After today it means charges of breaking and entering. Arson. This has gone beyond tame wannabe-superhero stuff. It's outright dangerous for everyone involved. There won't be a slap on the wrist. This means jail time. Even if it ends up being one of your friends."

I swallow and nod. Lawrence. Or one of my coworkers. Or major charges against *me* if someone—Rideout, the Golden Arrow, whoever—is trying to frame me like Matteo suggested. Serious business indeed. Suddenly the Golden Arrow seems scarier than the White Rabbit. More tangible. Closer to me, breathing down my neck. When did my superhero become a villain?

"I'm going to make sure your car starts." *Detective* Kildaire is back.

"I guess you'll call me when you have more information?"

He nods. "I'll be in touch. Don't say anything to anyone until you hear from me, okay?"

I open the door and step out into the night. After being ensconced in the car for more than an hour, it's chilly in the damp quiet of the sleeping city. I have the strangest urge to lean back in and tell Matteo it's going to be okay. My gut still says there's something tied to the warehouse. Something we missed tonight because the Golden Arrow had other plans.

True to his word, he waits until my car sputters to life. Rather than refreshed, I feel like my damage bar is lower than ever. My shields are down. My heart is battered. This Friday night definitely has not turned out at all like I thought. And somewhere out there, our masked friend still runs free.

CHAPTER 20

Lawrence buzzes like a bee, cleaning up the station where he trimmed my hair while I'm ensconced in one of those bubble-orbit hair dryers with my foils. It's too bad I'm here to ruin Lawrence's day and maybe our friendship. It's been three days since the fire at Marvelous Printing. The media has covered the fire as suspected arson and hasn't publicly announced the Golden Arrow's involvement. That doesn't stop pictures of the burning arrow from showing up on Twitter or blog posts the police probably don't want published. The Golden Arrow is gaining quite the cult following, truth be told. I've seen more than one post praising the person for "doing what the police couldn't" and a few about people trying to contact the Golden Arrow to see if he needs a sidekick. People aren't just fawning over him; they are contemplating following his example. Exactly what the police are hoping to avoid.

Radio silence from Matteo since Friday night, though I know Lawrence is on his short list. I've been on pins and needles, waiting for Matteo to show up at any moment, or at the very least call me to tell me he's arresting my bestie. Finally, I couldn't stand waiting. I told L I want to get a new color for the gala, and here I am. Lies of omission.

We're just finishing making my hair Power-Up Blue, and I couldn't love it more. Just shy of navy, and it screams superhero. Superman wishes he had hair this awesome.

I pretend to read through the new issue of *The Hooded Falcon*. The fire has set back production at Marvelous Printing. Nothing major damaged, but all the machines needed to be cleaned over the weekend. I got a call from Andy early this morning informing me that our limited run of *Hooded Falcon* origin books was lost in the fire. He dropped off a new test copy, straight off the press, just this morning, and he needs everyone on the team to sign off on the test copies *today*. It's the only way the issue will be released in time for the thirtieth anniversary.

"Weight-of-the-world-type stuff?" Lawrence catches me staring out the window into the waning late afternoon light. The Monday rush hour is winding down, and the roads are quieter. It's my favorite time of day—pensive. Not quite dark enough to need light, not quite light enough to see well, everything made of part shadow, part reflection. If I were a superhero, this would be the time of day I'd go crime fighting.

I sigh. "More like fate-of-the-world-type stuff."

L arches one perfectly drawn brow at me. He sets down the broom, spins the chair next to me, and settles in it. "This sounds serious. Is there a shortage of sequins for my dress?"

Despite my anxiety, laughter bubbles out of me, and I instantly feel better. "No, I have all the material I need for your dress, you tall drink of water."

"Is it Hot-Lanta?"

"Part of it."

"Your date didn't go well? I've been wondering why you haven't texted gushing. Bad kisser? Fish lips?"

I think back to the "date" where we saw a drag show, kissed in an alcove, and missed catching the person who set off an explosion at a printing press. "It's complicated. I like him. And he likes me. But the timing isn't right." Like we are just two normal people who met in a coffee shop. I sigh. Rip off the Band-Aid. "But that's not what's got me in a funk. Well, not all of it. L, we need to talk."

"Girl, you're not breaking up with me for that tramp down the street? He wouldn't know navy from cyan."

"No, definitely not. You're still my best friend, but . . . I may not be yours after this."

"I doubt you could make me hate you, M. What's up?"

I bite my lip and toss the test copy of *The Hooded Falcon* onto the countertop with L's styling tools. "Do you remember the journal you showed me? Well, I kind of broke my promise to you. I showed the copies to someone."

Lawrence frowns at me, an expression I see so rarely, it makes me swallow in nervousness. "You showed someone the copies I gave you?"

"Yes. I'm sorry."

"Michael-Grace, I knew you'd end up showing one of your nerdy friends. It's not a big deal. I still have my journal, and you got your research."

I close my eyes. "It wasn't a nerdy friend. It was the police."

"You . . . *the police*? Why on earth would you need to show sketches to the police?"

Go big or go home? If I'm going home, I'm going home big because everything tumbles out in a rush. "Because I've been helping investigate a rash of copycat comic book crimes. Matteo is a narcotics officer, and my boss was in for an interview. Matteo showed him the copies, and Casey Junior is convinced the new crimes are linked to drug dealers his dad was following before he died and that he was murdered by a crooked cop." I swallow, nearly tossing my cookies onto the floor. "And you . . . were there. Casey Junior said you were involved. And you have a journal, so now you're kind of a person of interest in the case, so I need to ask you some questions before the police show up to take you in for questioning."

We both look at the door. I half expect to see Matteo marching into the little shop, furious that I'm interfering *again*. That would probably be the nail in the coffin for us romantically, and Rideout would *definitely* have his proof that I'm meddling in the case.

I refuse to look in the mirror or at Lawrence. Long moments pass. I shut my eyes, contemplating becoming a praying woman.

"That's a lot to handle." No sass. No character. Pure unfiltered Lawrence.

I open one eye. He's still in the room with me and hasn't bludgeoned me with a curling iron, so that's a minor success. "I know."

"You've had *all* that going on and you haven't told me?"

My long-held breath explodes out of me. "The police told me to keep my involvement secret. There have been threats made against people involved in this case."

"I see." Sarcasm drips from his words. "Thanks for letting me know I'm involved." Cue internal eye roll.

"I'm really sorry, L." My voice sounds a little quavery. I will *not* cry.

He stands up, lets out a deep breath, and wipes his hands on his pants. "I guess what's done is done. What do you need from me?"

"Are you mad?"

"Beyond pissed."

"Are we okay, though?"

"We will be, eventually. Let's work on keeping my ass out of jail first, shall we? You owe me some damn fine costumes for at least a year to make up for this."

I offer a small smile that doesn't extend much past my lips. "Deal. I need to know if you have any other journals, and . . . well, the police are going to ask for the journal, and I want to see it before they have it. I think we should copy it in case the crooked cop gets his or her hands on it."

He moves off, removing his color-guard apron and tossing it on the counter as he goes. "I'll go grab it. Come with and ask me whatever else you need to know."

"Okay. Do you have any more journals or know where more of them are?"

"No, I was just given the one by Senior as a gift. Maybe he gave the others away. I don't know. He was pretty eccentric. Maybe he hid them in a safe or something."

That confirms my suspicions, but at least L is a second voice for that. I follow him up the narrow stairs in the back of the salon to his apartment. It's cluttered with what I can describe only as bachelor queen kitsch. Pieces of costumes, wigs, piles of workout magazines, and dirty dishes scattered around a one-color-palette living room dominated by a TV and gaming system. "Okay. I also need to know about your relationship with Edward Casey Senior. I know you said you worked for him and he helped out, but his son seems to feel like it was more. Not in *that* way, but as in you guys spent a lot of time together?"

Lawrence digs through a box on the kitchen counter, muttering to himself. "I didn't give you the journal, did I?"

"No, you made copies and took it back." A tingle starts at the base of my spine.

"Maybe I put it in my closet up here." He opens what should be a second smaller bedroom door to reveal his personal walk-in closet. Rows and rows of queen costumes. I rarely come in here; he keeps his current stuff downstairs. Lawrence has amassed an impressive collection of fabric.

I'm in awe, looking at a history of my costume design skills. I spy a hastily sewn drapey white evening gown with a stitch so crooked, my fingers itch to rework the entire thing. My first costume for L.

"L, do you keep *all* my costumes?"

"Of course I do. They're works of art. Listen, I mean it. When you're winning awards for costume design, I'm going to sell these for millions. MG originals." He's digging through a stack of papers on a side table.

It touches something inside me. I forget the case for a moment and run my hands along the fabric. This is why I love design. Each of these costumes allows the wearer to step into another skin. To be whoever they want for the night. It's part of what I want to do with my job, and I bite my lip thinking about the promotion I may or may not get. As written right now, it doesn't out-and-out include design time. I'd still be in limbo. If I, by some miracle, get the job, do I still want it?

"Do you think the queens were serious last night about paying me to make costumes?" My mind also flashes to Nina's offer to hire me for Kyle's costume. And her offer to introduce me to the theater costumers. Maybe there's a simpler way to do what I want. If I'm willing to give up wanting to be an executive at Genius.

"You are *my* secret weapon," he jokes. "Even if I'm pissed at you currently."

"I'm serious. Do you think they'd hire me? If I quit my job or went part-time?"

Lawrence studies me from over a half stack of papers. "You want to talk about this now?"

"Yes."

He shrugs. "You've been turning them down for years now. Most of them would jump at the chance. But you'd have to do mine *first* and then the others'."

Isn't this what Ryan was talking to me about? Being creative with my own solutions instead of hammering a square peg into a round hole? Who says I can't do both? *I have been.* If I can costume part-time and write part-time, I won't *have* to get the promotion. I won't have to massage the job description. I can continue my work as a writer on the projects I love, continuing to look for opportunities at work, but not let that stop me from designing. Suddenly the Miss Her Galaxy competition holds new meaning. It's not a test anymore. It's the inaugural flight of my new decision. Let Andy have the promotion and kiss executive ass. I'm going to do what *I* am good at. I'm going to go into business for myself and design things I love for people I adore.

"It's not here. Bedroom," Lawrence says.

A dash of cold water on my thoughts. My fashion future needs to wait. We're both moving quicker now, sensing something is off.

Lawrence may be bachelor-messy, but he's not careless. Especially not with a prized possession.

Lawrence practically tears through the box under his bed, tossing items onto his pillows. "I wouldn't have put it somewhere else."

"L . . ."

"Maybe in my closet." He heads over there and paws through the junk on the floor. Old tennis racquets, a medicine ball, layers of glitter-camo *something*.

"Lawrence. You know last week how you thought someone had been in your apartment?"

Lawrence stops digging and turns to me.

"What if the Golden Arrow got your notebook?" I finish.

"Girl, this is bad. How would he even *know* that thing existed?"

I hesitate. "I told the police, and Casey Junior *did* say he thought his dad was killed by a cop."

A shadow passes over Lawrence's face. I wait for it to lift, but the gloom stays put. "That was thirty years ago. But if Junior is right and this is about his father, this is bad. Like *really bad*. And if the police are in on it, or in on it again . . ." He trails off, rubbing his hands over his face. "Did your boss really say he thought Casey Senior was murdered?"

The weight of that idea hangs on Lawrence's frame, heavy as a millstone.

"Yes. He said he thinks the heart attack ruling on the police report was a cover-up."

"I'd *suspected*, but of course, I couldn't come forward. I was a homeless high-school-dropout drag queen. I figured everyone would think I was crazy." He runs his hands over his face again and looks at the ceiling. "Casey Senior was definitely playing superhero on his own time. I just never knew that it was what he put in his comic books or that it got him killed."

I sit on the bed in the purple-tinted sunshine streaming through the sheer paisley curtains, the roller shade beneath hanging lopsided and broken. Lawrence comes to sit next to me, and we both bask in the warmness of the sunshine for a moment, lost in thought.

L's voice breaks the silence. "I was always a good kid, but my parents didn't take kindly to me coming out. My dad was head of the psychology department at a state college, and my parents had dreams of me becoming a professor or a lawyer. I failed all my classes in school except theater. I've always known it's what I wanted to do. Long story short, they kicked me out when I told them that I preferred men to women. I didn't have anywhere to live or a way to pay for school, so I started doing drag shows. Back then it wasn't as popular as it is now, and it took me a while to meet my *real* drag family. I fell in with a bit of a rough crowd at first—drugs, meaningless sex, sabotage—but it was a place to live, and I loved the stage. Anyway, one of the things they'd have me do to earn my rent was to steal stuff for them to sell. I didn't love it, but I didn't really have any options."

"Lawrence, that is *awful*."

He nods. "It wasn't good. So there I was in this ritzy neighborhood, supposed to break into this house where the people were on vacation. I broke into a window, crawled in, and came face-to-face with Casey Senior. You can imagine my shock. I'd gotten the wrong house. I think he expected me to pull a gun or something, but I've never been made of material like that. So I apologized profusely, made up some ridiculous story about how I was dog-sitting for these people, forgot my key, and broke into the wrong house by mistake." L gives a humorless chuckle. "He knew I was lying, of course, but he invited me to sit with him like I was a *guest* and not some skinny black kid who had just busted his window. He asked me my name, and I told him my real one, and when he asked what I was *really* doing, I told him the truth too. All of it. My parents, the queens, the drugs, the stealing. How we'd hit several houses in the neighborhood. I can't explain it. The guy had this energy around him. He made you want to trust him with your story."

"I get that." It's what I could feel in his house. His spirit was still there for sure.

Lawrence takes a deep breath, then stretches his legs out in front of him. "Anyway, after hearing my story, this guy I'd never met offers *me* a place to live. He says he likes my story and that lots of superheroes have tough beginnings. He tells me that I'll have to work for him, help out with watching the house for break-ins from my old crew, and help around the house, but that if I did that, I could stay until I had enough money for college. So I did."

I put my arm around Lawrence and give him a squeeze. "I had no idea."

"I don't tell many people."

"So do you think the queens you lived with are the ones we're looking for? Do you think they could have killed Casey Senior?"

"No. But if that's what really happened, I have an idea who it could be. And . . . if it is them, then Casey Senior's death *is* on my hands."

I shift on the bed as a car door slams outside. I throw myself backward on the mattress and yank up the shade on the window over L's bed to see the street below. A quick glance assures me it's not Matteo, so I turn back to L and motion for him to continue.

He nods and continues, "Casey Senior was horrified to find out that there was so much crime going on right under his nose. You know, I believe he really did think he was a real superhero. Anyway, I told him about how we'd been stealing items from the houses and giving them to various drug dealers in exchange for drugs—all types. Heroin, weed, cocaine. I didn't even use the drugs, but I was the fetch-and-steal boy to support everyone else's habits. So after hearing my stories, Casey Senior decided that he was going to make a formal complaint to the police department and that I could give them all my inside knowledge so that they could crack down on the problem and stop it cold. It was a great idea, until the police officer arrived and I recognized him as one of the drug dealers I'd stolen stuff for."

"Yikes." My pulse speeds up. I've been right to worry about crooked cops. Lawrence has already had brushes with them in the past. Maybe even someone who is recognizable today.

"Yeah. I managed to make enough hand gestures that Mr. Casey realized there was something up. I slipped out of the room, and he ended up just reporting that someone had attempted to break in through the downstairs window, and the officer left. Mr. Casey got kind of . . . excited then. He loved a good story, and a dirty cop, in his mind, was the best kind of story line. He asked me all sorts of questions and . . . well, we sort of started following the drug dealers around."

I can see where this is going. "You followed them around, and he wrote about it."

"I guess he did. At the time I thought it was a game, sort of like my job working security was also my job to rid the neighborhood of my previous friends."

L tells me about some of their escapades, many of which ring eerily true to the comic. Following a dealer to a warehouse in LA. Watching boats unload cargo into the warehouse. How they followed dealers from different rings and how Casey Senior suspected that the rings were planning a showdown. Everything falls into place in my head like a huge game of *Tetris*.

"Lawrence, this is huge. You guys should *not* have been out there tailing these guys."

"I know that now. At the time, though . . . it just seemed *fun*. Mr. Casey would come back from these trips so excited to work, and before I moved in, I guess he'd been really down in the dumps, feeling like he didn't make enough of a difference in the world writing comics. I never paid attention to *what* he wrote. I just knew that spying on bad guys was fun."

"You were Swoosh."

"Who's that?"

"The Hooded Falcon's sidekick."

"I guess so."

I contemplate all that he's just revealed. "But after he died . . . surely you could have said something then. Especially if you thought maybe he got killed for investigating these guys."

"Mr. Casey had told me that he prepared evidence for the police. Now I think maybe he'd found proof of the cop's involvement, something the cop couldn't deny, though at the time I just thought it was general 'we followed drug dealers' stuff. He was going to seal it in an envelope and send it to three different detectives so that he could be sure it got addressed. When he died and that big bust happened, I just figured that he'd done what he promised. That his information had put all of those men in jail and that his spirit could rest well knowing he'd done what he'd set out to do."

"That's really romantic."

"It's stupid is what it is, if you're saying that these guys are still in business. I don't know how they avoided that bust, but it's apparent they'd kill to keep their secret."

"And you don't know where the information went?"

"Like I said, I thought he sent it. Then he died, and Casey Junior resented me. Thought I'd brought trouble into his house—and he was right. So then I got fired, and here I am." Lawrence stands and brushes his hands on his pants.

"Thank you for telling me, Lawrence." I stand and follow him down the stairs into the shop. Still no sign of Matteo, which is good. But now I have so much more to weigh in my head.

He turns to give me a brief hug. "Don't ever lie to me like that again, okay?"

"Deal. Thanks for the dye job. I'll just grab my comic and head to the office to sign off for Andy." But I pull Lawrence's apron off my proof copy and stop dead, staring at the front page. This is definitely *my* copy. There's the telltale splatter of coffee on the back cover from my breakfast that I ate in the car, so it's not like someone snuck in and put a new cover on it. This is the cover that came out of the test-print run, but it's *not* the cover I saw Andy send to the printer. I must have looked only at the back cover when I brought it in. Someone *changed* the test-print file after I'd seen Andy send it off. I flip forward to the second page—it's exactly as I remember it, but the first page is a single panel, which we never do. Not only that, it's not a finished drawing. It's a sketch. A sketch I've seen before.

It's the Hooded Falcon and Swoosh kneeling in the middle of a dark panel, one holding out the bow to the other. It's the same panel I admired in Lawrence's journal.

"This isn't the end . . ." written in bold comic script and the words "I know" are sketched in the Hooded Falcon's dialogue bubble. Underneath the panel are four typeset words I didn't see earlier. I read them now, and the bottom falls out from beneath my feet. "And I'll find you." It's signed with the drawing of an arrow.

I'm eyeing Lawrence, the sense of impending doom as thick as the scent of dye and shampoo in the air.

I hold up the comic and point to the panel signed by the Golden Arrow. "I guess we know who has your journal."

Lawrence mutters a string of curses a mile wide.

I pull out my phone to call Andy right this very moment but catch sight of a familiar car parking on the other side of the street. *Crap, crap, crap.* And a familiar gorgeous, hazel-eyed cop driving it.

"L, is your front door locked?" Usually when he has only one client, he locks it to avoid the homeless visitors.

"Yeah, why?" Lawrence picks up my frantic vibe and cranes his neck to see out the windows.

"Matteo's here." I do a bad impression of an army crawl, hit the one light switch that's still on, and get back to my feet. "We need somewhere to hide!" I grab Lawrence's hand and pull him along toward the back hallway.

"From your boyfriend?"

I chance a look over my shoulder. We have maybe ten seconds before Matteo can look in the front door. We'll never make the stairway.

"We need somewhere where he can't see us!" I'm hysterical now. "I'm *not* supposed to be here, and I'm definitely *not* supposed to be telling you everything I know about the case."

Lawrence grabs me around the waist, opens the door to our left, and all but throws me in. He whips the door almost closed behind us, then stands along the wall so he can peer out through the crack.

"Did he see us?" I pant the words, collapsed on the floor against a rack of clothes or coats. I can't tell in the dark.

Lawrence is silent for a long minute. "He looked in, knocked. Now he's going around the back." I can see only a sliver of his face. The room is pitch-dark otherwise. "Did you lock your bike up back there?"

"Yeah." Inwardly I groan. "Maybe he won't notice."

"Maybe." Lawrence sighs, shuts the door, and flicks on the light. "If they have a warrant, we can just say we didn't hear them knocking. You were helping me sort my costumes or something." He peeks back out. "But I don't think he saw us."

My mind goes directly to the warehouse. Last time we spoke, Matteo mentioned that they were dropping surveillance. But L needs to know what he's getting into. "If we do this, things could get sketchy. It involves breaking and entering. And perhaps narcotic smuggling."

"Average Monday night for me."

I laugh. "I shouldn't get you involved."

"Honey, that's what *real* family is. They're the people you call when the bodies pile up."

I hesitate again. I want him to be fully aware of the dangers. "There's a dirty cop. Someone leaked case info already. I'm really worried that if you go in for questioning, someone bad may recognize you. I think you should take a work vacation. I'll see how the investigation is going. See if I can figure out who's leaking info."

"You want me to evade police?"

"Not evade exactly. Well-timed trip to visit your drag mom?"

Lawrence thinks for a moment. "I can lay low. I've done it before."

I sigh. "Okay. Let's do this thing. We'll call anything related to this ridiculousness . . . Operation Janeway, okay? Like a code word."

"You know what this means, don't you?" Lawrence has his usual gleam and sass back, seeming more *excited* than worried about this whole fiasco.

"That we're both terrible decision makers and likely going to end up in jail for this, but at least we'll have each other?"

"Better." Lawrence flashes me a big smile. "It means that we need to go through my closet. We are going to be the fiercest, most fabulous crime-fighting duo this town has ever seen."

CHAPTER 21

Worrying about work should be illegal while your best friend is in hiding, your *pretend* boyfriend keeps asking if you've heard from him, and you're analyzing every fact you know about a thirty-year-old murder in your spare time. I've spent most of the last three days avoiding Matteo. I think he's convinced it's because of what he said after our kiss and the fact that he's trying to track down Lawrence to question him. I *know* it's because I'm lying to Matteo. Not that I know where Lawrence is *exactly*, but the fact that he's missing . . . that's all me. Instead of sketching, I've been researching obsessively about the drug culture surrounding Casey Senior's time of death.

I made some really interesting discoveries. Namely that Detective Rideout's father had been questioned in connection with one of the drug busts right before Casey was killed. He was cleared of all charges by the police chief, but it gave me a little tingle of foreboding.

There's a story here.

The fact that Rideout's father and the police chief were chums isn't lost on me. The chief, Tony Munez, became the star of Los Angeles for pulling off the biggest drug bust in LA history. Several rings, several head honchos, all at once. There was a freaking *parade* in his honor. So when he vouched for Rideout's father, the city dropped the charges. Rideout's father retired, but the Rideout I know trained directly with Tony Munez until the older man retired as well. Talk about hero worship.

"Paging Dr. House."

My head whips up, and I come face-to-face with Kyle. The red ball I've been throwing at the wall bounces away across the room. I forgot I was even throwing it.

"Sorry, was I bothering you?" I ask.

Simon's sarcastic reply comes from behind me: "A slightly better noise to work to than jackhammering, but not much."

Whoops. "I'm sorry, guys. I've got writer's block."

"We can tell." Kyle's annoyed expression melts, and he reaches forward to grasp my shoulder. "We've all been shaken up. This week has been crazy with that lunatic running around burning down buildings."

It's easier to agree, so I nod. "Yeah. That's it. I think I need some fresh air. I just can't get this villain right for the *Hero Girls* issue."

"Well, if you're stuck when you come back, let me take a look."

Usually I'd respond with an "I got this, no problem," but I am s-t-u-c-k *stuck*, and my brain can't seem to come up with anything original. New MG thinks that just *maybe* having Kyle help won't be so bad. My shoulders relax just a hair. "Okay. I'd like that. *If* I'm still stuck."

I head out the office door and toward the elevator. I don't know where I'm going exactly, but I have this constant need to move right now. Anything to alleviate the feeling of anticipation. Like the other shoe is about to drop and I'm not going to like it.

With a ding and a hiss, the doors slide open. I step inside, only to realize that Lelani already occupies the car. She's cool and poised in a tweed skirt suit. If Casey Junior hired her for affirmative action, at least he hired someone who looks the part of an executive.

"Hello, MG."

I offer a polite smile and turn to face the front. She may not be warm, but at least she doesn't call me Michael. "Ms. Kalapuani."

We wait for the doors to close, and I lean forward to press the "Close Door" button, even though it doesn't hasten any movement.

The awkward silence stretches, though it appears I'm the only one who feels the *awkward* part of that. "So, uh, how are you liking Genius Comics?"

Lelani smiles. I note that her smile is made up of small even white teeth. The effect should be charming, but something about her smile reminds me of a shark. "I like it very much, thank you."

I can't help myself from prying. I really want to know why Casey Junior hired her. Was it just to have a skirt among the pants? "So did you work for a comic business before this? How does Genius compare?"

Her smile doesn't falter. "No, I've never worked on this side of the industry. Before this, I acted in and helped market superhero adaptations for movies."

"So you were an actress?" No surprise there; she's gorgeous. But it's an unusual résumé for a marketing executive.

The elevator begins to move. Thank God. "Among other things. I've been meaning to come find you and check in about your *Hero Girls* issue. I have some ideas."

"Oh yeah?" And now she wants to meddle. Fantastic.

"Mr. Casey isn't the most fond of it, but I'd like to become an advocate. We girls need to stick together, right?"

I study her face. She *looks* sincere. She sounds sincere too, but I can't shake the feeling that Lelani's Cheshire smile doesn't reach her eyes. That she's calculating. Maybe she's sizing me up as much as I am her. Touché. "Right."

The elevator seems to be taking forever to descend five stories. I don't know that it's ever felt this long. It's on par with how I feel reading a *Sentry* issue.

Lelani breaks the silence first. "You're a good writer, MG. The best on your team."

I'm surprised at the straightforward compliment. Two points for no womanly, manipulative mind games. "Thanks."

"But you tend to isolate yourself."

Or not. *Ouch.* Has she been talking to Casey about our promotion? "Um . . ." is all I can manage. I'm not sure how to respond.

"Your characters, I mean." She offers another smile that has me thinking she may have a hidden agenda. "I'd like to see *Hero Girls* play more with some other characters. Maybe get them into a few of the special team issues with our big hitters. Stuff like that, maximize their exposure. It makes it harder to nix the project if it's not all by itself out on a limb."

Nix the project? I'm taken aback. Partly at what might be a veiled threat and partly at the genius of her idea. It's so simply stated, so . . . *spot-on,* that I can't believe I've never thought of it before. And her comments about being a team player. Either she's been reading my mind, or she's incredibly insightful. Eerily so. Didn't I just have this conversation with Ryan?

"And your villains. I think if we changed up what you're doing just a little, we'd have more commercial success."

And just like that, my hackles are back up. "My villains don't need to be 'changed up.'"

The elevator dings, the floor sways beneath my feet, and the doors open onto the polished marble floor of the lobby. I start to step out, planning on making a hasty excuse and exit, but Lelani's cool hand on my arm stops me cold.

"I've upset you. I didn't mean that. I only meant to say that your villains, your *world,* are so black and white. Good guys and bad guys."

I huff, resisting the urge to shake off her arm. Who cares if I write Supes instead of Bat? Sure, the Falcon is a bit of a rogue, but he operates within the law . . . usually. *He* certainly has never set anything on fire like the Golden Arrow has. And while I love a good Han Solo in my love life, this is *my* writing we are talking about. "Well, of course there are good guys and bad guys. That's what comics are all about." She has to know that, being an actress and all.

Her lips press together slightly, and she shakes her loose long dark hair over her shoulder. "That's what the *old* comics are about. I'm talking about the new breed of superheroes. The new breed of villains. The gray area. I think you need to broaden your views and your writings to think that your superheroes may not always be good and your villains may not always be bad."

My mouth snaps shut. Again Lelani's insight cuts through more than just my work persona. It goes straight to the core of what I've been struggling with on the case. The Golden Arrow. The White Rabbit. The dirty cop. Me. More shades of gray than I'm comfortable with. Good guys who are bad guys. Bad guys who aren't all bad. It's *not* my usual fodder. I'm a comic book purist. *But* Lelani has a point. The gray-area stuff makes a damn good story.

Her hand drops off my arm, and she walks forward into the lobby. With a little wave at someone near the front door, she turns to look at me again. Appraising. "Take my suggestions or leave them. I am simply suggesting giving your *Hero Girls* villains a more contemporary appeal. Let readers see a complicated villain that they can identify with. Let them explore the idea that every good guy makes mistakes. Does whatever it takes to get the job done. That every antagonist has his or her own story."

With that, she walks off toward the front door. I watch her go, stymied by the insight. By the laser-point focus that woman has. She nailed every problem on the head and gave me a way to work through them. She is a freaking *genius*.

Lelani rises on tiptoe to kiss the person she's meeting on the cheek before they head out. But I know that cheek. That brush of blondish hair under a backward hat. The person she's meeting is Ryan. My Ryan. I watch as they make their way to the parking lot. Seeing "a girl from the gaming group" indeed.

I stare after them for a long moment before performing an about-face and pushing the elevator call button again.

So Ryan and Lelani are a thing. *Interesting.* Ryan and I obviously haven't been talking enough lately, but I plan to jump on him about that tonight after work. Lawrence mentioned that Ryan had a date . . . but *Lelani*?

I shrug and step back on the elevator, no longer stuck for direction with my work. Lelani is worth her weight in gold as far as I'm concerned. She's given me lots to think about, and more importantly, she's given me the seeds of a story.

Date night. Or it would be if Matteo hadn't drawn our professional line in the sand seven days ago in a parking lot lit by a burning arrow. I've spent this entire last week throwing myself at my work and L's costume. I've caught up on all my *Hero Girls* sketches and have used every free moment to work on my design for Her Galaxy—anything to keep my mind from wandering to that kiss. Matteo made it clear he likes me. His lips certainly didn't lie. But until this case is solved, we can't be together, and if Rideout somehow convinces him I'm a suspect, I may lose Matteo for good.

At least Andy and I are back on speaking terms. The moment I realized that the Golden Arrow had planted the sketch into the test print of the comic book, I went straight to Andy. Screw the promotion or what going to Andy could do to my chances; this sketch *couldn't* get out to the general public. The drug lords would come after Genius for sure. I told Andy I'd screwed up the test proof and inserted a sketch from another project by mistake. We corrected the file with Marvelous Printing and ran the prints the next day.

I feel *awful* keeping something like this from Matteo, but if someone on Matteo's team is dirty—and my suspicion can't help but land on Rideout—I don't want them knowing the Golden Arrow has the journal and is trying to publish it. Best I can figure, the Golden Arrow set the fire with the express purpose of diverting attention so he could change a file on the printing press. Another connection. Another puzzle piece.

The news has also gone quiet; the Golden Arrow seems to have gone underground. The case is in a holding pattern while the arson team sorts out the fire and the burglary team sorts out Casey Senior's office. Agent Sosa is also reviewing Huong Yee's interview. On TV the justice system works so much faster than it does in real life.

I lean over the mirror, applying mascara for the second . . . third time? I've screwed it up at least twice now because my mind keeps going to Lawrence's story and wondering *why*, if all the drug ringleaders were busted in the eighties, it is coming back around now. Had someone gotten out of jail wanting revenge and the Golden Arrow got wind of it?

There's a knock, and I swallow hard, heat rising to my cheeks and the tips of my ears. When do I ever get nervous for a date? No, a *non-date* date. When it's with the most gorgeous man I've ever seen, who kissed me like he was heading into epic battle—that's when. I smooth the black lace of my bodice and hurry from the downstairs bathroom. I kick aside the black-tulle, green-sequin mess that is the scraps from L's Comic-Con bustier and nearly trip and fall into the door.

Matteo stands on the other side, ever dashing in his button-down shirt rolled at the cuffs. "I didn't think flowers would be appropriate, but I come bearing coffee." He holds out a paper cup to me, the scent of cinnamon in the air.

I take his offering and give him a small smile. The man knows me. I'd *much* rather have coffee than flowers. Much more appropriate and appreciated. A gift for all occasions.

"You look . . . really nice." Matteo's eyes burn as they travel down my length and back up. My heartbeat speeds up, faster than a speeding bullet. Despite my concern about how many secrets I'm juggling, Matteo is irresistible. I give in to the temptation to flirt. "What, this old thing? I've had it for years, and I just thought it needed to get out beside a suit for the evening." I give a slow twirl, letting him appreciate the costume. The way the black-lace sheath dress hugs my generous curves. I spent hours updating my old Ms. Genius costume from a con, replacing the skimpy leather leotard base of the costume with a forties-era lace-bodice dress. I added my homage to Ms. Genius's lightning bolt to the top of the dress in glimmering gold satin, and at my hips lies Ms. Genius's signature scarlet wrap. Comic book chic.

He watches my slow twirl, and I revel in satisfaction watching him watch me. Any guy who loves a dressed-up geek costume is okay in my book.

I make a show of asking him to do a twirl of his own in my entryway. "You, however, are *not* dressed properly for the gala. Matteo, this is a costume ball."

He shifts uncomfortably. "I brought this." He holds up a black plastic Zorro mask, complete with a single elastic band to hold it on his head.

"No."

"What do you suggest?"

"I was prepared for this too." I lean down and grab a plastic bag sitting by my feet near the door. I hand it to him, and he raises his eyebrows at me.

"My costume, I presume?"

"It may not fit perfectly, but it will do, and we'll go together with our forties-throwback stuff. You can only be one superhero. This is one of Ryan's. I made it for him a few years ago. Navy paratrooper pants. Navy army-inspired jacket with the insignia, and"—I back away a few steps and pick up the cardboard shield I made for Ryan—"*tada!*"

Matteo looks like he might argue with me, but he shrugs his shoulders and heads toward the downstairs bathroom. "When in Rome."

CHAPTER 22

We arrive at my office building twenty minutes late to the party, and I already can't focus. Matteo makes a really *hot* Captain America, and we touched-but-not-touched the whole car ride here. Every time I snuck a glance at him, I swear he was just turning his head from watching me. If I were a betting woman, I'd say he's just as hot and bothered as I am, judging by the sheer volume of times he's adjusted the neckline of his costume. So much for a calm professional front tonight.

The building glitters, lit up like the Eiffel Tower, from strings of Tivoli lights on the trees and strung up outside the main entrance. It's magical, surreal. A huge banner hangs in the lobby declaring the thirtieth anniversary of *The Hooded Falcon*.

We join the queue for coat check, and I nearly break my neck trying to see everything at once. Food stacked high on trays, carried by black-tie waitstaff. Buffet tables scattered around the perimeter of the large open lobby—I immediately spot my favorite artichoke dip. The very air in the room shimmers, from the lights strung across the ceiling, to the lights onstage where a live band assembles, and to the cocktail tables set up around the room with sequined tablecloths. A funky sixties-style chrome bar is set up for the occasion, flanked by two ice sculptures of the Hooded Falcon—one the original, one the current reboot. In short, it's magical, and it fills my geek heart to see hundreds of people in mostly Genius-inspired costumes turned out to celebrate my favorite fictional character.

When it's our turn, I hand the girl my long velvet coat with the maybe-real-I-don't-want-to-know fur collar—a treasured find from a thrift store. I fought Lawrence over it and won. The attendant hands me back a ticket. Then Matteo and I turn to face the room, shoulder to shoulder, Ms. Genius and Captain America among our caped compatriots.

It's all I can do not to grab his Captain America–clad hand and drag him to the dance floor to join the crush of people. The urge to be close to him distracts, though I know that Matteo is a professional; he's dedicated to keeping this about work tonight. I'm almost relieved as we push through the crowd to the bar. I need to keep my own head on a swivel. There's been no word from the Golden Arrow all week, and I can't help but *feel* he or she might be here tonight. This is, after all, a gala for superheroes.

The line for the bar is a million leagues long, so we settle in for the long wait. It gives us a good vantage point and a good reason to people-watch—how I like to label "spying on my coworkers" to myself. The guy in front of us wears an impressive adaptation of the original Hooded Falcon. His brown forest cape is draped expertly over one shoulder, and a quiver of *real* hand-fletched arrows sits on the opposite. I'm admiring the detailed stitching when I realize that I know this stitching. I *did* this stitching.

"Ryan!" I reach forward, grab the man's shoulder, and spin him around.

"Oh hey, MG!" Ryan's gaze flicks from me to Matteo, back to me, then across the room. He offers his hand to Matteo with a "Hey, man." We all stand awkwardly for a long stretch. I haven't had a chance to talk to him about Lelani. We've both been so busy this week. In fact, I've hardly seen Ryan all *month*. He's watching Matteo with a hostile look that makes me think I know why Ryan's being weird. I've never let a guy come between us before. It's a rule in our house. Yet for all he knows, I met this guy in the coffee shop and pretty much dropped off the planet.

Matteo clears his throat. "I see a colleague of mine. I'm going to go say hello. I'll be right back, MG?"

"Yeah, okay." No need to ask me twice. I want space to talk to Ryan.

Ryan's face jumps to life the second Matteo leaves. "Did you bring Lawrence? I need to talk to him, and he's not returning my calls."

"No, I—uh—think he went to visit his drag mom, right? He'll be back soon. I think he told me a week?"

Ryan frowns at me. He can *so* tell I'm lying. It's why I've avoided talking to anyone about Lawrence. With all I'm carrying around, I'm about to come apart at the seams, and Ryan knows me best.

"What did you need to tell him?" I ask.

Ryan studies my face for a minute, then glances around the room again. He looks back to me, and something odd happens. I realize that Ryan is deciding about whether to say something. Ryan, Lawrence, and I are *always* honest with one another. How has our relationship gotten to this point? I'm keeping secrets from him, and it looks like he might be keeping a secret of his own. Lelani.

I nearly hit my head with my hand. Of course, *Lelani*. He wants to talk to Lawrence about her, and he's not sure how I'll react because she's my boss. My shoulders relax.

"It's okay, Ry. I know what you've been keeping from me."

He looks startled—his eyes fly to my face, and I swear color drains from his cheeks.

I motion my hand forward. Jesus, the guy looks like he's about to have a heart attack. "About Lelani?"

Ryan still looks like I could knock him over with a feather. The line shuffles ahead, and I grab Ryan's arm and drag him up with me. "It's no big secret. I saw you guys leaving for lunch the other day. It's okay if you're seeing my boss."

Instantly Ryan relaxes. He shakes his hands slightly and blinks. "Oh . . . You saw that, did you? Yeah." He runs his hand down his face, then places it back on the thick leather belt that wraps over his cloak and costume beneath. "We're seeing each other. I'm sorry I didn't tell you."

"That's okay. I know it's a delicate situation."

Ryan's face hasn't regained all its color yet and still has that hesitant, watchful quality. He leans in closer to me. "Listen, while we're being honest, I looked into your boyfriend."

Ryan and his damn hacking.

I make some sort of noncommittal grunt. This shouldn't surprise me. Ryan and L are protective, but it *still* violates my privacy. Not to mention what he probably found out. Secrets revealed indeed.

"He's a cop."

I square my shoulders; no need to take this lying down. "Yeah, I know. I knew all along. He doesn't like telling people." It's as close to the truth as I can get in this setting. I should have been honest with Ryan from the beginning, saved us all this trouble.

"I can see why. He's working on that Golden Arrow case."

Ruh-roh. "Yeah, I guess." Time for distraction measures. "So what are you going to order? I'm thinking about getting a whiskey sour."

"MG." Ryan's hand isn't gentle on my arm, and he forces me to face him again. I'm eye-to-cloak with his costume, more specifically the large golden pin in the shape of an arrow that holds his cloak closed. Either Ryan has leveled up in his costume creation, or someone else has been fiddling with *my* costumes. Lelani. My thought derails when Ryan gives me a small shake. "This is serious. That case is dangerous."

I sigh. "I know. Ryan . . ." I glance around at the people near us in line. Almost everyone is on their cell phones, no one paying attention to us. "I've been helping a little on the case. It's how I actually met Matteo." There, closer to the truth without all the bells and whistles.

Ryan moves back a half step, taking me in. "You sure that's a good idea? The news reporters say that the drug lords are threatening anyone even *involved* with the case now. That's you, in case you're missing my point." That's Lawrence; that's Matteo too. It's probably even Ryan since he lives with me. I bite my lip so hard, I wince.

The line shuffles forward again, and I glimpse Matteo making his way back toward us. "I can't stop now, Ry. We're close to solving the case."

"But—"

I don't let Ryan finish. I paste a cheery smile on my face and reach a hand out for Matteo. "Oh good, just in time for a drink."

Matteo gives me a quizzical look but puts an answering smile on his own face. "How about that martini, then? Shaken not stirred?" He does a James Bond impression, and I like him just a *little* bit more for how bad it is.

Ryan looks between us, back stiff, face cold and impassive. "She doesn't like martinis. I think I've lost my date. I'll catch you later, MG." With a swirl of his cloak, Ryan melts into the crowd on the dance floor.

Matteo openly frowns at Ryan's back now. "What's that all about?"

Nothing is going my way tonight. "*That* was my roommate telling me that he found out I've been lying to him about you being a cop."

"Oh. But how did he—"

"Don't ask. Ryan has his ways." I will *not* get a second best friend arrested while I am still trying to protect the first. "Either way, he's mad at me, and not you."

"I'm sorry, MG." For a moment it's *Matteo* looking at me, not Detective Kildaire. "I've made things complicated."

I sigh. "Let's just catch the bad guy so we can move on, okay?" We step up to the bar, order our drinks, then turn to survey the room. There are so many people to watch, I don't even know where to start sleuthing.

"I guess we can go talk to Tej. He's the only other member of the team we haven't looked into. I can introduce you to all the marketing people."

We take a quick tour of the room and find Tej at a cocktail table eating Swedish meatballs with his wife. I let Matteo steer the conversation. I feel like I'm recovering from a one-two punch in my life: first, Lawrence has been forced into hiding because of *my* choices, and now, my other best friend is pissed—for good reason—that I lied to him about my boyfriend. And he doesn't even know the half of it.

With only partial attention, I listen as Matteo casually questions Tej about his alibi for the night of the explosion, then about the afternoon when I saw the Golden Arrow at the Casey mansion. I don't know how he sounds so *normal* asking people these things, but Tej and his wife are all smiles, sharing their alibis without a second thought. I can tell when Matteo starts using platitudes like "Maybe we'll see you next weekend for the movie marathon" that he's ready to move on. I look around for a suitable reason to drag Matteo off and find our next victim.

"I'm sorry about the promotion," Tej says, snapping my attention back to the conversation.

"Sorry?"

Tej's eyes widen, and he looks a bit like he wants to eat his words. "Yeah. Um . . . I guess they're going to announce it formally on Monday, but I thought they would have told you at the same time as Andy."

My eyes fly across the room to where Andy and Casey Junior are laughing over drinks. Most definitely celebratory, bro-hug, good-ol-boys-club, no-girls-allowed drinks. All around the table, everyone is frozen, watching my reaction. And I wait for the wave of anger, of injustice, of *anything* to crash over me. But it never comes. In my head, I'm clinging to the life raft of Ryan's words. And my conversation with Lawrence. I'm shocked to find I'm a little bummed, but . . . that's it.

"Andy was a good choice," I say carefully. "And sure, I'm bummed, but I guess this means that there's an opening for team leader now, right?" I shoot Matteo a look to gauge his reaction. He looks almost . . . proud of me. That's one I'm not used to seeing on my dates' faces.

The band strikes up a jazzy swing tune just as the conversation wraps up, and Tej's wife grabs his arm. I can tell they're looking for an easy way to extricate themselves from the awkward conversation, and I don't blame them. "We *have* to dance at least once. Come on. Maybe MG and Matteo will join us?"

In a complete reversal from the day in the lobby where he accepted the movie invitation without asking me, Matteo is hemming and hawing while I throw out a cheery "Sure, we'd love to." I know there's no other way to get Matteo on the dance floor, and the music drags at me. I want to just forget about Andy's promotion for a minute. I don't have the time to add that to my list of internal grievances right now, and dancing is the perfect way to achieve that.

"Come on, it's just one dance. We can scope out our next target while we're out there. And this music is perfect for our costumes." It may be a nerdy statement, but it's true. I can imagine no better music for our characters to dance to.

He protests but follows me out onto the floor, where he grabs my hand with one of his and my waist with the other. Slightly old-school, but I can dig it. We find a jazzy rhythm, and I shoot a shocked look up at him. "Matteo, you can *dance*."

"Why are you so surprised?" He frowns, and I can tell he's trying to keep this *professional*. It's starting to push my buttons because in this moment, I *dislike* Detective Kildaire. He's stuffy and focused on the case. Which is what I should be, except I'm swept away by the capes, the costumes, the jazz music, the dancing. I can't help myself. The story thread I'm picking up tonight is deeply *romantic*, in the old-fashioned sense.

I want Matteo back.

"Why am I surprised that you've got rhythm? You drive a Prius, and you drink tea."

He throws me a good-natured scowl, a piece of his dark messy hair falling across his forehead. My heartbeat accelerates. Not only is he a man in uniform tonight; he's a man in costumed uniform. I don't know that I've ever seen anything so sexy in my entire life.

"Are you really okay about the promotion? I know you really wanted it."

I think for a moment before meeting his gaze. "Yes, I think I really am. I've got some other pretty awesome things going on in my life right now, and it just seems kind of . . . small. Something I can work around."

His hand tightens on my back, and he pulls me just an inch closer. This case still stands like a wall between us, but Matteo and I are drawn together like magnets through it. If the case were over and I could finally be honest about everything, well, there wouldn't be *anything* between us anymore. My mind goes to all sorts of scenarios with nothing between us, and my face grows warm.

"Don't you look at me like that," he warns, a friendly smile plastered on his face. He spins me out, then back in, letting our bodies crash together just a smidge too much for propriety before setting me back on my feet. "We have work to do."

"I don't know what you mean. *I'm* looking for clues," I say, playing along. The music and the dancing and Matteo's hands on my waist are making me *giddy*, the heady atmosphere of the party not helping either.

"Sure you are—" Matteo drops my hand suddenly and looks over my shoulder. "Agent Sosa. I didn't know you'd be here."

"Apparently."

I turn around, schooling my features into a pleased surprise. "Oh, hello again. We met at the warehouse."

"Yes, I remember. You're consulting on the case." Her voice is chilly. There's the reminder. I can tell she doesn't approve of Matteo's conduct.

"Are you here as a guest? Or are you also here for research on the case?" I make sure to add a sweet smirk to cover my pointed explanation of *why* Matteo is here with me.

"I'm here with my husband and father. Purely pleasure tonight, I'm afraid." The corners of her lips go up in an approximation of a smile, but it doesn't reach her eyes, and her tone makes it clear she doesn't qualify our dancing as "business." I can't picture her coming from a family of comic book nerds, but you never know about people. I try not to let my judgment show.

Matteo gives a cough. “Glad you’re here anyhow. MG—er, Ms. Martin has made some really impressive headway on the case this week. A possible connection from the time the original *Hooded Falcon* was written. I can catch you up on Monday if you’d like.”

“Yes, I suppose I can make the time.” Wow, she’s *cranky* that Matteo is here. Her eyes flick to me. “I’m surprised you’re still working on the case. Detective Rideout seemed to think there was a—ah, what words did he use?—conflict of interest? Don’t let me get in the way of your . . . investigation, if that’s what you’re calling this.”

Well, that just throws a bucket of ice on the only fun I’ve had all night. Agent Sosa moves off toward the front of the room, and Matteo and I follow suit, the fun gone from the brief moment of letting go. My heart sinks. I’ve obviously lost the respect of Agent Sosa by acting so unprofessionally and made her think less of Matteo as well. We don’t talk about it. We just grab new drinks and snag a table near the front of the room to watch the speeches. A few friends from other departments stop by, and I introduce Matteo, but he’s distracted.

Not five minutes later, the lights dim off and on, and the general din of the room drops as people move to the cocktail tables. Casey Junior appears on the stage, dressed in a stunning black tuxedo.

“MG, your roommate Ryan, how did he know I’m a cop?”

I turn to him, surprised. “The speeches are about to begin.” I do *not* want to discuss Ryan’s illegal activities.

“I’m serious.” He has that look on his face like he’s piecing together a puzzle, and I don’t like it.

“Why? What are you thinking?”

“Well, he would have access to your stuff and Lawrence’s, right?”

I frown. “Yeah, I guess.”

“And he’d know the cops working on the case if he were . . . involved in the vigilante field of employ.”

Nausea threatens. "Matteo, no. That's not it at all. Ryan's a hacker. Please don't tell him I told you. I don't want *both* of my best friends in trouble with the law."

"But you said he's smart and good with computers." Matteo is on a roll now, an aha moment written all over his face. "Able to disable a security system maybe? And he obviously loves the comics." He holds up a finger. "*And* didn't you tell me that he's got costumes, capes, and tights, the whole lot?"

"So does every nerd in this place. You saw Kyle's closet. And don't you think I'd know it if my own roommate were parading around this city in tights and a cape? Well, other than tonight, I mean. *Everyone* is in tights tonight." I'm indignant on behalf of Ryan, but I'm also a little rattled. Matteo's words sink in, and my mind runs a mile a minute. Ryan *is* all of those things. Matteo has a point.

"You're forgetting what your profiler said, though," I say slowly, my mind rewinding to the words Rideout threw at me on the stairs. "They think you're chasing a woman. Well educated. Ties to the comics industry. Ryan is a guy, high-school dropout, and works in video games."

Matteo doesn't look convinced, so I rack my brain further.

"I mean, you can ask him about it yourself, but I'm pretty sure Lawrence and Ryan were at a gaming competition for at least one of the Golden Arrow crimes."

"They could be working together." Matteo leans in now, his voice hushed but passionate. I recognize the fervor I feel when something clicks for me in my stories; only this time Matteo is off his mark.

"*Neither* of them fits the profile. Plus, Lawrence was at the drag show the night of the explosion, remember? And . . ." I struggle to recall Ryan's schedule. I snap my fingers. "Lawrence mentioned that Ryan was missing the show because he had a date."

"That could just be a cover-up." Matteo sounds *victorious* now.

"No. Not made up. She's right over there, and she'll tell you herself. I saw them going out to lunch again this week. They're a real couple." I motion over to Lelani, and beside me Matteo goes still. His shoulders slump slightly. He's gone from victorious to . . . defeated? Wow, my argument must have been excellent. I've won this round, thank Thor.

The room hushes. I catch a flash of dark hair near the front of the stage and crane my neck to catch sight of Agent Sosa standing just off the front of the stage, drink in hand and sour face still in evidence. Standing beside her and schmoozing with several of the Genius executives is someone I recognize as one of LA's government officials . . . city manager maybe? I don't pay attention to politics when I can help it, but his face and name *do* seem familiar. Which puts to rest my curiosity about her coming from a comic book–loving family.

Casey Junior is checking the mic on the podium, and I turn to watch, glad we've settled the Ryan issue. Casey Junior leans forward and addresses the crowd, "Welcome, and thank you all for sharing this night with me. I wish my father was here to see how many came to celebrate." Usually I'd roll my eyes at this, assuming he's tugging at emotions to gain customers, but now I *know* he's serious. Suddenly I'm like the Grinch who grew a heart. I hardly recognize myself these days. Casey Junior gives a short account of how his father started the comic and how he's proud to carry on the family legacy. No mention of the controversy. No mention of his father's possible murder or crooked cops. I'm distracted and miss Casey Junior introducing the next speaker, but suddenly the crowd around me claps as Junior walks offstage and an older gentleman takes his place at the podium, his steps measured and careful. He uses the podium for balance, his wrinkled hands less than steady, even gripping the sides.

The crowd rustles like a celebrity has joined us. To me, it's just a guy in an old-fashioned captain's uniform. Apparently, to everyone else, this guy is *someone*. It finally dawns that I'm seeing the celebrity police captain I've read about in my research, in the flesh.

"Thank you, thank you," he says, waving down the applause. "I'm happy to be here to celebrate. I accepted the offer to speak tonight because while some people call me a real-life superhero"—he pauses again for more applause—"we all know that Edward Casey was the real superhero. He was a visionary, a man before his time. His comic inspired social change, and I can speak personally to that. But Edward Casey didn't just write about people fighting social injustice; he was a friend to the Los Angeles Police Department. Just before his unfortunate death, he had given a statement specifically to help end crime happening in his very own neighborhood. Edward Casey Senior is one of the many reasons we were successful with the biggest drug bust in LA's history. May we continue to honor his memory by supporting social justice, supporting our law enforcement, and encouraging those we love to wear a cape now and again." He continues to speak, and the crowd eats it up. He's charismatic despite his age and apparent frailty. There's a wave of laughter, and I look at Matteo. He's basically got stars in his eyes. This man is one of his heroes the way comic book superheroes are for me. I expect to be overtaken by the same wonder as everyone around me—this guy is as close to a real-life Superman as LA has ever had—but something prickles in the back of my head. Something that feels like the hints of a story. My Spidey sense.

The beginning of his speech has my mind wandering. The climate of the comic and the climate of LA were unbelievably similar. A drug war. A big bust. And in the comic, the reveal of a *superhero* who went rogue. A superhero, or a *cop* manipulating the drug war for his own benefit. A *superhero* who would benefit by having his competitors in the drug trade removed and who would kill any man who tried to unmask him.

Ice forms in the pit of my stomach. "How old is he?"

Matteo still claps, watching the older gentleman exit the stage. "What? Who?"

"Anthony Munez."

Matteo's brows crease in annoyance, and he answers in a hushed whisper, "I don't know. Seventy-five? Eighty?"

That would make him forty-five when he was police chief. I drum my fingers on the table. The puzzle pieces start fitting together, even though I don't love the picture they're painting. I need to make sure my hunch is correct. And I need to get back in that warehouse to conduct my own search before the White Rabbit realizes how close to him I am and disappears, or worse. My safety, Matteo's safety, and L's safety all depend on *proof*.

Applause rings out. I've missed the rest of his speech, and now the crush of the crowd threatens to keep me from acting on the idea I just had: Lawrence had seen the dirty cop all those years ago.

"I need a picture," I say to Matteo.

"Of?"

"Anthony Munez. Come on. Come take a picture with your idol." I reach into my small bag and produce my iPhone.

Matteo lets me shove my way through the crowd that has formed at the bottom of the stage. Captain Munez has just reached the last step, and we're only second, next to Agent Sosa, in his receiving line.

Matteo nods to her. "Agent Sosa. And I assume your husband?" Matteo shakes her hand first, then reaches for the hand of the gentleman next to her. "Ah, yes, it's City Councilman Sosa, right?" They must have assembled to greet Anthony Munez like, it seems, the entire room is on its way to do.

Ah. Councilman. I knew I'd seen his face on a bus stop somewhere. I shoulder away several of the gray-hairs who have convened to pay court to Munez. He's started down the line, first pausing for a picture near Agent Sosa and her husband.

I wait until after the flash of the camera has cleared from my eyes before lunging forward slightly, hand on Anthony Munez's arm. "Can we get a picture too, sir? Detective Kildaire is a huge fan."

"I hardly think that's appropriate." It's the acerbic tone of Agent Sosa's voice. Her husband's face is a similar mask of disapproval. What are they, the propriety police? They can get pictures with the fabled police chief, but Matteo can't?

Munez settles the stalemate with a gracious half bow. "Nonsense, nonsense. Happy to help. My public misses me, and I miss the spotlight."

Gotta get while the getting's good. "We'll be quick about it!" I shove Matteo toward Anthony Munez and step back to take the picture.

"One, two, three!" My cell phone hates the low light, but I manage to get a blurry one that should work. "Detective Kildaire, this should go in your office. Thank you, sir. It was so nice to meet you." I spin on my heels, texting Lawrence as fast as my fingers can fly over the keypad.

Meet me at Genius right now. Come alone. Operation Janeway.

Matteo grabs my arm just as I reach the line of people arriving at the coat check. "Hey, MG, stop. Hang on. Where are you going?" He drags me around to face him, perfect in his costume. How I wish I could spend the night dancing under the glittering crystal chandeliers with him. Except in this moment work is *really* between us more than he knows.

My hunch grows, and if I'm correct, the White Rabbit already knows or will soon know we're on his trail. Matteo will be in the line of fire. I'll be in the line of fire. I need to keep my next moves secret, even if just to protect him. After this is all over, I plan to kiss him silly for days.

I wrench my arm away. "I forgot about something I need to go do." I reach the coat queue and dash my hands through my hair because the line is *so* long.

"What? That's crazy." Matteo elbows into line behind me. "We're here to work."

"We are; we were. But I need to go." I grasp his arm, willing him to believe me. The crowd surges around us. I recognize Nina and Kyle, dressed as Wonder Woman and the Flash. I see Ryan over in the corner, deep in heated conversation with Lelani. *This* is where I wish I were staying. This is where I want to be. At this fancy party with Matteo in his hot costume, with my awesome friends. I feel an intense wave of longing that nearly knocks me off my heels. It's odd how I feel like I belong with these people when I've spent so many years building up a wall. All it took was one hazel-eyed narcotics detective to turn my world on its head. But I have a killer and a drug lord to catch. And there are too many damn people gathered around this coat check.

"You stay here, okay? Free booze. Check into my coworkers. Steal the canapes. Lots of fun to be had. And look, there's Ryan with my boss Lelani near the coat check. Maybe they're leaving too. Quick, you can go meet her. Ask her about the date. Do your thing."

Matteo's face is frozen and impassive. "I know who she is."

"You do? From researching Genius?"

Matteo clears his throat. "No, we were engaged."

It's like a punch in the gut. Engaged? Let's go ahead and rain on my parade with my *boss*, who is my roommate's girlfriend and hopeful alibi, is Matteo's ex-girlfriend, and happens to be goddess-model hot and super-brainy smart.

Matteo clears his throat again. "I, uh, didn't know she'd gotten a job here. I probably should go say hello."

It's as if everyone freezes for a moment as I absorb this, while inside my emotions run wild like Storm is wreaking havoc with my internal weather. What if he still has feelings for her? He might not be over her. She dumped *him*, right? And he planted an oasis for her at his house. And now I'm dealing with a wave of uncharacteristic jealousy. I don't have time to deal with my complicated reaction to this. Better to stuff my feelings into a padlocked box and focus on my mission. I turn toward the coat check. If nothing else, Matteo talking to Lelani will buy me time to meet Lawrence. "Yeah. You go do that." I'm going to go catch our killer.

Matteo hesitates, then takes a few steps toward Ryan and Lelani. My throat constricts—the locks on that padlock in my brain must not be very good. I can't watch—my gorgeous Matteo standing next to gorgeous Lelani. They would have stupidly perfect children.

I turn, push through the line of the coat room and up to the front, where a different girl is now dutifully tearing off tickets. "I lost mine," I announce.

"Some of us are in *line* here." An elderly woman in a truly spectacular forties-era pantsuit tries to push in front of me.

"This is an emergency. A life-or-death one," I say. That stops the pushing. A tad dramatic, but oh well.

"Do you remember what your coat looks like?" The girl chews her lip and looks unprepared for an *emergency* at the coat check. "I'm not supposed to let people back, but—"

I don't even wait for more permission. I skirt the table and head for the door to the conference room that masquerades as the coat closet. Not two seconds later, the door opens again, and Matteo nearly falls into the room behind me.

"Jesus, it's dark in here," he says.

"The coats don't seem to care." I click on my phone flashlight to add meager glow to the few amber-colored downlights turned on in the room. How would anyone find *any* coat in here? Of course, mine is long and black, just like the hundreds of long black coats hanging against the walls. I start checking collars. Fewer fur collars, so that should help.

Matteo's presence distracts me. I keep thinking about him with Lelani. It has me all tangled up inside in a way that terrifies me. We're not even a *real* couple. I have no claim on him. I'm not the jealous sort. So why am I all bent out of shape just because Matteo's ex is about as close to my opposite as the world can get?

Matteo's voice emanates close to my ear, and I jump. "Where are you *really* going? You're not off on another dangerous adventure without me, are you?" He intends it to be a joke, forcing a lightheartedness. I don't laugh. "Seriously, MG. Is this about earlier? The dancing? Or the case?" He sounds hurt, but I don't have time to sift through my emotions or his. Double-strength padlocks. I need to go. Now.

As if summoned by my thoughts, my phone buzzes. Lawrence. Five minutes out. I'll swing by the front?

I punch in the thumbs-up sign and continue searching.

Coat Check Girl enters with a pile of coats over her arm. "Find it?"

"Not yet!" I try to sound cheery instead of panicked. She gives me a weird look and exits again, while I grin like a maniac.

Matteo watches me search in silence. Finally I find my coat, in the darkest corner of *course*, and yank it off the hanger. I turn to leave the room, only to find Matteo standing behind me.

He's too close. I can't think straight. The scent of him—cinnamon and probably his hair gel—is an aphrodisiac to the part of me that wants *us* to be real. The part that wants to throw caution to the wind, tell him where I'm going, what I know, and who I suspect. I have to restrain myself from melting into him. It's an urge I need to resist. Until this drug lord, this *killer*, and this vigilante are behind bars, Matteo won't stop. It's his job to find them. And it's my job to help him.

"Michael-Grace, you're obviously upset. Can we talk about this?"

"I'm not upset. This is business, remember? No reason to be upset." Maybe I'm a *little* upset. Okay, a lot upset. The fact that I've just realized how invested my heart is in this fake relationship, how invested *I* am in this case, leaves me rattled.

"MG, look at me."

"I need to go."

"Look at me."

I do so defiantly. If it will speed up the process of me getting out of here, fine.

His hands reach out for me, fingers closing around my waist. He pulls me to him, though I fight for a few steps. "Michael-Grace Martin, come *here*."

I am at war with myself, but my full name on his lips is my undoing. I move forward until I'm nestled against his Captain America insignia.

"I know why you're upset. I know we said this was business, but it's clearly not just business." He sounds pained and unsure. Like he's not one to usually be vulnerable. It's hard for him to admit; I hear it in every note of his voice.

Clearly not just business. Our proximity allows me to feel his heart thudding a mile a minute, and I'm losing my resolve to run out of here at about the same pace.

I need to keep my mind on my plan. Leave. This is a distraction when the case may be going cold as we speak. "It's not?" I get suckered into the conversation. Emo MG wins this round.

"Not for me." He takes a breath. "Look. I'll lay it out there. I know this is messy. And I know there's the case. MG, I'm not good at this." His grip on my waist becomes stronger, more sure, like he's reached some decision. "I probably put work first too many times in my past relationships too. But you're different. I want you to know that." He licks his lips, and there's a small quiver in one of his fingers before he tightens his grip more and pulls me even closer. His voice gains surety, and I revel in his breath on my cheek. In our closeness. "If working this case means you're walking out on . . . us, whatever we are, I'll resign from it. I'll let Detective Rideout finish up. I'll take away the thing that's keeping us apart."

My heart hammers in response. He'd give up a case for me? Forget a one-two punch; this is a total knockout. One that leaves me weak-kneed and dizzy. I've *never* had a man offer to do something like that before. I'm used to boyfriends using me. There was the guy capitalizing on our dates. On a broader stage, the years I've felt undervalued by the executives at work. All the guys at cons who were interested only in my "finer assets," as Rideout said. Yet here's Matteo, knight in shining armor, willing to give everything up for *me*. It's something I thought

I'd never want, but I'm awash with how amazing and scary this feels. Because it's real.

Real. Reality crashes back in as I contemplate how *real* the case is too. I can't have Detective Rideout head up this investigation. Not only did he train under Anthony Munez and could very well be *the* dirty cop, but he'd have me in jail in less than twenty-four hours, guaranteed. Offering to give up the case proves Matteo is true. Honest. The double agent would never give up control, and I need an honest cop at the helm of this, no matter what happens.

I reach out and put my hand on his chest, right over his true-blue heart. "I want you to stay on the case. I want us to solve it. And no way you're letting Rideout lead this. The guy already thinks I'm the Golden Arrow. I'd end up in handcuffs for sure." The darkness presses in on us, and I run my hand up his arm. "I—I really appreciate you saying those things. You're worth waiting for, however long this case takes." The last words come out in an almost-whisper. I mean them to the very bottom of my stiletto heels and all the way back up again.

Matteo looks like I've given him Christmas. Then his lips are a breath from mine. "MG, I can't stop thinking about you." His wrists circle mine, and he lifts our hands above my head and presses me back into the pile of coats.

Our kiss isn't soft. We grasp at each other as if we're drowning. We fall into the coats, and I grab the bar above us to keep from falling all the way through. We shouldn't be doing this, but *oh* we should be doing this. I'm made for this kiss—costumes, coat closet, and all.

Matteo's breath is ragged as he drags his hands down over my coat and back up underneath, his hands hot against the lace of my dress. He leans down, kissing the pulse beating wildly at the base of my throat, and I nearly pass out from the sensation. My head swims, blood pounding in my ears. I can't get enough of this man. He's gotten under my skin, in my brain, and stolen my heart.

Coat Check Girl chooses this very moment to reappear. A triangle of light from the door falls across us, and she clears her throat in a loud and well-rehearsed manner. "Did you find your coat, miss?"

The coat rack nearly collapses beneath Matteo and me, and we part on a laugh.

"I—uh—yeah, I found it. Right here. Thanks for checking on us." *Not.* I push to stand, grab my coat where it has sagged to my elbows, and pull it back over my shoulders.

She throws me a look that says she's partly sorry she had to interrupt us. "I have more coats to hang," she says with one last appreciative look at Matteo. "Be back in a sec." The triangle of light disappears.

"I feel like I'm fifteen," Matteo says, his forehead coming to rest on mine.

"If you were kissing like this at fifteen, you needed to teach lessons." My phone buzzes again. "I really do have to go. But I'll call you later, okay?"

Matteo's hands settle back around my waist. Then he snuggles my coat around me further, buttoning the top button. He pulls me in for a sweet peck. "If you must."

Something in the pocket of my coat sticks into my side, and I frown. I haven't put anything in my pocket.

"What's wrong?"

"I don't know. There's something poking me in the side."

"I didn't think it was that obvious." Matteo gives a bawdy wink, and I laugh.

"No, I'm serious." I dig in my pocket. There's definitely something in there. Something like a book. I definitely didn't put a *book* in my pocket. I extricate it with difficulty and hold it up to the meager light.

It's a softcover journal.

It's a *black* softcover journal I've seen before. *Dammit, dammit, dammit.*

Matteo's eyes widen as I flip quickly through the journal. "Is that what I think it is?"

I snap the journal closed and shove it back into my pocket. "My journal of ideas? Yeah. I forgot I had this with me. Ideas for the new *Hero Girls*." But it definitely isn't my journal. It's Casey Senior's missing journal, the one whose sketches showed up in my test copy of *The Hooded Falcon*. What the hell? Who snuck this journal in my pocket?

Matteo knows something is up. I can see the light of suspicion dawn. "Are you *sure* that's your journal? Because if it belongs to someone else and you took evidence, you'd be a suspect and off the case."

The warning is clear. Come clean now and stay on the case. Lie and risk losing my freedom and the man offering me so much more. But he didn't see the note at the back of the journal. A note to *me*. It simply said,

MG, Rabbit in the Glen. Tonight, 11 p.m. Follow the arrows.

If I turn this over, the journal pretty much frames me as the Golden Arrow or, at the very least, an accomplice.

I offer a small smile. "I guess that would be one way to solve the problem between us?"

Matteo grits his teeth. "I can't *date* a suspect either."

My phone buzzes, reminding me of my appointment with fate, and now with a warehouse. I don't wait to see if he's hurt or angry. I'll deal with that fallout later. I square my shoulders. I give him a swift kiss on the cheek. "Then I guess it's a good thing I'm not one."

CHAPTER 23

I race out of Genius Comics as fast as I can without looking like I'm fleeing a fire and find the Millennium Turd in the parking lot, lights on, Lawrence at the helm. Thank God his drag family was close enough for him to make it up here in under an hour.

"What's shakin'?" Lawrence calls as I throw open the passenger door and fling myself into the car.

"A whole lotta shade," I respond, putting my arm over my eyes. So much has just happened, I don't know where to begin. "We need to carry out Operation Janeway tonight."

"Like right now?"

"Now. Well, right after I show you this." I fumble through my purse and retrieve my phone. My fingers slip on the device in my haste to pull up the picture I took inside. "Do you recognize this man?"

I hold out the picture, realizing now *just* how blurry it is. Photographer I am not.

L rubs his jaw and looks at the picture. "Maybe?"

I throw down my phone in frustration, and L shoots me a look. "What, MG? That picture sucks. Who is he? Why should I know him?"

"He's the old police chief. The one who was in charge when Casey Senior died."

"The one who cleaned up the streets in the eighties, single-handedly reduced crime rates, and took LA into a long stretch of peaceful living?"

I grit my teeth. "Yeah. That one. I think he's the White Rabbit. I wanted to see if you recognized him as the cop from Casey Senior's house or any of your superhero stuff."

Taking the phone from me, Lawrence studies the picture again. He gives a noncommittal shrug. "I mean, maybe. But it's hard to tell. And anyway, MG, are you *really* going to accuse someone like *that* of being the White Rabbit?"

"Not without proof, no."

Something occurs to me, so I snatch the phone back and navigate to an internet browser.

"What are you doing?"

"Googling."

"Girl, we don't have time for that—"

"L, you said that picture sucks, and I'm trying to find a better one. This guy was *all over* the news in the eighties. There *has* to be a better picture." The silence stretches as my phone maddeningly halts on the load screen. Stupid dead zones. "Come on, come on, come on."

Lawrence sits in silence maybe a full thirty seconds. "I thought you said we needed to be quick."

"We do!" I growl in frustration. The few pictures that have loaded are articles about tonight's gala, nothing about the younger Munez. I'm facing having to start the search over. Maybe *'80s Munez?* But what if all that come up are articles *about* the drug bust? I literally beat my forehead with the phone in frustration.

Lawrence sighs, watching me. "Even if you could find it online, this dude is so old. Highly doubt he's donning a cape and spankies."

"What if he has a protégé? L, I've been thinking. Rideout's dad worked with this guy. Munez got Rideout's dad out of some serious charges. Then Rideout trained with him for years until he retired. Maybe Munez is the original, but my hunch says that we're dealing with a younger cop, still on the force, and someone in Matteo's inner circle. Someone who took his ideas and runs the same operation. Maybe *this* is what the Golden Arrow is trying to tell us."

"That's a lot to prove, MG."

I give up and throw my phone—still stuck loading the fourth and fifth pictures on Google Images—into my lap. I'll have to try again later. "Yes, thank you for your assessment. Now let's go before Matteo comes out. He already suspects that I have the journal, and if he sees me with you, well, I'll be off the case for sure." His warning said as much. If he finds proof that I've taken the journal the police are looking for, I'll probably be arrested for impeding an investigation. I catch L's startled look at my mention of the journal. "I'll tell you about the journal on our way. We need to get to the warehouse by eleven p.m."

Lawrence shifts the car into drive, though we can't move forward yet. We have to wait for several people to meander across the road toward the party at an infuriatingly slow speed. Too late, I recognize Agent Sosa and her husband walking through the parking lot. I will her not to notice me, but my car's wheezing exhaust system is pretty noticeable in the sea of luxury automobiles. She catches my eye. I can't look away, even as they make their slow way in our direction.

Agent Sosa stops just outside my window. It seems intentional and threatening, even though I've done *nothing* to this woman but be polite tonight. "Leaving so soon, Ms. Martin?"

"Business to attend to," I answer through my open window. I make a move to roll it up. Having it down was a *big* mistake.

Her eyes slide to Lawrence, then back to me. Lawrence does his usual "haters gonna hate" ignore-them routine. I wish I could be as good at it as him. Instead, I reach across the middle of my car and grasp his hand with mine. I'm fighting off a strong case of the heebie-jeebies along with a ball of anxiety that would make Black Lightning nervous. I'm positive he can feel my hand shaking, and he squeezes back.

Her sour smile has turned into something of a Cheshire grin, and it doesn't sit well with me either. "Well, it was nice to see you again. Maybe we'll see you and your friend around. Lawrence, isn't it? I thought someone inside was asking about him. Have a nice night. I'm sure we'll be seeing both of you soon." She and her husband continue around the car, but I'm frozen in my seat.

"L, did she just use your name?"

"Yes. Shit. She doesn't seem friendly."

"She knows Matteo is looking for you." Dread seeps into my pores like one of Lawrence's ridiculous gel facial masks. This gets more *real*, more dangerous by the minute. "We need to go. She knows who you are. I'm with you, and I'll bet my spandex that she's going to tell Matteo. You could get arrested for evading police, and I could be arrested for obstructing justice. On so many counts." I think of the journal in my pocket. My heart sinks, and I fight a wave of nausea. But my job right now is to keep Matteo safe, keep L safe, and solve this crime so I can beg forgiveness. No way out but through. Sometimes you just have to go into the fight and throw a lot of elbows. "L, I need your help to put this whole puzzle together before someone I love gets hurt."

I know the comics. I know enough about the crime scenes to get me started. I'm going to have to be *very* careful not to get caught, but if anyone can catch the Golden Arrow at his own game, it is me. This is do or die, life or death.

Lawrence regards me, then revs the engine of my little car. "Game on, bitches."

We park two blocks away from the warehouse in an alley behind a dumpster, per Lawrence's insistence. Sometimes even Han took suggestions from Leia.

"I should have been more specific about Operation Janeway's uniform requirements." I push my black wig off my forehead and glare through the curls at Lawrence, who seems to be monitoring everything while still walking down a dark alley without tripping. There is no sign of a wiggle in his walk. This is game face for Lawrence, and if I'm right, he's carrying at least one gun on his person.

"I look like a castoff from *Saturday Night Fever*," I grumble. Truth be told, I rather love the maroon leather jumpsuit I'm rocking, and the knee-high brown boots are very *Kill Bill*. Better for a little B and E than my lace dress by a mile.

"I wish. I'd kill for some bling and a good pair of bell-bottoms right now," Lawrence answers. Beside me he looks right out of *The Matrix* in his black pants, black sparkle T-shirt with a hot pink "L" on it, trench coat, and *Blade Runner* black boots. "You don't want them to instantly recognize you on surveillance, do you?"

I glance around. "Who is *them*?"

Lawrence shrugs. "The police. Your boyfriend. The drug dealers."

We're standing just outside *the* alcove. It looks less mysterious and sexy tonight and more . . . trashy, filthy, and it smells like urine. I miss Matteo's strong presence and his Kevlar vest.

"So tell me again why we're here." Lawrence glances around.

I rattle the door and find that it's locked, as I expected. "We're looking for a way inside." I pull at the window to find it's fixed shut. "The journal said the White Rabbit was going to be here at eleven, and to follow the arrows." I pull the journal out of my pocket, and hand it to him so he can read the message.

While Lawrence is overjoyed to have his journal back, he's also beyond pissed that someone scribbled in it. Not just anyone. The Golden Arrow intentionally left evidence on my person that the police are looking for. Either our hero wants to help me find the White Rabbit, or the Golden Arrow wants me off the case. I've chosen to see this as an olive branch, but standing in the dark outside a warehouse makes me realize that it very well could be hemlock.

The sound of breaking glass has me whirling around to face Lawrence. His paisley head scarf is wrapped around his hand, and he's leaning against the building with a forced expression of innocence.

"What did you just do?"

"I slipped."

I peer around him. "Did you break that window?"

"It was already broken." He turns and studies it. "But yes, when I slipped, I did happen to make the hole bigger. Big enough that half of a crime-fighting duo can get in there and go let the bigger half in through the door."

"I thought you said I was in charge."

He shrugs. "I'm helping. My guess is since this one was already broken, they've turned the alarms off. Thank God it's not safety glass, or I would have broken my hand."

"Yeah, we'll see about that." I turn and study the window. I'm grateful now for the thicker material of my jumpsuit. "Okay, help me up." I ignore my pulse pounding in my ears and how my knees are knocking together. I'm about to commit a *real* crime.

Lawrence grunts as he cradles me in a basket hold, and I work to balance myself to get my feet through the hole without catching on the broken glass. My butt poses a bit of a problem now that my feet are dangling inside the building and my upper body is supported by L. "You're going to have to essentially *throw* me through this window."

"That doesn't sound like a good idea."

"It's either that or my back drags across broken glass. I need to go straight through." And *nothing* at all could go wrong with that. Right? "Okay, on three. One, two—"

Before I get to three, Lawrence tosses me as best he can through the broken portion of the window. Jagged glass grabs at my back, the shoulders of the suit, and a section of the wig. A sting on my cheek says something scratched my face. All told, the worst part of the entire trip is the landing. I wish I could say that, like my hero counterparts in the comics, I do a neat tuck-and-roll and shoot to my feet ready for action. Instead, the heel of my left boot skids to the side, I land hard on my right foot, my ankle rolls, and I end up spread-eagle on my stomach, my face inches from a wooden pallet.

"You okay? That sounded bad!" Lawrence's voice is an exaggerated stage whisper.

I peel myself off the floor and test my weight on my turned ankle. "It's not life-threatening," I announce in a similar whisper, limping my way over to the door. This door isn't locked on the inside, and I simply push open the panic bar. Though I'm cringing, no alarm sounds.

"Let's make this quick," Lawrence says, ducking in. The door closes behind us, and we're left in semidarkness. He clicks on a flashlight, hands it to me, then clicks one on for him.

The warehouse looks exactly like it did when I was here last week with Matteo, Rideout, and Agent Sosa, minus the fifty-odd police officers who were there that day. Everything is neat and orderly. I don't see anything or anyone who would indicate the White Rabbit is here, or any arrows to follow. I limp through the stacks of boxes and pallets to the general area where I stood with Matteo before. The floor is empty of the big crates, instead filled with towering plastic-wrapped boxes. "Stuff has moved."

It doesn't help that I don't know what I'm looking for, if anything.

"But you said you saw the guys were *unloading* boxes? Boxes, not crates of drugs? If they were with the drug ring, wouldn't they be picking up the crates to sell or loading them into a boat like you said?"

"That's what Matteo said too. I don't know. I'm still trying to figure this out too." I trail off as I walk around the plastic-wrapped tower and spot something down the large row of boxes. It's a large black arrow drawn onto the side. Usually I wouldn't have paid it any mind, but it's the first arrow I've seen. "I see an arrow."

There's a second arrow farther down the row, and a third that points halfway down another plastic-wrapped tower at a smaller stack of boxes.

"Don't touch anything," Lawrence warns as I use my flashlight to pick my way across to the boxes. "Especially if the DEA uses this as a sting to catch the person who comes for these."

"I can't tell, but I think these are the same kinds of boxes I saw the guys loading out of the truck the night of the explosion." I turn and sweep my light to the left. No more arrows to be seen. "But if the trucking company wasn't picking up the drugs from the bust and was just dropping off boxes, *why* was the Golden Arrow here?" I sigh and run a hand over my head, which skews the wig. The sound of a door shutting comes from another part of the building, and I freeze, a cold sweat forming on my brow. Lawrence and I both click off our flashlights.

When the sound doesn't repeat, a sneaking suspicion dawns. I whisper frantically to L, "What if this is a setup by the Golden Arrow? What if he called the police to tell them we're here? I don't want to get caught for nothing." It could be *so* much worse than the Golden Arrow planting evidence on me in the hopes of Matteo discovering it. The Golden Arrow could be out-and-out framing me for the crimes.

Lawrence has ducked and is fiddling with the nearest box. *We don't have time for fiddling. We need to get out.* There's the sound of tape ripping away from cardboard, as loud as a gunshot in the silence.

"Are you opening boxes? I thought *you* said we shouldn't touch anything."

"This box says 'Genius Comics.'" Or I think that's what he says, given the flashlight clutched in his teeth.

"What?" I crouch beside him and take in the pile of boxes, all neatly marked with Genius Comics packing tape and form shipping labels.

"Did you know Genius uses this warehouse?" L asks.

"No. But this can't be a coincidence, right?"

This time I *definitely* hear something from within the warehouse, and we freeze again after clicking off our lights.

"Do you think someone's here?" I hate that my voice quavers. The police? Matteo? I should have thought twice about following some stupid scribble in a notebook. I rushed in full bore, per my usual, which is probably just what the Golden Arrow wanted me to do.

"Could be a night guard," Lawrence says, though I can tell he's placating me. His eyes are worried too. "We probably should leave." He looks briefly at his phone before shoving it into his pocket. "Shift probably starts at ten, and it's nine forty-nine."

I've stopped listening. I'm too busy leaning around Lawrence and peering at the box he opened. I click on the flashlight but keep my hand over the top to stop it from lighting up our area of the warehouse. "They're *Hooded Falcon* comics."

I reach in, expecting to meet the resistance of stapled spines, but they're loose pages. "What the heck? It's just the covers of the comics." Old-school tear sheets—the ones bookstores send back to prove they haven't sold the comics. Returning the whole comic is too costly, so they just send back the cover torn off for a refund. I reach down to see if the whole box is made up of the single-page covers of *The Hooded Falcon* or if there are full comics at the bottom. My fingers encounter a different type of paper, or not really paper at all. I press harder, and it gives ever so slightly. A brick? Why would you put a brick at the bottom of a comic book tear-sheet box?

"I thought I said we needed to go, MG." The stack of boxes blocks us from the main aisle, but that doesn't stop a fidgety Lawrence from peering around them repeatedly.

Each time he looks, I'm sure we'll be discovered, but I can't stop now. "In a second. Give me your phone." I'm frantically pulling the tag off the box Lawrence opened.

"Use yours."

"Mine slid down my boot, and it's at my ankle. Give me yours."

"MG—"

I'm positively frantic now, and I have weird tremors running through my legs. I'm panting like I've just run an Iron Man. "I need to take a picture. I think this is it. This is *the* thing we're going to find," I hiss at him. Finally I feel the weight of his phone in my hand. "Are we clear? No one is around?"

"Well, not that I can see, but, MG, I worked security for years. I think we need to go. Now. Before the shift for the guards starts."

I flick up the camera icon on his screen and start madly fiddling with the functions of the camera. "Okay. I need five seconds, and then we can get out of here."

"Five seconds to what?" he asks as I take pictures of everything around us in rapid succession, the flash on the phone blinding us in the process. "Oh shit, girl. Warn a queen before you do something like that and get us caught."

I blink tears from my eyes as I blindly snap one more picture. We pause as a door closes somewhere. Footsteps.

I want to pee my pants the way I did when I got stage fright in my third-grade musical. I don't deal with stressful situations well at all. "Oh my God, do you think they saw the light?"

"MG, the Martians saw the flash from that phone." His head swings frantically side to side, gauging the boxes around us.

The squawk of a radio and heavier footsteps approach. *Oh no, oh no, oh no.* I am going to jail. *We* are going to jail. And that's if this is a *cop*. If it's the White Rabbit . . . well, it's curtains for us.

I must have said that last part out loud because L answers, "Not if I can help it. Up."

"Up?"

"Up." He puts his hands under my butt and boosts me up. I scramble as quietly as possible on top of the towering stack of boxes wrapped in plastic and go still. Beside me I don't hear anything but a grunt, and suddenly L is on top of a taller stack of boxes.

Immobility is the name of the game. I'm an icicle. I'm a statue. I'm a box. I'm Trogdor's Halloween costume. I'm sitting on top of a stack of plastic, and if the guard below us looks up, what am I going to say? "Oh, uh . . . hi. Lovely day for warehouse tanning." The wig on my head is stifling, and I fight every urge in my body to scratch the itch on my nose.

Outside the warehouse, I hear a car backfire and tires screech, and a bright flash of headlights beams through the window as the car pulls a U-turn. I look over at L. We're completely exposed, lit up as bright as daylight. I can't breathe. My muscles feel weak and stiff at the same time. And the bridge of my nose itches something fierce, impossible to ignore.

Directly below the stack I'm sitting on, someone coughs. Then the radio crackles to life again. "It's just kids spinning doughnuts outside again. Maybe call patrol and have them cruise by."

I feel like I've heard that voice before. I chance a look down. The guard looks an awful lot like the cop who took Casey Junior's statement. What is his name? Officer James?

Why would Officer James be working guard duty on a building the police aren't supposed to be watching anymore?

We sit there as he walks around the boxes, scuffing his feet. My heart is in my throat, my ears rushing and ringing with my pulse. My drink from the party threatens to make a repeat appearance.

Several long minutes pass, and just as I'm getting ready to break, a phone rings below us. Officer James answers with a clipped hello, then silence.

"Yes, sir, the boxes are here. Pickup at eleven o'clock." A pause. "No, sir, nothing out of the ordinary." A third pause, and this time the voice is lower and shaky when it replies. "I took care of it, sir. Made it look like he hung himself in jail. I don't think he'll be making his plea bargain anymore. I would say his father has been adequately warned about the dangers of discussing this matter with the police."

A fresh wave of nausea crashes over me. My fingers clench in reaction, and it's everything I can do to keep still and quiet. Lawrence must read it on my face because his eyes narrow to slits, and he shakes his head as forcefully as he can while lying on a pile of teetering boxes.

"Yes, sir, wire it to my offshore. Thank you." A click.

Oh my *God*. Officer James has killed someone. Someone in custody. Someone whose father needed warning about working with the police, and someone whose plea bargain was to trade information about the White Rabbit. It must have been Huong Yee. Son of the printing press owner. The kid who was going to out a cop and testify about the White Rabbit. *Bastard.*

Footfalls slowly fade, and I begin to breathe again. Feeling comes back to my fingers and toes as my oxygen reaches normal levels. After a few moments of intense silence, I hear Lawrence slide down, then feel a hand on my leg.

I step into his palms and, like some sort of ill-trained acrobat, manage to turn my ankle again, landing with my stomach on his head, then fall halfway down his back before he can catch me and right us both.

"You are a terrible cat burglar," L says as he pulls me toward the illuminated exit sign.

"I like to think of myself as a corgi burglar. I don't like cats." Corgis aren't graceful either.

He uses his phone to look at the door, then pushes through, pulling me after him, and we spill out into the night air. It's thick with the smell of burning rubber and exhaust. Somewhere inside the building, a sound rings out of the dark. An impossibly loud beeping.

"Come on, we need to go. Now. That must have been a fire exit. We just set off an alarm."

In the distance, a police siren wails to life.

I'm already limping down the street toward the car when L spins me around, grabs my hand, and starts running the opposite way. "Never lead them directly to your car! We'll go two blocks up and then two over, and then double back."

I'm out of breath already as we dash down side streets and through alleys. I'm sure we make as much noise as two bulls in a china shop, but we don't stop.

"Is that something you learned as a security guard?" I ask.

"No, it's something I learned from breaking up with dramatic men."

Lawrence huffs and puffs too as we sprint across the main street.

Twenty minutes later, I'm drenched in sweat, I have insta-blisters all over both feet, my ankle is on fire, my wig is tucked into the top of my shirt, and we *finally* circle back around to the car. It's untouched behind the dumpster, and truth be told, I'm glad we parked several blocks from the warehouse in question. It would have taken either a stroke of genius or a large police force to have searched this well already.

I slide into the driver's seat and coax the engine to life. Sputtering, the Millennium Turd makes a less-than-spectacular exit from the alley, and soon we're on our way home.

Lawrence slumps against the passenger window, already stripped down to his sparkly black T-shirt. I can tell he's not impressed with my sleuthing skills. More than unimpressed. He seems out and out ticked. "We're in trouble. I want you to take me home."

"I know. Lawrence, that guard is a cop. I saw him at the station with Matteo. He's got access to all of Matteo's stuff. He's going to know you worked for Casey. He's going to hear your interview. I . . . I think he killed a suspect, a *kid,* Lawrence. He killed a kid to keep him from talking."

"What you found in there had better be worth it, girl. This is *bad*."

I flip his phone to him as I skid around a curve. "Here, look through what I took. There's something in the bottom of that box. Those are tear sheets. They come back to Genius when comics are unsold as proof that the books have been destroyed. They're trash. They're counted, then discarded. There shouldn't *be* anything else in those boxes."

Lawrence flicks through his phone, scanning the pictures. He stops on one, then sits back. "That's cash. That's a big brick of cash."

"In a box of comics?"

"This has to be how they're moving the drugs around. MG, they're using your comics. My guess is they pack their product in these boxes after the comics are printed, send the boxes to China, sell the drugs, then send back the tear sheets with the cash. It's brilliant, really." The Yees *are* a part of this. They bought into the printing press so they could package the drugs with the comics bound for Asia. Didn't Ryan say just the other week that the comic was selling gangbusters overseas? Maybe not quite as well as heroin.

I nod slowly. "I need a name. I need *proof*, because if I show up at the LAPD with these pictures, guaranteed you and I are dead. Officer James isn't working alone. I *need* the other journals. Casey Junior thinks that his father named his murderer in them. You told me Casey Senior was amassing evidence against someone. I need it to prove that he was going to unmask the White Rabbit. It's got to have his *name* on it."

The journals. Everything comes down to a dead man's journals that have been missing for thirty years. And given the fact that I came face-to-face with our mystery man in Casey Senior's office, the Golden Arrow is looking for the evidence too. I wasn't sure what the Golden Arrow's game plan was upon finding them, but given the fact that he or she set fire to a building, I'm not sure murder is off the table. Either way, I need those journals first.

And now . . . well, I've probably tipped my hand to the White Rabbit too. If Matteo tells his team that he thinks I have the journals, the double agent will leak the information. The White Rabbit will then be looking for the journals, and for me, to get rid of us both. I need to get ahead of this thing. "How can I beat the Golden Arrow at this game when I've been two steps behind this whole time?"

Lawrence taps his chin. "If it were me, I'd put the journals in plain sight. Somewhere someone wouldn't expect. Not in a safe, but inside a boring book or something."

Think, think, think, MG. What was in the office? What would Casey Junior miss for *thirty years*? In the comic book, stuff was hidden behind a painting, in a wall safe. We *saw* the wall safe. It's the most obvious place to look. And it was behind a painting. Something shifts in my mind, just like something *shifted inside the frame when we moved it.* At the time, I thought it was a broken frame, but now I'm wondering if Casey Senior's spirit is reaching out yet again and delivering the story line.

Matteo said many of the paintings were being shipped to the charity auction at the San Diego Comic-Con. This is the connection between the two story lines. The printing press. The comic book, the painting, the wall safe. I guarantee the Golden Arrow is going to be at that auction, and so are we. In fact, I'm going to make sure the Golden Arrow is there, and the White Rabbit too. We're going to catch them and end this thing once and for all.

"I have a plan."

Lawrence nods as if he's been expecting it. "I'll call in my crew. You're not doing this alone."

I need to find that painting and whatever Casey Senior hid inside, and lucky for me, I'm already going to compete in the Miss Her Galaxy fashion competition. Perfect alibi.

CHAPTER 24

"You're sure that they'll find us?" I'm scanning the crowd outside the convention center, barely able to keep my tired eyes open. I've been up past midnight the last few nights putting the finishing touches on the six feet of sequined glory I've created for Miss Her Galaxy. My Band-Aided fingers tell the cautionary tale of sewing tulle while narcoleptic.

The crush of zany characters takes my breath away, costumes from every corner of geekdom. In our plain clothes, we're pretty much mosquitoes among a butterfly gathering: boring and invisible to everyone else.

"Girl, you worry too much. It's like gaydar. Queens can find each other anywhere."

Once L agreed to my plan, he insisted his drag family were the perfect ones to pull this off. And look fabulous doing it. I glance to the side, where Ryan is still getting a selfie with an amazingly adapted steampunk Legend of Zelda character. We weren't in line twenty minutes before he put our fangirling to shame. For all that he argued about coming, Ryan has already filled half his phone storage with pictures.

"Like a kid in a candy shop," Lawrence confirms, looking over my shoulder. The line shuffles forward, and we dutifully follow. I'm on pins and needles for so many reasons, I kind of feel like throwing up now that I'm forced to be mostly still in line for our badges. Kinda like that time I had three butterbeers, then went on the Flight of the Hippogriff at the Wizarding World of Harry Potter. Barf city.

"What did you end up telling Ryan? You didn't tell him . . . all of it, did you?" I eye Lawrence. I also can't help but go back to my last conversation with Matteo, where he all but told me he suspected Ryan of being the Golden Arrow. I almost convinced him—and myself—that it's impossible. Yet . . . Ryan and I haven't talked about our conversation at the gala either. Ryan has basically been MIA since the gala, though I saw him at work a few times. I've also been busy: watching the news, preparing for my fashion show, brainstorming with L, and actively avoiding Matteo while I'm meddling in his investigation . . . Well, I didn't have the time to track Ryan down to talk. In fact, this is already the most I've seen of Ryan in a week.

Lawrence makes a sound of disapproval in the back of his throat. "I said I wouldn't, didn't I? I just had him tell his girlfriend that our drag family does a mean after-party show. She pulled a few strings, and now the official Homage to Todrick Hall Disney Queens will be featured at the Genius Comics After-Party. Oh! There they are!" Lawrence raises his arm and waves.

"I still can't believe they found you badges. I bought mine in March."

"It pays to be me sometimes," Lawrence answers with a sassy hip toss. Even in his dark denim jeans and Captain America tee—whom L insists is a closet queen because, *girl*, have you seen his hair?—Lawrence manages to look perfectly put together and ever-so-slightly sultry.

"Okay, so you remember our main job today is to check out the auction items and get ready for the show." I'm chewing my nails to the quick now. This all has to go *perfectly*. Everything I've set up. Everything I've gambled and guessed on. All of my hopes wrapped up in the fashion design competition that brought me here. Everything.

"Recon. Check." Lawrence gives me a salute.

The line moves forward again, and I hold out my ID to the guy at the gate. No big deal. MG Martin. Undercover vigilante-hero-apprehender and hopeful fashion maven. Lawrence and Ryan follow, and soon we're standing inside the arched glass–ceilinged lobby of the convention center.

Lawrence looks around, using his height to his advantage. "Now all we're missing is my family."

"Darling!" Lawrence is swooped up in a hug from behind by a tall black queen whom I instantly peg as Lawrence's infamous drag mother. She's tall, thinner than L, and her close-cropped curls are dyed a platinum blonde.

I catch sight of another figure behind Shwanda before turning my attention to Lawrence. I guess it's probably one of L's drag family, though I don't recognize him.

L looks positively adoring introducing his Mother. "MG, Ryan, I'd like you to meet Shwanda."

"Shwanda Knuts," she says, extending a regal hand first to Ryan then to me. Rings glitter on every finger, bracelets jangle at her wrists, and a huge gold chain rests against the neck of her black eighties jumpsuit. Shwanda may not be in full costume, makeup, or character, but there's no missing that this queen is full-time fierce. Man or woman, *always* Shwanda.

"I can't believe we haven't met yet—either of you—after hearing so much about you, Ms. Knuts," I gush, trying to take in the spectacularness that is the drag mama.

"Just Shwanda, if you please. Like Cher. And this is Vince, or Amy Blondonis." Shwanda motions to an extremely tall and angular white guy, who I'm ashamed to admit I thought was a person waiting for another group. He's got intensely pale-blue eyes and is tattooed from head to toe. He looks nothing like a queen in a white T-shirt, baggy jeans, and a hat turned backward. Unlike the bubbly Shwanda, Vince is silent. He's intense. I can see why Lawrence invited him for a crime-solving mission.

I paste a cheery smile on my face even though I've literally never been this nervous in my life. It's not just the show that might make my new career. It's Matteo and the message I left him. It's the fact that I'm banking on Rideout being a leak. It's that I've based all of this on a rattle in a frame in a dead guy's office. "Okay, so are we ready to look at the exhibition hall?"

"I was born ready, darling." Shwanda kisses my cheek before bustling off toward the doors to the trade show.

"She's really something," I say to Lawrence as we trail behind. "But what about Vince?"

"Oh, that's just Vince. He's really quiet as a man, but he has the best singing voice as a queen. He's our secret weapon for the after-party."

As much as I'd like to keep our group together, it proves considerably difficult, bordering on impossible. We're pushed and pulled apart by the crowd, and two kids dressed as minions literally run between us. Then there's the draw of the shopping. The second Lawrence sets sights on the clothing alley, he squeals, "Ooo! Vintage bustiers!" and dashes off to the left.

I turn to Ryan. "Well, so much for—" But Ryan's already wandering away toward the large game banners that hang over the middle of the exhibition space. Likewise, Shwanda and Vince have dispersed. And I'm left all alone, swept along by the churning crowd, surrounded by life-size pink Wookiees, enough *Star Trek* uniforms to fill the *Enterprise*, hobbits, gremlins, and sexy gaming characters I don't recognize by name. The sights and sounds bombard my senses, the huge banners flying overhead catnip for every sort of nerd delight. A convincing droid walks behind me, and I hear her say to her companion, "You know, next year I think I'm going to do crossover cosplay. Maybe R2-D2 Wonder Woman."

I close my eyes, hold out my hands, take a deep breath, and let it out. For everything else that's going on . . . these are my people. I feel like I've come home.

I make my way through the clothing vendors to the heart of the exhibition hall, where I can see the Genius banner among some of the largest displayed. The superhero heart of the con beats large and strong this year. I fight the urge to stop and take pictures every four steps; people have taken Genius characters and created costumes that any designer would covet. As much as I'm anxious about the case, habit takes over. Cons for me are about costumes. And fabric. I feel that familiar pull, and I decide that it's okay to give in for just a little while. The auction isn't until tomorrow.

As I approach the sprawling Genius booth itself, a Red Cardinal costume literally stops me in my tracks. The Red Cardinal has her own series, but she's best known as the on-again–off-again love interest of the Hooded Falcon. This costume is beyond gorgeous—layers of red feathers create a striking one-shoulder gown bodice and gradually give way to pinned and tucked layers of bloodred ruched silk cut through with silvery, gauzy fabric. I might be drooling, and I am definitely stopping traffic.

"I love your dress," I can't help myself saying.

I'm absolutely mesmerized by the creation she's wearing, and I'm not the only one. All around her people are taking pictures. She's essentially holding court.

"Thank you." She smiles, and I move my fangirling upward from her gorgeous dress to the intricate way her glossy black hair piles around a jeweled circlet, complete with a bejeweled cardinal. Then I see her face. I take a step back, muffling an oath. Of course it would be perfect Lelani, ex-fiancée of the guy I may or may not be falling in love with.

"Oh, MG. Good to see you. What are you up to?" Andy appears behind Lelani, dressed in dark jeans and a black T-shirt that says "Genius Comics" across the front. I need to get my head back in the game of solving a thirty-year-old murder case.

"I was just telling Lelani how wonderful her costume is." I brush my hands on my dark skinny jeans and face Andy. "I didn't know you were working the booth this year. I thought it was mostly marketing people."

"I volunteered." It's Andy's turn to turn red, accentuated by his light-colored surfer curls. "You know, to help our company since now I'm . . ." His face pinkens as he trails off. Now that he's an executive. "I wanted to be here in case Lelani had questions or can't answer a fan since I've worked at Genius forever." Andy tries to act like he hasn't been staring at her ample cleavage, but hell, who *wouldn't* stare at Lelani? She's like a Pacific Island princess in that dress.

"I should get going," I say to them both.

Lelani waves, her smile not quite reaching her eyes. "I'm looking forward to seeing your work in the Her Galaxy show. It's my favorite event. And you'll be at the charity auction tomorrow, right?"

Behind us, someone calls for Lelani from the main Genius booth. I can't see who through the piles of clothes and toys and stands of comic books spilling into the aisleway.

"If you'll excuse me," Lelani says before turning and walking back to the booth in a cloud of red silk and feathers.

"Wow," I say, marveling at the train of the dress, which has hand-stitched feathers attached.

"Yeah," Andy agrees, his tone dreamy.

I cut him a glance. "I was talking about the dress."

A pause. "Yeah. Me too."

I debate about telling Andy that Ryan and Lelani are an item, but I'm not feeling *that* friendly toward Andy yet. "Come on, let's go back to the booth. I need information about the auction." I steer him between Captain Genius T-shirts and a stack of Justice League action figure sets. I need to find out where the auction items are being kept. That is Genius inside information.

I follow Andy into the main part of the booth where there are other costumed Genius characters posing with fans. Captain Genius is particularly popular this year since a movie just released a few months ago. The line to take pictures with him stretches into the aisle. Beyond that, a few of our popular characters mingle, including the new Hooded Falcon in his garish multicolored armorlike gear. Lelani returns to her line, fans waiting to take pictures with her.

"Hey, Tej." I grab a schedule off the back table and scan it until I find the auction set at 6:00 p.m. tomorrow. It's going to be tight to get there from the fashion show in enough time. A light turns on in my head. That's the *perfect* excuse. And the truth. "I want to come to the auction tomorrow. I'm hoping to get something for my personal collection. But I have the fashion show."

Tej nods. He's the only one of four people working the Genius booth whom I recognize. I feel a pang of nostalgia. Even though I worked hard to get to the point where I can enjoy cons instead of work them, I miss the camaraderie. I do *not* miss the requisite XXL black T-shirt emblazoned with "Genius Comics" they have to wear.

"I was hoping I could see the stuff that's getting sold. In case I need to have someone bid for me."

"Oh yeah, no problem." Tej pushes his thick-rimmed glasses up his nose.

"Really?"

"Yeah, there's this really handy catalog . . ." His voice is muffled as he digs under the back table. "Ah. Here it is." He hands me a three-ring binder with pages of pictures and descriptions in it.

"Oh." I try to look pleased. "Yay. Perfect. Thanks, Tej." Inside, my stomach sinks. I really need to inspect the items themselves. I stand at the back table for a stretch thumbing through the binder. First editions, action figures, set pieces from the first TV adaptation—there really are some interesting items being sold, but I'm looking for something specific. The painting with the frame that went clunk. I hand the binder back to Tej.

"So what ballroom is it in? You know, so I can get there after my show?"

Tej points toward a far wall. "I think it's over there. Andy helped them set up yesterday. He would know. Oh hey, that kid is messing with those toys again. Little bastards." Tej bolts to the front of the booth, where someone is perilously close to toppling a stack of figurine boxes.

I glance at the schedule and note the ballroom number. Wading across the sea of people, I make my way over to the bank of doors on the other side of the hall. "One-oh-two, one-oh-three . . ." *Crap.* Standing in front of the door to ballroom 103 is a uniformed security guard. I think he's meant to look like he's casually placed there, watching the con, but I know better. And I'm going to need a way to get around him. I head to room 102 and jiggle the handle. Locked.

"And just what do you think you're doing?" a voice comes from behind me.

Busted. I whirl to find a smirking Lawrence.

I gasp, hand over my heart. "You scared the bejesus out of me."

"Well, you're not going to get anywhere looking as guilty as you do."

"Thanks for the pro tip," I mutter.

"What did you find out?"

"The auction goods aren't at the Genius booth like I hoped. They already set up the auction in ballroom 103, which has a guard. So I'm going to get into this one and try to get to 103 from inside."

"Nope. Not going to work."

"Why on earth not?"

Lawrence shifts some bags in his hands. He's been busy shopping already. "Because, like I said, you look too guilty. Best way to do this is straight on."

He digs in his bags and produces a thick pair of black lensless frames.

I try to look merely confused instead of annoyed as hell, which is how I feel. "Clark Kent glasses? I'm wearing my contacts today, and I don't see how this will get us past a guard."

He shrugs and, without asking permission, pulls out a purple pashmina and wraps it around my shoulders. "If we have to try getting in another way, it will be harder to determine you're the same person. We'll just switch your costume . . . Oh, that damn hair." He glances up at the recognizable shock of blue. Rummaging around in the bag, he produces a too-big black top hat, which he puts on my head in a pushed-back manner.

"I look ridiculous."

"It's Comic-Con. You look downright normal."

Touché. I roll my eyes at him, square my shoulders, and march up to the guard. He eyes me as I approach.

"Hello," I say in my best businesslike manner. "Andy sent me over to check one of the auction items." I reach under the pashmina and pull out my Genius lanyard displaying my picture ID.

The guard shifts on his feet. "I'm not supposed to let anyone in."

"And you're doing a fine job." *Jerk.* I smile. Time to unleash the Force. My "these aren't the droids you're looking for" tactic. "It's okay. I can come back later. Or I could go get Lelani to talk to you. Would that work? Or Edward Casey. He's the one who wants me to check to make sure one of the items wasn't damaged." I'm inventing wildly at this point and decide to add humor. "I could go get a teacher's note from him if you need."

The guard hesitates.

"It will take three seconds," I say, sensing weakness. "Andy says one of the frames might have cracked in transport. We might have to fix it before the auction tomorrow. But like I said, I can come back later if you need a note or something."

He saw my badge. He knows I work for Genius. He wavers and finally steps aside. "A few minutes?"

"Or less," I say, doing my best to keep a straight face. "I appreciate your diligence. We wouldn't want anything in here to go missing."

I slip through the door and into the dark, quiet ballroom. In here, the buzz from the hall is diminished, sounding like a faraway swarm of bees. A row of covered folding tables is set up on the stage, lined with various groups of items, each one with an official-looking placard describing the lot. I waste no time ascending the stairs, bypassing the podium, and walking quickly down the line of elements.

My fingers itch to touch everything, including early editions of *The Hooded Falcon*. Signed pen-and-ink drawings on card stock. I'm passing the first large framed piece when I hear a noise in the room. Instantly I am on alert, and I straighten.

"Find anything?"

Guard Guy pokes his head into the room and regards me uneasily. I can tell he's still not sure he should have let me in.

I make a show of pointing to the large framed piece in front of me. It's the same one that sat behind Casey Senior's desk, and the last time I saw it, it was on the floor of Casey's office. Thor's hammer, the sight of it has me buzzing with excited energy. "I think this is the one Andy told me about. I'm just going to have to inspect it for damage." I brandish my phone, turn on the flashlight function, and proceed to check over the frame front and back, hoping the guard will get the hint and leave again.

Instead, he walks up the dark aisle toward the stage. No, no, no. I cannot properly look at this frame with him in the room. I feel like crying. I'm *this close*.

It's going to be hard to fake a damaged frame if it looks perfect.

"Oh, I see what you're looking at," he says, motioning to the frame.

He does? I blink. "Oh yeah." I lean over the frame with my phone flashlight. "It's just easier to see with some light . . ." But he's right. From this angle, I notice that the black paper covering the back of the frame is torn. About the right size tear for someone to slip a journal through. My heart does a victory dance.

Not only my heart, but I execute a tiny shimmy of joy. I just cannot contain my excitement. "I, uh, just need to look inside and see if the cornice pieces are affected." I have no idea what I'm talking about, but I'm a writer. Making up stuff is my job. I make up monsters daily; surely I can fool one measly guard. "It's okay if the outer layer tears, but you don't want the protective layer to be punctured; the integrity of the structural layer holding the cornice pieces has to stay intact."

I'm positive he's going to call my bluff. He's most certainly the son of a professional painting framer. He probably knows what cornice pieces are, which I don't. I hold my breath.

"Oh *yeah,* that sounds serious."

"I'll just take a few pictures, and then I'll be on my way. We won't need to fix it if the structural layer still protects the art."

I use my pen to hold the torn piece away from the frame and snap a picture. There is *something* in there, but I don't want to pull it out in front of Guard Guy. I squint harder. The corner of a black journal is barely distinguishable inside the tear. I squint harder, thinking I make out a second black corner . . . so, possibly two journals. Not only that, I catch the flash of something manila colored. *Please, oh please, let that be Casey Senior's evidence.*

If it is, my plan will work. I texted Matteo yesterday and told him there is a journal in the memorabilia, possibly inside this picture, and that I am worried about it going to auction and will try to buy it. If he behaved as expected, he'd have told the whole team—most importantly Rideout—and the information would get to the White Rabbit. Hopefully the Golden Arrow too. All the players in this chess game would be present. All I have to do is sit back and see who's intent on bidding for the painting that only a few select people *know* contains a journal. Brilliance, if I do say so myself.

"So is it bad?" The guard's face hovers right next to mine now. I can't let him see the journal.

"Nope. No. Not at all. Just a little tear. Nothing to worry about. This piece won't need to be touched. Or fixed. By anyone. At all. I took a picture for insurance purposes, so we're all good here." I tap my phone importantly. The last thing I need is Andy coming in and fiddling with the frame. I nearly drag Guard Guy out of the room with me.

"Well?" Lawrence pounces on me the minute I wave at the guard and walk back toward the Genius booth.

"I found it." I can hardly keep my voice steady. I manage to stop shaking long enough to pull up the picture on my phone and zoom in. It's no work of art, but the picture *does* show the spines of the journals. Bazinga. "And I sure hope you're going to buy me dinner because I'm going to have to spend a year's salary to win it at auction. And now it's time to focus on the fashion show because there's nothing much more we can do until tomorrow."

"What happens if you don't win the journals?" Lawrence is frowning now.

"We have to win. That's what Operation Janeway is all about. And if we don't, well, I hope you like wearing orange."

CHAPTER 25

The wheels of the suitcase I'm dragging protest against the concrete ramp outside the Hyatt hotel, just next door to the convention center. "What did you pack in here? Bricks?" The bag in question lurches side to side as we level off near the lobby, and I drop the second bag slung over my shoulder.

"That's my makeup case, so be *careful* with it."

"L, you packed an entire suitcase of makeup? I packed one bag total." I open the door for L and hold it as he wheels in the rolling garment hanger we snagged from the valet.

"The next time you're the star of a fashion show and responsible for the future of a talented designer, you can let me know how much makeup *you* pack."

"L, we're in a competition. There isn't a 'star.'"

"So you say. I look so delicious in this thing. Everyone else is just a side dish." He eyes me over the oversize garment bag holding the wig. "But I promise to share the spotlight with you, sugar."

I chortle as we walk down the deeply padded floral carpet, following the signs to the fashion show backstage. My stomach is a mess of knots, and not just because I'll be racing to an auction after my show to apprehend a criminal. That should be enough, but I've spent months prepping for this, plus the cost of travel, and my future plans to go into business for myself hinge on today's results. I'll either leave with valuable feedback about areas I need to work on as a designer, or I could leave with the offer to help a well-known chain of stores develop a line of geek clothing for their customers. Either way, this contest is a launching point for MG version 3.0.

My fingers inch their way to my phone, and I find it in my hand, Matteo's number pulled up. For the fifth time in the same number of minutes, I stick it back in my pocket. I want to know if he's coming. I want to know if he's mad I'm here and I'm pulling strings on the case. I want to know if the information has been leaked. I need to play this cool, but it's damn hard.

"Come on, L." I stop outside the backstage door and show my badge, my ID, and my pass for the fashion show. "Let's go get you dressed."

I survey L's final touches on the drag makeup and breathe a huge sigh of relief and appreciation. Latifah Nile is a vision. Well, if Ursula the Sea Witch can be a vision instead of a nightmare.

All around us, girls are scrambling to finish costumes, stitch pieces that have come loose, touch up mascara. The nervous energy is unreal. I haven't had much time to talk to the other designers; we're all focused on helping our creations look spectacular.

"You're freaking out." It's not a question. L looks at me in the rectangular mirror that is propped on the folding table given to us by the fashion show. "Look at me. *Look at me*, Michael-Grace Martin. You've got this. *We've* got this. This is who we are, and that's all we can be today, okay? We've got *all* of this."

I let out a breath. L isn't just talking about the show. It's the auction. The case. Matteo. My job. So much at stake everywhere. "How do you know exactly what I'm thinking?"

"Because I know you." Latifah squeezes my shoulders, then turns back to the mirror to fluff her spectacularly tall wig.

"Michael-Grace Martin and . . . Latifah Nile?" The crew member reading our names stumbles over L's and gives us a double take. I don't blame her. With the wig, L is six foot five of sea-witch fashion fabulousness.

"Let's go," I mutter, straightening my own simple white pantsuit, accented with bright-blue stilettos, a chunky gold necklace, and my fire-engine-red glasses. The blue has faded in my hair, but I dabbed in some blue powder near the roots this morning for an intense ombré effect. Though I wear my makeup more toned down than Lawrence's, I've penciled in my lighter brows with a blue tint and wear blue-purple lipstick. My battle armor is on, and I'm ready to go kick some ass.

We wait for what seems like forever in a decidedly *unglamorous* back hallway while the show proceeds in the ballroom. Slowly our line inches forward, and finally it's our turn.

"Right in here. Watch your . . . hair." A girl dressed in black and carrying a clipboard holds open a side door in the hallway so L can duck slightly into the well-lit runway. The glare of the lights blocks most of my vision of the large ballroom, but it doesn't matter. I watch every strutting step Latifah takes up and down the catwalk. She *owns* it like no other model could. My Ursula the Sea Witch costume looks fantastic under the lights. The bodice is hand-dyed black-green tulle with glitter, woven and overlapped to create the effect of seaweed around the neckline. The frothy neckline gives way to a leather bustier with shell buttons up the front and laces up the back, giving Latifah an even fuller figure. The leather wraps over L's hips, giving way to a sexy, seductive mermaid-style skirt, green parachute material peeking through the darts just enough to look like seaweed underneath sheathed tentacles.

At the end of the catwalk, L executes a perfect spin, revealing the last surprise of the costume. The skirt flares out at the bottom in points, mimicking tentacles reaching out. The crowd breaks into applause, and L grins as she shimmies back toward me. I cannot fathom this costume on any other person. L embodies my vision for it perfectly.

We're the last runway model, so we don't have too long to wait until we're all called back up onstage to showcase the amazing costumes shown. The bright stage lights are glaring, and I can't really see many people past the front row. I wonder briefly if the Golden Arrow is in attendance, watching me.

We stand up front while the judges tally their votes, and I lean in to L. "So we're all set? For afterward?"

"Everyone's dressed in their appropriate costumes and ready for action."

The host, Auburn Elo—well-known geek fashion maven and my personal hero right now—approaches the mic. Her voice booms out as she thanks the audience for attending and announces that there will be two winners. The judges' pick and the audience pick.

"The judges' pick is . . ."

I hold my breath. I can imagine her saying my name. Several times over.

"Kelsey Maya, for the Black Widow!"

The crowd yells, but I deflate. I didn't win. Tears fill my eyes. Everything I've done. Everything I've worked for. But I square my shoulders, a ray of sunshine breaking through the clouds. This isn't the end. I'm still *here*. I still did this, and I'm still going to do this as a business. This exposure can only help me, even without a crown. I don't need any more proof that I should take a chance on myself. L is hugging me fiercely. I pat her arm.

"I'm sorry, L," I say.

"What are you talking about?" She picks me up and swings me around. "Aren't you listening? We just won the Audience Favorite!"

I look around in astonishment. Latifah hugs me to the glue-scented tulle neckline of her dress, and I am shocked to find I'm crying. Zero to sixty. I'm so excited and happy. Everything is a blur of disco lights, thumping music, and happy tears.

"We won!" I say, leaning against the wall backstage and closing my eyes. I don't even care that it wasn't the judges' favorite. My heart doesn't know the difference. I'm basking in the euphoria of knowing I'm *finally* on the right track scaling back on the writing and pursuing costuming. It's not what I ever planned, but it feels like the universe gives its nod of approval. In a world of mortals, I most definitely feel like Wonder Woman right now.

"I wish we had time to soak it in." L's already at the makeup station, though she's not disrobing like I thought she would be. "Vince just texted me and said that someone wearing a T-shirt with a golden arrow painted on it just walked into the auction and asked about the painting."

Right. That whole freaking fate-of-the-world thing. *Crap.* No big deal, I just won my first national fashion competition, but I still have hidden journals to buy, a masked avenger and a murderer to identify, and a man to win over.

"It's like sardines in here," L mutters as we push our way into the packed ballroom for the auction. Edward Casey Junior is already onstage, introducing the curator for the museum, who will be retaining one of the pieces and gaining the charitable funds.

My gaze sweeps the crowded room, already too warm, or maybe that's from my sprint over here. The first queen I spot is Shwanda, L's drag mama, dressed as much like a security guard as L and I could costume her on short notice. She's standing along the back wall, looking official and important, and meets my eye immediately. She motions with a nod toward one section of the room, so I pull L along with me through the crowd.

It takes a bit to get there, and by the time I locate two empty seats, Edward Casey Junior finishes his speech. I face forward and groan. He's shaking hands and posing for a photograph with the piece he's donating to the museum, and it's the large print. The one with the journals in it. Donated, *not* for auction. I apparently misread the stupid booklet Tej had given me. Dammit.

They set the painting—nay, my carefully placed criminal trap, now rendered *useless*—to the side, and the auction starts in earnest.

"This is all wrong," I say to L. I feel crushing defeat for the second time in as many hours. "That's it. This plan will never work now. I won't be able to see who bids on it because nobody gets to."

Someone slides into the chair on my left, and I whip my head to the side, ready for combat. My adrenaline and nerves are just about shot. "Ryan, you scared me stupid!"

"Sorry. Has the auction started? This place is a zoo." Ryan picks up on my nervous energy, evidenced by my fidgeting like a kindergartner on a Fruit Roll-Up high. I follow his gaze to Lelani, who's standing near Shwanda. Lelani's brows are pulled down, her face in a scowl. I'd be mad too if my huge dress kept me from being able to take a seat.

"No, it's just starting. You didn't miss anything." Except my plan to capture one or two suspects in my case going up in flames. Suddenly suffocating in my suit coat, I peel it off and toss it across the back of my chair. It leaves me in only my white silk camisole, but in this stifling room, I'd give anything to be wearing less. Or maybe it's nerves. Or both. I swallow noisily, panic rising in my throat.

L leans in, whispering so just I can hear, "Just sit tight. I'm sure we can get up there after the auction. We've got other problems. There are at least three Golden Arrows here."

"What?" My eyes scan the room, and dread fills my limbs.

There are several people here dressed like the Golden Arrow. The social superhero has been in the media long enough that people have made costumes based on it. Not that I'm even sure the Golden Arrow will be dressed like the Golden Arrow. There are Hooded Falcons in the crowd too. Considering this is a Hooded Falcon memorabilia auction, it's to be expected. And surely the White Rabbit won't be wearing a costume that says, "I'm a drug lord and murderer." I'm not sure why I thought I'd be able to pick them out.

I search for Amy Blondonis, the last queen on our private crew. I spot her by the back door, easy to pinpoint because of the copious tattoos on her person. The long half-black, half–icy blonde wig sticks straight with blunt bangs. It complements her huge fur stole and signature Cruella de Vil slinky black dress. Amy meets my eyes, and I suppress a shiver—I'm glad she's on our side; Amy is intense.

How are we ever going to identify anyone in here? There have to be a thousand people.

I turn forward and sink in my chair. An air of electricity charges in the room, and it doesn't have anything to do with the action figure that makes up the first lot at auction. "I guess we just wait and see," I say to L. "Something will work out; I feel sure of it. Hold your sweet black tauntauns. All hope isn't lost." *Or I'm wrong, and we're both in a huge pile of crap.*

A hush falls as the auctioneer steps up on the stage. Bidding starts, and I sneak looks around. No one seems particularly suspicious or familiar. Well, that I can tell anyway. One of the bidders is Groot, and I can't see even a bit of face.

"L, maybe you're right. With the costumes, I can't even tell who anyone is; this whole plan is a bust . . ." I trail off and turn to look behind me. A scuffle has broken out in the back among bidders. I'm not the only one to pause. The auctioneer slows the bidding, obviously unsure if he should continue. The scuffle increases in intensity. It's odd for a fight to break out *before* the auction has even really started. A chill snakes down my spine, and I get the inkling of an idea that this is no mere scuffle just seconds before the entire room plunges into darkness.

CHAPTER 26

Instantly, L pulls me to my feet. "Get to the door!" I can barely hear her over the screams of the patrons around me. I hear a strange whizzing as something flies by my head and an *ooof* as the item that grazes my head goes on to hit Ryan. Something sharp scrapes my face, and I feel the instant ooze of blood. Between this and the damn warehouse break-in, I am going to look like Deadpool when this is finished. I'm aware of Ryan climbing straight over the chairs in front of us, making his way to the stage. He seems pissed, which is so completely odd, I just stop and stare for a moment.

There's a brief loud ripping sound, then a crash and a thump that sounds a *lot* like someone falling off a chair onstage. *The hell?* This isn't in Operation Janeway anywhere.

L pulls my arm out of my socket, requiring me to climb over people to get out of our seats. All around me in the dark, mass hysteria reigns. Chairs clatter to the floor. I can only vaguely see L's form as we plow through the rest of the row into the aisleway. The emergency exit is the only source of light in the ballroom now.

The auctioneer tries feebly to calm people using the PA system, talking about an orderly exit, when all the lights flood back on. Pandemonium ceases; everyone freezes midflight. Chairs are everywhere, people and costume pieces scattered. The auctioneer waves a hand. "It's okay, it's okay. Someone just bumped the bank of lights. We can all settle down now and return to order."

I think I see Ryan hurtling past the hulking form of Casey Junior, sitting and moaning on the stage like he's been sucker punched in the dark.

"That was weird," I grouse, rubbing at my temple.

L is still on high alert. I can feel her vibrating next to me. "More than weird. That was a diversion. Look at the stage."

My eyes trail over the covered tables to the round one where they set the large print after the presentation. *My* print. The one with the journals and the evidence in it . . . or the remnant of what was once the beautiful piece. I gasp. *No, no, no.* The canvas sags open, a gaping slice straight through the middle. The top and bottom curl away, revealing the back of the frame. No journals. Nothing. Gone. But . . . I didn't see anyone. Not a White Rabbit. Not a Golden Arrow. Not a damn thing.

"The painting! The journals!" I spin to L. "What do we do?"

"Hang on." L looks to Shwanda's corner, then to the corner with Amy Blondonis. They exchange complicated hand gestures, and her shoulders relax a fraction. "Unless someone went through the ceiling, I don't think anyone made it through an exit. The girls gave me the all clear, which means the doors haven't been opened. The thief is still here."

And I still have a chance to slay this monster. Good thing I have my ass-kicking heels on. "I need to get to that microphone."

I make my way as fast as I can up the side of the stage and walk across to the auctioneer, who eyes me with alarm. It could be the blood oozing down my face. Or my disheveled appearance. Who knows?

"It's okay; I work for Genius. I need to make an announcement." I step up to the microphone and address the audience. "Someone call security. We need to keep the doors closed. One of the items has been destroyed, and the person responsible may have an item of interest—"

I don't even get to finish. There is a second scuffle, this time by the back door. Abandoning my announcement, I race to the edge of the stage in time to see the long blonde hair of Amy Blondonis diving into the center of a circle of costumed bystanders, her fingers grasping just shy of the shirt of a figure who bolts through the back door.

"L! We have to go! He's getting away!" I leap off the stage, only to find Latifah already racing through the crowd, her ample curves and ample height no match for the flummoxed herd of attendees. Behind me I hear several people take up the cry as they see the damaged painting, but we're already off and away, chasing after our villain.

"Which one is it? Arrow or Rabbit?"

"I don't know!" I'm yelling to be heard over the pandemonium as we careen around a group of six-foot dragons and scramble through the back door. Amy and Shwanda are in hot pursuit, just the glimpse of a figure up ahead, wearing a big black leather jacket and a black ball cap pulled low over the face.

I'm impressed at the speed Latifah manages in her five-inch stilettos. Mine are inches shorter, and I'm barely making muster. Amy Blondonis dodges costumed folks in the small hallway, yelling something I can't hear or understand.

"What do we do?" I gasp, already tiring. We're approaching the exhibition hall, and I groan inwardly. There's no way to track this person if they make it in there. We're sunk.

"In gaming terms, we are going to Leeroy Jenkins the *shit* out of this bitch," Latifah yells. "Hold my wig." She yanks the confection right off her head, exposing the wig cap as she runs, and throws it over her shoulder at me. "You find a way to navigate. I'm going to catch this mother." In an unbelievable burst of speed, L is at the heels of Amy Blondonis.

"Navigate. Navigate. I've got to *navigate*?" I'm not even sure what that means. Eyes on the ground, maybe? *Up.* I need to get up above to see the Golden Arrow. I need the Genius booth.

Not two seconds later, Shwanda screeches past, taking an alternate route. I hope L is trying to circle around to cover the other exits.

Yells and a large crash explode from within Artists' Alley, likely our villain having a hell of a time shaking Amy and Latifah. My suspicions are confirmed when a shout rises above the general murmur of the crowd and I see a booth topple not two hundred yards to my right.

I *need* to find something to climb on. My eyes alight on the huge Genius banner. It's held by a PVC frame and attached to the ceiling with cables. There is *no* way it's safe, but it's sitting on top of the booth, so I sprint for it.

"MG!" I hear my name shouted, but I can't spare time to look. I need to get eyes on the ground, and it needs to be *now*. Not even bothering to explain, I burst through the line of people waiting for pictures with characters, practically bowling over Captain Genius before I right myself and race to the back table.

Tej stands ramrod straight, his eyes round with fear. "MG, what the *hell* are you doing?"

I don't answer; I vault—well, really I slide and bounce—over the folding table into the back area and grab on to the booth frame.

"Lift me up." I pull Tej's arm.

"What? No! What the—" The last words are muffled because I've used the table to climb onto Tej's shoulders before hefting myself onto the roof of the booth. It sways underneath my feet, and I grab the PVC frame holding the banner, praying that it will hold my weight steady. It does, and I breathe a visceral sigh of relief, even with the floor swaying many feet below me.

I gather my bearings and recognize a huge Sea Witch racing down the next aisle. "Up here! L!" I frantically wave until Latifah looks up and catches sight of me.

"Which way?" Latifah searches the crowd in front of the Genius booth.

"I don't know! I . . ." I'm scanning the crowd and happen to catch sight of a dark jacket turning the corner. "Over that way! Artists' Alley, wearing a red top hat now!" The jacket looks to be the same size and shape as the one I saw in our chase.

Surely L can catch our thief. I have clear eyes on the figure, and we have hundreds of feet to the main entrance. I glance up again, pondering why the figure in the jacket doesn't seem to be going *toward* the main entrance, and freeze.

"Latifah! The fire exit! He's headed to the fire exit!" *There's no way L heard me.* I can't think of anything else to do, so I yell, "Stop that masked—er, hatted man!" I've always wanted to say that. Too bad we're in a *room* full of masked men. Chaos breaks out beneath me.

And now there's nothing left to do but shimmy down the booth, chuck my heels to the side, and sprint as fast as I can toward the fire exit.

It's not pretty. I'm tearing through booths, clothing and toys are flying everywhere, and I'm just yelling blanket apologies as I run. I careen around a corner and spot the fire door. No one has gone through yet, or the alarm would be ringing. I slide on the floor, intent on my goal. In front of me, a dark figure bursts through the back curtain of a booth and sails into the aisleway looking over his shoulder.

I glance too and see an irate Amy Blondonis hopping through the mess of a booth, her dress caught on the booth itself. Our thief in the jacket straightens, looks at the door, then bolts. I'm outdistanced and outpaced, and there's no way I can reach the figure before he's in the open.

"Stop!" I scream, nothing else at my disposal. I take a risk. "We know you're the White Rabbit! There are police outside that door. This is a setup!"

The hat turns in my direction, and the person's steps falter. It's enough to shift their focus to me, just enough time for L to save the day.

In slow motion, a monstrous Sea Witch rises from the tangled curtain of a booth. Latifah steps forward, holds her arm out the booth exit and across the narrow aisle, and clotheslines the fleeing thief. At the same time, a black stiletto heel flies in from the other direction, landing with a solid thunk against the back of our perpetrator's head. It's enough to knock the person to the ground, facedown on the carpet.

"That's right, *bitch*. You don't mess with Shwanda!"

Shwanda fishes Amy out of the crumpled booth, sans one shoe.

L is already using one of the belts from a clothing booth we demolished to truss up the victim.

The world rushes in, and I look around, realizing we've essentially stopped San Diego Comic-Con. There are at least five cell phone cameras pointed in our direction and not a small number of irate booth owners storming toward us.

"We need to call the police," I say.

"Shouldn't we look for the journals first? You know, since we're trying to use them to keep ourselves out of jail?" L's chest heaves, my gorgeous creation hanging half off her body. The costume looks like it's been hit by a tsunami.

"Right. Yes." I surge forward. I want those journals. I *need* those journals.

L grunts as she flips the squirming body on the ground over, then goes still. I pounce, searching the outside jacket pockets for the journals. For *anything* when I realize that L's not just waiting. She's . . . freaked out.

"What—" The words die on my lips the moment I see the criminal's face.

It's not Rideout. It's not Tony Munez. It's not even Officer James.

Her face.

Agent Sosa's dark-brown eyes meet mine from the floor. "Hello, Ms. Martin," she says conversationally. As if we've just run into each other in a bar and not run through countless booths and over countless Wookiees in a chase scene that should be in some campy meta musical episode of *Supernatural*.

But it doesn't make any sense. Why would Agent Sosa be involved in this? Did we tackle an officer giving chase by mistake? I don't think so. Why would *she* want the journals? My first inclination is to let her up, but my gut churns. She's the *one* person I dismissed because she wasn't an integral part of Matteo's team. But she'd been at *every* scene with the DEA. And has access to the interviews and the *suspects. And probably Matteo's text about my suspicions of the painting at auction.* My heart flips over as I think about Song Yee. The dawning crashes like the space shuttle in *The Martian*—I want to hit my own head with my hand, but my hands are still splayed on her jacket, holding her down.

I don't have to wonder what to do for long, because from behind me a voice I recognize very, *very* well rises above the chaos.

"Don't *anyone* move. I'm Detective Kildaire of the LAPD, and as far as I'm concerned, *all* of you are under arrest."

CHAPTER 27

"Matteo!" I'm delighted and *mortified* to see him in front of me. "You came!" I note with distaste that Detective Rideout is present, along with a few other police wearing San Diego uniforms.

"Yes, I got your text . . . I also found you on a surveillance tape at a warehouse, as well as your fingerprints on some items of interest in a box of comic tear sheets. You failed to mention that when you told me about the painting."

I wince.

He spares me a quick glance, then back to Agent Sosa. His eyebrows shoot up as recognition dawns on his face.

"Kildaire, get this crazy woman off of me. We're in pursuit of a suspect; they tackled me by mistake." The police behind Matteo shuffle around, gearing up for action, instantly on alert for a person of interest.

"No, you *are* the suspect," I argue back, turning to Matteo. "Don't let her go. I promise I'm right." It makes sense. She had access to the drugs. She had access to the reports. Matteo asked her to watch Yee's interview, and she probably saw the Casey interview too. Enough to know we were on her trail. This explains her icy disdain for me at the party. How she didn't want me taking a picture of Anthony Munez. Maybe afraid I'd put two and two together and recognize the similar dark eyes, the same straight nose. Only I didn't. Not until now, when I could study her face up close. Sosa. A married name. I'd been looking for *one* White Rabbit, but she is the protégé—a family business. I remember the day James handed her a baggie at the warehouse. And when I heard Officer James admit to interfering in the case, potentially committing *murder*. And though I was wrong in assuming Rideout, I was right on all other counts.

Matteo's gaze rakes my face, taking in the blood covering my cheek. His shoulders relax momentarily when he realizes I'm not mortally wounded, but the royally pissed look doesn't take long to surface again. He helps me up, then squats down next to Sosa, placing a restraining hand on her back to keep her prone while he continues speaking. "I am going to give you thirty seconds to explain what went on here before you're all taken to the station. MG, you told me you wouldn't do anything stupid. Assaulting an officer qualifies as *really* stupid." There's no hint of a smile or smirk in his gorgeous hazel eyes.

I have to gather myself, heart hammering inside my chest. I'm surprised my ribs contain it. This is where the rubber meets the road. I need to lay it all out and hope Matteo believes me. Forgives me for doing it on my own. I take a breath and recap how I texted him to encourage the leak and lure the Golden Arrow and/or the White Rabbit to the auction.

The story tumbles from my lips. The auction, the chase.

"I was *attacked*," Sosa interjects. "I arrived just as the lights went out. Someone shoved me through that doorway. I was giving chase." She does have a lump rising on her cheek. But so do I. Shit went *down* in that room; it's not a stretch of the imagination that someone's elbow caught her face as she dove out the door.

She's pretty convincing. I have the slightest moment of self-doubt. Could I have seen this wrong? No. The story fits.

I can't read Matteo's face. He's *Detective Kildaire* all the way right now. He looks to each of us in turn. Weighing my testimony. Assessing. "And you all"—Matteo motions to Amy, Shwanda, and Latifah—"just thought that rather than waiting for security or calling the police, you'd ruin merchandise and put lives at risk by chasing a thief through a convention by yourselves?"

No one answers, but all eyes turn to me. *The captain goes down with the ship.* "It's my fault. Waiting at the auction. This whole idea. The chase just . . . happened. I'm sorry about that." But I caught one of the suspects we've been searching for. That has to count for something, right?

I can hardly bring myself to meet Matteo's eyes, but when I do, I wince. There's condemnation in his gaze, but beyond that, there's hurt. Betrayal. Maybe a semibroken heart. And definitely broken trust. I feel as badly about that as anything. It's hard to breathe, like someone is sitting on my chest. I did the right thing, but I'll have to pay the price.

Matteo's mouth is a thin line. "You're going to have to come in for questioning."

My shoulders sink slightly, but I take a deep breath. "I realize that. And I'm ready to accept my punishment."

Matteo's gaze flicks away like he can't keep looking at me. He grunts and rises to his feet. "Fine. Rideout, call Officer James. Tell him we need holding cells for questioning." He motions to two officers who step forward and lift Agent Sosa off the ground. The snap of handcuffs is audible as they tighten around her wrists.

But I can't get past the mention of Officer James. We can*not* go into custody with him around. We'll end up dead for sure. "Wait! You can't!"

The cops stop what they're doing and face me again, most wearing expressions that say they clearly think I'm off my rocker. I clear my throat and drop my voice so that only Matteo can hear me. "Um, you can't have Officer James involved. He's been working with the White Rabbit."

Matteo rocks back on his heels like I've slammed him bodily. "What?"

"Lawrence and I saw him in the warehouse."

"Officer James has been doing patrols. That does *not* mean he's dealing drugs."

My head shakes back and forth before he's finished speaking. "We heard him say that he'd helped make it look like Yee hung himself in his cell."

Matteo's eyes widen, a hint I'm breaking through the natural detective skepticism. I get the sense that not many people know the details about that, certainly not the public.

Feeling faint hope he'll believe me, I continue, "Look, all I can tell you is what I heard. I know it's my word against his, but—no, wait. I heard something else. Something you can use to check it out. He asked that money be wired to his offshore account. Matteo, that would be proof, right?"

Matteo's expression is still shuttered. He is silent for a count of five, in which I don't move or breathe. Then he turns to his partner and says, "Rideout, call the captain. Apprise her of the situation. Have Officer James put into custody pending investigation as well. We can cite two eyewitnesses until we get a look at his financials. Better yet, ask her to confiscate his phone also."

Rideout studies me, and I'm expecting some sort of remark, but he just looks . . . rattled. Ashen-faced, he turns and lifts his cell to his ear, presumably to make a call to the captain.

Sosa has apparently been able to hear some of what we said because she struggles against the officers holding her, cheeks a bright red. "Kildaire, this is ludicrous. This whole fairy tale about a White Rabbit is stupid. I'm just out here trying to chase down a guy who stole a painting. Look, let me go. I am a fellow officer, and we are letting our true perpetrator get away."

Matteo hesitates again.

It's zero hour. And she's about to talk her way out of this because I have no proof. I snap my fingers, startling everyone beside me. *Proof.*

"It's not a fairy tale, and I can prove it. Matteo, if she's who we were chasing, she hasn't had time to ditch the journals. She's got them on her somewhere. I swear." I've never been so sure of anything in my entire life. I *will* Matteo to believe me.

Matteo reaches forward and unzips her jacket. A manila envelope falls out, along with a journal.

Bazinga.

Agent Sosa screeches, face beet red now. "That's not *mine*. Someone planted those there. Why would I have some journal? That huge sea beast put it in my jacket when I fell! You're arresting the wrong person!"

She's right. We can't *prove* she took them. Another thought occurs to me as I eye her open coat. The painting. The ripped canvas. "Look for a knife," I tell Matteo as he pulls on a glove and scoops up the envelope. "Do officers carry knives? Anything sharp that could, say, slice through a canvas?"

Silence stretches as he pats her pockets and produces a small folding utility knife, black in color. It looks like military issue, and I'd be willing to believe it's Sosa's personal knife. He drops it into a baggie while Sosa glares at me.

The yelling has gathered a crowd, and though the officers are doing their best to keep people out, I see a multitude of cell-phone cameras pointed in our direction. For better or for worse, the Golden Arrow and the White Rabbit—and me and my crew—are evening news fodder. A familiar face pushing through the crowd draws my attention.

Ryan's face is white. He's sans coat and bag of freebies, and he all but launches himself to land near Matteo. "MG, what the *hell* is going on?"

I cut a glance at Latifah, cuffs placed on her beefy arms. "Minor misunderstanding. It seems we happened upon a bad guy—er—girl and got in the way of her escape. Ry, you're going to have to feed Trog for me until this is cleared up, okay?"

Ryan looks around, sees the rest of his party being handcuffed, and swings his gaze back to me. "No, I'm coming with you guys. I'll witness to . . . whatever."

"Actually, that's a great idea," Matteo cuts in. He turns to Ryan. "Were you involved in this chase too?"

Ryan raises his eyebrows. "Chase? No. I was in the auction room. Everyone was panicking, and I got stuck in the crowd. Didn't see where anyone went."

I squint my eyes. That's not exactly how I remember it.

"I want you to come give a statement. Sit for questioning anyhow." Matteo says this like a challenge.

Ryan shrugs like it's no big deal. "Sure. I'll meet you at the station." He turns to me. "And I'll call the neighbor to let Trog out."

Matteo rolls his shoulders back, rocks his head side to side, and faces Agent Sosa. "Okay. Back to you. I think this notebook is enough to hold you until we take a look at this evidence. Book her."

"Kildaire, are you sure about this?" It's Rideout. But he's not being an ass. He sounds nervous. I mean, we're accusing two people on his team—and his idol's daughter—of drug dealing, murder, and smuggling. Big stuff.

Matteo searches my face, and I nod, pointing to the journal. "Read it. Open the manila envelope. Everything you need is in there."

He nods and rips open the manila paper, which almost disintegrates. A VHS tape falls out, along with some photography prints and another journal.

The prints show a young man weighing bricks of heroin. The man's features had aged by the time of the anniversary party, but it's unmistakably Agent Sosa's father, Anthony Munez.

"So, your dad is the White Rabbit." I know she won't answer me. "Is that why you blocked this case at every turn?"

Agent Sosa won't meet my eye.

I press on. "Was Huong Yee going to out your father? Or was it you he'd seen—the *new* White Rabbit?"

She is still silent, but her chest rises and falls at a rapid rate.

I shrug and look at the group gathered around us in silence. This feels so *dramatic*. "Fine. Stay quiet. I don't know what's on this video, but I'm guessing it's going to incriminate your father. It's why your father killed Edward Casey Senior."

The crowd does an impressive imitation of a movie scene: a collective gasp, complete with an outbreak of rabid conversation.

I turn to Matteo, guilt melting all my bravado. We're back to the fact that this man is now well aware that I lied to him, withheld evidence, aided a suspect in eluding police, and set up a sting operation on my own. Quite the little superhero story line of my own. "I couldn't tell you because . . . well, I thought Rideout was the double agent. I was wrong about that." My eyes flick to Rideout and his ashen face. "Anthony Munez not only killed Casey Senior to protect his identity but claimed to have used the information Casey sent to the police department to fake a drug war, round up his competition, and put them all away. It really was brilliant. For thirty years, it worked. But Edward Casey's journal resurfaced. He got his revenge. He got his justice in the end."

"That's quite the story," Rideout says. No condemnation. Just fact.

I shrug. "It *is* just a story at this point, but I'm pretty good with stories. I bet you'll find that I'm right when you do the hard work of pulling together the evidence."

"I want a lawyer," Agent Sosa announces as she's escorted ahead of us.

"I bet you do."

I nearly crack a smile at Rideout's dry response. At least he's a jerk to everyone, and not just me.

"The only thing I *can't* figure out," I say more to myself, "is where the other journal went. Either Sosa ditched it, which could be possible, *or* . . ."

"Or what?" Rideout barks, a touch of his old bite in evidence. "Spill it, story girl."

"Or the Golden Arrow was here and tried to nab the envelope. Maybe that's what the scuffle was. If you find the journal, maybe you'll find our vigilante. They might not even know we've caught Sosa or that she had the envelope."

"Or you're the Golden Arrow and trying to draw up a ruse."

The accusation is so simple, it takes my breath away. "Why would I go to all the trouble of pointing out a loose end if I was hoping to get away with it?"

"Criminal brilliance?"

I look down, my slinky white slacks and rumpled thin cami clinging to my body. "And just where do you think I'd be keeping it?"

Rideout has the decency to look away and mutters something about a pat-down at the station.

"I'm fairly certain there's another journal missing. I took a picture when I snuck in to see the painting—sorry," I mutter as Matteo shoots me a look. "My cell phone is in my jacket pocket. But I know I have a picture showing two journals. My jacket is back in the auction room," I say, and a police officer is dispatched while we wait.

Matteo holds up his hand to Rideout and signals another cop forward. "If MG is right and Sosa doesn't have both journals on her, then maybe it's true that someone attempted to stop her, or she dropped one of them. Engage the con security team, and let's do a sweep for the item. *And* hope to God that there are two sets of prints on the journal if we find it," he adds, cutting off Rideout's retort before he can voice it. "Since MG doesn't have a journal on her person, I'm going to go with innocent until proven guilty." He turns an eye to me. "You'll have to come in for formal questioning, though, and your cell will be kept as evidence until you're cleared."

I hold out my wrists to Matteo. "I'll come willingly to the station for questioning, but you can cuff me if you'd like."

"Maybe later." He still looks *pissed*, but there's a hint of a smile tugging at the corner of his lips.

CHAPTER 28

I ring the doorbell on the exterior of the metal gate. It's an old-fashioned one that rings a real bell, nothing digital, nothing electric. I have to ring it twice before I get a response from the house. The blinds move slightly as someone looks out; then the door cracks open.

Dragons dance in my belly; I wonder if he's going to shut the door in my face. If he's going to dismiss me before I can explain. It's been two months of hell—seeing him interrogated in the hearings for the trial—and not getting to talk to him or touch him. Explain myself other than through my testimony.

"Hey, I wasn't expecting you." Matteo is in bare feet and pajama pants. He looks relaxed and scrump-diddly-umptious. That is, minus the frown lines that crease his face and the set of his shoulders. Those say that he's nervous to see me too.

"I'm officially not a suspect anymore. I just thought I'd let you know. I know a guy who says face-to-face is best for important conversations."

Matteo smirks. He studies me for a moment, then sighs and opens the door wide, allowing me into his house. "In that case, let me welcome you into my home, *normal civilian*."

His shoes sit by the door, and I take care to place my bright-purple kitten heels right next to his neat brown shoes. The living room is dark, save for the glow from a TV—he *does* have one!—tucked away on the far wall. I note the scene paused on the TV, and I laugh. "*The Princess Bride*?"

Matteo shrugs. "Kyle recommended it."

"I bet he did." This time Matteo returns my grin with a small one of his own, and the world seems a lot friendlier.

He shuffles his feet in the carpet. "So how does it feel to be 'not a person of interest'?" It's a simple question, but it carries weight.

I lift my hands out to the side and shrug. "Glad it's over. So lovely, I guess. But I'm a little sad it's over. I feel like I *was* the superhero. I got to be the Golden Arrow, or the Hooded Falcon. I did a little vigilante justice, brought a double agent to her knees." I need to get to my point, though. "But, um, I kinda hurt someone I like in the process, and I want to apologize."

Matteo's eyes flick to the ground then back up to mine. "Apologies are quite the work of art, so I hear."

Great, he isn't going to let me off easy. I give a dramatic sigh, run my hands through my hair—I've returned it to my natural white blonde for the hearings—and square my shoulders to him. "I'm sorry I didn't tell you about the journal. Or Lawrence." I tick them off on my fingers. "Or Officer James. Or call you when I found the drug money in the warehouse. Sorry about breaking into a warehouse too. Probably a bad call."

He raises his eyebrows and rolls his hand forward to indicate that I should continue.

I squint one eye. "I'm also sorry I set up a sting without your knowledge or permission and that I attempted to catch a dangerous criminal on my own, making this case messy and a logistical nightmare." I had to sit through hearing after hearing while it was sorted through. I *know* I made this a tough one for Matteo to wrap up neatly.

He still doesn't look appeased. "And?"

I rack my brain. "And . . . Matteo, I think that's everything. I swear."

He sighs and crosses his arms. He's standing with his feet shoulder width apart, and even in his pajamas, I recognize *Detective Kildaire*. "Michael-Grace Martin, you need to apologize for putting *yourself* in an inordinate amount of danger. I couldn't protect you from the bad guys. Hell, I couldn't even protect you from *you* because I was in the goddamn bloody dark." Color rises to his cheeks, and he swipes his hand over his face.

I'd like to sink into the carpet. "I know."

Detective Kildaire isn't done. "You're my partner. We're supposed to have each other's backs, be honest with each other, even when it's hard. That's what *partners* do."

I feel like my heart is coming out of my chest like in the old cartoons. He said "you *are*," not "*were*."

"I was a crappy partner."

"Damn right you were."

"But it's because of the dirty cop, Matteo. I was afraid Lawrence would end up dead or *I* would end up in jail. I didn't know who to trust, and I was worried about you too, getting in trouble because of me. I just thought it best to keep my own counsel."

"You couldn't trust me to keep you safe? You thought I was the dirty cop?" His stance hasn't changed, but I hear the hurt in his voice. Ah, this is the crux of it. He thinks I didn't trust him.

My voice comes out small, but I'm being honest. "I suspected you for about thirty seconds, and then it was obvious that you're the least crooked cop that ever existed. I tried to protect *you.* I was wrong not to trust you. I'm sorry. I'll be a better partner in the future, I promise, if you'll still have me?"

I hold my breath, terrified for having put myself out there for rejection that openly. He could stomp all over my heart now if he wants.

"You didn't just catch one double agent."

I blink. "What?"

"Two of them, as I recall from the hearing." There's a note of pride in his voice now.

"Yes, two of them." I lean forward. "So does this mean I'm forgiven?"

Matteo studies me, then rolls his eyes to the ceiling and mutters what looks like a prayer for patience. "I guess so. And I never suspected. I just showed that text to the team without thinking. Does this make us both crazy?" He reaches forward and hauls me to his chest. I breathe in the smell of toothpaste and revel in the static cling of his pajama pants against my jeans.

I speak into his chest, anxious to discuss the case, since I haven't been able to for two long months. "It's crazy to me that Agent Sosa would take over her father's business like that. The drugs, the lies, the false reports, tossing out cases, deflecting suspicion." I sat in on only two hearings with Munez and Sosa present, but now that I'm cleared of all my charges, I'd get to sit in on more. I'm now a witness for the prosecution, though the lawyers are thinking this case could take *years* to sort through in court.

His arms are still wrapped around me like a vise, and he leans his chin against my head. "She did it because she loves him. His health is bad—very bad. He won't live to see his sentencing, I don't think. Dementia is a terrible thing, even worse when you're a kingpin. From what I've heard in the hearings you missed, he had started to make business mistakes. His mind was going. She didn't want him to get caught, so she took on more and more gradually. At first just to keep him out of jail, and then . . . well, money can be a powerful motivator. Unfortunately, she was good at what she did." He pauses for a moment.

"I don't think she knew that he had killed Casey until we discovered it. Then she knew for certain he'd die in jail if the case was solved. She was just trying to protect her father. In fact, had she not been falsifying the test results from this specific case, I don't know that we'd have enough to hold her on. Officer James agreed to identify her in exchange for a plea deal, and that helps. Though he'll still get close to life for killing Yee. His only chance is to hope he drops that sentence for parole."

"All of this has been so crazy. The costumes, the crimes, the real-life superheroes. I'm ready for my life to settle down a bit."

A rumble starts in his chest, and his shoulders shake beneath my cheek. He still hasn't loosened his hold on me. "It's been pretty crazy. But I have a feeling that life with you isn't calm and boring."

I grin against his chest and slip my hands into his. "No, probably not. Actually, did you see the latest copy of *The Hooded Falcon*?" I look up to gauge his reaction.

Matteo's mouth presses into a line. "Yes, we've seen it." A month ago, an independently produced comic showed up online and in retail stores bearing the name of *The Hooded Falcon*. Instead of it being a rip-off of ours, though, it was a slim comic containing the cleaned-up sketches of the original Falcon. The sketches from the journals that had been in the frame. The Golden Arrow had presumably managed to somehow take the journals, clean them up, and publish them as close to what Casey would have done as possible.

"You'll go after the Golden Arrow now?"

Matteo eyes me. "Are you *sure* it's not you?"

I laugh. "I've been cleared by the courts of men and God."

"I mean, yes . . . but we have no leads at this point, although we're looking. We're still busting the drug rings involved with the White Rabbit. I think things will quiet down a bit with Sosa and her father behind bars." Matteo looks shell-shocked as he shakes his head in wonder at me. "Anthony was *the* purveyor of heroin in LA for thirty years, and we never knew."

I nod. The waves of this case touch every part of the LAPD. Everyone has been in for questioning, Matteo and Rideout included.

"How are Lawrence and Ryan?" Matteo's question pulls me back to the present.

I shrug, and he wraps his arms around me and rubs slowly up and down my back with one hand. "Okay. Everyone's shaken up about this. No one's acting normally. But I think we'll get there." Lawrence and Ryan had the charges of aiding and abetting dropped when their alibis panned out. Lelani had actually been a huge help in backing up Ryan's story. I guess she wasn't just good in the boardroom; she was good in the courtroom too.

I'm hesitant to share my next bit of information, but Matteo has just said that honesty is everything. "I have to admit, I kind of like the idea of our masked avenger still being out there. Instead of these journals rotting in evidence, they're seeing the light of day. I know it's not how the case should be. But it's a little bit like Robin Hood, don't you think? Rob from the rich—er, police, and give to the masses? Everyone gets to find out how the comics would have ended. Anyhow, I told you I'm *not* a suspect anymore. I don't want to talk about the case."

I want to talk about *us*. I want to talk about how my hands don't ever want to stop holding his. I want to talk about our partnership and where we're going to go from here.

Matteo pulls me to the sofa and scoots closer until our thighs are pressed together. "No work talk?"

My heart races, and I have trouble focusing on his actual words.

"No." I reach out, wrap my arm around his neck, and pull him to me. I breathe him in, so happy to find that he's real and warm and willing to forgive me. We sit like that, cozy in the couch corner, for a long moment, and I drink in his presence. I feel like I'm home, something I've never felt with anyone else. I take the time to sort through the fact that Matteo *isn't* my type. Instead, he balances me out. He doesn't have to fit into my standards for a boyfriend . . . He cares about me. He may not know enough to ask me to watch a *Doctor Who* marathon yet, but he'll watch it with me because he knows it will make me happy. I spent so much time pushing people away because they didn't fit what I was looking for, and in the end what I needed was someone to bring *me* out of *my* prejudices. Open my eyes to the world. To realize that the perfect person will support my fashion design, my wacky hair, my comics, my job, because those things are all a part of me.

Thank God for the Hooded Falcon. Yet again, he knew exactly what I needed in my life. He led me from original and unhappy MG to MG

2.0, who kicked ass at Genius but was a little lonely. Now, through this case, and through Casey Senior's presence in my life yet again, MG 3.0 is ready to be released into the world.

Here I am with a gorgeous Muggle, and the world still has magic in it. *The Princess Bride* is on TV, and there is a masked vigilante still out there in the world if things get too crazy. The universe is just about perfect.

I roll my shoulders back. "You know what I'm really in the mood for?" I give him my best bedroom eyes.

"What's that?" His thumbs are already on my rib cage, his mouth inches from mine.

"Herbal tea."

"You minx."

"All right, fine. I don't want tea. I just want to be Matteo and MG for a bit. No capes, no costumes, no crimes, just . . . us. Can we do that?" I run my hand up his arm, feeling the goose bumps rise on his skin in the wake of my touch.

He leans forward and seals my query with a kiss. "What does the hero say now? Oh yes. 'As you wish.'"

ACKNOWLEDGMENTS

First off, a huge thanks to Kristi—the "real" MG. Without you and your zany life, this book would never have existed.

This book was a lark, a "fun" project to work on while I was supposed to be revising my "real" book for submission. A huge thank-you to the team of friends who convinced me that *this* project was the one that deserved my attention. To "the Girls," for reading the first version chapter by chapter. Thanks to Erin, for listening to me talk about this project ad nauseam and cheerleading the whole journey, and Trisha, for the insane late-night plotting that you've done with me. Thanks for being my partner in crime, as you put it! A thank-you to John, for spending hours telling me what it was *really* like to be a narcotics detective, and to my sensitivity readers. To my husband, for both laughing out loud at the dream that inspired the book and for pushing me to write it because "this is probably going to be the one that sells, because it's ridiculous and awesome." He was right! (Don't tell him I said that.) For my family, who continue to be completely supportive of me and my crazy dreams, even though I'm often overtired and cranky from pursuing them at all hours of the night/day. And thanks to my son, Noah, who is absolutely a real superhero and reminds me daily why the world needs laughter, fun, and "real people" in literature.

This book wouldn't exist without my amazing professional support system. First and foremost, my agent, Joanna MacKenzie, who felt like an old friend the first time we talked. She's the (more capable) other half of my awesome nerd team, and I cannot imagine my book ending up in better hands. And, of course, my inimitable mentor, Kelly Siskind. This book took shape because she took a chance on my manuscript in Pitchwars. I never would have been able to accomplish those initial revisions on my own (plus, her writing and dedication to the craft and business of writing are second to none!), and her tireless optimism in the project kept me afloat. To my editor(s) Adrienne, Jason, and Jaym: you guys have made this debut process so enjoyable and easy.

Last but not least, a thanks to Brenda Drake and my Pitchwars community. Specifically to my critique partner and comic guru, Ian, for always being there to vent/celebrate/send corgi gifs/give guidance on pages. To the rest of my writing crew I gained from PW—Christine, Elise, Kelli, Helen, Suzie, Jen, Julie, and the whole "Raptor Pack." You all are the gift that keeps on giving, my coworkers, my inspiration, my confidants, and my peers. I can't imagine this journey without you.

ABOUT THE AUTHOR

Photo © 2018 Julie Patton Photography

Meghan Scott Molin loves all kinds of storytelling. After studying architecture and opera at college, she worked as a barn manager before becoming a professional photographer. *The Frame-Up* is her first published book. An avid lover of all the nerd things—*Star Wars*, *Star Trek*, hobbits, *Doctor Who*, and more—Meghan also enjoys cooking, dreaming of travel, coveting more corgis, and listening to audiobooks in the barn. She lives in Colorado with her husband (and fellow zookeeper), her sons, two horses, a cat, and a rambunctious corgi. For more information about Meghan, visit her website at www.MeghanScottMolin.com or follow her on Twitter (@megfuzzle).